Dee

Rachel Lynch is an author of crime fiction whose books have sold more than one million copies. She grew up in Cumbria and the lakes and fells are never far away from her. London pulled her away to teach History and marry an Army Officer, whom she followed around the globe for thirteen years. A change of career after children led to personal training and sports therapy, but writing was always the overwhelming force driving the future. The human capacity for compassion as well as its descent into the brutal and murky world of crime are fundamental to her work.

Also by Rachel Lynch

The Rich
The Famous

Helen Scott Royal Military Police Thrillers

The Rift
The Line

Detective Kelly Porter

Dark Game
Deep Fear
Dead End
Bitter Edge
Bold Lies
Blood Rites
Little Doubt
Lost Cause
Lying Ways
Sudden Death
Silent Bones
Shared Remains

RACHEL LYNCH

DEEP FEAR

CANELOCRIME

DK | Penguin Random House

First published in the United Kingdom in 2018 by Canelo

This edition published in the United Kingdom in 2025 by

Canelo Crime, an imprint of
Canelo Digital Publishing Limited,
20 Vauxhall Bridge Road,
London SW1V 2SA
United Kingdom

A Penguin Random House Company
The authorised representative in the EEA is Dorling Kindersley Verlag GmbH.
Arnulfstr. 124, 80636 Munich, Germany

A CIP catalogue record for this book is available from the British Library.

Print ISBN 978 1 83598 290 7
Ebook ISBN 978 1 78863 017 7

Printed and bound in Great Britain by Clays Ltd, Elcograf S.p.A.

Look for more great books at
www.canelo.co | www.dk.com

Chapter 1

Conrad Walker left his house in Watermillock, to head off for his morning swim across Lake Ullswater: an activity he'd been doing for fifty-three years. He'd only missed the ritual on a handful of occasions that he could recollect. One was because of the biggest storm in living memory. The wind and rain had battered the steamers and caused thousands of pounds worth of damage. Conrad had been fifteen years old. His mother hadn't allowed him near the Lake on that day, but he'd climbed out of his bedroom window anyway, to walk down to the shore and watch the fierce anger of the tempestuous water.

Nugget padded on ahead of him. She was his third Collie, and all three of them had swum the lake with him every day until, one by one, they could no longer manage it. He didn't go as far as he used to, but it was far enough for him and Nugget. The July sun shone in a clear, piercing sky, and Conrad figured the lake might be twenty degrees today, on its surface at least. The road was quiet, as it always was at this hour. He'd parked in one of the bays scattered along the lake's shore, and he opened the back to throw in his towel and pull on a pair of loose trousers and a jumper. Nugget waited faithfully by his side, knowing that her turn would come; she'd get a rub and a treat, and she looked up expectantly. When that was done, she jumped in to the passenger seat. Conrad could have walked but that wasn't the point. It was a daily ritual, and for the last nine years, after his swim, his next stop was to visit his wife and bid her good morning. He'd take his flask with him and have a cup of tea.

Driving up the hill, the small village was quiet, with the farmers having left for the day, and the tourists still in bed. Nugget let her tongue soak up the rushing air from the Land Rover's open windows for the short journey to the church.

He parked opposite the Victorian version of the consecrated site, built of red sandstone and slate, to replace the dilapidated Tudor structure. The church stood proudly watching over the lake beyond, and Conrad came here often to absorb the stillness of her grounds. In the summer, there were huge, shady canopies under which to sit; in the winter, there were sheltered benches to spend time upon, contemplating anything that took his fancy. He rarely saw anyone else, except the reverend, if he was up at this hour.

Nugget jumped out of the Land Rover, and ran straight over the road to the gate.

Conrad paused. In all her eleven years, she'd never done that. Every morning, she jumped out of the passenger seat and waited at his heel until he signalled for her to cross the road. Conrad looked at the seat, wondering if she was losing her ability to hold on. He looked for a stain but there was none.

He shrugged and closed the door; he never locked it. He was perplexed and tutted; he liked routine. He looked both ways up and down the lane, then crossed to where Nugget was sitting. She stood up and began to bark, turning round and round as if she'd sniffed a trail.

'You seen a squirrel, Nugget?' he asked. He opened the gate and the dog shot off into the churchyard, with Conrad following, shaking his head. She must be chasing something, he thought. The barking got louder and Conrad chuckled; those damned cheeky rodents, they tease her so. He spotted a fat grey sat at the top of a branch, goading the canine, as it devoured nuts and cared nothing for the chaos it was causing to Conrad's morning. He followed the barking; it was in the same direction as Ada's gravestone anyhow. He had commissioned a bench to be placed in front of her, so he could stay as long as he wished without stiffening up. In colder months, he brought a blanket and a flask of tea.

He continued around the church to where he thought the barking was coming from and he thought that it might be under the massive old oak that stood majestically to the east of the church entrance, guarding the graveyard. It had been just as big when he was a young lad, singing in the choir, and his father had said that it was more than five hundred years old. Conrad half expected Reverend Neil to come out, asking what all the fuss was about, but then he remembered that Neil was away in Whitehaven on some Diocesan conference. He wasn't a bad egg, the reverend; they'd had worse. He was a decent chap who always had time for his flock; not that Conrad counted himself as one of the flock, not since Ada had died.

He shielded his eyes against the sun, which rose quickly at this time of year. It shone a deep orange and made him squint. It was going to be another belter of a day. He shouted the dog's name over again; he'd never known Nugget to be so disobedient. Her barks grew louder, and Conrad was sure now that it was coming from the oak tree.

He took two more steps but then stopped. Nugget's barking rang in his ears and Conrad swayed slightly. He rubbed his eyes and took another step, and then he was sure. He held onto the dry stone wall, and his eyes continued around the churchyard to see if anyone else was about. He was alone. Well, sort of. The flask slipped from his grasp and he covered his mouth.

Nugget was standing over the body of a lady, but the lady wasn't moving. She was still. Conrad started to panic and his first thought was to go back to his car for a coat to put over the poor woman, who was completely naked. He tried not to look at her and he thought how awful it would be if she realised that a stranger had seen her that way.

But all the way back to the car, he knew.

He knew because of Ada. He knew because of the flies.

But he got the coat anyway.

Half way back to the church with his coat, with Nugget still going crazy, he tutted and went back to the car for his mobile phone, which he never used but his daughter had bought for him. He had no idea if it had any juice in it, as he rarely charged the bloody thing.

He dialled 999.

When he got back to the body, he threw the coat over her, and pulled Nugget away. He made a decision, and turned back towards her and knelt down. He touched her skin and pulled away.

He knew she was dead.

Conrad said a prayer, not because he was religious, or because he believed in God, but more to give the woman some dignity, and to allow her soul to rest in peace.

When the ambulance arrived, he was sat on Ada's bench, under an apple tree, holding a hot cup of tea from his flask. Nugget sat faithfully at his side, and the only sound was of insects buzzing, and distant twittering birds feeding their young.

Chapter 2

Kelly Porter was chewing a piece of cold toast when she got the call. Her jacket was half on, and she struggled to manoeuvre it, as well as her handbag and briefcase. Watermillock would be a mere ten minute drive at this time of the morning, and she decided to go straight there rather than to Eden House. She threw her belongings onto the passenger seat of her car, decided against the jacket, put on her sunglasses, and started the engine. It sounded like she'd need her trainers for this one, and she threw them in as well.

As she pulled away, a familiar knot formed under her ribcage, and she concentrated on the road. At a red light, anticipation made her toes tap the floor of the car. Blues weren't necessary. The woman was dead. The forensic team was already there, and the area secured by uniformed police officers.

She gripped the steering wheel tightly and willed the lights to change. She drove east and traced the north shore of Ullswater, wondering how long the body had lain in this weather, but trying not to speculate too much; she had no idea what she was about to find. All she knew was that there was a body, it was female, a paramedic had confirmed life extinct, and it probably hadn't been a natural death. Her job was to assess the scene to aid the coroner.

For the first time in a long time, she found herself thinking about London. A body. No-one expected it round here. A thousand questions raced through her head, and she tried not to get ahead of herself. As she turned off the main road and followed the lane, up the hill, away from the lake, which led to the tiny hamlet of Watermillock, she'd already worked through the next few hours in her head: what she'd need, how she'd allocate jobs, how she'd sketch the scene, and how to handle the press.

She parked at the church, where a small group of tourists had gathered. She popped her sunglasses on the top of her head and looked towards the lake, which sat in serenity, blissfully unaware of what was unfolding a mere mile away. She quickly bent over and slipped on a pair of ankle socks and her trainers, taking a deep breath before heading out in front of the audience. Police tape sealed the church entrance, but the onlookers were still craning their necks to see what was going on. News travelled fast on holiday. Kelly remembered swimming across the lake as a kid, and cycling up here afterwards, just so they could race back down again. Apparently, the old man who'd made the discovery had just been for his morning swim before coming to pay his respects to his wife, like he did every day. Poor bastard, Kelly thought. She checked her ponytail and moved it over her left shoulder, over her back pack that she carried when out of the office. It meant she could leave her handbag and briefcase in the car where they couldn't get in the way.

A white tent had been erected, and Kelly flashed her badge to two uniforms manning the immediate area. It was a place of unique quietness, but, Kelly noted, it was also very public. The church was the centre of the village, if it could be called a village; it was more a collection of residences, hotels and self-catering holiday homes scattered between the lake and Little Mell Fell. The man who'd found the body was giving a statement to a third uniform. They were sat on a bench under a tree, and it swayed in the breeze. The old man was perhaps in his sixties and he was shaking his head, his face looked pained. Kelly waited to introduce herself and put away her sunglasses.

The man stood up and took Kelly's hand. He looked into her eyes and Kelly realised that he was in shock. Nonetheless, he stood erect, and his demeanour smacked of old fashioned propriety and pride. The woman had been found naked, and Kelly could tell that it'd had a dreadful impact on him.

'I put my coat over her,' Conrad said.

Oh fuck, thought Kelly. Forensics would be made up with that nice bit of contamination. Now they'd have to rule him out as a suspect because he'd put his fingerprints and DNA right on top of her. Poor bloke. Unless he'd done it. She eyed him for a fleeting second as she would a suspect, but immediately dismissed the thought; his eyes were too kind.

A collie sat obediently at the man's legs and Kelly bent to stroke her. Its tongue lolled out and she looked as though she were smiling. 'She likes you,' the old man said. Kelly smiled.

'Are you local to Watermillock, sir?' she asked. He nodded. It was a shame that he'd probably never walk past the church again without remembering today, and for all the wrong reasons.

'Yes. I've lived here all my life,' he said.

Damn, Kelly thought. At least if he was a tourist, he could go home and put some distance between him and what he'd seen. But he'd be reminded of his grim find every day, as long as he lived in the village. It wasn't something that would be forgotten in a hurry, in a place like this.

'And you swim every day, at the same time, and then come and visit your wife's grave?'

'Yes, I do. Every day. She's over there, by that bench.'

'I'm sorry that she's been disturbed,' Kelly said. Conrad looked at her and his face lifted a little. He nodded.

'Thank you so much.'

Kelly looked towards the tent, said farewell to Mr Walker, giving him the usual line of getting in touch after handing him her card, and walked towards the giant oak. By the way the man described the body, insect activity had already begun. And sure enough, she could hear the familiar hum of thick-bodied flies, looking for a good place to land.

The uniform had a full statement, and the old man signed it and gave his address. He was then told that he could leave. Kelly felt a pang of sorrow for him; people who came across bodies weren't customarily kept informed of how an investigation panned out; they were usually forgotten, but something told her that Conrad Walker might have trouble sticking to his routine from now on. He took a handkerchief from his pocket and held it to the corner of his eye as he walked away, with the dog following obediently.

A forensic officer was bent over just outside the entrance to the tent. As Kelly approached, she saw that he was making a cast of a print in the small patch of mud by the path. The cast was dry and was being pulled back as Kelly got closer. It was the print of a shoe.

'Fresh?' she asked the officer. He removed his mask.

'Fresher than anything else around here, and it didn't rain last night,' he said. She nodded and approached the tent.

Kelly smelled the odour of the dead before she saw the body. It was sweet and fresh. She reached into her bag and pulled out a bottle of perfume and sprayed it onto her fingers, rubbing underneath her nose.

With sheep numbering around three million in these parts, and outnumbering humans by six to one, the blow fly, with its distinct hairy, blue bottle back, thrived year on year. The first of nature's hungry scavengers to arrive on a scene of death, the animal soon left its tell-tale mark: writhing masses of pure white maggots that grew fatter and fatter until they could eat no more. In summer conditions, flies could be on a corpse within an hour. Within twelve hours, the maggots have begun to hatch and eat their meal, found so lovingly by their mother. There, they fed happily for six weeks until pupation and adulthood. And it was this cycle that would help estimate the body's time of expiry; basic forensic entomology that every detective studied. The smell wasn't too bad, yet, so maybe the body was fresh, thought Kelly. It made sense that in such a public place, a body would attract attention straight away, and Conrad Walker had confirmed that he walked Nugget here daily. The church itself was a tourist attraction, with visitors coming to view its bold architecture and pretty interior, as well as of course the view to the lake, and beyond.

She went inside the tent.

Another forensic officer greeted her and gave her some covers for her shoes. She had gloves in her pocket.

'Homicide,' the officer said. Kelly looked at the body. A photographer clicked her camera.

Kelly reckoned the body hadn't laid there long, but they wouldn't know for sure until after the autopsy, and the entomologist's report. She walked around the victim, looking for small burrows in the soil, where satiated fully grown maggots might have buried themselves to pupate. There were none.

The woman's nakedness struck Kelly, and again, she noted the sense of public humiliation. But more so, now that Kelly saw the woman in the flesh: she'd not only had her life taken, but, perhaps more importantly, her dignity.

Someone wanted her found. Quickly.

Kelly went closer inside the tent and held her breath momentarily. The aromatic, pungent cocktail of dead, congealed blood penetrated her perfume and caught her off guard.

The woman's white flesh, against the earth, looked like a fat juicy mushroom, ready for picking. She was face down, head to the side, and Kelly took in the details.

'We're not turning her over. I want her bagged and off to the mortuary as soon as we're done. But I can tell by her skin that she's less than twenty-four hours old. It's just starting to slip, but the weather doesn't help. Her mouth, ears and nose have been stuffed with soil, but it's not from here – well, it doesn't look like it is. The soil here is dark and dense: great for fruit trees. Her fingertips have been removed.'

'What?' asked Kelly.

'The tops of her fingers are missing,' he repeated.

'To prevent prints?' asked Kelly.

'Perhaps. Might be something else to it. Anyway, please take a look,' he said. Damn, she thought, the stuff found under fingernails often produced golden nuggets of forensic information. And they'd have no prints for ID.

'Sexual assault?' Kelly asked.

'It'll have to be confirmed by the rape kit, but I'd say yes, and pretty brutal. Look for yourself,' he said.

Kelly approached the victim and the smell became more arresting. It was nothing compared to a rotting body that had laid abandoned for weeks, but it was bad enough. Kelly looked at the victim's face, or as much as she could see, and she got an idea of what the woman looked like in life. She also noticed bruising around the woman's neck. Kelly guessed that the victim was in her fifties, and she took care of herself: her skin was good and she had nicely coloured hair; just a millimetre of grey could be seen at the root.

The crime hadn't been motivated by robbery. The woman wore a nice looking, gold Tag watch, and she had some rather large diamonds in a ring on her right hand. She also wore a large gold band on her wedding finger. Murders were usually motivated by one of three things: possession, passion or pleasure, and Kelly got the distinct feeling that the latter was looking possible.

She walked to the rear of the victim and crouched down. She shook her head when she saw what was in between the woman's legs. Kelly covered her nose and peered more closely, not completely believing what she was seeing. She beckoned the forensic officer over and he simply said, 'I know. Bank notes.'

It was a disturbing MO. Not just the implied manner of death, but the brazen dumping ground, and Kelly couldn't help but conclude that the perpetrator was bragging. Like an excited child showing off his painting, the perp was actually showing off his work; and sending them a message.

A series of events was taking shape in Kelly's mind, as well as dozens of questions. Investigations always threw up more questions than they answered, but that's where they started; and that's all they had, for now. She strongly suspected that the killer knew this woman, and his work was methodical and organised. Apart from the soil, she was clean, and oddly taken care of.

But one word kept coming back to her as she walked around the victim: punishment.

This woman had suffered horribly, and the killer had wanted her to. Kelly hoped that she was dead when he sliced off the tops of her fingers. She remembered a similar case from ten years ago. It was equally brutal and brazen. A serial rapist and murderer had terrorised Leytonstone in 2006, until he was apprehended on some traffic misdemeanour, and willingly offered his DNA. The guy was about as brain dead as anyone could be, and the depths of his psychopathy stunned anyone who interviewed him. He stared ahead with dead eyes, and said his victims deserved what they got, because they teased him. He was a great lumbering man who the local press had dubbed 'The Hammer', due to the fact that he smashed his victims' skulls in as he abused them. The Hammer was impenetrable as a human being, and for the first time in her career, he'd convinced Kelly that evil did exist.

Before that, she'd met bad people and good people. Bad people did bad things, and good people did good things and, sometimes, they overlapped. But The Hammer wasn't human, he was an animal, and Kelly had nightmares about what he put women through, in the hours before they were allowed to die. Now, as she stood inside a tent at a popular tourist destination, which was about to get extremely busy, she wondered how long it had taken for this poor woman to meet her end.

For now, Kelly had a nameless body, which had been tortured and mutilated. The first thing she needed was a name, and that would be down to dentals, given the absence of fingerprints. Today, she could start questioning in the local area and keep badgering the coroner. She hoped it was still Ted Wallis. They hadn't spoken in months.

She heard plastic wrapping and watched as the woman's head, hands and feet were secured for her journey. As the body was lifted into a black bag, and the zip closed, Kelly looked around. She was standing in the spot where a sadist had said goodbye to his kill. She was certain that the woman hadn't been killed here. The scene was too tidy. They'd have to check the dirt to see if that threw them a lead. The woman's position made her look like she was sleeping and, if disturbed, or in a rush, the killer wouldn't have been able to achieve this.

Plus, the money had stayed where it was put. If she'd been dropped, kicked out of a car, or dumped in haste, some of it would have dislodged. Sick bastard. Kelly shivered, despite the day heating up. Maybe now she'd put on her cardigan that she'd tucked into her bag. She needed to keep the details out of the press. She was sure that they could count on Mr Walker to respect their wishes.

Kelly left the tent and removed her gloves and shoe covers. She smelled of death.

The church was closed.

Chapter 3

Brandy Carter swaggered into the children's play area, and made her way over to a group of kids, who were playing on the swings.

'Got some pocket money for me, then?' Brandy said. Her chin jutted out and her eyes were menacing. The younger kids stopped playing, and several of them dug their hands into pockets. There were no adults around; Brandy was the oldest there. She half smiled, revealing stained teeth, and she coughed, forcing her hand out of her pocket to catch whatever landed on it; she wiped it on her jeans. She wore a hoody and this only served to make her look more sinister to her innocent victims. One boy, of perhaps nine years old, moved towards the front of the group and stood up to her.

'We don't have to give you anything,' he said.

For a moment, the other children stopped digging around for something with which to pay off their tormentor, and watched to see what would happen. They didn't have to wait long.

Brandy shot a hand out and grabbed the boy's hair. He didn't resist and his eyes filled with terror. He'd tried to stand up for his mates, but had only succeeded in making an idiot of himself. He wished his mam was here.

'Anyone else want a piece of me?' Brandy growled.

The children shook their heads and Brandy let the nine-year-old go. The boy rubbed his head and handed Brandy a pound coin. The older girl smiled again and the other children followed suit.

'What's this shit?' Brandy held up a packet of sweets.

'I haven't got any money,' a small girl said.

'Well, fucking make sure you bring some next time, you little bitch.' Brandy swiped her hand across the girl's ear, making the girl wince and tears come to her eyes.

The language shocked the children and made them compliant. They heard stuff like it on You Tube, but this was right in front of them, here in Arogan Park, Penrith, and they froze in fear. Several of them started to cry, and Brandy made baby noises in response. Nobody moved as Brandy counted her booty, she'd stolen the best part of seven pounds and she lumbered off, pleased with herself.

After leaving the park, she made her way across the recreation field, towards a block of flats that was a home of sorts. She rarely went back to her mam's. Brandy's mother, when sober, was a violent creature and liked to throw cigarette butts at her daughter. The new man in her mother's life liked to go a little further with his girlfriend's daughter, and threatened her with his fists. At first, Brandy had been grateful for the notes he gave her for quick blow jobs, but the money had stopped and he'd begun to expect it for free.

So she'd kind of moved in with Bick. His flat was grubby, but it was warm, and he gave her free drugs in kind. He was rough, but he always said sorry afterwards. For now, she had enough to buy a packet of smokes, and she was happy. She scratched at the angry red spots under her nose, and her eyes went watery when she lit up a cigarette.

When she opened the door to Bick's place, three of his mates were playing Xbox. Brandy didn't understand what attracted them to the games, but at least it kept them off her case.

'Give us a smoke, Brands,' one of them asked. She flicked one over to him; another ploy to keep them away. The boys played the same games over and over again, and Brandy wondered why none of them ever got bored. Boys: they're so dumb, she thought. The TV rocked with gunshots and cars screeching, as well as the odd scream of a woman being brutalised.

Nice. No wonder they all turned out dickheads, she thought.

Bick came in and tutted when he saw her. She knew that she wasn't the best looking girl in his life, but she helped around the flat, keeping it as clean as she could with dirty men coming and going through it. She watched him as he took off his jacket, which he wore every day, regardless of the temperature. It was a Golddigga parka, and Bick thought he looked like a You Tuber who posted videos out of Compton, LA.

Idiot.

Bick kept his cap on, but turned it the wrong way round. His jeans slipped past his butt and he walked with an arrogant swagger. He went over to the other lads and picked up a fourth controller, and began to play.

Brandy sat and smoked for a while, but was soon bored, so she asked Bick if she could have a wrap.

'Jesus, girl, you fucking eat that stuff! Your brain gonna fry, Brands,' Bick said, and he went back to the console. Over the years she'd known him, he'd perfected a kind of Jamaican street slang that he heard on the games he played, his friends did the same.

'Please, Bick, I'll pay you back,' Brandy said.

She could see that he was thinking about it. He was so engrossed in the game with Monk and Tinny, that he ignored her for a few minutes until he remembered that she was still there.

'Fine, go take a shower.' He reached into his pocket and threw her a wrap. It was worth a tenner, and he was giving it to her for free, but nothing from Bick was ever free. She looked at him and slowly, a smirk began to spread across his face. She didn't like it, and she felt vulnerable suddenly. Monk and Tinny could take things a little too far, and she had no other place to go, besides; she needed a hit. Her tummy turned over. She hoped they wouldn't hurt her.

Outside, across the street from the block of flats where Bick, Monk and Tinny waited for Brandy to have her shower, a figure turned and walked away. Brandy Carter had just become a candidate.

Chapter 4

Carleton Hall, usually a quiet and plodding place, was awash with activity as Kelly strode in to meet with DCI Cane. It was a dull but necessary task. Usually, she avoided her boss, but she needed him onside to secure a team for this case, and she wanted to get started as soon as possible. Cumbria might be the biggest constabulary geographically, but it was woefully underfunded. She'd have to beg for extra officers. On the outskirts of Penrith, the old pile exuded an air of importance slightly elevated to that of Eden House in the centre of town.

It was larger, quieter and more serious. Kelly didn't care for it at all. She knew that if she ever made DCI, she wouldn't be able to stand the static containment of HQ. She'd go mad. She was an operational officer.

She felt slightly anxious, and her biggest worry was that Cane would want the case for himself. It could be argued that a crime such as this shouldn't be investigated by one DI alone, and Kelly wondered if she'd be paired with someone, or if she'd lose it to a senior member of the force. Technically, it should be hers, and that's what she was playing for. She was the DI in charge of the Serious Crime Unit for North Lakes, and intended on staying so. However, Cane might want to court the press, and play the big cheese. She was ready for a fight. She'd already proved her team's mettle last year in one of the biggest police investigations outside London. Old colleagues had even called her to congratulate her, and she'd gained back some respect. Matt had even called, but she hadn't acted upon his request to call back. He was still a twat.

She still hadn't briefed her team, and her aim was to be made Senior Investigating Officer of the dead woman's case, and allocate jobs this afternoon. She poked her head around Cane's open door. He looked perplexed, but not hostile. Kelly suspected that the older officer had grown lazy, cossetted by his desk, and he looked too comfortable in his huge office chair. She wondered when he'd last been on an active case. Years ago, by the look of it. But operational work wasn't for everyone, she reminded herself.

She steeled herself, and took a deep breath.

'Kelly, come in.' He managed a smile, but it was difficult to read. 'Nasty murder. Really nasty. Name your team. We need this one caught ASAP.'

Kelly was relieved, and surprised.

'Sir. There was a shoe print at the scene, as well as several items inserted into the victim. My priority is processing them, so I'll need more uniforms on the ground, asking questions in the local area. We've got three working the houses already. I haven't got a name for the victim yet, but I've been on the phone to dentals, and I'm hoping to have an ID by tomorrow. The autopsy will be carried out tomorrow, first thing, by Ted Wallis, in Carlisle.' Kelly spoke like rapid fire bouncing off the walls of a farmhouse, under siege in an old cowboy movie. She expected everybody's brain to work as fast as her own. Her face was tanned from running on the fells, and she stood waiting, like a fresh reporter, eager for a lead.

'Ah, yes. The chief coroner. I wonder if he's seen anything like this one before.'

Kelly thought of ten-year-old Lottie Davis and guessed that, after that, not much shocked Ted Wallis anymore.

'I'll give you free rein, Kelly. That's one screwed-up bastard out there,' Cane said, finally. Kelly calmed a little; the expected tussle hadn't happened, and she found herself a little deflated. It meant that her visit to Carleton Hall would be delightfully quick, and she wondered why Cane hadn't told her all this over the damn phone. Perhaps there was a catch.

'Sit down, Kelly. You're too energetic. Tell me what you know. I need the distraction. I haven't asked you all the way over here for you to disappear after a minute. Tell me some good news, brighten my day. You happy with your immediate team? We could always pull some more officers from Carlisle or even here at HQ.'

Kelly did as she was told and sat down. So she was expected to provide a diversion to his lacklustre day? She could play the game for a little while, if that's what it took. She looked at her watch.

'My team is excellent, sir. It'll be a baptism for the new kid on the block. DS Umshaw is superb and the safest pair of hands outside the Sale Sharks. DC Phillips and DC Hide are quality; I wouldn't change the dream team, sir.'

'Right, then. Let me know as your needs might change. Who's the new kid?'

'DC Shawcross. Rookie, straight out of exams. Good listener.'

Cane nodded.

Kelly shivered. It was colder in here than it was outside and Kelly wished she had more on.

'Let me make you a coffee, walk with me.' Cane left the room and Kelly rolled her eyes; he'd just told her to sit down. She got up and followed him.

'Sir, I've been thinking about the MO, and it smacks of serial psychopathy: no remorse, judgement, superiority, God complex etcetera,' said Kelly. She was getting ahead of herself entirely, but her mind was racing, as it had been all morning.

'I know, Kelly, but I hope you're wrong. Be careful using the word "serial". It's inflammatory and plain incorrect. Don't throw words like that around your team. However, between me and you, I agree, this type of sophistication isn't usually displayed on a primary murder. They've usually been at it for years.' They were thinking the same thing, but Kelly didn't like being told to rein herself in. It reminded her of her mother and the way she'd been treated as a wayward rebel all her life. She was passionate, that was all. If that was seen as a nuisance, then tough.

'I'm thinking of flagging up missing persons, sir,' she said.

'Go ahead. Just keep me updated,' Cane said. He placed a cup under the nozzle and pressed the Cappuccino button. It smelled good. She tapped her leg against a unit. Cane watched with interest.

'How many murders did you work in London, Kelly?' he asked. She was taken aback by the question.

'Erm, I'm not sure, sir. Probably in the twenties,' she said.

'Go with your instinct.' He smiled at her. 'Trust yourself. I do.' He handed her the coffee and she took it. 'You have my complete faith. I hear your mother is ill,' he said.

She winced.

'Yes, sir, but that won't impact my ability to...' she said.
Cane held up his hand.

'That's not what I meant. I just wanted to offer my thoughts that's all,' he said.

'Thank you, sir.'

'Put your requirements in an email and get it to me as soon as you can so I can make the necessary arrangements. Let's hope we get a name soon,' he said.

'Yes, sir,' she said.

'Have you distributed work load yet? I'm being asked almost hourly for updates, and at least one senior officer has pointed out to me that this is work for a DCI. I told them to tell you that themselves, and they shut up.'

'Thanks, sir.' The corners of Kelly's mouth curled up.

'Not at all. Now, call me as soon as you get a name.'

She finished her coffee and walked with him back to his office. They said goodbye and she went back out into the sunshine.

She'd a missed call from her sister, Nikki, which she ignored, and two from the estate agent.

Shit! She'd missed another viewing. She called him to grovel and promised to rearrange.

She drove back to Eden House in a brooding mood and thought about the case. Her new Audi drove well, and she felt less conspicuous than she had in her convertible BMW. It was more practical but also had a lot more space to clutter. Her phone rang again and she answered it, hands free. It was the hospital: her mother was being discharged tonight.

That was good news at least. Wendy Porter had spent three days being tested for irregular heart rhythms, and now she'd stabilised. It would give Kelly some breathing space while she threw herself into this new investigation.

Nikki would no doubt accuse her of putting her work first, but she'd gone beyond trying to defend herself. Dad had come under the same heavy fire for his commitment to the force. She was damned either way.

Kelly's thoughts turned back to Ted Wallis. Perhaps he'd find something on their victim's body to link her with where she'd taken her last breath, because Kelly was convinced that it hadn't been Watermillock. It was impossible to remove every trace of contact. Locard's Exchange Principal rang true every time; that the perp always brought something to a crime scene and always left with something too, but the difficult bit was finding someone to match the evidence to. If they had no crime scene, then they had no suspects.

So she'd just have to find some.

The lack of a classic crime scene would make the investigation harder. She knew that hunches were dangerous but she couldn't help feeling that, wherever it was, it would be used again. When she thought of the time and consideration taken to punish and extinguish the life of the woman found at Watermillock, Kelly came back to the same conclusion: the killer had enjoyed it. They'd have to concentrate on the dump site instead.

Kelly sat back in her car seat and thought about what she would tell her team. She imagined a man kneeling in the dirt, in the half light, arranging the body of a middle-aged woman with expensive jewellery. The man was strong and deliberate, he was also a huge risk taker, and possessor of an arrogance only reserved for the insane.

But there she stopped herself, and had to remember the one thing she'd never been able to understand about psychology: that psychopaths aren't crazy.

They know exactly what they're doing.

Chapter 5

Kelly was exhausted, and the last thing she felt like was a fight with her sister. She parked at The Penrith and Lakes Hospital, and took a chip coin. She always found the experience of hospitals sapping, and it had already been a long day. Her feet ached in her heeled sandals, and she could do with a freshen-up.

She needed a run, but that probably wouldn't happen now.

They'd worked with what they had all day, and had made a promising start, but they still didn't have a name. She had three officers working Watermillock and taking statements, but nothing interesting had been flagged up so far. Not one resident, tourist or passer-by had reported anything unusual: there was no car sighting, nothing out of place, and no mention of anything that marked the last twenty-four hours as out of the ordinary. There wasn't a sniff of a car parked too long, a noise in the night, anything where it shouldn't be, something missing from where it should be, or any hint that a body had been dumped there. Of course, any one of those statements could come from a liar. Either that, or Kelly's murderer was dauntingly slick. She phoned forensic dentistry again, and still there was no result.

The cardiac ward at The Penrith and Lakes Hospital was utterly depressing. Old people, smokers for years, hacked their lives out of their chests, and others wheezed and rattled around the corridors. The ward wrapped around a courtyard, and each patient had their own room. Wendy Porter was dozing. Kelly looked at her mother and felt regret. They were close in some ways but not in others. Kelly knew from DS Umshaw that being a mother was a tough job and children often believed that you were taking sides. The moment offered Kelly room to breathe and she watched as her mother's chest rose and fell gently. She looked peaceful in sleep. An urge to take her hand gripped Kelly, but it passed when she heard the carping voice of her sister. She rolled her eyes.

Kelly knew that she had to move out of her childhood home, and she made a note to herself to try to squeeze in a viewing tomorrow. But even as the thought came and went, she knew she wouldn't have time. Already the case was taking over. Damn it, she had to make time.

There had been a time when Kelly had worried about why she always seemed to disappoint her mother – to the satisfaction of her sister – but now she had more important things to consider, such as finding a house of her own, so she didn't need to listen to it. As well as needing her own space, Nikki had a key to her mother's house and barged in unannounced, whenever it pleased her, and Kelly felt suffocated. And now Kelly was public enemy number one. She'd not only put Dave Crawley away for fifteen years, but his father had been found guilty and sent down, only to spend the last pathetic days of his existence in the prison infirmary, being tended to by palliative care nurses. He'd died merely two months into his sentence. Of course it was all her fault, rather than the fact that they were both fucking toe rags. It still pained her that she'd shared a bed with Dave. She still felt unclean.

Nikki had lived in Penrith all her life; she'd never left. She finished college here, married a boy from here, and now she was raising kids here. Maybe that was the problem. Kelly had known for years, all the way through college and university, that she'd leave the Lakes one day. It wasn't that she didn't love the place, not at all – it was more that it made her feel trapped somehow. Before London, all she'd ever known was lakes and mountains; the same boys, marrying the same girls, and the same conversations around the same bars and the same nightclubs. Kelly wanted more, that was all, but Nikki called her arrogant and selfish. London did its job: Kelly found the life she'd craved, the freedom, the spontaneity, the vastness and the anonymity; they all intoxicated her, and when she came back, her sister was exactly the same. But with a vicious edge. Kelly hadn't known what to make of it, and had tried to comfort her sister, thinking the cause of her annoyance to be grief over their father.

She was wrong.

And now she'd rocked the boat on a monumental scale. Nikki's best friend was Dave's wife, and was finding life on the knuckles of her arse, without the trappings of Dave's extra-curricular activities, challenging.

Now, Nikki made it clear that she blamed her sibling, not only for not being there when their father passed away, but for the fate of one of Penrith's greatest families. The irony was lost on her, and when the sisters clashed, it was never pretty.

Kelly followed the noise and found Nikki berating a male nurse with a clipboard.

'Nikki, Mum wants you,' Kelly lied.

Nikki spun round and the nurse slipped away. Kelly turned to go back to the room, ignoring anything her sister might have had to say. Nikki turned back to where the nurse had been standing and, realising they'd gone, tutted indignantly. Kelly couldn't help smile as Nikki clacked towards their mother's room in her impossible heels. It must be exhausting being that pissed off all the time, Kelly thought.

Their mother was now awake, and having her vitals checked by the young male nurse who'd been debriefed by Nikki, just a moment ago. Nikki glared at him. Kelly wondered what on earth he might have done wrong. Offence; everyone is so easily offended, she thought. Kelly found the nurse polite and efficient, but then Nikki wouldn't be happy unless there was a problem. Kelly folded her arms, accepting that she'd have to share space with her sister for a while, and examined her. She wore black leggings, high white boots, and a baggy sweatshirt with some logo on it, several bangles around her wrists – which jangled infuriatingly – plenty of makeup, and a sullen expression. Her dyed hair was piled high on her head and she chewed gum. She stood in a strop, arms folded, glaring at the nurse.

'How are you feeling, Mrs Porter?' the nurse asked.

'Better now. You're very handsome,' Wendy said.

Kelly found her mother's blunt honesty (a result of the drugs she was taking) hugely amusing: it left her with no filters, and stuff simply fell out of her mouth. The nurse laughed, used to the effects of the drugs. But Nikki was appalled.

'Mum!' Nikki said. The nurse left.

'It's true,' Wendy said.

'Right, are you all ready, Mum?' Kelly asked.

'No, she's not,' said Nikki curtly. 'That's why I was raising the issue with that idiot,' she added, indicating the departing nurse. Kelly was puzzled.

'The consultant is busy, Kelly. I think I might have to stay another night,' Wendy Porter said.

'Oh, I'm sorry, Mum. These things happen,' Kelly said.

Nikki glared at her. 'It's disgusting! Who do these consultants think they are?' she spat.

'Calm down! You're not exactly helping. If there's no-one to discharge her, then we just have to accept that. At least she's got a bed,' Kelly said.

'Are you saying she's not entitled to a bed?' Nikki asked, head cocked to one side, looking for a fight. Kelly held her sister's gaze, and weighed up the pros and cons of bothering to answer. There was no point.

'Can you two stop it?' Wendy said.

Kelly looked at her watch. She had time for a run if she went now. She went to her mother and kissed her forehead.

'I'll come back tomorrow, I'm sorry, Mum, I'm not staying here to listen to this shit,' Kelly said, and walked out, past a nurse bringing tea. They shuffled past one another, and Kelly headed in to the relative peace in the corridor. Should she stay another minute in Nikki's company, she'd get under her skin, and it wasn't worth it. Her thoughts turned to her desperate need to move out of the house. Nikki was the main reason, she admitted, and it irked her – well, that along with the fact that she was a thirty-seven-year-old woman unable to bring a man back to the house anytime she wanted. They'd set up a hospital bed in the front room for Mum, and there was nowhere to breathe. She'd outgrown her girlhood home. The move was only ever supposed to be temporary, but then Mum got ill. Kelly walked quickly and made a lift that was just about to leave. Waiting for one could be interminable in this place.

Once back to her car, she felt no guilt as she pulled out of the multi-storey car park; just an all too familiar annoyance. She'd neither the time nor the inclination for petty squabbles, and the body of a naked woman with missing fingertips filled her mind. Soon, she'd be in her running kit and free of the ambient noise that crowded her head.

She reached the house in under five minutes, parked on the street and let herself in, running straight upstairs to change. As always, when she went back to the house where she grew up, she felt foolish and something of a failure. Her life had become a transitory existence between office, hospital and a spare room, and out of all three, she was saddened to admit that she preferred her office. That's where she fitted best, at least.

It felt good to be out of her office kit, and she drove to Pooley Bridge, where it was quieter and more peaceful than a town run. The drive only took ten minutes and she parked by The Crown. The centre was busy with tourists but once she got out on to the hills, she'd be able to forget them. She made sure she had her phone, and strapped it to her arm. The headphones were connected wirelessly and she selected a hard-core playlist that would help release the pent up tension in her body and her mind.

There was no doubt the village was lovely, nestled on the eastern shore of Ullswater. It would be a pleasant place to live, and this is where the planned viewing had been today; the one she'd missed. Penrith wasn't unpleasant, it was just sprawling and depressing at times, because that's where she worked. Last year had made her an unwilling minor celebrity, and she hated it. Here, lodged between the lake and fells, could be her escape. If it hadn't already gone. The property had a terrace overlooking the River Eamont, which fed the lake, and it was private. More importantly, it was within budget.

She ran over the bridge to the lake.

The last steamers were pulling in, and she ran against the tide of tourists, flocking four deep, all looking for an evening meal before they headed back to their hotels. Faces were tanned from a day on the fells and Kelly watched as tired toddlers screamed and wriggled in prams, alongside stroppy teenages who trailed behind uncool parents, and she smiled. A few tourists glanced her way as she headed to the fells behind Pooley Bridge, on the north shore of Ullswater. If she lived here, she could do this every day, and then jump in the lake to cool off. The idea became more and more appealing, the further she got.

Kelly's body was strong, and she'd been a runner for twenty years, but it had to be outside. In London, Victoria Park had been her preferred running track, but nothing came close to the fells and lakes that were now her private gym. As she passed the jetty, she received a lone wolf whistle from a young guy–probably a student working the summer season – but Kelly didn't hear it. She ran up the hill away from the steamer, and found emptiness.

Ullswater tapered off in the distance like a vast blue serpent, and the fells drew her eyes. Mountains framed the lake on each side and the sky sat in-between. No wonder so many artists painted here. Her only companions were the beat of the music and the rhythm of her breath. There wasn't a hint of technology or man's footprint anywhere:

not a plane, not a car, not a mast, not a building, and not a sound of an iPhone.

Kelly thought of Johnny.

She wondered if he still lived in Pooley Bridge, and if that would even be a problem. They were both adults. It hadn't worked out, but it was a free country. She could live wherever she wanted to, she told herself. A stab of guilt disturbed her rhythm; she'd liked him, a lot. He was strong, independent and, most of all, he made her laugh. But it hadn't gone at all well when she'd finally been introduced to his daughter, Josie. They'd argued, and eventually realised that they were too similar. Neither would back down; Kelly thought he was wrapped around his daughter's finger, and giving the girl her own credit card was irresponsible; on the other hand, Johnny believed that it was his job to look after his only child. In the end, there was only one choice, and Josie was going nowhere. The girl won.

Pushing thoughts of him aside, her mind turned to the woman who was probably laid in a morgue fridge right now, ready to be sliced open and prodded by Ted Wallis tomorrow morning. A fleeting thought distracted her, and it was a nagging doubt that she should be running by herself, when a woman had been murdered and dumped just seven miles from here. She could be running past the farmhouse, shack, hotel or caravan where the crime had been committed. Goosebumps formed on her honey coloured skin.

'Stop it, Kelly!' she told herself in admonishment. It was easy to become dramatic and paranoid when in charge of a murder case, and she pushed the thoughts from her mind, as she reached a steep incline. She dug in, on her toes, and used her arms to pump, with small powerful thrusts from her hamstring muscles aiding her climb. When she reached the top, she jogged on the spot to catch her breath and turned back towards Ullswater. The lake reflected the dark orange sun of early evening, and she felt better.

By the time she'd reached the car again, the sun had waned behind the fells, and shadows made her shiver. She threw on a sweater and jumped into the driving seat to make the short journey home. But first she phoned the estate agent and asked what time they opened in the morning, and if the property overlooking the river was still available.

It was.

Chapter 6

They had a name.

Dental records had been traced to Mrs Moira Tate. Fifty-nine years of age, white-Caucasian, born in Halifax and, now living in Kendal. She hadn't been reported missing, and her passport photo, pulled from the database confirmed it: Mrs Tate was the woman dumped outside The Parish Church of All Saints in Watermillock.

Coiffed and serious, Moira, in life, looked wealthy and accomplished, and that's pretty much all they knew. Checks had traced a monthly deal with Vodaphone, who were scouring phone masts to see when Moira's iPhone 6S was last used, and where. Now the investigation had life.

Kelly chose the M6 route to Kendal, she was in no mood for sightseeing. She'd brought along her new rookie, DC Rob Shawcross. He was a young Detective Constable, fresh from his National Investigators' Examination course, and had reacted like an excited puppy when she'd selected him.

'Should we grab a coffee?' she asked the young male officer, as she drove.

'Sure, Guv,' he replied. It was procedure to notify the family of a homicide in twos, if possible. Kelly preferred it that way. It was an opportunity for the young officer, and one that she'd have jumped at when she was his age. Shawcross was twenty-seven and had everything to learn.

The young officer was affable, if a little star struck. Kelly Porter had a reputation: she kicked arse, and Rob saw it in the way she handled the Audi. This was his dream: to work a homicide, and he didn't want to screw up in front of his new boss. Everybody had followed the case last year on the news, and Rob knew that she'd come across some pretty nasty characters, and she'd emerged the winner.

'So, why did you choose the investigator's route, Rob?' she asked. Kelly could tell that he was excited, and a little nervous, and that was good: it meant that he cared. She tried to relax him.

'I knew I wanted to join the police when I was seven years old,' he began. Kelly was interested; it was her turf and she wanted to know what motivated anyone who worked for her. She'd been the same, watching her father leave every morning in his handsome uniform.

'So that's what I did. Then, later, as a uniform, I was involved in searching for a back packer who went missing five years ago,' he carried on. Kelly watched the traffic, but listened intently. She spotted a motorway café sign and signalled to pull in.

'I wanted to do what the detective did,' he said. Kelly smiled and nodded knowingly. She pulled into the garage and parked up, keeping the engine running to take advantage of the air conditioning.

'I was part of something, but not, if you know what I mean. And afterwards, when I'd searched for three days and taken dozens of statements, and confiscated cars, caravans and a few weapons, I was told to go back to my beat, and it…' he stopped, trying to find the words.

'It pissed you off?' Kelly asked, looking at him.

He laughed. 'Yep, that's exactly it. I wanted to see that investigation through, rather than just being a pair of boots on the ground,' he said. Kelly turned off the engine.

'So, was the back packer found?' she asked.

'I followed the news and asked around, but I don't think she ever was. I think, in the end, it was assumed that she'd left the county,' Rob replied.

'Ah, assumption: the mother of all fuck ups,' Kelly said. Rob looked at his boss, as if he was seeking some kind of indication of what she would say next; it didn't come.

'Sorry, it's an army term. It's like the seven Ps,' she said. Rob continued to search her face, nonplussed. Kelly had learned a lot of army slang from Johnny, and she used it affectionately. That was the second time in two days that she'd thought about him.

'Prior preparation and planning prevents piss poor performance,' she said, and smiled, as though expecting a round of applause. Rob didn't know what to do. Kelly opened the car door. She logged the information about the back packer away in her mind for another day. Rob stopped her.

'I'll get these,' he said. Kelly could have taken the gesture as misplaced chivalry, and been affronted, but she didn't, and instead took it as a sign of respect.

'Ok, thanks.'

Hot air blew from outside as Rob opened his door and slammed it behind him. She watched him go. He was tall and strong, and she wondered if he'd been picked on at school for wanting to be a pig, like she had. He had an open face, and Kelly admired his enthusiasm: it was infectious and reminded her of herself at twenty-seven: all keen eyes and energy, but little experience.

He came back to the car with two coffees, and got back in.

'I brought sugar,' he said. She took one and opened it, pouring sugar into the cup and stirring. She sipped a little and replaced the lid, popping the coffee into a holder by her door. She started the engine and they put their belts back on.

'Where do you see yourself in five years, then, Rob?' Kelly asked. He didn't hesitate.

'In charge of a case, like you.' It was the kind of answer she'd have given at twenty-seven, before she knew better.

'So, have you notified before?' she asked, bringing him down to earth.

'No,' he replied.

'Alright, just observe. It can be rough, especially with a homicide.' Rob nodded. He was nervous, but excited.

Kelly remembered when she'd been given a chance to tag along with the boss, as a junior officer over ten years ago now, and the exact day was fresh in her mind. It'd been a burglary gone wrong, and an old woman had been beaten to death. That day, she'd watched her DCI examine the first dead body she'd seen, and she'd wished to be like him one day.

It was good to have the company, too.

'Have you always worked for the constabulary, Rob?'

'Yes, Guv. It's where I grew up. I can't imagine leaving. What about you?' He'd heard that she'd worked in the Met. The idea of that fascinated him, but he knew he'd never go. Mia wouldn't hear of it.

'No. I worked for The Met for fifteen years. I moved back last year,' she said.

'Bit of a shock?' he asked. Kelly laughed.

'It's different. I think anyone who works murder squads in any city can't keep it up for ever, it gets to you.'

'I bet. I'm guessing this kind of thing is routine for you then?'

'Well, I see why you'd say that, but, you know, this homicide is pretty unique. I never saw anything like it in London, I saw loads of drug related homicides and sexual violence, but this is more about the ritual, I think.'

'But it's sexual too, isn't it?'

'Yes, you're right, but it's not the main characteristic. We'll have to wait for DNA to know for sure. I hope you haven't got much planned for the next few months, we'll be eating and sleeping this one,' she said.

'That's why I went the detective route. My girlfriend knows that.'

'Understanding girlfriend. I'll try to go easy on you,' she added, knowing she wouldn't. 'So, when not chasing homicide investigations, do you get into the Lakes much?'

'Every chance I get,' he said.

'Yeah? What's your sport?'

'In the summer, I windsurf. In the winter, I climb. Have you ever tried paragliding?' he asked.

'No, I haven't, have you?' she replied.

'Yeah, it's amazing. I did this flight over Arthur's Pike and the view was spectacular, I mean, just perfect. It gives you the best view of Ullswater, it was incredible. This summer I've done Brock Crags and some of the fells down Borrowdale. You should try it, honestly, it's so peaceful up there, and the view… it's incredible,' he said.

Kelly remembered when all she cared about was climbing and fell running, before she ran away to London to throw herself into something that couldn't ask questions or make demands on her heart. Rob's love of the Lakes touched her, and maybe she'd give paragliding a go one day. Slowly but surely she was falling in love with her childhood playground all over again.

'I might do that. I love the Borrowdale Fells. Could you do it off Scafell Pike?' she asked.

'Are you nuts?' he said, without thinking. Kelly looked at him and he froze. She knew he thought he'd just insulted her by the look on his face. He needed to get to know her a bit better; it'd come in time.

'Yes, I am nuts, I find it helps, when you're chasing nutters.' She smiled, and took another slurp of coffee.

They entered Kendal and followed satnav to the residence of Mr James Tate, husband of Moira. Their mood changed, and their thoughts turned to the victim's husband: it was possibly the worst job of any police personnel; informing the family of the death of a loved one, and in such horrible circumstances. However, they might also be about to meet their first suspect.

'I'll do the talking,' Kelly said, as they walked up the driveway, towards the front door. The property was handsome, and Kelly imagined that it wasn't cheap. It matched what they already knew about Moira Tate. They were in the most desirable part of Kendal. A Mercedes sat in the driveway and it had a new plate. Flowers hung in pots and boasted the best of the summer. Kelly carried a small handbag and Rob a notepad. He was dressed smartly like her, in a shirt and tie, and Kelly wondered if, like her, he preferred sport's kit and jeans. She wished she was paragliding off Scafell Pike. Kelly heard Rob take a deep breath and she tapped his arm in reassurance.

The Georgian property was double fronted and the windows were clean; it was well tended. Like Moira. Kelly knocked and they stood back.

A man, who looked to be in his sixties, answered, and smiled at them. He was disarming. He stood straight and tall as he took a pair of glasses off the end of his nose. He had a mass of white hair and reminded Kelly of The BFG. This would be hard. But then it always was.

'Mr James Tate?'

'That's me,' he said, still smiling. 'Can I help you?' he asked.

'Mr Tate. I'm Inspector Porter and this is Detective Constable Shawcross. We're from North Lakes Police. May we come in?' Kelly spoke gently and showed her badge. Rob watched.

Mr Tate's face sank, and he stayed, unmoved, for several seconds. He was puzzled, and a little worried. They had his attention. He'd been listening to Classic FM, wondering why Moira hadn't called.

'Of course,' he said finally, and stood back, beckoning them into the hallway. It was as grand as Kelly had expected. The floor was a beautiful mosaic of oak, and the staircase swept away from it majestically. A chandelier hung from the high ceiling, and Kelly fancied herself in a magazine shoot. They stepped inside.

'Please, come in,' Mr Tate said again. He led them into a spacious drawing room and it was obvious that he'd been enjoying tea and cake when they'd called. Kelly wondered why he hadn't reported his wife missing.

'Please sit down,' Mr Tate said. They did.

'Mr Tate, do you recognise these items?'

Kelly showed the man a clear plastic bag, inside which were Moira's watch and rings.

'Of course, they belong to my wife. Why…?' He floundered.

'Mr Tate, I'm sorry. There's no easy way to say this. We're here to inform you of your wife's death. We had to make sure. I'm terribly sorry.'

The man's face wrinkled and his mouth opened and closed. 'Why? What? Where?' Questions poured out of him. 'It's not possible.' He attempted to laugh: a common response to horror.

Mr Tate's head sunk into his hands and he sobbed. 'It can't be, I… I saw her only two days ago. I'll ring her, see, you've made a mistake.' Mr Tate went to get up.

'Mr Tate, is this your wife, Moira?' Kelly showed him a copy of Moira's passport photo and he stopped dead. It was Moira. They hadn't made a mistake.

'Where is she?' Mr Tate brought himself back under control and wiped his eyes. He coughed and straightened, embarrassed by his earlier outburst.

'Carlisle. We need to perform an autopsy, Mr Tate. Your wife was murdered.'

James Tate half sat, half fell into his armchair. His elbow knocked his newspaper, and that knocked the cup of tea, and it fell on to the carpet. For a moment, no-one moved. Mr Tate was oblivious to what had just happened, and Kelly left the room to try to find a kitchen that might have towels. Rob didn't know what to do, so he sat down opposite the old man and simply said, 'I'm so sorry.'

Chapter 7

Brandy Carter was bored.

Bick snored next to her and she looked at her watch: ten p.m. She went to the fridge and took another beer; she needed to get all the freebies she could while Bick was asleep. She was mad with him and he owed her anyway. They said they'd be easy on her. Bastards: they thought it was funny, at first.

He must have felt guilty because he'd given her two wraps plus twenty quid. The money was in her purse. The corner shop would still be open, and she was out of cigarettes. Maybe there'd be some kids playing on the street still, despite the hour. The light nights always gave them leeway with their stupid parents, who only started to pretend to care when something went wrong.

She remembered when her and Bick made a boy strip and then ran off with his clothes; that had been cool. But, now she couldn't rouse Bick from his pissed slumber, and the others had gone. It looked as though she'd have to go out on her own.

She felt unsteady on her feet. And she was sore. They'd said sorry in the end and they'd shared beers. She'd even laughed. But she wasn't laughing now and, as she downed her beer, she felt the need to vomit, so she made her way to the bathroom. She lifted the toilet lid and knelt down, steadying herself with her free hand. She retched but nothing came so she put her fingers down her throat and she had more success, but it didn't make her feel any better. She flushed and stood up, and she felt less shaky.

She didn't expect it to be cold outside, and so left her jacket, grabbed her bag, and went to the door. The sky was turning dark, but the last of the sun made it dark purple and orange. Brandy's vision was slightly blurred, so she didn't stop to admire it. She was unaware that she was staggering. There was no-one about and she felt disappointed. She was in the mood to make someone feel pain, to assuage her own. The park was empty, and the Rec, as far as she could see, was deserted.

She walked to the corner and entered the shop; a bell alerted the owner. An elderly man approached the counter and looked disapprovingly at the girl who swayed.

'Ztwenty Lam-bertnbudler,' she slurred. Brandy squeezed one eye; the guy was shaking his head.

'Give 'em to me...' Her voice was interrupted by hiccups and the man reached out to offer his assistance. Brandy recoiled. 'Off me!' She stumbled.

'You're drunk. Go home. Do your parents know you're out? A young girl shouldn't be out at this hour, on her own in the dark.'

Brandy went to retort, but she hiccupped instead.

'Fucker.'

'Jesus,' the man swore under his breath and figured the easiest way to get rid of her would be to sell her the goddamn cigarettes. Which he did. He shook his head; these kids threw their lives away. This one was probably no more than seventeen, judging by her size and face, but her eyes and teeth belonged to a corpse.

'£7.49, please.'

Brandy handed over the twenty and received her change. She dropped some of the coins and the man went to help her.

'Get yourself home, do you hear me? You need to get yourself to bed and take care of yourself.'

'Get off me!'

She staggered backwards and the man held his hands up, away from her. He knew that he was wasting his time, and went back behind the counter, watching her stagger away. A few coins remained on the floor. When she'd gone, he went to the door and locked up, toying with the idea of whether to ring the police or not. He sighed.

Outside, Brandy opened the packet and took out a cigarette to light. She fumbled with the wrapping and tottered across the road to the Rec. She managed to get the lighter to her mouth without setting anything on fire and took a deep drag. It hit her bloodstream with a furious wave and she had to sit down. The cocktail of chemicals, mixed with the alcohol and the coke, made her want to vomit again. She'd be alright, if she could just stand up, she willed herself. She was sitting under a tree and she leant back on the trunk.

The sky was now totally dark. She needed to get up, but the grass was so comfortable. If she could just have a little rest... Nausea caught her off guard again and she took another deep drag on her cigarette, thinking that might help.

Before she could exhale, though, a great force wrapped around her and held something over her mouth. For a moment, she thought Bick had followed her and was helping her stand. Or perhaps it was one of the other boys: Monk or Tinny, wanting some more, out of the way of Bick's charge. Fear gripped her as she struggled to breathe. Yes, it was Monk, she could feel his strength. She fought as hard as she could, but her body went heavy and she couldn't seem to coordinate herself. Maybe it was all three of them.

Brandy passed out.

When she came to, it took what felt like ages for her senses to sharpen. Her head banged, she was terribly cold, and it was dark. She was lying down, or that's how it felt. Her arms sent messages to her confused brain that she couldn't move them; more than that, she was restrained. Seconds passed and her body flooded with adrenaline as her endocrine system contemplated flight, but she couldn't flee, she was tied down.

To a bed that wasn't hers.

Or Bick's.

Maybe it was Monk's.

Now, she was fully awake.

She went to shout, but her mouth was taped over tightly. This panicked her further and her heart jumped beneath her chest. Her head hurt and she needed to pee. Then she felt the chill. She was completely naked, and her legs were bound as well. She was on a bed, of that much she was pretty sure, and each limb was tied at one of the four corners, leaving her terribly exposed, and she felt like an animal. She tried to focus and her eyes darted about frantically, but the light was so dim, and she could barely make out the ceiling and walls. She recognised nothing. The lack of oxygen, caused by the tape, was making her dizzy and she passed out again.

When she came to for the second time, it took several long seconds to remember the information she'd processed the last time. Her brain registered that she was still restrained. Bick and his mates watched a lot of porn, and some of it, she'd seen, involved tying up games. Her chest heaved up and down. Then she became aware that she was laying on a plastic sheet. Her heart rate increased again and she pulled harder at her straps, but it hurt too much. She willed herself to think.

A door opened and closed.

Brandy went to speak again, but she'd forgotten about the tape, and it was just a weird mumble. If she could have spoken, she would have screamed, '*Bick you fucking bastard, I'm gonna rip your dick off!*'

'Hello, Brandy,' said a voice.

It wasn't Bick. Or Monk, or Tinny. Her knees trembled.

'You're a bully, aren't you, Brandy? I don't like bullies.'

She struggled against her straps.

'You need to be made clean, Brandy, because all that hate and nastiness has made you dirty, do you understand?'

Brandy decided to agree with whatever the person said. They were speaking in riddles that made no sense. She nodded emphatically.

'Good.'

The person left the room.

But not for long.

Chapter 8

'Mr Tate. I know that this is an extremely difficult time. It's never the time to ask questions, but it would help Moira.' Kelly's voice was gentle and easy.

Rob paid attention as he watched his boss select her language and approach carefully. The old guy was clearly distraught. There was no way he was a suspect, at least that's what Rob decided, in his haste: he examined DI Porter to see if he could work out what she thought.

They knew that relatives would have questions of their own, but they would come in time. Some loved ones wanted to hear everything – every gory detail – so they could go forward and process; others wanted to know nothing, in an attempt to remember their dearest as they were: before their bodies were ripped apart. Some relatives were staggeringly dignified after the brutalisation of a loved one – like Jenny Davis – but others swore revenge and flew into murderous rages. James Tate didn't look like the latter; he was broken and inside the moment. Rob daren't say a word. Then Mr Tate spoke.

'Anything. Ask me anything. I'll help in any way I can. I don't know anyone who might want to harm Moira, it must be an accident. A mistake perhaps?' His face was pained, and the detectives knew that's how it'd be for a long time to come. Kelly remembered what she'd seen outside the church in Watermillock this morning, and she

47

doubted very much that it had been a mistake. She looked at Rob to check on how he was holding up; he was doing a great job. There was no easy way to experience this.

'That was going to be my first question, Mr Tate, thank you. Can you tell us why she wasn't reported as missing?' Kelly asked.

'She wasn't missing. She was staying in Penrith for a few days, while she visited her mother in the hospital. It saved her driving every day, and her mother hasn't long to live, Miss Porter. Oh God, how can I tell her?' Mr Tate's voice was tinged with panic now, as well as grief.

'We can do that,' Kelly said. She imagined an old woman preparing for her own death, only to be told that her daughter had beaten her to it. Well, at least now they had their answer.

'Do you know where Moira was staying?' Kelly asked. Rob's eyes followed, first one, then the other, like a game of interrogation tennis.

'Inglewood Hall. I insisted. It's the best.' A glaze of pride descended onto Mr Tate's face, but quickly disappeared, when he remembered that Moira wouldn't be staying at the Inglewood anymore, and neither would he.

Kelly glanced at Rob, to make sure he was getting everything down, onto his pad. He was diligent, and scribbled away.

'What is your mother-in-Law's name, Mr Tate? I presume she's in the Penrith and Lakes Hospital?' asked Kelly.

'Catherine Tring, yes she is,' he replied. Kelly noted that, like many people in shock, he was glad to be useful, because answering their questions kept him occupied.

'Do you have any children?' She carried on.

'Not together. She had Warren from her previous marriage. I have Sarah and Colin from my previous marriage,' he said. Rob wrote this down.

'I'll need names and addresses, please.'

'I'll go and get my diary. Moira's ex-partner died of cancer. Mine, sadly, is still alive. If you'll excuse me.' He left the room and Kelly looked at Rob, raising her eyebrows.

'Complicated family, some animosity there. If there's tension between him and the ex, then my guess is the children wouldn't take well to Moira, waltzing in and enjoying the fruits of their father's labour. Classic wicked stepmother,' said Kelly. Rob jotted some notes.

Mr Tate came back into the room with a book, found the relevant pages, and reeled off names and addresses. He had no idea where Warren lived, or if he'd seen his mother recently, his surname was Downs.

'They had an acrimonious relationship, and Warren was closer to his grandmother,' said Mr Tate.

More family dramas, thought Kelly. It certainly suited the circumstances of Moira's state that she had a relationship with her killer: the nakedness, the intimacy of throttling, and the care taken over her arrangement – as well as the pleasure gained from her shame at being found naked and exposed in a public place.

Their list of persons of interest was growing.

'When was the last time you saw Moira, Mr Tate?' Kelly asked.

'She left here on Sunday, after the hospice called. They said Catherine didn't have long to live, and for Moira to come quickly. They said she'd been admitted to The Penrith and Lakes. I spoke to Moira on Monday afternoon,' he said. The story struck a chord with Kelly, who

49

also found herself journeying back and forth, to and from The Penrith and Lakes, visiting her sickly mother.

'It would be very helpful if you could remember what items of clothing she'd packed for her stay.'

Mr Tate nodded, deep in thought. His eyes glazed over again, and he wiped them with his hands.

'How did she seem, when you spoke to her?'

Mr Tate took some time to think about his answer. 'She was upset. She'd argued with her mother but she didn't elaborate,' he said.

'Did that happen a lot?'

'If I'm honest, yes. Catherine isn't the easiest of people, detective.'

'Did she say she'd be visiting anyone else whilst in the Penrith area?' Kelly asked.

'No. She was just going to see her mother.' Mr Tate seemed sure of this.

'Could we take a look around, Mr Tate? Perhaps Moira's room? To get an impression of her personality? It can help immensely with our enquiries,' Kelly asked. 'Perhaps you could show us her wardrobe and think about what she took with her?'

'Of course.' Mr Tate led them upstairs, which was just as grand as the ground floor. The stair carpet was thick and lush, the soft furnishings oozed femininity, and art work adorned the walls. The place was immaculate. Mr Tate led them to a bedroom and indicated for them to go inside. Like the rest of the house, the room was opulently decorated and expensive.

'She didn't have much luggage. She had her cashmere coat, and the scarf which I bought for her last winter.' He faltered. 'I'm sorry,' he said.

'We understand, Mr Tate. Perhaps it's too much for now?' Kelly asked.

'I'll be downstairs. Unless you need me?' he asked.

'We'll be fine, thank you,' said Kelly. Mr Tate disappeared.

'You take that half, I'll take this. We're looking for photos, keepsakes, letters, diaries etc.' Kelly moved quickly, but left virtually no mess, and Rob tried to do the same. Mr Tate had invited them into the room and indicated that they could help themselves: that amounted to owner's permission.

By the time they'd finished, they had three photos, a diary, and some snapshots on Kelly's phone. As they thought, Moira wore a lot of jewellery, fine clothes and accessories, and owned countless designer handbags. She wouldn't go anywhere without her baubles and so, wherever she'd been prior to her demise (or during it), she'd left a lot behind. They went back downstairs, and found Mr Tate sat in an armchair, staring out of a window. It was time to go. The family liaison officer would be here soon.

Kelly was careful to show Mr Tate the items, for his approval, and he nodded simply.

'Thank you, Mr Tate. I think that's all for now. I'll leave you my personal number, if you think of anything else, anything at all, please call me. And if Warren gets in touch, I'd like to speak to him.'

'When can I see her?' he asked. His face was heavy, and his eyes had stopped twinkling.

Kelly knew he'd get round to this eventually, like they all did, but it was important to leave it to him, as next of kin, to decide. Moira wouldn't look that bad, once the mud was removed from her nose, mouth and ears.

The blood vessels in her eyes had ruptured, but the eyes themselves were intact, and Mr Tate wouldn't need to see the rest of her; the undertaker could be instructed to tuck her hands underneath her body to hide the damaged fingers.

'I'll let you know as soon as I can. We have professional officers, specially trained in bereavement as a result of violent crime, Mr Tate, should you wish to take advantage of it; they'll be calling on you as well. Or we can arrange for a friend to come for you.'

Kelly hated this bit: the housekeeping end of death, but it was mandatory. Mr Tate insisted that he wanted to be left alone, and it wasn't unusual, for his age and gender, to request exactly that. The liaison officers would deal with that when they arrived. For her, it was time to hand over.

'I'm so sorry, Mr Tate. Please be assured that we're working all leads, and finding Moira's killer is the constabulary's absolute priority.' She wanted to give him a cuddle; her dad would be about the same age now. He looked lost, and she didn't want to leave.

They left in silence. It was the worst part: walking away from the fallout of the nuclear bomb that she'd just dropped.

'So what d'you think, Rob?'

'I think he really loved her,' was all he said.

They walked to the car and Kelly's phone rang. It was her sister, Nikki.

'Kelly.'

'Nikki.'

'Mum's got cancer.'

Chapter 9

Coroner Ted Wallis washed his hands. It was a force of habit, rather than a necessity; the next patient was unlikely to catch any diseases as a result of her surgeon's hygiene.

She'd been called Moira, the notes read.

He could see, straightaway, that she'd suffered a horrid end. Ted was more used to performing autopsies on eighty-year-olds for the purposes of medical science, but this was different. Every now and again, a body would land on his slab that took the wind from him. Moira Tate fell into this category.

Ted spoke into his microphone, as he walked around the body, and his photographer clicked away, at his behest. She'd already been weighed, and now he measured her for the record. He also took her temperature. It had been taken at the scene, and taking it again would give him an idea of how quickly Moira had cooled after death.

He carefully scraped away the dirt from her nostrils and bagged it; he did the same with her ears and mouth, and checked her throat. The dirt was pretty superficial, and the thing that came to Ted's mind first, was a vision of a young child tidying up a misdemeanour, so he wouldn't get scolded by his mummy. He dismissed the idea, but it stuck. He'd read about it: a killer plugging orifices in an attempt to tidy up his mess, and it sprung from guilt.

The victim's eyes showed clear signs of trauma: it was as if the vessels had exploded, and Ted expected to find further evidence of asphyxiation. Sure enough, ligature marks tracked all the way around her neck, and Ted knew from experience that Moira had been throttled, and from the front: a bold move; the killer wanted to behold the moment of death. And it would take great strength to do so.

Ted was taken back to Med School, to a lecture on Criminal Psychology. If he hadn't gone into pathology, forensic psychology would've been his second choice, but he couldn't stand all the feathery pirouetting around people's feelings: they were murderers, plain and simple. He was better cut out for communing with dead bodies, not the tortured souls of live ones.

But one case stood out: the American serial killer, Michael Bruce Ross, who used to stop, mid-kill, to massage his fingers whilst strangulating his victims; because the effort was too great to achieve in one go. Ted had a vision of an all American kid, sat over a body that he'd just abused, because he 'couldn't help his urges', casually massaging his fingers, ready for the next go, all the while, his terrified young victim wondering when, and if, she would meet her end. Ted knew that he'd entered the right profession; he couldn't have counselled a monster like that.

His mind came back to his current killer, who'd managed manual strangulation, albeit with a strap of some kind, but he was still clearly a man of incredible strength. Moira was a lady of generous proportions; and dead, she'd have been even more cumbersome. The ligature marks looked as though they came from a belt, to Ted, but the lab would confirm that. He measured the marks and had them photographed.

Ted noted swelling around Moira's shoulders and more marks around her wrists and ankles, indicating restraint. He concluded she'd been killed somewhere else other than the dump site, but the detective would work that one out. Kelly Porter had been assigned the case, and with her record, they all counted on her to bring the killer to justice, and fast.

Ted turned to the mutilated fingers, and satisfied himself that, due to the way the blood had coagulated, it was done post-mortem. Be thankful for small mercies, he thought. The cuts were clean and precise, this wouldn't be the case if it had been done to a live victim in the throes of agony and terror. The procedure was performed so well that Moira's red nail polish had been sliced clean through. Ted was impressed. Perhaps the killer had experience.

Unmoving clumps of little white eggs clung to the wounds: they'd been rendered soporific by the fridge in which Moira had been kept overnight. He collected a few specimens and placed them carefully into pre-prepared plastic tubes, each containing amounts of formalin. They'd be sent off to entomology. Blow fly eggs generally hatched into flesh hungry maggots within a day, so Ted knew straight away that Moira had been dumped recently, probably the previous evening. It was a brazen act of daring, and Ted shook his head. He'd examined many bodies laden with third generation fat maggots that had liquefied their meal to almost nothing. Moira, by comparison, was in good shape. The smell of ammonia wasn't that bad either: another indication that the critters hadn't been at their buffet for long.

Next, he turned to her toes, and scraped beneath the nails. A small stiff fibre adhered to a tiny residue of dead skin cells, and he looked through a magnifying glass. He held the specimen between tweezers and held his hand steady. The fibre looked synthetic, not human, and it was grey. He wouldn't know for sure until it'd been examined properly. He bagged and labelled it.

Then, he turned to the money between Moira's legs. He swabbed the area and removed the bank notes, one by one. They were neatly rolled up, side by side, as if stored. 'Likely sexual assault,' he said into his mic. In all, there were seven ten-pound notes. Finally, what he thought was number eight, looked different. It was a piece of paper, covered with plastic, and it too was rolled up. Ted unrolled it and saw that something was written on it. The writing was clear and precise, and it could easily have been printed from a writing font. Whoever put it there had taken care over it to preserve it. Ted held it up to the light. It was barely two lines.

> '*Whilst yet the calm hours creep,*
> *Dream thou – and from thy sleep,*
> *Then wake to weep.*'

Ted bagged it, but his hands began to shake gently. He decided to call the detective as soon as he finished up. But first, he placed a chainmail glove over his left hand to protect himself from the saw, and began eviscerating Moira's body. He had a hunch that Moira's internal organs were completely irrelevant in this homicide. The killer had damaged her from the outside for a reason.

Ted was keen to look at the victim's cervical vertebrae and larynx: none of the superficial wounds had killed this woman, and Ted reckoned that the actual cause of death would be strangulation, but he had to find solid evidence first.

Once inside her body, Ted knew that he might find an enlarged liver, due to a few too many red wines; he might find a cancerous tumour; and he might even find the beginning of heart disease, but he knew that these wouldn't be related to Moira's demise. She'd been blotted out and used as a vessel: a message; and he had the note to prove it. He took samples of various bodily fluids for the lab, but he'd already arrived at his conclusion. He wondered what Moira had done to deserve such a demise, or, more specifically, what someone *thought* she'd done.

Chapter 10

The Female Medical Ward was quiet.

Kelly waited at the nurses' station and, after about five minutes, a junior nurse padded down the hall, carrying a jug of juice. Kelly had instructed Rob to get back to Eden House and check with DS Umshaw about the progress at Watermillock. Meanwhile, she would talk to Catherine Tring. Kelly needed time to process the news that her sister had given her. Nikki had driven Mum home. There was no solid prognosis, only that her mother would have to be subjected to more invasive tests. All they could do was wait. Kelly had spoken to her mother on the phone and she was adamant that she wanted no fuss.

'I've known for months, Kelly.'

It was the most vicious sentence Kelly thought she'd ever heard. Kelly considered going against her mother's wishes and driving straight home, but Wendy Porter was firm. She'd see her mother later, once her sister had gone home. Kelly wondered if she could perhaps find someone to have a beer with after work, so she could avoid Nikki. The last thing her mum would want to listen to was her daughters bickering.

'Afternoon,' the nurse said, brightly.

Behind her, the ward sister appeared, along with a man Kelly presumed was a doctor: he wore a stethoscope around his neck and he carried a clipboard, although he couldn't have been older than twenty-five. But it was the ward sister who was firmly in charge.

Kelly spoke to the junior nurse loudly – making sure the sister's ears pricked up – and sure enough, they did, as soon as the word 'detective' was mentioned.

The sister stopped what she was doing and took over. She reminded Kelly of an old style matron.

'Can I help? I'm Sister Grey, did I hear you say you'd like to see Mrs Tring?' Sister Grey asked.

'Yes, I'm Detective Porter, and I'd like to ask Mrs Tring a few questions about her daughter,' Kelly said.

'I'm afraid that's not possible,' the sister said, with finality.

'I'm sorry, why not?' asked Kelly.

'She's very poorly, detective. I doubt you'll get any sense out of her at all. She's terminally ill and beyond even palliative care. We're just keeping her comfortable. She's a non-resuscitation case too.'

'On whose authority?'

'Her own. Excuse me.'

A bell interrupted them, and Sister Grey, plus two others, including the young doctor, rushed away. Kelly followed, her interest piqued. She stood outside the room they'd rushed to, and the bell fell silent. A white plastic board was screwed to the wall next to the door at eye height, as they were outside every room. Three names were written in green washable ink. The last one was Tring. Kelly waited.

When they emerged, the sister dished out instructions, and nurses scurried off in different directions. Kelly was frustrated, and used to getting what she wanted. She followed Sister Grey, who stopped and turned around.

'You definitely won't be getting to talk to her now, Detective,' said Sister Grey. 'That was Mrs Tring's respirator. I'm afraid she's passed away.'

'What? Just now?'

'Yes. I told you she was gravely ill. It's such a shame her daughter wasn't here. But she wasn't alone. One of our staff was with her to the end.'

Kelly was bitterly disappointed. But then, she supposed, the old lady had been spared hearing the news of her daughter's brutal murder. But, nonetheless, Kelly had lost a witness: someone who might have been the last person to see Moira alive.

'Sister?' she asked.

'Yes?' The sister was striding away from Kelly, barking instructions, but Kelly persevered.

'May I ask you a few questions?' Kelly asked. Sister Grey tutted and thought for a moment.

'You have five minutes. I've got paperwork to do.' It was non-negotiable.

'You obviously know Mrs Tring's daughter?'

'Of course. She was here a lot. She hadn't been for a couple of days though, which we all thought odd. But she obviously had other things to do, I need to call her, she was Catherine's next of kin.'

'That was why I wanted to speak to Mrs Tring actually, Sister. Moira was found dead this morning.'

Now it was the nurse's turn to stop in her tracks, and she shook her head. 'Really? How on earth…?'

'She was murdered.' Kelly let the news settle in, and she watched. It was vital to build a picture of her victim, and by questioning and watching those who'd had contact with her, she could do just that.

'Christ. Excuse my language. She was only here – when was it? – Monday, I think.'

'Sister Grey?' Kelly asked.

'Yes, yes.' The nurse was obviously shaken.

'I need to get as much information about Mrs Tring's daughter's last movements as I can. I'd like to speak to your staff. I have reason to believe that Mr Warren Downs visited his grandmother too?'

The nurse thought. 'I'm not sure. You're better asking Nurse Richmond. I remember the daughter well. And I remember them arguing. But I don't remember a young man. I think Nurse Richmond had more to do with Mrs Tring, you'll need to ask her.'

'Arguing?' Kelly asked. 'Is Nurse Richmond on shift?'

'They argued a lot. I don't know what about. Nurse Richmond is in with Mrs Tring, laying out the body. She was with her when she passed, thankfully. I'll get her.' Sister Grey walked away.

Nurse Richmond came out of the room with the sister, and walked towards Kelly. The two nurses appeared to have a good relationship and talked animatedly. Sister ran a tight ship. With formalities over, she left them to complete her duties, and Kelly asked the nurse about Warren.

'Yes, he did come a few times,' the nurse said.

'And Mrs Tring's daughter?'

'She was here a lot, but they fought constantly, so she spent most of her time in the canteen,' said the nurse. Kelly made notes.

'Did you hear what the arguments were about?' Kelly looked at the nurse's badge. 'May I call you Amy?'

The nurse nodded. She was clearly put out, and probably had a million things to do, but she also wanted to be helpful. She ran her hand through her short hair and put her hands on her ample hips. Together with Sister Grey, these two were a formidable force.

'Yes. I do. It was always money. I didn't eavesdrop; it was obvious – I mean, the whole ward heard it. So when I next went in, I asked Mrs Tring if she was alright – after her daughter had gone – and she told me that she wanted to leave her money to her grandson, and that she'd changed her will. It hadn't gone down well with her daughter.' Nurse Amy raised her eye brows knowingly as she spoke. Kelly figured that the nurse enjoyed a bit of gossip, and it was something to talk about when she was changing beds.

'Thank you, Amy. Can I give you my card, in case you remember anything? Especially if Warren turns up, I'd really like to speak with him. Anything at all. Did she have any other visitors?' Kelly asked.

The nurse thought carefully. 'No. She didn't. Can I go now?' she asked.

'Just one more thing. When did Mrs Tring become dazed and confused? She seemed to have deteriorated quickly,' Kelly said.

'She started to slip away yesterday. She'd asked for her daughter.' The nurse smiled and walked away, keen to get on with her duties.

Kelly closed her notebook and made her way out of the ward.

Chapter 11

Kelly drove back to Eden House. She was keen to assemble her team and get an update.

DS Umshaw had managed to get hold of the reverend of the church in Watermillock. He'd been on holiday when Moira was found, which explained the closure of the church. He was in shock, but keen to help the inquiry, and he was due back tomorrow.

The sun was beginning to lower in the sky, shining brightly through every window in Eden House, and it made everything the familiar orange of summer. The red sandstone of Penrith became more vibrant, and the town slowed for the evening. Most offices were closing up, but Kelly had a lot of work to do. She had no intention of going home early, but as long as her team had written their reports for the day, then there was no reason why they couldn't be allowed to leave. She wanted to give them as much time as she could now, because if the case dragged on, none of them would be leaving early.

There'd been nothing of interest flagged up from interviews in and around Watermillock, and most of the day's jobs had been collated. The whiteboard, as well as HOLMES was up to date, and Kelly decided to let her team go home and get some rest. They couldn't live without the dynamic reasoning engine named after the celebrated sleuth. Kelly marvelled at how much manpower it would take to check and double check the facts that the software was able to churn around electronically without breaks or sleep. Their mood was sombre. A press release had been given from Carleton Hall and Kelly picked up the phone to call Cane. She had plenty of things to do, but they all had an order and none of them (at the moment) could be done in the middle of the night.

Journalists from as far as Manchester had begun arriving in the area: it wasn't just the rarity of such a crime in the Lake District, it was the nature of it. They had an attention seeker on their hands, and with twenty-four hour news on loop; it was bees to a honey pot.

After her call, Kelly sat alone in the incident room, sipping from a cup of water, wishing it was something stronger, and began drawing diagrams and links on a piece of paper around Moira Tate's name. Personally, she'd discounted James Tate after meeting him, but his name would stay on the board until his involvement was disproven. She wrote the names of the reverend, the nurses caring for Catherine Tring, and Warren Downs, as well as James Tate's first wife and their children. They'd been interviewed and Kelly read the transcripts. Nothing of note flagged up, and the interviewing officers had recorded their impressions that the family wasn't overly moved by the horrific news. Kelly's theory was panning out: there was no love between James Tate's first and second wives. Moira emerged as a woman who had opinions, and cared little for those she offended.

An MO formed in Kelly's mind, but she'd need the autopsy results to flesh it out. She took off her shoes and stretched. She sat back deeply in the chair, put her bare feet up on a table, and looked at Moira's photo – taken when she'd been alive. She then flicked through the photos taken at the dump scene, and she noticed that the essence of Moira – her character – had been preserved. The vision of the woman alive was very similar to the vision of the woman dead, in the sense that her personality hadn't been rubbed out. She was proud and confident. The body hadn't been hacked, ruined, or destroyed in a rage. Apart from the dirt in the nose and mouth (which had been done very neatly), and the missing fingertips, which had again been done expertly, Moira was… tidy. Yes, that was the word, thought Kelly… she'd been left tidy.

But Kelly didn't pretend to know what it meant, she was merely the observer and gatherer of evidence. Only when the two began to match, would she be able to interpret any of the information at all.

She wondered if Ted Wallis had finished the autopsy yet, she knew he'd call her as soon as he had, and they were well overdue a catch up. Ted Wallis was a man who was good to be around, he had the ability to slow things down, so they meant something, he made Kelly feel calm – and not many people could do that. Maybe it was something to do with his profession: the phlegmatic composure needed to work through a body and all its parts, not missing a single fibre or residue. The purity of examining life at its very tiniest form: tissue.

Kelly had seen one autopsy and that was enough.

The first thing that had hit her was the smell. It was the same smell that had taken her by surprise (it always did) under the tarpaulin at Watermillock: the sweet waft of dead blood. In her haste, she'd forgotten to put Vicks under her nostrils. The second thing that struck Kelly about an autopsy was the quiet. The morgue was such a peaceful place – and so should it be – and business was mostly conducted in silence. Of course, the coroner spoke into his or her microphone from time to time, but even that was done gently, and assistants worked autonomously and diligently in the background.

She guessed that the operation performed on the dead was less frenetic than those performed on the living. She'd witnessed operating theatres in full swing, full of professionals – all fulfilling different roles – buzzing around the place, barking instructions and shouting statistics. A postmortem operation was different. There was no rush: the patient wouldn't go into cardiac arrest, nor would they react badly to the anaesthesia. An autopsy couldn't save a life, but it might explain a death.

The next thing she remembered was the saw. Kelly had never had a weak stomach: she'd shot, plucked and drawn countless game birds with her father, and the touch of butchered meat didn't disturb her, in fact the penchant for veganism in the capital positively disturbed her, and it was good to be back among carnivores again.

But watching a human being butchered was not what Kelly had expected, and she knew that whoever had sliced the tops of Moira's fingers off had a taste for it: they were not only unshrinking in the face of atrocity, they were also precise and talented.

She padded over to her bookcase and retrieved a book written by an eminent crime scene investigator called Margaret Steiner, because something had jogged her memory. Kelly had loved reference books since she was a little girl, and it didn't really matter what they were about; it wasn't so much the topic that impelled her to trawl through a thousand pages of facts, it was the consuming of them. And most of it stuck. Occasionally, like now, something would trigger a fact learned long ago that became relevant, and she'd flick through her collection until she found it.

There it was. 1992: the murder of five young women in Massachusetts, USA. All the women had dirt pushed into their various orifices: eyes, nose, mouth and even anus. Margaret Steiner's theory was that the murderer was tidying up. Death was a messy business and bodily fluids drained everywhere at the moment of expiration. So, the slicing was tidy, the body was tidy, and the orifices were tidy. Someone who went to such lengths to keep their work so methodical and well ordered, must be very proud indeed. A bit like Moira herself.

And pride always precedes a fall.

Chapter 12

Ted Wallis was more than happy to meet for a pint.

It was a happy diversion for Kelly, but it meant that she could work at the same time. She'd checked in with her mother, and she and Nikki were happily eating fish and chips. For tonight, at least, there was calm, and she decided that she could afford the time away from the house. She may get judged later, but she didn't really care. Kelly surmised that as soon as her mum texted her and said that she was ready for her bed, then Nikki wouldn't be there for much longer, and it'd be safe for her to return, but not before.

Kelly kept a few toiletries at work, and she went to the bathroom to freshen up. She topped up her makeup and sprayed some perfume. As she looked in the mirror, she noticed a few lines under her eyes and she accentuated her smile to see how deep they were. Her large brown eyes didn't need much mascara but she put it on anyway, and swept a little blush on her cheeks. Her suntan made her look fresh, but she applied some lipstick anyway. She took down her hair and ran her fingers through it to plump it up. Despite having worn the skirt and blouse for close to twelve hours, she was happy with the way she looked. Not that it would matter to Ted Wallis, who was thirty years her senior, but it wasn't about that; it was about how she felt. It was like body armour: the better she felt about herself, the less shit could stick. The tinge of pain, felt when she thought about London, was fading.

She walked to the pub in the centre of town; she could grab a cab home. Ted said he could make it by around eight o'clock, as he was driving from Carlisle. He'd bought a place in Penrith and this surprised Kelly. She didn't know much about his personal life, and she wondered that, if he was married, did his wife know he had a place in Penrith?

The air was cooler now, but it was still warm enough for Kelly not to need her jacket, she carried it over her arm for later. Traffic was negligible, as most workers had left the centre, but there were still plenty of tourists milling about and at this time of year, the shops closed late, the light from their dressed windows flooding onto the streets. The best views were to be had from the Beacon, but on a clear day like today, tourists posed for photographs with the mountains as a backdrop all over town. She was used to being asked to take photos for people, and she did it with pleasure. For fifteen years she'd forgotten about the same views, and it still bemused her. Now, after only a year, they were her backdrop again, and she felt at home. She was forgetting the smell and the shapes of the city.

The pub was fairly busy and, as always, a woman alone attracted attention. Kelly had enjoyed the anonymity of the capital: no-one cared if a woman walked into a bar alone, but here, it raised eyebrows, and it made Kelly smile. Men moved aside for her, and allowed her to get to the front of the queue, it was such a dated gesture, but one that amused her. It was reassuringly familiar.

She ordered a pint of Bray, locally brewed across the M6, and a few men nodded their approval. She took her drink and found a seat with a table. She looked at her watch, and it was gone eight. Ted should be here any minute. She watched the frequenters of the pub and ten minutes had passed without her realising it. The clientele was eclectic. A group of youngsters played pool, walkers compared photos on their iPhones, and singles eyed each other up.

She saw Ted come in and caught his eye. He was a man who looked exactly how one would expect a senior pathologist and Home Office Coroner to look: deliberate, well dressed, and in charge. She stood up and he strode towards her. She couldn't imagine him doing anything else. He kissed her on both cheeks and this was one thing that reminded her of London: everyone kissed in greeting. Up here, it was still seen as namby-pamby or 'posh'. To Ted, it was just good manners.

'I see you're alright for a drink, Kelly. It's good to see you, it's been too long,' he said. Some of the men at the bar watched them, and Kelly could tell that it was assumed that she was meeting her older sugar daddy for a date. Let them think it, she thought.

'It's good to see you too, Ted,' she replied. He went to the bar, and the men parted once more, jealous of the much older man.

When he came back, he sat down opposite her and took off his tie. 'That's better,' he said. His face was tanned, despite spending long hours in his vault. Kelly assumed he played golf or something equally fitting for his age and demeanour. He wore a tailored suit, with a white shirt, and the tie he'd taken off was expensive. His cuff links were gold and he smelled of a decently branded cologne. His smile was wide and genuine, and he immediately disarmed Kelly. His hair was a soft grey and Kelly imagined that he was quite the catch in his day. He had large brown eyes and well-manicured hands; like a lawyer or a banker.

'So tell me, Kelly, how've you been?' he said.

'It's all good, Ted,' she lied, and instantly regretted it. 'In fact, that's not entirely true. We found out that Mum has cancer,' she said. She felt at ease with him and the words came out naturally.

'That's terrible news, Kelly. So soon after your father,' he said.

It had been three years, but it felt like less. Ted put his hand on top of hers and he didn't have to say much at all. She knew that he was well meaning, and, at his age, he must be thanking something up above that he was fit and well. He wasn't even seventy, and so nowhere near old, but cancer didn't tend to check details first. He must be the same age as Wendy, but she'd been down that route before: the unfairness of it all, the random nature of cancer's rampage, and it got her nowhere. There was simply no sense to it.

'Did you know my dad?'

Ted paused. He remembered Wendy well. He recalled her long emerald green dress, dancing with her husband at Wasdale Hall. Kelly had the same look: the intense brown eyes, the honey-tinged auburn hair, and the nipped-in waist. It must have been twenty years ago.

'Barely, but I met him on a few occasions. The old Earl, at Wasdale Hall, used to throw grand balls every year and I was invited. Your father, being a respected member of the force, was invited too and I remember your mother. You look like her.'

Ted's voice was comforting. It was slow and measured, unlike any other around Kelly at the moment. She was surrounded by people who shouted down hospital wards, barked into phones, dominated meetings, and demanded answers. This was different and most welcome. She sipped her pint.

'I'll tell her.'

Ted nodded at Kelly's beer.

'Good choice, I've got the same,' he said.

'I didn't know you owned a place in Penrith,' she said. She was prying but she couldn't help it.

'I like the place,' he said. 'I'm no longer with my wife, so I thought I deserved a treat, I come and walk in the Lakes when I can. I'm doing the 214 Wainwrights.'

'I'm impressed, Ted. I'd love to do them all. It'll probably take me twenty years, the way I'm going. I'm sorry about your wife.'

Kelly was intrigued. She assumed that people who divorced in their late sixties had simply grown tired of one another. She wondered what Ted's story was.

'I'm not, Kelly, I should have done it years ago,' he said. Kelly showed mock irreverence and Ted spread his hands.

'The children aren't children anymore, it was time,' he said.

'Fair enough.' Kelly thought of the tension between her own parents, and wondered if John and Wendy Porter would have been happier apart. Nowadays, everybody gets divorced, or that's how it feels. But two generations ago, it wasn't like that. People stayed together for life. For better or for worse.

She was glad she wasn't married. Maybe that's what pissed her sister off so much; that Kelly had only herself to think about. Matt, Nikki's husband, was a bit of a twat – like her own Matt the Twat in London – how ironic that she had to go all that way to find her own.

She and Ted were essentially colleagues, here to discuss murder, but it felt like they were just two people sharing space and time. They'd spent so much time together last year, and all for the wrong reasons. They'd met for drinks occasionally, and they'd discussed the weather and the fells. But they always got round to murder.

'So, Moira Tate,' Kelly spoke first. Ted shook his head.

'Can you stop sending me bodies, Kelly?' It was light hearted and Kelly wasn't offended. She understood.

'Weirdo, this one, Ted,' she said. He nodded and took a gulp of his beer.

'That's the word. He arranged her pretty good, didn't he? It was well planned. I'm no detective, Kelly, it's my job to tell you what the body went through – it's your job to say why.'

'I know you think that, but your opinion is important to me. I agree, it was well orchestrated.'

'I thought you'd like to know something I found today. I've emailed you the report, and I'm sure you'll go through it with a fine tooth comb, but a few things stood out for me.'

'Go on,' she said. He had her full attention.

'Apart from what I've already said, about the planning, it struck me that the sexual activity was subsidiary – as if an afterthought. The main point was the way she was left and what was left with her.'

'I see where you're going, but I disagree. The sexual activity is rushed, violent and full of rage, whereas the arrangement, messages and care taken, are all deliberate. I think they're equally important but different.'

'Well, that's why I'm not a detective,' Ted laughed.

'I saw some of the money in-situ before she was bagged, I knew it was there. To me, that's something you would do to someone who's cheap; to make a point.'

73

'Or money grabbing – remember the fingers,' he said. Kelly nodded. The bar was busier now, but all their attention was on each other. 'I see some of the worst things mankind can do to one another, Kelly, but I still get shocked. The money inside the victim, well it wasn't just money. I found something else. It was a piece of paper with verse written on it. I looked it up. It's from a poem by Shelley.'

'One of the Lakes poets,' she said.

'Exactly.'

Chapter 13

Kelly woke in a good mood, and when she went down-stairs to make her mother a cup of tea, Wendy was already up and sat at the table. She looked well. Kelly had missed her sister last night, and for that she was thankful. Her mother had been in no mood to discuss her health, and so Kelly had respected her wishes and tried to act as normal; but she'd forgotten suddenly what normal was. Instead, she'd given her mother a lingering hug and helped her in to bed. Even this was too fussy for Wendy who had ordered her daughter to bed.

'Morning, Mum,' she said, and kissed her.

'Morning, love, did you sleep well?' Wendy asked. Kelly wished that her mother wouldn't be quite as gracious, she certainly wouldn't be if she'd just been told that she had cancer. Kelly supposed it was the stoicism of the generation: but, to her, she couldn't understand it. If cancer came knocking on her door, she'd slam her fist into it.

'I did, thanks, Mum. I slept brilliantly. So well in fact, that I feel a bit groggy. What about you?'

'I did. It was a good night. I feel like going for a walk today.'

'That's great, Mum. But I don't know if I'll make it back for lunch,' Kelly said.

'Don't worry, love. I'll go on my own. I think I'll walk to Nikki's.'

'Why don't you call Nikki and ask her if she'll come and get you, and then walk back? I'd feel much better,' Kelly suggested. She had a crazy day ahead, but surely Nikki could find time to take their mother for a walk. 'I'm not around at all, Mum. I'm driving to Inglewood Hall today, and then I'll be in Watermillock.'

'Will you call her for me?' Wendy asked her daughter. Kelly didn't relish the idea of speaking to Nikki this early in the morning: it could potentially ruin her whole day.

'Of course I will, I'll do it now,' she said, sounding breezy. She called her sister.

'Kelly? Is Mum ok?' Nikki asked.

'Yes, she's fine. Nothing to worry about. Mum would like to go for a walk later, I was wondering if you could take her? I'm out all day,' Kelly said.

She closed her eyes and prayed that Nikki said yes. She wandered in to the other room and sat on her mother's bed, in case the conversation turned into an argument. The bed was a great ugly thing and Kelly had tried to improve it by draping it in sheets, buying fresh flowers, and pretty cushions, but it was still depressing. She waited.

'I'm busy too, you know,' Nikki said. Kelly's heart sank.

'I appreciate that, Nikki, I'm only asking because Mum would really like to get out,' Kelly said. She used all of her self-control to keep her voice monotone and passionless. She had little experience of children, but reckoned it wasn't far off this.

Nikki sighed, as if Kelly had asked her to walk to Manchester to collect a speck of dust.

Wendy eavesdropped from the kitchen, and she figured she knew how the conversation was going. She didn't blame Nikki; she was indeed becoming a burden, and it must be irritating looking after an old woman who couldn't even walk round the block on her own. She wished John were here, or that she was with him, dead already, pain free and away from the squabbles.

She didn't blame Kelly either, although she could be abrupt. It was as a result of remaining a spinster that did it; it made one hard. In her day it was called being 'on the shelf', and anything left on a shelf went stale eventually.

Wendy had checked her will only last week. Everything was split down the middle: the girls would get half each. That shouldn't cause too many problems, she thought. Her bank manager was her executor, and she'd made her instructions clear: the house was to be sold straight away to minimise arguments. She continued to listen to Kelly, who sounded tense, as always.

'I'll see what I can do,' Nikki said, uncommitted. It was the best Kelly could do and she hung up. She walked back to the kitchen.

'She's going to see how her day goes, Mum. I'm sorry,' she added.

'It's not your fault, Kelly, you've got a job to do. I'm guessing you're dealing with the body that was on the news last night?'

Kelly had forgotten that finding a body in the open in the Lakes, during peak season, would cause a stir. In London it would have been just one more news item in a stream of pessimism.

'Yes, I am, Mum.'

'What happened to her?'

'It was a murder, Mum. Pretty gruesome. You don't want to know what some weirdos get up to.'

'I hope you're being careful, Kelly. You work with some horrible people don't you?' Wendy said. She didn't add that she'd be better off getting married and having children.

'I know, Mum. Of course I'm careful. We'll catch him soon, don't worry, it's my job,' Kelly said.

'That's why I worry. Did you bring all these criminals back from London? It doesn't seem as though you've had a moment's peace since you came back.'

'That's a slight exaggeration, Mum. And you don't need to worry about me. I'm not Dad.'

'What is that supposed to mean?'

'Nothing. I mean, we're different. I'm not your husband. You shouldn't worry.'

'But, you're my daughter.'

Wendy was overcautious by nature. Kelly shook her head and grabbed a flapjack and finished her coffee. She kissed her mother on her head and decided she didn't need her jacket again, she could get used to this weather. The sky shone blue outside, and all the forecasts said it would be another scorcher, reaching twenty-nine degrees. The traffic would be horrendous, with tourists everywhere, blocking the roads with their caravans and four-by-fours. Kelly swore it wasn't this busy in the summer when she'd been growing up, but everything had seemed smaller and children take little notice of such worries, too busy jumping in lakes and running up and down hills.

That reminded her that she'd had a message to call the Tourist Board. Murder was bad for business.

'I've laid out all your pills, Mum.'

Kelly went to the door.

'I know, I've seen them. Off you go. Call me later,' Wendy said.

Kelly left. She unlocked the Audi Q5 and jumped in. It still smelled new. The Z4 she used to have couldn't navigate the fell roads, though it was a dream to drive. The Audi was better suited and more practical.

Kelly sighed, aware that she might be growing up.

Chapter 14

Kelly's team was assembled at eight-thirty, sharp, armed with coffee and note pads. The room was airless and she felt sorry for the men in ties. Her policy was to allow them to take them off in the office, but they must wear them out on business. It was easier for the women who could wear loose fitting skirts and blouses. She cleaned the white board and scribbled notes under titles. Officers busily arranged photos to put on the board, and others collated witness statements and items bagged from the area, around where the body had been dumped.

Kelly handed copies of the coroner's report around. A hush descended. DS Umshaw entered the room last minute after a quick cigarette and with her she brought a smoky odour that lingered around her. Kelly began.

'As suspected, Moira Tate died between eight and twelve hours before she was found. That gives us potentially thirty-six hours unaccounted for, before her actual death. This indicates a length of time where Moira was held against her will and tortured. A newsagent's vendor near The Penrith and Lakes has stated – on record – that Moira always popped in for polo mints either in the morning, or late afternoon. She wasn't particularly talkative, but the vendor remembers her because of her attire and general appearance standing out as 'posh'. I hate that word, but that's what he said. He distinctly remembers

Moira buying mints on Monday afternoon at around five p.m. but not on Tuesday morning. But there's something else I want to draw your attention to.'

Everybody watched their DI as she wrote the lines from the Shelley poem, found on a piece of paper inside Moira Tate, on the incident board. Kelly then walked to her computer and pressed a few buttons, bringing a photograph of the item up on the white board alongside.

Whilst yet the calm hours creep, dream thou, and from thy sleep, then wake to weep.

'It's from a poem by Percy Shelley, called *The flower that smiles today, Tomorrow dies.* Along with the money, it was found inside Moira, written on a piece of paper. Thoughts please,' she said, and waited for the news to sink in.

She liked to catch people fresh, and she wanted to know what they would make of the unusual find. It was rare that a killer wanted to converse with their enemy: the people bent on catching and punishing them. It was even rarer that a murderer left what was known as a calling card. Kelly had seen it only once before: an acronym scrawled above a body in a flat in Shoreditch.

'Grim,' said DC Phillips. 'I've never seen anything like it. It's like a warning or something.' Will Phillips who'd impressed Kelly so much last year was quickly becoming her go-to. He'd been permanently transferred to her team, from Kendal, and was catching her eye for promotion. A DC for four years, it was about time he made DS.

Kelly nodded.

'I thought the Lakes' Poets were always spaced out on opium and blissfully happy, Guv, not signposts to murder,' DS Umshaw said, and she got a laugh.

'Exactly. So why has their poetry been used?' asked Kelly. 'I want to know everything about Percy Bysshe Shelley. What sort of poetry did he write? Was it just Lakes/Romantic? What was it about? You know poetry always has a deep meaning, did anyone study English Literature? Does anyone have a burning desire to get on this? It's a direct communication with our killer; I think it's vital.'

DC Emma Hide volunteered. 'I studied English at Lancaster, Guv. I'll give it a go. I'm still in touch with some of my old professors.'

'Thanks, Emma. A copy has already been sent to a handwriting expert in Manchester, and, of course, that will take time. I'll be at Watermillock most of the day, as well as Inglewood Hall. Rob, give us an update on Watermillock, please,' she said.

DC Shawcross approached the white board and stuck photos of various items onto it. He turned around and addressed the room. He was a natural, thought Kelly. He wasn't nervous (or at least didn't show it), and he got straight to the point. He was fitting in well.

'The shoe is a Nike, size 7, general cross trainer. The lab has identified several manufacturing details as well as unique defining factors, only found on this shoe.' He pointed to a clear black and white enlarged print. 'See, here, the tread is cracked. And here, there is a stone lodged in the heel. Any suspect we identify, we'll be looking to collect and compare a selection of shoes. The footwear database didn't give us a match sadly. We also recovered quite a lot of general rubbish, none of it specific or obviously useful, but it's all gone to the lab, just in case,' Rob said.

'Good work,' said Kelly. Rob left his photos on the board and went to sit down. She carried on.

'We're waiting for results on the dirt, we don't think it's from the dump site. The coroner confirmed that the time of death preceded exposure to the evening temperature, so we're talking about someone who has the privacy to do this. We're waiting for DNA from the victim and from fibres found in her hair. We all know how long this takes and so, today, it's all about pushing the names we have so far. The hospital is phoning me if Warren Downs turns up. I did a PNC search on him and it turned up nothing, he's got no record. You all know what you've got to do. We'll meet same time tomorrow. Oh, can someone call the Tourist Board and calm them down? They've been on to Carleton Hall saying this is all going to affect business. If I call them, I won't be responsible for my language. Emma? You're way more tactful than I am. I'll let you do it. I never knew you were an English grad. Knock 'em out.'

Kelly smiled. No-one disagreed that their boss used colourful language; and it only got worse when she became frustrated.

'Have we got statements from the hospital staff nursing Catherine Tring?' Kelly moved on.

'I swung by the hospital this morning. Not all of them were on shift, but I got a list of exactly who had access to her from the ward sister,' DC Phillips said.

'Nurse Grey?' Kelly asked.

'Yes.'

'I can't imagine anything getting past her. I caught up with the coroner last night. You all have a copy of his report. It turns out that he's quite a Lakeland enthusiast.'

Kelly didn't add that Ted Wallis was also a Thai enthu-siast and they'd gone to The Thai Rack and eaten green curry and noodles. She hadn't lied to her mother this morning when she told her she'd slept well; but it was more to do with three excellent pints and the food, rather than feeling rested.

'We're lucky to have him, he's unique in the sense that he's a thinker. Most pathologists and coroners are fantastic at what they do, but they deal in facts. Ted Wallis likes the investigative part as well,' she said.

'Don't we deal in facts?' Rob asked. A few other officers stared at him but Kelly didn't mind his forward, inquisitive nature.

'Of course, but we need to watch out for links and red herrings, and that takes foresight and insight. The forensic stuff is only useful if we can pin it to a person or a place. Right, I think everyone is clear about their jobs for today. Rob you can come with me to Inglewood Hall. We better get going, the traffic will be building up by now. Have a good day everyone,' she added. The others filed out, keen to get started. Despite the horrific circumstances surrounding Moira's death, the undercurrent in the office was positive, and there was a collective desire to nail the bastard quickly. A buzz was forming in the media and Kelly had warned her officers off social sites, if they had accounts. All the journos knew was that Moira was naked, and that it was a homicide. Panic had to be contained. More could always be leaked later, in their own time, to stir interest and also, if needed, piss off their killer. Kelly grabbed her bag and jacket, and Rob followed her. They left the building and went to her car.

'Here, take this. I want you to read every word to me out loud while we're driving. It makes a difference,' she said, handing him a copy of the coroner's report.

'Haven't you read it?' he asked.

'Of course I have. But you haven't, and it's an opportunity for me to take it in from a different angle. I might have missed something,' she said.

Rob felt foolish. He'd discussed the case with Mia last night and she'd asked him all sorts of questions. She hadn't really been interested in his job when he'd been in uniform – apart from the uniform of course. But since he'd gone over to being a detective after passing his exams, she wanted to know everything. She was obsessed with crime channels and thought she was helping when she offered leads, methods and guesses. In fact, the murder of Moira Tate seemed to be gripping the whole of the Lakes. A whole host of people – strangers for the most part – were giving interviews to news channels and newspapers, and giving their opinions. It was the first time that Rob had experienced media attention, and he wasn't sure about it. Mia had got so much wrong already, but perhaps that was Kelly's intention when she chose what to feed the press in the first place. She was playing a game to irritate the killer – if he watched the news, and that was a big if.

Several things had been kept away from the public arena, such as Moira's fingers, the money, and the soil. And now they had the poem.

'Will you let the press know about the poetry?'

Kelly drove with the windows down, and the air that rushed in was warm. It was their best summer weather for years, and when the blue sky brought days and days of temperatures above twenty-five degrees, there was no better place on earth to be.

'No. It's titillation. The killer is a proud narcissist. He'll be watching the news for some kind of recognition. I want to play it down, it'll irritate him.' Rob was chuffed that he'd guessed this correctly.

'So you're a fan of profiling then?' he asked. Mia had plagued him with her take on the mind of a murderer, and he'd listened patiently, flabbergasted at how a little information could be so dangerously wrong. But, then, that was drama. He waited for Kelly to reply. He could listen to her all shift; she was serious but witty; formal but fair; accurate but inclusive; but most of all, she was a walking mecca of facts and knowledge.

'I am, yes. But I'm not obsessive about it. Like everything, it has its place. Don't get caught up in the sexiness of profiling, Rob. That's my advice to you. It can go terribly wrong. But, in small doses, I do find it helps,' she said.

Rob watched his boss. She was so different to Mia. Kelly Porter was confident, commanding and a little intimidating. She was athletic, strong and had an air of confidence, in her tailored skirt and loose, green blouse. Her auburn hair, tied to the side as always, shone in the sun, and it was tinged with blonde at the front. She wore sunglasses and concentrated on the traffic. Her face was always focused on one thing, and her jaw intimated that she didn't suffer fools: her time was too precious. Mia, by comparison, was slight and gentle; homely and open. Rob couldn't imagine getting close to Kelly Porter and he wondered if she allowed anyone in. But that was the point: they were at work, and she only had eyes for the case, and she was exactly the kind of detective that he wanted to become.

Chapter 15

Inglewood Hall Country Club and Spa was one of the best in the Lakes, and it sat half way between Ullswater and Penrith: the perfect retreat in which to luxuriate indoors, or visit the lakes and mountains of the National Park. James Tate obviously had expensive tastes, and Kelly got the impression that Moira didn't complain about it, but that someone close to her did. Neither Kelly nor Rob had been there, but they'd looked it up and seen pictures.

As Kelly drove, Rob read aloud from the coroner's report, as he'd been instructed to do. It was mostly dull, talking about lateral this, anterior that, and various weights of organs that would never catch their killer. Occasionally, Kelly stopped him and made him repeat something, then she'd fire questions at him and either nod or tut.

'Rob, this afternoon, I want you to throw everything in to finding out who Moira Tate was. It's clear that she was targeted for a reason. I want to know her habits, her routine, her friends, her style, and her views. Understand? Classic victimology. Messages don't usually get left with strangers.'

'Yes, Guv. What about the scene reconstruction?' Rob wanted to watch and learn from his boss, and he'd like to spend the whole day with her; there was an energy around her that kept him charged, but she was the boss and he'd do as he was told.

'I'll go to Watermillock and do that. I need you to get to know Moira. I'll get to know our killer.' Her mind was made up. In her head, she had specific roles for everyone. Rob was lucky to be assisting in such a small team: he was seeing much more than a regular DC in a major city would. Their team was so small that each member had the luxury of witnessing developments as they happened. In London, only the SIO joined all the dots. DCs found them.

They approached the driveway entrance and Kelly slowed the vehicle. She proceeded up the long driveway and their first glimpse of the residence was impressive. Trees lined the paths, and a great fountain stood in front of the grand entrance. The splashing water sparkled in the sunlight and gravel crunched as Kelly followed the signs to the car park. It reminded her of period dramas, in which Kate Winslet and Emma Thompson ran, in Edwardian dresses, in and amongst the trees, carrying baskets of fruit and flowers.

The house had once been a stately home. Sold off long ago, it commanded six hundred pounds per night, for some suites. Kelly wondered who could afford it. Mr James Tate for one. Her mind went back to Moira's jewellery, and the fact that she'd ruled out robbery; but looking at Inglewood Hall, and the money needed to stay there, maybe the motive was money, but just lots more of it.

'Rob, make a note to check Moira's bank accounts for large withdrawals,' she said. He put down the coroner's report, that he'd finished reading fifteen minutes ago, and got his notepad ready. They parked up alongside Mercedes, Range Rovers and a few Bentleys.

As they came to a halt, they couldn't help taking in the imposing stone, pillared entrance. They got out and their feet left imprints in the tiny stones. A concierge in uniform opened the door for them. Inside, it was cool, and Kelly removed her sunglasses. Rob did the same. She slipped on her thin jacket and took in the surroundings. Walking regalia was available in the foyer for guests to borrow should they have arrived under-prepared.

Guests sat in comfy chairs sipping coffee and reading papers. Flowers sat arranged on every table, and the receptionist smiled sweetly, as she'd no doubt been taught on a very expensive course, at a Holiday Inn, off the M6. The pair attracted attention; their garb was not typical summer attire and they looked too dour and practical to be tourists: business partners perhaps. It was in the way they looked around, as if looking for something.

A great atrium allowed the sun to flood in above them, but open windows allowed a breeze, too. The receptionist found Mr Terrance Johnson, the Day Manager, and he strode towards them. He was immaculately turned out, as one would expect from such an establishment. They shook hands.

'It's terrible,' said the manager, quietly. Kelly was mindful that he'd want to keep the murder of one of his guests as quiet as possible. He looked like the kind of man who'd be terrible at keeping secrets, and Kelly wondered what the staff had already discussed before her arrival. He whispered just a little too loudly, and he smiled inappropriately, given the nature of the call. Kelly decided that he was enjoying the fuss.

'Can we go somewhere private?' she asked. The manager guided them to a conference room and they sat down. Rob took out a pad. Terrance Johnson ordered coffee without asking if they wanted any. He wafted his hand to a waif-like waitress, and she scuttled away. The manager was a little eccentric and was probably hired because of it. Lots of Americans stayed here and enjoyed the quintessential English quirks on offer.

'So, Mr Johnson, Mrs Tate was booked in for how long?' Kelly began the interview. Terrance Johnson was nervous and kept looking at the door. Kelly noticed that his shoe looked around size seven: small for a man, but not uncommon. His manner was nervy, and his strong hands were pressed tightly together. His suit was beautifully pressed and accessorised with a handkerchief, gold wrist-watch and strong cologne. Kelly had extensive knowledge of the gym, and she could spot muscle tone from miles away. This guy was strong.

'Her husband had paid for three weeks,' the manager said, fiddling with his hands. Every now and again, he'd look at Rob and lingered a little too long.

'Cash, up front?' Kelly was surprised. She noted his wandering eye. So did Rob.

'Yes. We deal with the high end of the industry,' Johnson smiled smugly. Kelly didn't like him. But that didn't make him a murderer.

'How did you find Mrs Tate? Her character, her habits, her routine. What was she like? What did she do?' It was a lot of questions, but Kelly knew that this man's mind was whirring around all of them: he was highly intelligent, and therefore capable of contriving a story very quickly.

'She was friendly. She liked to show off, you know, she gave large tips and spoke about expensive things to other guests. It was quite embarrassing.'

'Why is that embarrassing?' Kelly wanted to know what made the manager so uncomfortable about somebody displaying their wealth. It happened all the time, it wasn't unusual or a cause for alarm, especially in an establishment such as Inglewood Hall, but, to this man, it was significant. Surely the wealthy were his bread and butter.

'Well, it wasn't hers was it? I mean, all of them are the same, the money comes from either Daddy, or sugar daddy.' Kelly didn't like the way that Terrance Johnson was smirking. She made up her mind very quickly that he was, in fact, a prize bitch who loved to gossip. Kelly wondered who else, among his guests, he'd taken a dislike to.

'Do you have a lot of rich ladies on their own staying with you, Mr Johnson? Any others who you don't particularly like?'

'I wouldn't say I didn't like them. More, I'm not fooled by them. But they tip well, so I smile and get on with it.' The coffee arrived. Johnson wafted again, and the waitress poured.

'And did Mrs Tate get along with the other guests, or was it just you who had a distaste for her?' Kelly asked, her face unmoved. Johnson looked offended. The question was timed to perfection; the waitress stared at him and kept her head down. Kelly surmised that Johnson's staff were not exactly afraid of him, but wary.

'Did you ever hear her argue with another guest?' she asked.

'No, I don't think so.'

'I think we'll see her room now.'

'Don't you want coffee?' Johnson asked.

'No thank you,' Kelly said. She wanted to make an enemy of this man to see how far she could push him. It worked. The manager took affront and stropped away, coming back with a card key.

'I'll take you,' he said, sassily.

'That's alright, we'll find our own way, if you give us directions,' she said. He did so, albeit unwillingly, and they went to find the lift.

'If looks could kill,' said Rob, when they were in the lift.

'I know, I bet he knows all sorts of secret goings on from these corridors. Bitter, isn't he?' Kelly said.

'I wonder what's eating him,' said Rob.

'Jealousy probably, he finds it hard to be around all this money, and none of it finds its way to him. But maybe it did. From Moira.'

They found the room and went in. It smelled pleasant: like a woman. The bed was made and the curtains open. The view was spectacular: they could see the mountains in the distance and Kelly reckoned that Mr Tate had paid a premium for it.

'I wonder why she was so pissed off that her mother was giving away her inheritance, when she was clearly well off enough anyway,' Rob vocalised his thought process.

'But that's her husband's money, isn't it?' Kelly said. 'Her inheritance would've been hers in her own right, and the old girl was worth around four hundred grand.'

'Enough to go it alone?' asked Rob.

'Maybe, but not in the style to which she'd become accustomed. There's more to it. We need to find Warren.'

They rummaged around the room, but found nothing of any interest. There was no handbag, phone, lap top, iPad, or anything that would have given them a link to Moira alive. They looked through her clothes and jewellery and, as expected, they were suitably expensive, and if the room had been gone through before their arrival, anything distinguishable would have been taken. A newspaper sat on the dressing table and was dated Monday July 8th. Satisfied that they'd seen enough, they left, and found Terrance Johnson talking to a female guest. She threw back her head and laughed. They wondered how much he earned in tips and if it topped up his salary significantly. They approached him, and he excused himself.

'Mr Johnson. Did Mrs Tate order a newspaper every day?'

'Yes. Every day. Always.' Johnson was serious again.

'So didn't you think it strange when she failed to order one on Tuesday?'

'I wasn't at work on Tuesday.'

'What did you do on your day off?' Kelly asked.

'I went walking.'

'Where?' she asked.

'I did the three Dodds. Not much.' He was vague.

'Could you write that down for me? I'm not familiar with the fells, I don't like walking much,' she said. Rob didn't move his face. Kelly handed Johnson a card and turned it over, she also offered him a pen. Johnson took it and did as he was asked, but he looked at the detective oddly. Before he could question why on earth she would want the names of three of the most famous Wainwrights in the park, he'd handed it back to her.

'Thank you. Can anyone confirm that you were out walking all day, or were you alone?'

Johnson looked uncomfortable. 'I was alone.'

'Right.' Kelly held his gaze until he looked away first. 'We'll be in touch.' Kelly gave him a new card. 'Maybe next time we'll have time for that coffee,' she said and smiled. 'Oh, and Mr Johnson, what is your shoe size?'

He looked down at his feet, and like all men with small feet: he lied. 'Size eight,' he said.

Kelly took a long time to look at his shoes. 'Really?'

'Well, these are a seven and a half, but...'

'Do you live on site, Terrance?' she asked.

'Yes, I have a room here.' Kelly noticed a few beads of sweat on his brow that hadn't been there before.

'So you wouldn't mind allowing us to have a look around, so that we can eliminate you from our enquiry, you understand?'

'Me?' he said, a little too loudly.

'Like I said, to eliminate you.' Rob was impressed; it was Hobson's choice. Johnson was thinking. Finally he nodded and beckoned them.

'This way,' he said. They followed him through the hotel to the back, near the kitchens. Behind a door was a corridor of first floor rooms, which were not as well decorated as the rest of the hotel they'd seen so far. Paint was scuffed off the woodwork, and wall paper peeled off the walls. Food smells wafted from the kitchen, and it was uncomfortably warm. He stopped at a door, and took out a key. He opened it and went inside. The room was light and tidy, and Kelly could see from the door, that it was small and just big enough for its sole occupant. The single bed was rather forlorn and Terrance's cheeks burned.

'We don't have to come in, Terrance, I just need a pair of your trainers,' she said. He was now at her mercy having agreed to open his door to her, and he walked to his single wardrobe and took out his only pair of trainers. He handed them to her and she took them and smiled.

'Thank you so much, we'll get them back to you as soon as we can,' she said. 'If you'll show us back to reception,' she said. Terrance locked his door and took them back the way they'd come. In the foyer, Kelly stopped and looked at the day manager.

'Thank you, Terrance. Goodbye for now,' Kelly said.

Terrance Johnson watched the two officers leave knowing they hadn't believed him.

Chapter 16

Watermillock had almost gone back to normal after being invaded by press, police dogs, forensic teams in plastic suits, yellow tape, and groups of residents and tourists, standing around theorising about what might have happened to the woman in the churchyard.

Kelly and Rob had eaten sandwiches from Waitrose at the M6 services. They'd drunk coffee and cold water. Holidaymakers came into the shops and cafes, happy, tanned and relaxed, and looking forward to the final leg of their journey. It was a hub of activity and one of the best gateways into the Lakes.

She dropped Rob back at Eden House and carried on to the A66. He would have to sit at his desk making phone calls this afternoon, like most of the others. It wasn't that she didn't want him with her, it was always good to bounce ideas from person to person, but she just couldn't afford the officers. She didn't have an endless pit, and if they were all to go home at night and get some rest, she had to spread them thinly. She knew he wasn't impressed, and neither would she have been at his age. Rob was good company and he was keen to learn. There was often much to acquire from a young fresh pair of eyes, which saw things that tired ones missed. But she'd made her decision, and had come to Watermillock on her own. Her team knew that she tried to give equal experience to everyone, but that experience included number crunching and screen time. Cane wasn't about to yield more officers yet; she'd have to unearth some critical evidence first.

Kelly parked as close as she could to the church gates. The building was typical of the Lakes: sandstone craftsmanship coupled with quiet serenity. It had almost returned to peaceful calm once more and Kelly thought back to the last time she'd been here. Since then, fifty-two statements had been taken, turning up very little of interest.

The graveyard was full and Kelly could see, without going up close, that most of the headstones were hundreds of years old. Some of them lolled to the side, others crumbled away, and some were covered in vegetation, relatives having passed long ago. Several benches were dotted around and Kelly wondered if Conrad Walker had been to that of his wife recently. She hoped so. The place was arrestingly soothing, like many churchyards, but with the trees bouncing gently in the soft breeze, and the smell of Ullswater close by, it was a place of singular beauty, and this struck Kelly as important. She walked around the back, looking for possible ways that a body (a hefty one at that) could have been transported here. The trainer print had been found in the mud, by the gate. They had no guarantees that it belonged to a killer, as opposed to a member of the congregation, but it had looked fresh, and so it was a lead.

The imprint of Terrance Johnson's shoe was not a match.

Uniforms still manned the spot where Moira had been found, but the tarp, tape and markers would be soon gone.

This was Kelly's last chance to replay the scene in her head, in peace, without being disturbed. There was only one road in to the village, so she had to assume that the body had been transported by car. It would've had to have parked. She looked around. There were no street lights in a churchyard and, sadly, no CCTV.

Kelly calculated the closest place where a car could have parked, and it was pretty much where she had parked herself. She measured it: it was twenty-three feet away. Moira weighed over two hundred pounds. Kelly had once squatted ninety kilograms in the gym, egged on by three male colleagues, whose testosterone levels would challenge those of the Marvel team put together, and she'd managed two repetitions. She'd been twenty-six at the time.

She looked around, and confirmed there were no cameras, houses, or shops in the line of sight. There was no play area, pub, bench, or bus stops nearby. Kelly's heart sank when she contemplated the endless list of options presented in the Lakes to a killer who wanted privacy, isolation and tranquillity. It had it in spades. Once out of Watermillock, the killer could have driven east or west. East led back to Penrith, and west, deeper into the Lakes National Park.

The reverend had agreed to meet her, and she walked to the entrance and opened the large oak door. He'd already given a statement, but Kelly wanted to meet him personally. He'd stated that he'd never met Moira and, indeed, no-one in the village knew her.

The church was cold, and Kelly appreciated the break from the sun. The contrast between the hot summer outside, and the cool, cavernous mausoleum interior was striking. The place was vast inside, thanks to high ceilings and huge stained glass windows. Her small heels made a racket on the stone floor. There was a desk to one side, and she checked her watch and waited, absently flicking through leaflets and flyers. For such a quiet village, it would seem that it had an active community.

Kelly was struck by the stillness, and it instantly impelled one to quiet. The smell of incense wafted around and she noticed a metal and glass burner near the pulpit. A cloud must have passed outside because light, in shades of blues and yellows, hit the stone floor, as it flooded through stained glass windows. If she'd been religious – which she wasn't – she might have been moved by the significance. The reverend was late, and she studied the images splayed all over the church more carefully. Images of saints and sinners, and hell's pitfalls, were everywhere. The potential religious significance of Moira's death nagged her.

She heard a door creak, and a man in a long black cassock with a white dog collar round his neck, came towards her. He smiled and held out his hand. He was a small man but thick-set, and Kelly wondered when and how he'd found his calling. He wore glasses but they couldn't hide his open face.

'Reverend Neil Thomas?' she said.

'Kelly Porter? Pleasure. Please, let's go to my office, unless you'd like to walk in the grounds? It's a wonderful day,' he said.

'Yes, that would be fine. It is gorgeous out there,' Kelly said, relieved. He beckoned her to lead and she did so. The Reverend Thomas was proud of his church and he pointed out details for her as they wandered towards a bench. It had a metal plate screwed onto the back of the backrest and an inscription: 'For Hilda Alty. 1909-1973. Missed every day.'

They sat. Birds chirped, and the reverend waited.

'Reverend, I'd like to ask you some questions about the place. You must know a lot about the village, and, I'm guessing, its inhabitants. How long have you been here?'

'Twelve years. I couldn't believe my luck, being sent here. But now, I'm afraid visitors might come here for something entirely different,' he said.

Kelly was sure that if visitors came here on some weird pilgrimage tour of a gruesome murder, then the reverend wouldn't mind the extra traffic. They could set up a tea shop.

'I'm wondering if there was a reason why the woman was left here. I have reason to believe that this place was chosen on purpose, but from what I can make out, she had no connection with Watermillock,' she said.

Kelly didn't mention the relevance of dump sites, or the fact that she believed it to be a punishment killing – thus flagging up a whiff of religion at least.

The reverend looked at the sky, as if God would provide him with the key to her quandary. She wished that He would.

'It's a beautiful place, Miss Porter,' he began.

'Please call me Kelly,' she insisted. He carried on.

'I suppose one could think that she was brought here to make peace with God. You could think that it was an act of mercy. Or, it could have been an accident,' he said.

'I don't think it was an accident, and I don't think it was mercy. The lady's husband told us that she was not at all religious, in fact, she was vehemently against it,' said Kelly.

'So a conversion perhaps?' said the reverend.

It was an attractive theory, and Kelly did believe that Moira knew her killer, because he was making a statement about her personality and character. Kelly wondered if the reverend had ever considered becoming a forensic psychologist.

'What do you know about the Romantic Poets, Reverend? Specifically the Lakes poets. I noticed you had some of their work for sale at the entrance.' The trinkets, pamphlets, maps, guides and sweets for sale in churches had become a normal sight, and there was nothing unusual about this one.

He looked at her oddly. 'Has that got something to do with your enquiries, detective, or are you just making conversation?'

'I have reason to believe that they might be relevant.'

He looked at her questioningly but Kelly divulged nothing further. He knew the score. He looked at the sky once more, thoughtful and introspect, then answered.

'Well, they loved the Lakes. They loved the majesty, the vastness and the fact that in such a wilderness, one was closer to God. Well, perhaps not God, but a god of sorts: their god. The creator, whatever form that came in for them. I think Wordsworth was religious, but they were all more believers in the human spirit. Or they thought they were. In reality, I think they all believed in the God who created all of this.' He wafted his hands around the church-yard and beyond, to the fells. It was singularly romantic, and Kelly could sit and listen to this man for hours. He must spend much of his time alone, in contemplation and study, but he didn't seem to mind. His speech was calm and measured. A bit like Ted Wallis.

'I think they were tortured souls, Kelly, looking for the meaning of life, escaping the evils of the time,' he said.

The word torture jarred her. 'What were they escaping from? What tortured them?'

'The degeneracy of industrialisation. Lust for money and capital. The slide of man into a hedonistic and politically crooked existence, where nature was forgotten. Why?' he asked.

'You seem to know a lot about them, Reverend, is it a hobby of yours?' she asked. She thought about Moira's fingers again, and an image of miserly money lenders in Grimm nursery tales came to her, their fingers sticky with money and corruption.

'Absolutely. I love any literature or art to do with the Lakes, it's the most beautiful place on Earth! I take guided walks on trails following in the footsteps of poets like Wordsworth, and artists like De Breanski.'

His enthusiasm was infectious. She felt like staying here in this alluring place, discussing poetry and the meaning of life, all day long. But she had a job to do, and despite wanting to spend hours with this reverend–cum–professor, she had to pull herself away. She wondered if, at some point, she could join one of his tours – it could be relevant. Indulgent, but relevant.

'What do you think of this? It's from Shelley's "The Flower that Smiles Today, Tomorrow dies".' She showed him the lines that had only yesterday been retrieved from the cavity of a murder victim, and today copied onto clean note paper, and he read them, engrossed.

'This is one of the more depressing elements of Lakes poetry, Kelly. They were all guilty of it: Wordsworth, Coleridge, and Keats, although there's no evidence that Keats ever stayed here for any length of time. They couldn't help themselves, it was their way of trying to make sense of man's existence. The Age of Reason tried to do it with science, and the Romantics tried to do it with feelings. It drove a lot of them to opium, I can tell you.' He laughed.

'So what's depressing about it? I always thought that the Lakes poets just wrote about the beautiful scenery. What am I missing?' she asked.

Kelly had a vision of Coleridge, Shelley and Southey, wasted on hard drugs, on top of Wordsworth's cottage roof on a heady summer evening, swigging from bottles of Port and reciting their poems to one another. But she still didn't understand the meaning of the verse clearly.

'I suppose they compared themselves to nature, and always fell short. Ironically, though, they were all narcissists. They espoused poetry that came from the heart, but they were still members of the privileged elite, like all philosophers. Champagne socialists, shall we say.'

'So they were hypocrites?' Kelly asked.

The reverend laughed.

'Yes, you could say that. Look, it's about innocence, and not being as beautiful as we once thought, and about losing something because it's essentially tainted.' He looked at her. His eyes were soft, and his face deeply etched with experience; real and theological. His face was tanned and she imagined him taking groups of walkers around the major sights, reciting lines from verse as they listened attentively. A philosophical theologian was a rarity indeed, well at least one who was so balanced. In all the time he'd taken to answer her questions, he hadn't once tried to preach to her.

Kelly was no English graduate like Emma. She'd majored in Biology. But it was beginning to make sense. Especially the notion of being judged.

Punished.

'How regular are your tours, Reverend?' she asked. 'Does anyone help you?'

'Every Friday morning, and yes, my good friend, Professor John Derrent, at the University of Lancaster, comes along now and again, and when he does, he always puts his own spin on things; the walkers love it.' The reverend was enthused once more, and he became more animated.

'And you follow in the footsteps of the poets?'

He nodded. 'Most of them,' he said.

'Percy Bysshe Shelley?'

'Yes, when we go to Keswick. But he was only here for three months. He didn't like it and he moved on, finding it not in the least romantic, but tainted and full of tourists. A bit like today, some would argue,' he said, mischievously.

'And is that what you think, Reverend?' she asked.

He thought for a moment before he replied.

'Anything that is beautiful is sought after, and one would like to think that we are the only pursuer. It's like going to The Louvre to see the Mona Lisa, and getting there, only to find that you have to queue up behind a thousand other people to get a glimpse, when your fantasy was you sitting in front of it, on your own, taking it in, and appreciating the beauty like no-one else could,' he said. Kelly shivered.

'So their idea of perfection was tainted after all?' she asked.

'Exactly!' he said, his eyes twinkling. His accent was from the midlands somewhere, and Kelly wondered if he had a family.

'Do you stay alone in the Vicarage, Reverend?'

'I do. Divorce isn't picky like God is,' he said. Sadness tinged the corners of his mouth and his eyes looked glassy.

'Well, I really could stay here all day, but I need to get back to work, I'll contact you should I need anything further, and please don't hesitate to get in touch should anything jog your memory – anything at all, even if it doesn't seem important,' she said.

'Of course I will. I'll walk you to your car.'

'Could you write down the name of your professor for me, and your phone number?' she asked, and passed him a card and her pen.

He did so. The reverend was right handed.

She stood up and held out her hand.

'Thank you so much, Reverend. I'll join one of your tours one day.'

'I do hope so, that would be very fine indeed.'

As she walked back to her car with him, Kelly thought to herself that she hoped he hadn't always been religious. It seemed such a waste. She hoped he'd smoked weed and necked vodka at university. She did that a lot with people who fascinated her: made up stories about their past.

They arrived at her car.

'Is it a close community, Reverend?' she asked.

'Oh yes, and everybody is in deep shock. I'm organising meetings to bring everyone together so we can grieve as a community. We didn't know her, but she came to rest here, and it will never be the same,' he said.

'Have you seen Mr Walker?'

'Yes, we've been for several pints of the strong stuff. He's taken it badly, but he's a survivor, Conrad is, he's made of tough stuff.'

'I hope it doesn't put him off his morning routine of coming to sit with his wife.'

'No, he's here like clockwork, every morning.'

'Good, I was worried about him.'

They said their goodbyes and Kelly drove away. The lake glimmered in the distance and she considered that the killer had chosen somewhere fairly remote: it wasn't random. Had he planned the timing too? Perhaps he had watched Conrad Walker go into the churchyard every morning, and placed Moira near his bench. If the community was as close as he said it was, then Kelly wondered why on earth no-one seemed to have seen anything at all. It's as if Moira was brought here under circumstances shrouded in absolute secrecy, and the whole village had been asleep.

Chapter 17

The nurse had been true to her word, and phoned Kelly as soon as Warren Downs appeared at the hospital to visit his grandmother. Instead, the poor bastard had been told that both his mother and grandmother were dead, and one at the hands of a brutal murderer.

He'd been prepared for the passing of his grandmother – people over eighty were supposed to die, even if you loved them more than anything in the world. But Warren Downs was struggling to process the death of his mother: the finality of it as well as the savagery of it. It wasn't grief; just shock. The nurse didn't know the details, and so Warren waited patiently for the detective.

Kelly was beginning to detest the Penrith and Lakes Hospital. It was a sprawling place, half new, half ancient and crumbling, with corridor after corridor of pale looking people, shuffling along in a half-dead stream of malady and despair. The people in the café looked no happier or better; mothers looked at their iPhones and ignored toddlers demanding more cake, wives worried about husbands, and mothers worried about sons; all looked anguished and dog tired. Kelly made her way to the female medical ward, and was shown to the day room. It was a sparse room, badly decorated, airless, and boasting only one tiny window that overlooked a brick wall. The TV blared out something, albeit quietly, and a man got up from a shabby sofa as Kelly walked in. She knew the room well; her mother had resided on the very same ward, twice.

He was in his late twenties, tall, with hunched shoulders, and a mass of shaggy hair. He looked as though he'd die of a heart attack, should you speak too loudly, or too directly to him. He looked like the son of a domineering mother. He also looked as though the exertion needed to carry a chair would be too traumatic for him. Pending evidence, she discounted him straight away.

'Warren? I'm Detective Kelly Porter. Pleased to meet you,' she said, and held out her hand. He took it and it was a limp comparison to hers. He didn't speak.

'You've had quite a shock, Warren, I know. I'm sorry.' Kelly waited. Warren went to sit back on the shabby sofa. He bit his nails. His hair was unkempt, and Kelly guessed that, by habit, he didn't wash every day.

'Warren, I'd like to ask you some questions about your mother,' she said. He looked at her, and for the first time, Kelly saw emotion. It was a mixture of disgust and defiance.

'What was your relationship like with your mother, Warren?'

'What kind of question is that?' His voice caught Kelly off guard. It was quiet, but aggressive and bitter. It was bigger than him.

'It's just a question. Some of the nurses have told me that you didn't visit when your mother was here,' she carried on.

'It's none of their business. Why are they telling you stuff?' He was angry.

'They kind of have to, Warren. I'm a police officer, so it's in everyone's best interests to tell me what they know.

It'll help me catch your mother's killer quicker.' Kelly had decided that Warren Downs was tougher than he looked, and she played hard. 'Why did you avoid her, Warren?'

'I couldn't stand the old bitch. She was a money grabbing leech,' he spat.

Kelly remained calm. She thought of the money stuffed into Moira's vagina. It was a personal, intimate act, full of hate and rage. *Fingers sticky with money. The flower that smiles...* Vanity.

'To the extent that someone would want to kill her?' Kelly asked.

'I wouldn't know. It wouldn't surprise me if she had loads of enemies. Start with her stepchildren, they hated her,' he said, and looked away.

'As did you, it would seem,' Kelly suggested.

'Yes. I did. It's no secret. She... she let everyone down,' Warren said, quieter now. He softened and looked at his hands.

'Warren, did you kill your mother?' Kelly pushed him.

'No! Are you accusing me? Jesus Christ, I couldn't... I...' He floundered, as if the thought of being seen as a suspect was ludicrous.

In fact, it was the most natural thing in the world for the victim's family to be investigated, one by one, until the police were satisfied that they were innocent. The police were used to being lied to by relatives, and investigating them was a matter of course. Only last month, yet another live TV plea had gone out in Leicester for a missing ten-year-old girl. A week later, the police discovered that she'd been killed by her own father: the same father who'd appeared on TV in tears.

But Warren Downs displayed too much passion to be faking it. His reactions were instant, not contrived.

'So, who do you think did?' she asked. He wasn't off the hook yet. 'Where were you between eight p.m. on Monday, to two a.m. on Wednesday? Can you account for all that time, Warren?'

'No, I can't. I'm sure that for most of it I was alone, and that looks bad. I didn't know where my mother was staying. I didn't see her the whole time Gran was here. I work on the other side of town, in a warehouse, I can give you my shifts. But I live alone, so I can't get anyone to verify the evenings.'

The lad was talking as if to a lawyer, and Kelly was inclined to believe him. His body was open, and more relaxed now. But whoever killed Moira was capable of more than mere story-telling, so even if Kelly stared the killer in the face, she wouldn't be sure.

Society was full of functional psychopaths, holding down jobs, having families, going on holiday, and buying fried chicken. Whoever killed Moira Tate, Kelly surmised, was probably a damned good actor.

Her team had yet to formally put a profile together – apart from the narcissistic angle – and so she was relying on instinct. Warren Downs seemed disinterested in his mother, as if he'd given up years ago, and he didn't seem to have a burning hatred that consumed him and everything he did. When Kelly looked at his shoes, she estimated that he wore a size ten, at least.

'When did you fall out with your mother, Warren?' She was analysing him, and he knew it.

'Probably shortly after birth, officer.' He was no longer intimidated by her enquiries. Kelly thought the joke funny, but didn't laugh.

'When was the last time?' she ploughed on.

He sighed. 'About two years ago. She was ashamed of me, after finding a husband who believed she was of better stock than she actually is,' he paused and smiled. 'He still has no idea that she was raised on a council estate. Gran called her Mrs Bouquet,' he laughed and his eyes wandered off.

'You were close to your Gran?' she asked softly.

He nodded. 'I didn't expect it this quick, the nurse said at least a week or two.' He stopped and put his head in his hands.

'Do you know that your Gran's will names you as sole beneficiary to her estate, Warren?'

Warren looked at her and his mouth opened, but nothing came out for a moment.

'She said that's what she'd do, but I never believed her. I told her not to,' he said.

'Well, she went ahead and did it, Warren. Do you know how much her estate is worth? Did you ever discuss it?' she asked.

'No, I'm not interested,' he said, and Kelly believed him. She had what she needed for now, but she'd like to visit his home.

'Where do you live? Could you write it down for me? In case I need to get hold of you, you could add your phone number too, please.'

He did so. Kelly looked at the erratic effeminate handwriting. It was another sample to add to the others she'd gathered so far. He was right handed.

'I'll be in touch. I might need your help again. And of course, I'll keep you updated on our investigation,' she said.

Warren looked confused; he'd expected to be dragged into the back of a black police van, there and then.

'Officer?'

'Yes?'

'Can I ask you something?'

'Of course. Anything.'

'Was it… bad? I mean, I don't want to sound weird, but, after everything, it's a bad way to go. Was it really bad?'

'You mean, did she suffer?'

The young man nodded. He displayed compassion, and Kelly admired it. His grandmother obviously thought the world of him, and from what she'd gathered so far, not many thought the same about Moira Tate.

'I think it was quick. She won't have known a lot,' she lied. He seemed relieved. She left him to his thoughts and left the room, looking at her notepad.

James Tate's ex-wife, Emily, lived in Windermere. Preliminary visits had turned up nothing. It was another line of enquiry. The traffic would be horrendous, but she'd still have time to cook for Mum and perhaps a quick pint afterwards to unwind. She'd got into the habit of playing pool in the Goose and Gun with two old school pals who hadn't grown up either. One was divorced and the other had never married, preferring instead to impregnate ladies and pay maintenance.

Before she got back into her car, she spoke to an officer whom she'd tasked with running the name of Terrance Johnson through the PNC. He'd been caught in a lewd act in public toilets in Bowness three years ago and let off with a caution.

Chapter 18

Kelly collected Rob from Eden House. He was the one the least tied down when she'd strode in to look for a colleague to accompany her to Windermere for the last job of the day. DS Kate Umshaw watched with interest as the rookie fumbled with note books and pens, and she found it amusing. It wasn't so long ago that she'd been all keenness and enthusiasm, until she'd had three babies and begun to spend more time thinking about chicken nuggets than work. She'd learned that, no matter how many hours one put in to this job, bastards kept doing awful things.

The drive to Windermere wasn't as bad as Kelly had anticipated, and they drove with the windows down; the air was still warm as it rushed into the vehicle. Rob was buoyant.

'So, tell me what you've learned about Moira.' She was ascending Kirkstone Pass, and she looked in her rear view mirror to catch a sight of Brotherswater. Past the inn, she began to descend, and that was when they hit traffic. Caravans, estates with trailers, motorbikes and minibuses choked the route south, and Kelly began to worry about her plans for the evening.

Rob distracted her.

'I've spent pretty much three hours on the phone to people in her diary, and it's weird,' he said.

'What's weird?' she asked.

'I just get the impression that she was either a really shallow person with no friends, or she was leading a double life. There's nothing there to suggest a closeness to anyone. She had shopping partners, tennis partners, bridge partners, and golf partners, but none of them were distraught at the news. Shocked, yes, but none of them broke down or cried. They didn't speak about her in a way you would expect from friends. I think she was incredibly private.'

Kelly processed the information. 'I spoke to the son.'

'What was he like?'

'Well, he confirmed that he pretty much hated his mother, but he was very close to his gran. There was real emotion there. He's probably nine stone wet through. Not someone who will give us a headache I'm sure. He called Moira a — and I quote — a money grabbing bitch.'

'Motive?' he asked.

'Yes, but I wasn't convinced. There was something gentle about him,' she said, as she peered around traffic, willing it to move. Finally, they picked up speed and Windermere was only five minutes away.

'Gentle?'

'I don't know. There was something about him,' she said, distracted with the traffic.

'Can't all killers be charming when they want to be?' he asked.

He was challenging her judgement and it irritated her. She fell silent, and Rob was embarrassed.

'I'm sorry,' he said.

This irritated her further.

'Don't be. It's early days. It's too easy to see guilt in everyone at this stage, I like to watch people and discount them, rather than try to make them fit. So what else did you find out about Moira, apart from that she had super-ficial friends? How many people are you close to? Apart from your mother and father, and your new wife? Moira was fifty-nine years old, Rob, similar to my mother, and after raising two kids and sacrificing her life to her family, she doesn't have many friends either. Rather than thinking why she has no friends, look elsewhere. What about friends she made through her current husband, maybe she cut herself off from friends in the past as she moved up the social ladder, she was quite a climber according to her son.' Kelly concentrated on the traffic, and wished she'd come alone. She was tired and felt she'd spent the day in her car. At least it wasn't the M25 though.

She glanced sideways and saw Rob's cheeks burning.

'I'll ask Mr Tate about that then,' he said.

Kelly felt a pang of guilt, but it was fleeting. A junior officer had to learn to think big, and not get bogged down in details. Cases were processes of elimination, not blank pieces of paper, ripe for any old theory that can be made to fit.

'What else?' She decided to distract him, surprised by his fragile ego. Rob looked at his notes.

'On Monday evening, about nine o'clock, Moira tried the same mobile number over and over again, and that was the last number she called,' he said. 'It was pinging off the mast near the hospital in Penrith.'

'And, do we know who the number belongs to?' she asked.

'I've searched her diary, and it's under a man's name called Tim Cole. I looked him up and he's a surgeon at the hospital in Penrith. At first, I thought he was something to do with her mother's care, but he's not an oncology consultant, he's an orthopaedic surgeon. He specialises in ankle injuries. I called him, and he got all cagey, playing down the phone calls, and the extent of his relationship with Moira. So I went to see him. He's married, and he begged me to be discreet. It turns out that he and Moira were having an affair.'

'Really? Well, well, well. Good work! What was he like?' she asked.

'He's tall, looks as though he takes care of himself. In his late forties. He was pretty embarrassed; he kept asking me not to involve his wife,' Rob said.

'I don't suppose you got hold of his handwriting?' she asked.

'Well, he did have to nip out for five minutes, to assess an emergency, and I might have taken a quick photo of his notepad.'

'Unconventional but resourceful. What was his character like? Did you trust him?' she asked.

'He came across as someone who rarely found himself in a situation over which he had no control,' said Rob.

'How long had he been seeing her?'

'Four months,' Rob said.

'Did you ask how they met?'

'Yes, in the chapel, apparently. That's what he said,' said Rob.

'But, Moira wasn't religious. What was she doing in the chapel?'

'I don't know,' Rob said.

Chapter 19

Emily Tate was a rotund woman in her sixties, and she gave Kelly the impression that she carried a weighty resentment on her shoulders. The neglected appearance and the lines curving from her mouth made the woman look dreadfully unhappy, as if she was delivered life changing, awful news on a daily basis. She looked immediately suspicious, and the glasses perched on the top of her nose were shoved back with a single finger, at the same time as flicking hair back from her face. She wore jeans and a baggy t-shirt covered with a cardigan more suited to a man.

It was none of Kelly's business, but stood before her was a woman who either cared not for what anyone thought of her; or had no inkling of how unattractive she was. However, in the three seconds they'd been standing in the doorway, Kelly had noticed a flicker of a past happiness in the woman's eyes. Kelly got the distinct impression that rot had set in when James Tate dumped her for a younger model.

Kelly introduced herself and Rob, and the woman invited them in. She didn't look surprised by the visit. They were invited in to the small reception room off the hallway, and Kelly took everything in. The house matched the character of its owner: it was drab, unloved, worn and had seen better days. There was a malaise that pervaded the small space, and an untidiness that evoked sadness. Still, Kelly kept her mind open. From the moment she'd opened the door, to showing them into her home, Emily Tate hadn't smiled once.

'Come through,' she said.

The house was large for one person, and Kelly guessed that James Tate paid a sizeable sum to keep it going. Their children were grown up, but Mr Tate had confirmed that he still paid maintenance to his ex-wife, because it was the decent thing to do. But, despite the size, and obvious value of the place, it was unloved. The décor was functional. The walls were painted magnolia, and the furnishings were dated. Kelly wondered how long the woman had been on her own. There was no noise – not even a radio, or a spinning washing machine. There were no cooking smells or evidence of anything familiar or comforting that would make the place a home.

'Do you work, Ms Tate?' Kelly asked.

'No, I gave up two careers for the children, and it left with me with no marketable skills,' Emily said. She was like a succubus. Any life in the room had deserted it years ago, and Kelly was beginning to feel the same way. Kelly wondered if Emily sat in her lounge all day feeling sorry for herself. It must be exhausting, she thought.

'Can I get you a drink?' Emily finally offered. The question was primarily directed at Rob, to whom Emily had begun to pay attention. Kelly watched as Emily smiled for the first time at him, and he smiled back. It was a little pained, and Rob looked awkward.

'I'll have water, please,' Kelly said.

'Could I have a coffee?' asked Rob.

'Of course, sit down in there and I'll bring it,' Emily said, and left the room. Kelly turned to Rob and he spread his hands in mock helplessness.

'You've got a new fan. Keep it up! I'll watch, you're distracting her,' Kelly said.

'You want to use me as a human shield!' Rob feigned indignity.

'Yup.'

Emily came back in to the room, followed by the waft of coffee. A tray was laid with sugar and milk. Kelly's water was lukewarm, and the glass dirty. She placed it on the table, untouched. Rob accepted his coffee gratefully, and Kelly decided it was time to start. Emily sat heavily on an armchair opposite them. Now and again she'd steal a glance at Rob, and Kelly couldn't work out if it was on purpose, to buy time to think, or the woman was genuinely taken with him. He was an attractive guy – that was for sure. He was tall, smart, athletic, and in possession of a disarming smile. He could be a valuable asset to Kelly. He wasn't her type: he was too young, too perfect, and too clean-looking. Her mind briefly wandered back to Johnny and she pushed him out of it.

'Mr Tate told me that you've been made aware of the death of Moira,' Kelly said. She waited. Emily nodded, but looked at Rob. She gave no impression that she was in the slightest bit interested in Moira Tate's death.

'Did you know anyone who might want to harm Moira?' Kelly asked.

Emily looked at her as if Kelly had blasphemed in a holy place. 'Well, I don't know anyone who liked her, let's put it that way.'

Kelly was saddened that the victimology that was rapidly coming together in her investigation was of Moira as a woman who few people actually liked, let alone loved.

'Does that include your children?' Kelly asked.

'That woman took their home,' Emily said. Her chin jutted out, and her hate made her ugly.

'Are you telling me she deserved to die?' Kelly asked.

'No. I'm telling you I'm not surprised.' The answer was measured. Emily Tate made no apology for her feelings.

'What's your relationship with your son like?' Kelly continued. The question seemed to catch Emily Tate off guard. She looked at Rob. Kelly could tell that she was thinking. Rob smiled and sipped his coffee.

'Lovely coffee,' he said. Kelly carried on.

'The reason I ask is because he is ignoring my calls and not answering his door. I've sent officers to his address on two separate occasions. Is he away?' Kelly asked.

Emily switched her gaze to the female detective who was obviously in charge. Her voice was clipped. Kelly knew that she was rattled. Her son was a touchy subject.

'No, he's about. He works long hours. He wouldn't be rude on purpose,' Emily added. 'What are you accusing him of?'

'Nothing. I need to speak to him, that's all. Do you have a recent photo of your son?'

Emily stuttered. 'No,' she lied.

'Who might that be in the hallway, on the occasional table, the one with the lamp on it?' Kelly asked.

'Oh, that one,' Emily said. 'Of course, I'd forgotten about that,' she said. Kelly went back to the hall and retrieved the item. She held it up to Emily. Rob remained where he was.

'Yes, that's Colin, with his sister, Sarah,' said Emily.

'I believe that Colin spent some time in a juvenile home for boys? Can you tell me about that?' Statistics were sadly against Colin Tate: children from care homes rarely broke the mould, and delinquents were rarely cured.

Emily swallowed. It was harsh, Kelly knew it, but she had to explore all angles, and Colin Tate was avoiding the police for a reason.

'He did nothing wrong. He had a tough start in life. When he came to us, he was an angry young man, but that all changed. He's got nothing to do with this, if that's what you're implying.'

'When was the last time you saw him?' Kelly ignored the statement. No-one knew who had anything to do with Moira's death, apart from the killer. Kelly was aware that both Colin and Sarah were adopted. It shouldn't matter.

'You just don't care do you? You're all the same. You lot have preyed on him all his life because of his problems. He's vulnerable. He responds well to care, not being hounded. If he knows you're always at the door, then I'm not surprised he's worried. He's probably thinking the same as me.'

'His file said he suffered anger management issues. Are you telling me that this has changed?'

'If you treat him right, he has no so-called "issues".'

'And what if someone doesn't treat him right?'

Emily Tate was showing signs of distress. 'He was a confused boy. He struggled with pretty much everything. I don't think it's fair to judge someone by their past. He's better now.' She was unconvincing.

'Can you have him call me as soon as you speak to him, please? It's essential that we talk to him. He's not in any trouble, but I have to interview every person who knew Moira, surely you understand that? My officers have spoken to dozens of people connected with the inquiry, and he's on my list, that's all.' Kelly was making little headway. 'Does he live alone?' Kelly pushed on. It was safer territory and she'd pushed Emily Tate about as far as she could.

'Yes, he does.'

'Does he read poetry?'

'I don't know. He has a lot of books, but I've never been interested in them,' Emily said. 'Is that important?' She was puzzled.

'It might be, we don't know yet. Well, thank you for your hospitality. That's all for now. I'm getting the impression that Moira caused your family quite a lot of upset. I know you think she caused pain wherever she went, but I'm assuming that's a sweeping statement? Unless you know of anyone specific who had a grudge?'

'No.'

'Right, well if you do, here's my card. I'll expect a call from Colin by the end of the day. It's vital that he doesn't avoid us; it will only make it worse for him.'

Emily Tate didn't reply, but got up to see them out.

When the officers were gone, Emily Tate dialled a number on her mobile phone that was answered quickly.

'You better come here now, and get your story straight, the police know about the home.' She ended the call.

Chapter 20

The Goose and Gun was busy but not packed. Kelly had changed clothes at home and she wore a light summer dress and heels. Her hair fell to her shoulders and she felt unburdened.

She'd left her mother watching TV. The lounge resembled a bedroom more and more, and Kelly had made sure she was comfortable before she left. Kelly imagined cancer to have a plan: you got it; it was treated; if successfully, you survived; if not, you died. That's how it had been with Dad. Kelly had no idea that it could come and go, and that doctors might be in two minds about what they could or could not treat, and how. It was a confusing mine-field. One minute, Mum felt fine, and the next, she slept all day long and woke up looking thirty years older than she was. One thing was for sure: Wendy made it clear that Kelly was not to fuss over her. So, it was easy to forget that her mother was in fact ill, especially when the subject of Nikki came up.

'I know I couldn't take you for a walk today, Mum, but it wouldn't have taken much for her to take half an hour of her day for you. It's selfish and she's just making a point,' Kelly had said.

'I know what you think, Kelly, but I don't want to hear it. I've listened to you two bickering for the past twenty years and I've had enough!' Wendy had replied.

She shook with vehemence and it took Kelly by surprise. The enormity of her mother's situation hit her, and she felt wretched. It was one of those times when she just remembered that she had cancer. It was one of those times that she imagined what it must be like to be the mother of two bickering children. In other words: perspective dawned on her, and she felt like a naughty teenager. The shame galvanised her and she apologised. The usual upshot was a knee jerk reaction to needing to move out. The flip side was guilt. Neither felt good.

'Has it always been like this?' Kelly asked.

Wendy took a deep breath.

'Yes, as far as I can remember. You just didn't… well… get on. It's not illegal − not everyone gets on − I understand that. And we accepted that you were always very different, the two of you, but don't you think it's time you gave it up?' Her mother had never been so forward, so transparently blunt. It made it a 'thing' − open and out there to be discussed and even dealt with. It made Kelly react badly.

'Me? Christ, Mum, all I asked was for her to take you for a walk around the sodding block!'

'Don't you swear at me!' Wendy said.

'I'm not swearing at you, Mum, I'm frustrated. Can't you see how she manipulates everything to make herself the victim! It's pathetic. She could have made different choices, but she'd rather whine, and you fall for it every time! It's the same at the hospital, it's embarrassing! I've moved on from all of this. I don't need such pre-pubescent drama in my life.'

'And you are just like your father, shouting your way to the end of an argument, without first stopping to think if what you're saying is correct!' They stood staring at one another. Cancer forgotten.

'You've always hated it when I stand up for myself. Why is it that when a man stands up for himself, he's heroic, but when a woman does it, it's reckless and offensive?'

'Don't trick me with your riddles. I've no idea what you mean. It's the truth: you always have to be right, like your father, Kelly. But sometimes, you're not.'

'Mum, I'm not going to sit back and let Nikki get away with wrapping you round her finger. She could have taken you out, that's all I'm saying. It annoys me that you can't see that.'

'Most mothers don't see the child in front of them, just the one they love.' Wendy's shoulders dropped and she sat on her bed. Kelly couldn't bear the theatre, but it had hit a nerve. She couldn't possibly ask her mother – any mother – to take sides. She had to accept that it was never going to happen.

'Mum, this is also about Dave Crawley. I don't really care anymore what Nikki thinks about me, Mum – it's true. But what I did last year had to happen. I had no choice. Dave was guilty as hell, and so was his dad. I make no apologies for it.'

'I know, love. Katy has been struggling. I think Nikki has been giving her money.'

'How is that my fault?'

'Ah, you know, Kelly. Your Dad had the same. No-one likes a clever copper. I'm proud of you.'

Kelly hadn't responded. It was progress. She'd heard it with her own ears.

There was only one thing left to do: go out. She couldn't sit simmering in the spare room all night, and her mother needed some space. Kelly needed some too.

She went to the kitchen and made a pot of tea, and brought it through on a tray along with two packets of biscuits. By the time she'd done so, Wendy had climbed into bed, and she was propped up on pillows. She looked forlorn.

'I'm sorry, Mum.'

'So am I, love. You go and have a fun evening. Don't check on me when you get in.'

They embraced and Kelly left. The warm night air on her skin intensified the relief she felt at leaving the house, and she walked to the pub.

Andy and Karl were at the bar.

There was a time when all she'd want to do was get pissed and forget. That's what they'd all done in London. Everything was different now. Her work had overlapped with her life, and there was no going back. Things had settled; fewer people stared at her and whispered into their pints. Andy and Karl never judged. They'd been mates since school, and occasionally, she'd shoot pool with them to wind down.

'Porter, what's your poison? Has someone died? You look miserable as shit,' said Karl, before realising his blunder.

'Oh, Christ, Kell, I'm sorry...' he said.

'It doesn't matter, no-one has died – or not yet anyway – I just need a drink.'

'Your wish is our command,' said Andy.

'I'll have a pint of Bray,' she said.

'Come here,' said Andy, and he pulled her towards him. They'd been friends since they were seven years old and they'd met at the art sink; they were the only two kids who enjoyed the job because they'd worked out that it got them out of extra work. After working out that they lived two streets away from each other, they began calling on one another, and climbing trees. They met Karl at secondary school, and the three of them smoked at the end of the athletics field.

She allowed herself to sink into Andy's chest and it was pleasant there.

'You're looking fit tonight, girl,' he said. He meant it, but as a genuine compliment, not as a come on. The thought of sleeping with Kelly Porter was incestuous, but the same couldn't be said of Karl, who'd done everything to get her into his bed since they'd met up again, last November, in this very pub, by the same pool table they were about to play on. That night, eight months ago, Andy and Karl had delivered Kelly back to her mother's house in a cab, and had rolled her inside the doorway, giggling and shushing.

The look on Wendy Porter's face had been priceless. But Kelly had given up trying to win her mother's affections through behaving properly; it never worked.

'What's up?' Andy asked, pulling Kelly back to the moment. 'Don't tell me you're the one trying to find the psycho who killed that woman?' he asked.

She didn't have to respond; her face said it all.

Andy smelled good, and he'd always worn the same aftershave. One of his hugs was about as good as it got: and it was the closest she'd come to a brother. Funny that in London, she hadn't thought of him all that often. Everybody grew up and drifted apart, she'd thought. But he hadn't changed. He'd married a local girl – from the year below them in school – and they'd had a couple of kids. Boredom set in and Andy decided he wanted to learn to ski. Kelly had almost fallen over when he'd told her. He left his wife and kids, and ended up doing three ski seasons back-to-back in the Alps. It was a singularly selfish thing to do, but he'd had to get it out of his system, and so he did.

By the time he got back, his wife had remarried and his children hated him. So he hung out playing pool, planning his next trip. His chest was broad and strong, and his t-shirt smelled of comfort. His hair had begun to be kissed by salt and pepper, but his eyes were just as playful as they'd been almost thirty years ago. Karl, on the other hand, was smaller but just as well built – they all seemed to be gym fanatics up here – but he wasn't as good looking as Andy, and he knew it. Andy was the one who attracted the ladies; Karl hung on for the ride. Both were good company and just what Kelly needed tonight. But appearances could deceive; they were good for bouncing off too, unlikely as they seemed. A couple of grown men in a bar – apparently hanging on to their youth, unwilling to let it go – smacked of emotional ineptness. But that's not what Kelly found at all. They'd all moved on in their own ways, but just found each other again.

They took their drinks to the pool table and piled a couple of twenty-pence pieces onto the side, by the slot, to bag the next turns. A group of young teenage boys were playing and taking their time about it. They laughed loudly and swaggered brashly when girls walked past – which was often. Kelly watched, amused. She was so glad that she wasn't in that gig anymore: under twenty-five and desperate to be liked. She'd never been one for cruising bars, but she remembered the insecurity that came with the lack of experience, and she wished she'd possessed the same amount of confidence then as now. She watched them interact and wished the girls wouldn't make it so obvious that they were available.

In her day, they'd be called slags, but that had all changed, and now it was acceptable for women to predate around dark pubs and pool tables. Kelly found it off-putting and she fancied herself old fashioned; for once, her mother at least would approve.

'Why do you want to chase psychos anyway, Kell?' Karl asked.

'For the same reason you keep having babies with strangers.'

Andy laughed. Karl spread his hands. 'It's not my fault if they tell me they're on the pill,' he said.

'God, are you serious? And you believe them?' Kelly said, incredulous. 'You shouldn't be doing it without a condom anyway, you're an idiot and you're lucky you haven't caught anything. When will you grow up?'

Karl was used to Kelly's candour. That's why he'd fancied her since third year Geography class, every Thursday, fourth period. He looked sheepish.

'Oh no, you have caught something? Bloody hell, Karl!' she said.

'I didn't say that! The doc said I could've got it from a dirty toilet,' he said.

'Bullshit!' said Kelly. 'And you believed him?' She shook her head and caught the attention of a group at the bar. Her stomach turned over but she knew she couldn't avoid it. Paul 'Flash' Gordon stood at the bar looking at her. It wasn't a look of aggression, or threat, but Andy followed her gaze and stood beside her.

'Don't worry, Andy.' She held the gaze of Dave Crawley's best pal. To her surprise, he smiled and walked towards her. She didn't know what to expect. It was the first time they'd set eyes on each other since the trial. Dave had tried to use Flash as an alibi. It stank.

'Kelly.'

'Paul.'

They spoke together, over one another. 'How are you…? Sorry. You go first.'

'I haven't seen you to say sorry, Paul.'

'You don't need to, Kelly. I had no idea. You caught him fair and square. But his old man, Christ, no-one knew.'

Kelly knew this to be false. Plenty knew, but she didn't elaborate. She let it go.

'I came back and spoilt the party.'

'No you didn't. He was an idiot. He fooled us all.'

'I was just doing my job.'

'I know.' He turned round. His friends were waiting, and she knew none of them. He smiled and walked away. She went back to the pool table.

The music was turned up and the bar began to fill up, and she lost sight of him. It was their turn to play pool, and Kelly and Andy teamed up against Karl, who was by far the better player, thanks to the amount of time spent in bars since leaving school.

Three girls made their third circuit of the pool table and Kelly watched them watching Andy. One of them caught his eye and Kelly felt the stirrings of jealousy: she wanted to protect him but she had no right to interfere. Besides, it was none of her business who he took home. Andy had bought a ski chalet two years ago and turned it into a successful business. Now he owned five, and they supported his ex-wife, his kids and himself very nicely;

and he could sleep with whoever he wanted. Kelly stood next to him and eyed the girls, who moved away quickly.

'You're spoiling my fun,' he whispered to her.

'I know, but I'm having loads,' she whispered back. He put his arm round her and squeezed. Kelly wished she had a brother rather than Nikki, but at least she had Andy.

Karl won, and they drank to misspent youth.

After three pints, a few wines and six rounds of pool, Kelly decided that it was time to leave. She'd got what she came for: to offload, and she looked at her watch. Her body told her it was late, her watch confirmed it, and she was swaying slightly. Karl and Andy had swapped beer for Jack Daniels and she'd drunk at least two glasses of wine on top of three pints. She nipped to the toilet before ordering a taxi. The bar was heaving and the music had got steadily louder throughout the evening. The atmosphere of the bar was changing from late afternoon drinkers to hard core pursuit between the sexes, and it was Kelly's signal to leave. Finally she made it to the toilets and went in. She looked hazily into the mirror and touched up her makeup, satisfied with the reflection. Other women and girls did the same, and some gossiped and giggled. Others swayed, but a lot worse than Kelly. She made her way out of the door, and avoided a girl who looked as though she was going to throw up.

Back in the bar, she stood still and stared ahead in front of her.

There was no mistaking. The flip flops, the baggy jumper sneakily hiding a tanned, hard body, and the greying hair, flopping to one side. Later, she wouldn't remember why she didn't simply turn around, and leave, but she didn't. She watched as he stopped talking to the guy next to him, and turned around. He walked towards her.

'Kelly, you're looking well,' he said. She couldn't read what he was thinking, and she felt foolish for being a bit worse for wear.

'Hi, Johnny. How are you?'

'Who are you with?' he asked.

'Some friends, I was just about to leave, I've had enough.'

'That's a shame, I was going to buy you a drink.'

'I've got work tomorrow.'

'That never stopped you.'

'You got me there, but I do need to go. It's good to see you, Johnny, maybe buy me that drink another time soon?'

'I will. You still on the same number?'

'Yes, I am,' she said. They stood for half a second, neither really wanting to leave, but Kelly made the first move, and she walked past him towards the boys. Johnny watched her. She said something to the bigger of the two, and they embraced. He watched her as she made her way towards the door.

Chapter 21

A young family trudged away from Aira Force car park. They'd started later than they'd hoped because the youngest child had projectile vomited into his car seat. However, after raiding the steamer office toilet for tissues, administering Calpol, buying coke to cheer the team, and promising ice cream on the way back, they'd managed to set off. The sun beat down on them, and they looked forward to the promised shade of their destination.

Not for the first time did the couple question their sanity. A walking holiday in the Lakes had sounded a splendid idea, but the reality was turning out to be trickier, and not as much fun, as they'd expected. The children whined that their feet hurt, they were thirsty, they were tired, and they were hungry.

It wasn't long, though, before they were walking through enchanting woodland, away from the road and the crowds, and away from the lake. Dad told stories to keep the children interested, and pointed out red squirrels and interesting ferns. The oldest child, at seven years old, wasn't fooled, and his shoulders continued to droop. The youngest, exhausted from the purge of his stomach contents, was asleep in his carrier. The middle child whimpered slightly, and stopped every now and again to wipe his face with a cool leaf. The Lake District was basking in record temperatures, and the shade of Aira Force was welcome.

The base of the waterfall had held their attention for a while: the sheer awe of it transfixed them, and the air around it was deliciously cool. But every tourist in Cumbria had the same idea, and they looked for a quieter part; they had to keep going higher, it was the only way to find a secluded spot. The children had hoped that the waterfall was the finale, and they could turn around and go back to the comforts of their hotel, and Wi-Fi.

On they went.

The view from the top of the falls was impressive, and, again, the children believed that this would be the end of their adventure, and soon they'd be able to go back the way they'd come. But Dad still ploughed on. He was jabbering on about the height of the waterfall and the family who'd planted the woods. He'd promised they'd see deer, and they'd seen none. Finally, the throngs of sightseers started to subside, and they came to a glade where the water was calm and inviting. At the top, way above the waterfall, the water gathered in pools, and there were rocks to sunbathe on.

'Here,' said Dad. The mother spread a blanket and gave the older boys towels. The toddler was released from his tethers and even the older boy smiled as he splashed water onto his mother. The sun only penetrated in patches here, and the air was cool. Dad smiled: his mission accomplished. They saw only four other people walking past, and now they could enjoy the fruits of their labour.

Toby, the oldest child, threw himself fully into the water and dunked his head under. His father chased him and his mother shook her head: she had no clean clothes for the boy. Well, she thought, he would dry off eventually, especially in this heat. She began to unpack a small picnic. She dangled her feet in to the water and it felt spectacular.

She jumped when she heard her son shriek. She could see her husband splashing water to him and she shook her head. But he made the noise again and it didn't sound like fun; the tone of his howls had changed. Her instinct was piqued and she stood up. She looked to where her husband had chased her eldest child, and she could make out her husband's figure in the trees, but not her son's. She panicked. She picked up the toddler.

'Roger!' she squealed. 'Roger!'

Her husband couldn't hear her, above the distant waterfall and their son's cries. He followed the boy as quickly as he could. The woods were thick, and he didn't want to lose sight of him.

But then he saw what Toby saw.

The boy was bent over double, retching into the water. Roger went to him and forced his son's head into his shoulder. The boy heaved and shook, and Roger held him. They shivered, as the extent of their soaking, unimportant before, made them icy cold. Roger looked over the shoulder of his son, and stared into the eyes of a dead girl.

Her body lay slumped against a tree, staring at them. Her skin was whitish grey, and her hair was straggly with reeds and debris. She looked like a doll, but Roger knew that she wasn't a doll. She was naked and Roger turned away. He hugged the boy, who wouldn't sleep properly for the next eighteen months.

Only now did Roger hear his wife's cries. He shouted to her.

'Lyn! It's ok. I've got him. We're ok. We're on our way back now!' he shouted.

Roger stood up and picked up his son, who, soaked in water, weighed a ton. He was deathly pale and his body was limp, and Roger tightened his grip.

When he got back to his wife, Lyn was beside herself. She momentarily put the toddler on the blanket and took Toby from his father.

'He's ok, Lyn. It's not him. We found… we found…' he couldn't finish. He managed to mouth the words, 'a body', and Lyn's eyes grew round. He left the boy with her, found his mobile phone, and dialled 999. He walked away from his family, not wanting them to hear the call. Apparently there was a car park near to where they were, to the west. Roger wished he'd researched the walk better and parked there. The emergency services and the police would be there in under ten minutes.

Meanwhile, the toddler waddled over to his mother, spat out some water, and then vomited all over her.

Chapter 22

That morning, Kelly had woken groggy. She'd called Eden House to check with the officer on call that there were no developments overnight, and made a decision to go for a run to clear her head. She preferred working late when the office was quieter anyhow, and she'd already decided to work that afternoon. She'd fix lunch for Mum, who was spending the evening at Nikki's with her grandchildren, and head off. At the moment, there was no reason to haul in her team at the weekend, and they were still crunching leads.

She decided to drive to Little Mell Fell. Colin Tate had been tracked down and she'd dispatched junior officers to take a statement. An hour or so on the fells would clear her head in more ways than one. Doctor Timothy Cole had been invited to give a statement for the inquiry, and she was to meet him at midday, at Eden House. She could easily have tasked a junior officer to do it, but, at this stage, she wanted to give her team their weekends. As she parked up by a quiet layby on the Dockray Road, she mulled over questions she had for him.

The ground was boggy and her trainers sank in places, but it was a relatively short incline to the top. It was one of her favourite views in the area, and she could see all the way down the Helvellyn range. As she reached the summit of the tiny peak, she felt her hangover disperse, and she breathed deeply as she bounced from foot to foot at the top. She could see beyond Gowbarrow Fell, to the south and would love to pay a quick visit to Aira Force to cool off, but she needed to get back.

As she descended and came within a hundred yards of her car, her phone started to go crazy. She stopped and fiddled with it, as she got her breath. She'd missed seven calls. She'd yet to get used to the intermittent reception in the Lakes. She called Eden House and spoke to DS Umshaw.

It wasn't the start to the weekend she'd envisaged.

'It's a body, Boss. Cause undetermined. Pretty tricky location, access by foot only.'

'Suicide?'

'Could be. Forensics are at the scene now, as well as medics. Carleton Hall want you there, but I couldn't get hold of you. I knew you couldn't be far. Where are you?'

'I'm on Little Mell. Great day for it. Typical. I'm on my way. Where is it?'

'Aira Force.'

The little hairs on Kelly's arms stood up and she jerked her head in that direction. It would take her five minutes to get there.

She parked at the top car park and showed her ID to the uniforms guarding the area behind the police tape. The deceased was female, and, by all accounts, young. Kelly had two questions bugging her: why was she alone, here of all places? And how long had she been here? She'd know soon enough.

She was led through the dense undergrowth that led to the girl; memories of exploring these hidden rock pools and bushes as a child flooded back to her. Tarpaulin had been erected but DS Umshaw was right: the site was inhospitable and the structure wasn't ideal. As she approached, and thanked the uniform for guiding her, Kelly's first impression was that perhaps the girl had got lost. Maybe she was on a drugs high, and wandered from a party, disoriented and hallucinating. It had happened before. But when she saw the body, she had other hypotheses.

The victim was naked and arranged, setting off warning sirens in her head. She spoke briefly to the forensic officers present, and they'd taken a good load of photos, which were on their way to her email right now. Kelly took in the scene. The girl was young but she didn't look innocent, but Kelly didn't know why she thought that; the victim had a hard face: one that had seen stuff. She bent down close to the victim and tried to see if there were any glaring anomalies. There appeared to be nothing, apart from, of course, the victim was dead, and, it would appear, from unnatural causes. Something about the nakedness and location disturbed Kelly, and the forensic officers agreed. It was a homicide.

The girl looked like a mannequin, and Kelly was mesmerised by her. She was sat upright in the water; propped up like a doll, as if she'd become weary and was laid there to rest. Her skin was pale and blotchy, and the body looked emaciated and malnourished. It would have taken much effort to get her here, despite her apparent frailty, and time to tidy up her belongings and leave no trace of how she'd arrived. Another commendable stage production, Kelly thought. But she had some way to go to discover if this woman and Moira were connected. She nodded briefly to the victim, as if paying her respects, and shook her head. If this was the beginning of a spree of female victims, and Moira and this new nameless poor girl were part of it, they had one sick fuck out there on the fells. Fells she'd just been running on alone, with headphones in. She had a stern word with herself and decided to recommend that alerts be sent to the media to ward females off being alone out here. The tourist board was going to go mental. But first she must tell Cane.

Kelly decided to get back to Eden House. She'd seen enough. She didn't bother going home for a shower. There was a single shower in the ladies toilet at Eden House, and Kelly always kept odds and sods in her car for such eventualities. Running gear would have to do right now. She might have to cry off lunch, though. It was only going to be what her mother affectionately called 'cold table': ham, cheese, pate, bread and pickles. Mum would understand.

No sooner had she walked into her office at Eden House, than DS Umshaw poked her head round her door and indicated the land line.

'DCI Cane.'

'Great, thanks.'

Kelly held the phone away from her ear.

'I'm aware of all of that, sir. I need more boots for this one. Even combing the area is going to be a challenge with all that water. Yes, it's closed. I know it does.' She nodded and shrugged her shoulders at DS Umshaw. The office was noisy, and computerised jobs lists had been belching out of the system all morning. One of them was getting hold of the coroner's report. It might not happen today though. She'd called in DC Emma Hide, but that was all at the moment. They didn't even have a name.

'ID is my priority, sir. Fingerprints are being rolled urgently. She's in Carlisle. Yes, sir. Right. No.'

Finally, Cane stopped barking out questions and Kelly was able to hang up. He was only doing his job, and was probably the recipient of identical phone calls from up above; murders are big news in any constabulary, but in Cumbria – and in summer – even bigger. Two was uncharted water.

The tourist trade was worth almost three billion pounds to Cumbria, and Kelly felt the pressure gather over Eden House as she replaced the receiver. She beckoned Umshaw and Hide, who followed her in to the incident room.

'Kate, get me missing persons. Emma, I'm afraid I'm going to task you with babysitting the database for a fingerprint match. We can't do anything without a name. I'm going to Carlisle. Kate, you'll have to do the Tim Cole interview. My notes are all ready.'

Back in her office, she called Ted Wallis.

'Sorry, Kelly, I've had five missed calls from you, I assume this is to do with the young girl brought in this morning?' he asked.

'Hi Ted, yes, you're bang on, I was wondering if you'd done the autopsy? We don't have ID yet, but I need to know if she's connected in any way to Moira Tate, and you are the only one who can tell me that right now. Other than that, I have nothing. It's not what I'd choose to be doing on a Saturday morning, but I need to see this one in person, Ted.'

'I've scheduled her in for around one p.m. I appreciate the need to get this done. I do have things that I don't want to put off, but the gravity of this isn't lost on me. One o'clock is the earliest I can do I'm afraid.'

'Thank you.'

'Not at all, I'd welcome the company. It will make the task more bearable shall we say. I hope, for your sake, they're not connected. Can you be here by one?'

'Yes, I'm leaving now.'

'Super, I'll see you later.' They hung up. Kelly went to find DS Umshaw.

'Missing persons?'

'Nothing.'

'Ok. Call in every half hour. I'll be on the road. I'm going to the autopsy.'

Kate Umshaw grimaced. 'Ugh. Rather you than me. Have you got some Vicks?'

'And perfume. Wish me luck. You're in charge. Cane might breathe down your neck but he'll probably call my mobile rather than here, once he knows where I've gone. Something tells me we're about to get busier, Kate.'

Umshaw nodded. Her girls were old enough to help look after each other, and she quite enjoyed staying at work late these days. Kelly continued.

'First thing is ploughing through these photos. How is the appeal for witnesses going?'

'We've got three uniforms down there now.'

'Good. I've been through a lot of these and annotated. You know what to do. Let me know what you think about Timothy Cole. Rob thought he was a control freak but that doesn't make him a sadist, does it?'

'Nothing surprises me anymore. I'll be nice, I promise.'

'Don't go that far.' Kelly knew that the office was in expert hands.

'I'm sorry you weren't promoted this time round, Kate.'

'I'm not. I'm happy being told what to do, seriously; you give me a job, and I do it. Put me in charge and I'd hate it. I'm happy where I am. You're born to do this racing round malarkey, but for me, I'll get your back.'

'Thanks, Kate. I thought you might be disappointed.'

'No worries, Boss. I'll sort it.'

Kelly didn't need to say anymore. She went back to her office and packed her iPad into her bag, along with a bottle of water. She left the building and a knot of excitement, mixed with dread, formed under her rib cage. Her phone rang as she climbed into the Audi, and she looked at her screen. It was DCI Cane. She ignored it. She wasn't in the mood for his questions. He'd given her the nod for more boots, and that's all she cared about. If it was important, he'd leave a message. He could get a SitRep by getting his arse to Eden House. He was bricking it because media was about to go through the roof, now they potentially had a second body. That's what this was all about. Her job was to work the leads, not get embroiled in media spin. She had no idea if her constitution would hold for the duration of the autopsy, but she'd soon find out.

The M6 north of Penrith was wild and barren, but beautiful. The mountains loomed to the west all the way up to the border, and she wondered where, in all the vastness, her killer was, and what he was up to today. He might already have another victim in mind. He might already be working on them as she drove. She held onto the steering wheel tightly and turned up the music, reminding herself to unfluster her thoughts until Ted Wallis gave her something concrete.

Chapter 23

Ted was fresh and alert and pleased to see Kelly, who looked nervous and distracted. Well she might be; it wasn't every day one got to witness a live autopsy on a murder victim.

'Are you feeling alright, Kelly?' he asked, as they strode along the corridor to the mortuary, which was situated underneath the hospital. Ted had worked here, in its bowels, for almost forty years: half of that as the Home Office Coroner for the North West. Members of staff greeted him wherever he went, and their conversation was broken by pleasantries.

'Between me and you, I was out late last night and now I'm paying for it. I'll give it my best shot,' she said.

'Well, good for you, I hope it was worth it. Was it a gentleman?' he asked. Kelly was only slightly taken by surprise by the question, but she enjoyed his forthrightness.

'No, just friends. I haven't got time for men, Ted, with this bloody job.' But it was tongue in cheek, and they both smiled.

'You need to take care of yourself, and going out with friends is no bad thing. I should have done more of it at your age.' They neared the morgue. 'Are you ready?' he asked.

'I think so.' They went into a room and he showed her which garments she should put over her clothes. She'd forgotten how cold morgues were, and she shivered.

'You can leave any time you want to,' he said.

'I know. Thank you.' She smeared Vicks under her nose and sprayed perfume on her hands and rubbed it in so she could hold them up to her nose at any time.

Ted looked different in his scrubs: more masterful and completely in charge.

'When did you think you might want to follow this line of work, Ted?' She followed him through to another room, trying to fill gaps in conversation to delay the inevitable. Ted opened another door and they were inside the examination room. A body-shaped lump lay inside a black body bag on top of a table, and Kelly's pulse began to rise. The last time she'd seen the girl, she'd been in an entirely different environment. Kelly swallowed as she realised that the lump was somebody's daughter, somebody's sister perhaps, maybe even someone's mother. A technician was busy making notes and preparing equipment.

'Let's get on with it then,' said Ted. He adjusted a head set on his head, and tested it by speaking into it. He then unzipped the bag. The metal against metal, caused by the zip's teeth, was like a chainsaw in Kelly's mind. Ted didn't react. Kelly's pulse quickened.

The girl was wrapped in plastic. Ted's first job was to see if anything had been dislodged during the girl's journey here, and trapped by the plastic. He cut it open carefully.

Kelly put her hand over her mouth but forced herself to look. At least the smell was slightly dulled by refrigeration. And the Vicks. But she could still smell it: it was like wet dog, even over her Chanel: the strongest of her perfumes.

The first thing Kelly noticed, apart from the mass of exposed flesh, was the tracking marks up the girl's arms: drugs. She hadn't spotted them at the waterfall. Kelly's pulse calmed, and she said to herself that she'd got over the hardest part. Now she had to focus. When Ted went for his saw, she'd perhaps re-evaluate.

Ted was now in his zone, and the room fell into silence, apart from the odd clink of equipment and Ted's rhythmic activity of investigation. He examined every inch of the body, externally to begin with. He was completely meticulous, and utterly focused. He spoke slowly and quietly into his head set, and every now and again, he'd give instructions to the technician, which were carried out straight away. They were comfortable with one another, and Kelly guessed they'd worked together for some time.

Next, Ted cut off the bags around the girl's hands and head, preserved thus due to the cornucopia of matter found amongst nails and hair. The fingers were stained black, where forensics had taken prints at the scene; Kelly prayed that the girl was on their system. She checked her phone: nothing yet.

She watched as Ted called for photos to be taken, and removed items with tweezers, for bagging and tagging. Up to now, Kelly was more fascinated than repulsed, and she found herself carried away with the intensity.

'That's odd,' said Ted.

'What?'

'Her mouth won't open,' Ted said. Kelly went closer.

'I think there's some kind of adherent holding her lips together.' Ted picked up a scalpel and sliced between the girl's lips. A puff of air fizzed out and it sounded like a sigh. Kelly's guts churned, but she kept watching.

'Oh dear,' Ted said.

Kelly didn't say a word, she just watched, and listened.

'The tongue has been surgically removed, almost down to the glossoepiglottic folds. It was done with something extremely sharp – my guess is a scalpel, and it was done well, probably post-mortem. The wound suggests lack of blood flow vitality at the time of the incision.'

Kelly tasted bile in her oesophagus.

Ted fiddled around in the girl's mouth, and Kelly's insides turned over a little. She regretted not having breakfast, and she could murder a coffee: anything to take away the metallic, vile smell. She shivered.

'There's no evidence of the tongue in the throat, so it looks like it's been taken.'

'Another trophy.'

'Wait a minute. There's something in there.' Ted fiddled a bit more and pulled out a plastic bag. He opened it on the table and took out its contents with a pair of tweezers. Kelly moved closer.

It was a piece of paper. Kelly closed her eyes, and waited for Ted to unfold the delicate dried-brown sample.

'*And much it grieved my heart to think, what man has made of man.*' Ted read aloud, his glasses perched on the end of his nose.

Kelly pulled out her phone and googled the lines.

'It's Wordsworth.'

'I think you have your answer, Kelly.'

'Oh, Christ.'

Ted looked at her, wishing he could do something to help, unaware that he just had. She was desperately sorrowful that she'd come, but grateful too.

'Anything else?'

Ted focused on the body.

Kelly's foot tapped and she was freezing. She rubbed her hands and went from one foot to the other, wishing she had a jacket or at least a scarf. As Ted carried on, Kelly read about the poem on her phone. It was entitled simply 'Lines Written in Early Spring'. It was depressing. She remembered what the reverend had said about the Lakeland Poets. She envisaged a man in a Victorian suit, sat uncomfortably on the bank of a lake, paper and quill in hand, pouring his despair into lines about birds hopping and twigs snapping. Perhaps he wore a top hat. Ted's voice snapped her back to the present.

'Clear evidence of asphyxiation with a strap of some sort. If memory serves, the marks are exactly the same as the ones found on Moira Tate, Kelly,' Ted said. Kelly was surprised by the reference to herself and was caught off guard. She put her phone back into her pocket, and went to look at the marks, and confirmed the similarity. Ted measured and recorded the marks.

A couple of maggots, not completely stupefied by freezing, still wriggled and dropped off the slab to the floor. Ted collected them as Kelly watched in horror. She was reminded of a trip she'd had to Coniston Old Man with her father when she'd found some caterpillars in a bush and insisted on collecting them, only to find, later that day, the little critters hatching into wasps.

Ted turned to the girl's hair, which was matted with river detritus and Kelly tried to concentrate. The perfume was wearing off. The girl wasn't as tidy as Moira, but she might have been when she was dumped there. Nature had got in the way. Ted bagged various leaves, twigs and dirt, and he removed several hairs from her head. She'd been blonde, perhaps not natural.

'The cold water of the river has delayed putrefaction and so we may not get an accurate time of death. Note, insect activity only in areas where body was exposed, this might be helpful,' Ted said.

He took a scraper and began working on her nails. He scraped each one carefully and reached for a magnifying glass.

'Single fibre, looks synthetic, unlike a human or animal hair,' he said.

'Does it look grey?' Kelly asked, excited by having something to distract her.

'Now, now, Kelly. I'll send it off,' Ted said, wise and measured as ever.

'There's evidence of sexual activity, but it's not overly traumatic. The river has taken much of the fluid usually found inside. Swabbing for DNA evidence now, but I doubt we'll get a result,' said Ted.

Ted and his technician turned the girl over, and the body made a slopping sound as it settled. Her back was purple and black, and, even though Kelly knew that this was blood pooling, it still looked revolting; as if she'd been beaten to death.

Happy with the external search, Ted asked for help getting the girl back on her back. They'd bagged a fair amount of material, including stuff from the eyes and nose, which Kelly didn't have a clue as to its identity, along with some big fat juicy maggots. But the final straw was Ted reaching for his saw. Kelly told herself she'd see it through, but when the blades whirred and screeched, she decided she'd had enough.

'Sorry, Ted, I need to make a phone call.'

He looked at her through his visor. 'Of course. I'll come and find you.'

Her last image of the girl, was of the saw entering her body, opening her trunk like a can of beans.

Kelly closed the door behind her as the first rib was snapped.

She took off her overalls and left the inner changing room. She walked as quickly as she could to the main entrance of the hospital, and the warm outside air hit her, taking away her chill slightly. She found a bench outside, sat on it, and regulated her breathing. She stared up at the sun with closed eyes and let her body calm itself. She felt as though she'd been smeared in fish guts.

Moira's crime was her hands – money grabbing, Ted had said it. This girl's crime was her tongue. Perhaps she was a bully, perhaps she was a gobshite. Neither deserved to die.

She called Kate Umshaw.

'We've got another poem. The handwriting is the same, pending confirmation from our professor if he ever gets back to us. The girl's tongue was surgically removed.'

'Doctor Timothy Cole?'

'Surgeon Timothy Cole. Has Emma got a name yet?'

'She's checking in every half an hour. I'll call you as soon as.'

'Right, I'm coming back now.' She hung up. She couldn't get warm, despite the sunshine, and she believed herself to be reeking of death. It was minutes before Kate Umshaw called back with a name.

The girl was called Brandy Carter, and she'd had a minor op on her ankle a few years ago. The consultant's list on which she'd found herself was none other than Timothy Cole.

Chapter 24

Kelly rummaged around the locker at the back of her office, looking for something suitable to change into to interview Mr Timothy Cole, eminent surgeon, trusted employee, public speaker and life giver. Narcissist and God complex came to mind too, but she knew the danger of presumption.

After her shower, she felt ready and DS Umshaw had already prepared the room. Timothy Cole was on his way: a willing and graceful witness; thankful for the tact of the detective in choosing a private venue, thus enabling him to protect his family. Or that's what he thought.

Kelly was notified when he was inside the building, and he was escorted to the main interview room in Eden House. It was a comfortable enough space, in as much as the chairs were new and the blue upholstery was comfortable; not like the old brown plastic that perps had to sit on. Coffee and water would be on tap, within reason, but there was still no window: an old policy that still held true to the traditional belief that, if a suspect was allowed to feel too comfortable, they'd be less likely to make a mistake. An enclosed space without natural light was still deemed the best possible way to coerce.

Kelly met DS Umshaw in the corridor and they spoke briefly. The interview would be recorded and videoed. Of course, Mr Cole was entitled to a lawyer present, but, as yet, he wasn't aware that he might need one.

DC Will Phillips and Rob Shawcross had been dragged in on their days off, and were tasked with searching the surgeon's property, when – and only when – Kelly gave the go ahead. The circumstantial evidence against Cole was enough to get a search warrant, though it wasn't quite enough to arrest. Kelly saw arrest without potential charge as a waste of her valuable time.

They entered the interview room. Mr Cole stood up. It was a dated behaviour, showing respect to the two female detectives, and Kelly noted it. They shook hands. A uniform stood behind the door – procedure.

'Mr Cole, I am Detective Porter, and this is Detective Umshaw, we'll be recording your witness statement today. Please sit down.'

He did so, and Kelly was thankful because he towered above them. He wore an expensive dark navy suit, along with an immaculately pressed shirt, perfectly crafted tie and gold cufflinks. His shoes were polished and he smelled of pricey cologne. His skin was tanned; no doubt he could afford several exotic holidays per year. A glance at his earnings told them that the surgeon was in demand and earned the bulk of his money from private clients. His pad on the shores of Lake Ullswater was sizeable and boasted a pool and mature gardens and outhouses. He also owned a squad of flashy cars, including an Aston Martin DB9. They knew that the motive behind the killings wasn't robbery.

'Thank you for coming in voluntarily, Mr Cole.' Kelly used the official title of a surgeon, rather than 'Doctor'. She might use it later to annoy him.

'Of course, anything to help.' He looked down at his hands. Hands that had saved countless lives, and delved into the depths of hundreds of crippled and smashed bodies. They were large, manicured and strong.

'For the record, Mr Cole, could you state your place, and date of birth.'

The interview began formally. Kelly glanced up and down at her notes, remaining pedestrian.

'I see you have water.'

Cole nodded gratefully. Small beads of sweat sat on his forehead. The room wasn't cool, and it was an unnerving position for anyone to find themselves in. They always made allowances for that.

'Mr Cole. Would you like to explain to us, in your own words, your relationship to the deceased, Mrs Moira Tate?'

Cole coughed and retrieved a tightly folded handkerchief from a pocket. Kelly noticed his watch. Rob had already told her that he wore an Omega Seamaster. *Men and watches*. He reckoned it was worth about four grand: not a huge amount for Cole's wealth, but it was probably his work watch. Everything about the man smacked of success, wealth, measure and control. Apart from his reaction to this interview, which was way out of his comfort zone.

'I met Moira casually, and we were friends.'

It was going to be a long interview.

'Friends? Were you having sexual intercourse?'

Cole's eyes widened, which Kelly found amusing. For a man who was engaging in an extra marital affair on a regular basis (who knew if it was just one), he was a veritable prude, a paradox that might be relevant.

'Yes.' His cheeks reddened.

'Thank you. When was the last time you had sex with Moira?'

'I don't see what this has to...'

'It has everything to do with it.'

'Oh, Jesus, was she raped?'

Clever boy.

'We need to rule out your DNA, yes.'

Cole put his head in his hands.

'Mr Cole?'

'Saturday. We saw each other on Saturday.'

'The 6th?'

'Yes.'

'Where?'

'We used a hotel.'

'Name?'

'It's a guesthouse on the outskirts of Town. It's called The Mountain View.'

'Was it ordinary sex?'

'What?' He looked between the two women. They could have been asking him if he liked sugar in his coffee.

'I'm sorry, Mr Cole, if it's a line of enquiry you weren't expecting, and I appreciate your embarrassment. It's a sensitive subject but we really need to know the details.'

'Christ. Ordinary. Always.'

'Thank you. So when you met, was she behaving normally? Was she planning to meet anyone else while she was in town?'

'It wasn't amicable. I finished the relationship. We argued.'

'Was she upset?'

'Yes, very. She called me constantly after that. Every day until Monday night, when I last spoke to her.'

Kelly knew that Moira had called the same number several times on Monday night: the last calls she ever made.

'Did you use an unregistered phone for your relationship with Moira?'

'Yes.' Now they had their explanation. 'So, this number here is you?' She showed him the print out of Moira's phone calls, and he nodded. 'That's mine.'

'How was she? What did you talk about?'

'The same. I hung up in the end. I should have gone to get her. Oh God.' He buried his head again and loosened his tie.

'Where did she call from?' The phone had pinged off the main Penrith mast, but it couldn't pin point exactly where she'd been.

'She was walking the streets.' The desperation now apparent in the doctor's voice was pitiful. He realised, in that moment, that it was shortly after he'd abandoned her, by hanging up his phone for the last time, that she'd come to harm. Unless he was involved.

'Where?'

'Close to the hospital. She'd been to see her mother.'

'Where were you?'

'At work.'

'Until what time?'

'Ten p.m.'

Kelly looked at her print out. Umshaw scribbled notes and studied the doctor.

'She called you just after ten.'

'I know, I was getting out of my scrubs. That's the last one.'

'Where did you go after that?'

'Home.'

'Can your wife corroborate that?'

'Yes, but I thought… my coming here would prevent her being involved. Detective, please, I…'

'Mr Cole, I have a problem.'

Cole looked between the two detectives again. His face looked panicked. And well it might.

'Mr Cole, did you know Brandy Carter?'

'Er… the name rings a bell. I'm not sure. There's something about the name. Why?'

'She broke a metatarsal two years ago, it wasn't a significant break, but she needed a cast, and you were the consultant on her notes.'

'Ah, there we go. Forgive me, I can see twenty people a day sometimes.'

'Brandy was a regular visitor to The Penrith and Lakes. She suffered various ailments, including methadone addiction. Her last visit was for the treatment of gardnerella, a sexually transmitted disease.'

'I know what gardnerella is.' Cole's eyes narrowed. 'You said *did* I know her?'

'Yes. Her body was found this morning, Mr Cole. She was murdered.'

Cole's eyes widened and his mouth moved: his composure was deserting him in treacherous ways, making his hands shake and his feet point towards the door.

'Perhaps you took Brandy to hotels too?'

Cole shot up, and the uniform stepped towards him from behind.

'No! My God! What are you saying? You think I did this?'

'Now you see my problem. Please sit down. I've obtained a warrant to search your property on Lake Ullswater, Mr Cole. Is anyone home?'

'My wife. Oh no, oh please.'

'Mr Cole. Is there anything you'd like to tell us now? If there is, this is the time to do it. We're not accusing you, or charging you; we simply want to know your involvement with both deceased women.'

'I need to get home.'

'I'm afraid I can't let you do that, Mr Cole. You don't have permission to be present at the search. However, if you'd like to call your wife, then of course, you are free to do that.'

'I want a lawyer.'

'You're entitled to that, too. We'd like to request a voluntary sample of DNA and a handwriting sample, please.'

Cole licked his lips; they were dry and he looked as though he might faint. He sipped some water.

'Ok.'

Umshaw went towards him with a swab and asked him to open his mouth, which he did. Next, Kelly gave him a pad of paper.

'What shall I write?'

'Anything. Try Wordsworth. Do you like poetry?'

Cole's face grimaced. He took the pen and scrawled the name Wordsworth on the pad and shoved it back to Kelly.

'I do, but not him.'

'Thank you. You may call your wife.'

Chapter 25

Brandy Carter's address was registered as Flat 2B, 24 Askham Manor, Penrith. The flats were part of a 1960s drive to save space and move unfortunate souls into what would soon become ghettos of crime and tension. Why no-one predicted it at the time is anyone's guess, but they were depressing places: perfect sites to hide, stay hidden and reoffend. They were any constabulary's nightmare. Not as big as some, Askham Manor was still notorious for gangs and the police, though they'd never admit it, hated going there. Overpasses, underpasses, stairwells and concrete; all encouraged endemic crime. DC Emma Hide was on her guard, despite having a burly uniform accompanying her. She pulled in to the car park, which smelled of piss. But at least they were in the shade.

DI Porter had filled her in on some of Brandy's background, and none of it had evoked surprise, just pity. The girl had dropped out of college almost as soon as she began. The Headmaster had spoken about her as a scourge on his record. He'd recalled a problem student from the get-go. Brandy Carter was a vicious bully. She'd got a record too: drugs and vandalism, which is why her prints had shown up so quickly. The mother, Sharon Carter, possessed a reputation similar to that of her daughter. And that was to whose flat they'd come to pay a visit.

'Sharon Carter is a known alcoholic and general waster, so I'm not sure what we'll find,' Emma said to her companion. He nodded.

'Come on, let's see if she's noticed her daughter's missing,' she added.

The uniform knocked on the door of Flat 2B. There was no answer, so he tried again, harder. Emma looked around. They heard a male voice and, when the door finally opened, a waft of stale air escaped from inside. Emma introduced herself and the man's brow furrowed. He was a big, strapping guy with a large belly. That was most likely beer-induced, given the smell. His clothes looked unwashed and his teeth were stained. He had mean eyes and looked at Emma in a way that a lot of male persons of interest did: repugnance that she was on the force, and shock that she was a woman. Emma Hide was a petite woman, not yet thirty, but her stature belied her skill and experience, which is why she'd been sent.

The man puffed out his chest, and the uniform rolled his eyes.

'What's she done now?' the man asked. Emma couldn't tell if he was referring to the mother or daughter. Clearly he expected both to cause trouble.

'May we speak to Sharon Carter please? Is she in?' Emma asked.

'She is, but you won't wake her. She's pissed up, as usual. Good luck, I'm off out,' he said. The man had clearly been at the back of the queue in charm school. He tried to push past them.

'I'm afraid that's out of the question, Mr...?' Emma said.

'Me?' he asked, jutting his chin towards them.

'Yes, you,' said Emma. She thought she'd like to knee this man in his fat groin, and watch him wobble. The uniform's money was on his colleague.

'I'm a… friend,' he finally said, cagily.

'Name?' Emma insisted again.

The man looked evasive. 'Dave,' he said, finally.

'Surname, Dave? Don't waste my time.'

'Kent,' he replied. His chest deflated a little.

'Thank you, that wasn't so hard was it? Excuse me. Stay here please,' she said, and squeezed past him, walking into the flat. It smelled of stale cigarettes and was laden with dirty air. In the living area, a woman lay on the sofa. She was laid on her side, and Emma could only see her back. When the uniform walked in behind her the woman farted but, other than that, remained comatose.

Emma walked over to the woman and put her hand on her arm, still she didn't move. Emma shook her gently and the woman rolled over, just a little, and Emma saw her face. It was haggard and too old; deep wrinkles cris-scrossed the yellow, puffy skin and broken veins slivered across the woman's nose and cheeks. Emma didn't need to be close to smell the alcohol.

Dave Kent appeared behind them, and Emma turned around.

'Mr Kent, we need to speak with Mrs Carter as soon as possible. What was your relationship to her daughter, Brandy?' she said.

'Was?' he asked, warily.

Emma said nothing and waited.

'She moved out ages ago, I haven't seen her in months. She was shacked up with her boyfriend. Sharon hasn't seen her either,' he said.

'Do you live here, Mr Kent?'

'Kind of, yes.'

'What does that mean?' The man was evasive to the point of suspicious.

'I stay here sometimes but not all the time,' he said.

'Right, so were you here for the past week?' Emma ploughed on.

'No. I was on the road. I'm a driver,' he said.

Drivers had poor alibis.

'Mr Kent, we need to speak to Mrs Carter because Brandy is dead. Her body was found this morning near Aira Force.'

Dave Kent bent his head but didn't appear overly bothered; more shifty and uncomfortable.

'As soon as she sobers up, can you call me?' Emma asked. Dave Kent nodded and took the card offered by the detective.

'When was the last time you saw Brandy?' Emma asked.

He shifted from foot to foot and ran his fingers through his thinning hair.

'Erm… I'd say about two months ago, she was round here after money from her mother, I…' he stopped.

'You what?'

'Nothing, I… are you sure?' he asked. A chink of compassion glanced over his face, then disappeared.

'Yes, we're sure. But Mrs Carter will have to formally identify her daughter for our records. So you say she was likely staying with a boyfriend? Where might that be? Name?'

'I don't know, she was always hanging around with the wrong people. I saw her with a crowd over Scaws Estate a lot. Someone told me she was hanging round with Brian

Wick, he's a nasty piece of work if ever I knew one,' he said.

The irony, Emma thought.

Chapter 26

Karen Cole answered the phone.

'Karen.'

'Tim? Are you alright?'

'Look,' he said. He paced up and down the street outside Eden House. He was thankful to be out of that wretched room, and he'd been toying with what to tell his wife. The detectives would be there soon, and he didn't have much time to warn her, and come up with a plausible excuse. He ran his fingers through his hair, and to a passer-by he looked like an office worker, stressed and perhaps in trouble, having got some figures wrong.

Sweat stained under his arms, and he'd completely removed his tie. He was free to go, and the only place he could think of was back to work. The priority, though, was coming up with a suitable story. Thank God the kids were at school; on Saturday mornings they were submersed in sports and revision and wouldn't be home for hours.

'Karen, I haven't got a lot of time, and I've got to get back to work, but something has happened and I don't want you to panic. You know that woman who they found up at Watermillock recently?'

'Yes, of course I do. It's in all the papers.'

'Well, she was a patient of mine. Now they've found another one. Another body, Karen. She was my patient too.'

'Tim, you're scaring me. What do you mean they've found another body?'

'A young girl was found this morning, up at Aira Force. I operated on her two years ago. They think they're connected.'

'What?' Her voice was pitched. He had to be careful. Karen wasn't known for her calm nature under duress.

'Karen, calm down. I need you to think. They have a search warrant for the house.'

'What?' she screamed.

'Karen! Karen! Listen to me. It doesn't mean anything. They aren't charging me with anything. They don't think it was me, I'm their only connection because I'm a fucking doctor, sorry – a doctor: I was their doctor, but look, everything will be alright. They're the police, Karen; I can't keep them away. They can do what they want, and, right now, what they want is to snoop around our house.'

'You've got to come home!'

'Karen, I can't. You have to stay calm. You can do this. They just want to look around. I have to get back to work. I'm operating on a twelve-year-old and if he doesn't get this operation, chances are he'll never walk again.' It was a white lie. He'd already operated on said twelve-year-old, saving his legs, yesterday. But neither Karen nor the police needed to know that.

Karen whimpered. Tim closed his eyes. 'The children.'

'They'll be gone when they get home.'

'What are they looking for, Tim? Is there something you haven't told me?'

'No! I don't know. They might take some stuff, Christ, Karen, can you just hold it together, for once? Please?'

It was a low blow.

She hung up.

He went to work, calling the best lawyer he knew, on his way.

DC Will Phillips and DC Rob Shawcross were virtually five minutes away from the property when Tim Cole's wife slammed the phone on to its port. She heard the gravel on the driveway and went to the curtains to peek outside. They were obviously coppers; they wore cheap suits, drove an inexpensive Ford, and looked generally as though they were on sub-fifty grand salaries.

Besides, no-one else was expected.

She wrung her hands, took a deep breath and went to the door.

'Good afternoon.' The shorter one was in charge.

He handed her a piece of paper, like Tim told her he would, and she stepped aside.

'We need you to stay inside the property, ma'am. We don't want to disturb you any more than we have to.' The true reason was so if they were accused of planting evidence, they could testify in court that the homeowner was present during the search. They'd decided to go ahead in the absence of Mr Cole, though, firstly because DI Porter had him, and secondly, so he couldn't tamper with anything. It was a big house, including a pool house and various wings used for games and leisure. The guy was loaded. They waited for her to read the document.

Karen read the sheet of paper. It gave them free rein to search everywhere. She hadn't even had time to tidy up. All the beds were unmade. Last night's dishes were in the sink, and several empty bottles of wine sat on the counter. She blushed.

She watched as the two men carried in two hefty satchels, opened them, and took out plastic covers for their feet. They also put on gloves.

Once inside, Will and Rob spread out. There was a rigid protocol surrounding searches under warrant, and it was all to do with protecting the integrity of the scene, should, in the future, the evidence be challenged in court. If the scene were to be compromised, then it could ruin a case. Everything – from a sweet paper in a waste paper bin, to evidence of bodily fluid – would be photographed, logged, written up, sent to the lab, and witnessed three times. Lawyers made a living off derailing investigations and suing on behalf of clients who are guilty as hell, and it was a nightmare for any force.

Methodology was their best friend, and they set about combing each room at a time. They'd get to the out houses soon enough. They'd brought everything they needed, from evidence bags and dusting kit, to swabs and ultra-violet torches. They were tasked with performing a regular search, plus looking for particular items such as straps, medical equipment, literature and DNA. By his own admission, Tim Cole had regular sex with Moira, so DNA evidence would be defunct. They needed more to make a charge, something linked to Brandy perhaps.

In the study, a cursory rummage showed that Tim Cole was the landlord of several Penrith rental properties and was in fact quite a real estate magnate. They took the details and photographed relevant documents. The bookcase was photographed. It contained various medical journals, and works by obscure physicians.

The inside search took over an hour, and in that time, Karen Cole hadn't moved. She watched as their search went outside to the garage and sheds. There, they found what any garage might contain: rope, tarpaulin, garden tools and cable ties. A quick ultra-violet test confirmed that no blood was present. Two cars were parked in there and both were unlocked. A thorough search of them was carried out, and fibres, litter and the boot contents were collected. It was all very pedestrian. The tyres of both vehicles were photographed for their prints. The prints from Tim Cole's private vehicle – the Aston Martin – had been done at Eden House.

DC Phillips called DI Porter.

'We're pretty much done here, Guv.'

'Anything of interest?'

'Not on first glance.'

'Ok, come in and let's process the lot.'

After the officers had gone, Karen Cole closed the door and leant against the cold wood. She felt violated. Her watch told her that, in under an hour, her children would return home, and she'd have to begin thinking about their dinner. Her priority was to make sure that their rooms all looked normal. She found toothbrushes missing, as well as some personal items, and even underwear. She could make excuses for everything. Besides, the children wouldn't even notice.

Her main focus was waiting for her husband to come home.

He had some explaining to do.

Chapter 27

They had to wait until gone eleven o'clock for the sun to completely disappear over the mountains to the north of Aira Force.

Kelly had explained her reasons to her team and had asked for a volunteer. Of course Rob had offered straight away, but she'd made sure the others weren't overly keen to tag along; she didn't want anyone thinking that she was favouring the young man who was swiftly fancying himself her protégé. The moon was in a new phase and the waxing sliver of silver shone brightly in the clear sky. As they pulled off the A592, there was no other vehicle about, and the road was eerily quiet. Perhaps the same had been true the night Brandy Carter had been driven here. Ted Wallis had given her time of death as approximately fifteen to twenty-four hours before she was found, and Kelly believed that she'd been dumped at night: the tourist attraction would be far too busy during the day. Even for a narcissistic giant ego, it was too risky.

'I want to see what it's like without any ambient light,' she said to Rob, who yawned. They'd worked fifteen hours straight, but Kelly was still bright, and she pulled off the road and parked. The uniform whose unfortunate job it was to make sure no-one passed the police tape at night, nodded, and untied one end to let the vehicle enter the car park. Rob got his jacket from the back. The day had been a scorcher, but without the sun, the temperature soon fell, and he guessed it to be around ten degrees. Kelly pulled on a hooded sweater. They both wore casual clothes and footwear; they weren't strictly on duty.

They got out and Kelly walked to the uniform behind the police tape.

'All quiet?' she asked. He nodded. He had a vehicle to shelter in when he felt like it, and probably a few flasks of coffee to keep him going.

'On your own?' Kelly asked.

'Yes, ma'am. My partner rang in sick and she wasn't replaced. I'm fine,' he said, reading her concern.

'We're just going to have a look around,' she said to him.

'At night, ma'am?' he asked, curious.

'It's a different perspective,' she said, and the young copper nodded. If it was him, he'd be at the pub or in front of the TV, but he'd heard that the detective liked to do things her way. Strange lot, detectives, he thought. Rob shook the policeman's hand and they headed off to the trees. Kelly held a large diving torch because it was the most powerful she had.

She'd walked the route during the day a thousand times, but it was so different at night. She'd expected it to be so, but was still surprised at how it changed the senses. The noises were different, the smells were different, it felt different under foot, and it made progress slow. There were so many invisible obstacles to tackle without daylight.

'Fuck!' she said, as she tripped over a hidden root and tumbled into a bush. Rob came to her aid and, between them, they got her back on her feet. She had twigs and leaves in her hair, and her hands were muddy.

'How the hell did someone carry a body through this lot?' she asked.

'No idea, Guv. I haven't been up here for years but I have to say, there are so many other places which are easier to get to,' Rob said.

'I suppose that's the point. It would have taken extraordinary focus and local knowledge. I wonder how long it took,' she thought aloud. Rob looked at his watch.

'We've been walking for twenty minutes already,' he said.

'How heavy was Brandy?' she asked. Her whole team knew Brandy's autopsy report inside out. Kelly knew the answer but was vocalising her train of thought. Rob was used to the way she did this now, and he didn't answer.

'Seven and a half stone wet through,' she answered herself. 'Could you carry a dead weight of fifty kilos this far, Rob?' she asked.

'No, I don't think so.'

'And you work out, don't you?'

'Yes, but it's the terrain, Guv. Not the weight. He would have had to have taken it pretty slow, either that or fallen over a few times.'

'There weren't any superficial scratches on Brandy, so my guess is that she was wrapped up. I wonder if he dragged her.'

They made it through the narrow pathway to where it opened out, and it was a relief. The next part was fairly easy. Kelly shone her torch around the path in case she spotted something. She was looking for anything – a caught piece of material perhaps, a scrap of fabric or a drag mark. There was nothing. After fifteen hours, Brandy might not necessarily have had any rigor mortis.

'Why go to all this trouble?'

'Maybe it's something to do with the poem, Guv,' Rob suggested.

'But the poem isn't about Aira Force is it?'

'Not that I know of, Guv,' Rob said. 'It is pretty dramatic though. The first poem wasn't about Watermillock, or a church,' he added. Kelly agreed.

'The reverend said something about the Lakeland Poets having their own kind of religion: in nature.'

'It's certainly no accident, you wouldn't stumble on this place and say to yourself: oh this is a good spot.'

Kelly agreed. But a church and a waterfall. She couldn't make the connection.

The sound of the water became all encompassing, and Kelly wondered if the killer found it comforting. It didn't seem as though one was alone up here, with the water roaring as a constant reminder of life. The air was fresher nearer the water, and it pushed gusts outwards and upwards. The moon was shrouded in cloud and the night was blacker than anything Kelly had witnessed before. So much for choosing a new moon. The view of the stars was outstanding though, and Kelly believed their killer to be a lover of nature, and extremely comfortable in its company.

Kelly felt chilly as they neared the top. She felt exposed and every one of the sixty-five foot drop beckoned her. If she didn't know better, she would have said that it was an extraordinary mark of respect to leave someone here, but they knew the opposite to be true. No-one who tortured and maimed like their killer, knew any respect at all. They'd talked to the rangers, who hadn't seen a thing, as well as appealing for tourists to come forward who'd visited the attraction recently. The family who'd made the grim find had packed up and gone home early, put off the Lakes for life.

They reached the little bridge, and the might of the falls assaulted them. White water, clear in the little light available, tumbled endlessly into the depths below them. The power of it was staggering.

'I wonder if he stopped to admire the view,' Kelly said.

'Where was she?' Rob asked. Kelly knew the area better than he did.

'Up here,' she said, and he followed. She guided him above the waterfall, to a quieter glade of trees, where the water ran slower and calmer. Kelly stopped and shone her light towards some trees. 'There,' she said.

'Christ,' Rob said. 'What an effort,' he added.

Kelly nodded. This is what she'd come for, at such an unsociable hour: to witness, like the killer himself, the isolation and staggering atmosphere of the place. She imagined him dropping the body while he took in the beauty and majesty of the spot. He *must* care, she thought. He *had* to care about the place. It was so significant that Kelly was convinced that their killer planned every detail to precision. He had a relationship with this place, as well as the church where he'd left Moira. Kelly bit her lip.

It was those links that would eventually trip him up.

Chapter 28

A brief run of the name Brian Wick on the PNC didn't take long to throw out a result. Brian 'Bick' Wick had a decent criminal history, but more importantly, a known address. Kelly tasked DC Emma Hide and DC Shawcross to pay him a visit. Rob drove through Penrith towards the Scaws Estate and DC Hide sat in the passenger seat. She was a very different companion to Kelly, Rob noticed. The young DC was quiet and measured, and rarely spoke. She was petite, like Mia, but like a Jack Russell: not to be messed with.

'So what do we have on him so far?' Rob broke the silence.

Emma glanced at her notes. 'He's a local thug, that's for sure. Hangs around in the same gang he's hung with since dropping out of school. Twenty-seven, unemployed, various drug-related cautions and arrests. A bit of a local legend. Tough guy. He definitely attracts the dross,' she said.

'What are the links to Brandy Carter?' Rob wanted to keep the conversation going, he didn't like silences, and he was used to DI Porter pushing him on journeys like this. She'd quiz him to try and catch him out, trying to coax him into thinking outside of his comfortable box. Like last night: she'd got him to carry her as far as he could, and he'd stopped, panting and out of breath, after ten yards.

'He looks a beast in his mug shot.'

It was true. Brian Wick looked like a con. A professional. He snarled at the camera, thick-necked and gnarly, the stuff of nightmares.

'She must have been desperate to dig with him,' Rob said. Emma looked out of the window.

'Desperate enough to trust him, at least. He obviously did Brandy a favour, letting her crash in his flat; I wonder what she did in return. Mother seems a waste of space, and she was obviously never home, if it can be called home. I feel sorry for her. What a life,' she said. Emma's compassion touched Rob and he thought about Brandy as a person and how her life had been snuffed out and not many people – so far – seemed to care.

The news of the second body was on the radio, and Rob shook his head. 'How do they get it so quickly?' he asked.

'Social media, it can't be controlled. A statement was given from Carleton Hall, but the press will be hounding anyone who knew her for the foreseeable future.'

Their advantage was that the press didn't know that Brandy had stayed with Brian Wick, and that made their day infinitely easier. For now, they were press-free. It gave them a small window, until they inevitably found out.

'So have you turned up anything with the notes?'

Rob referred to the poetry left on the two victims. For his part, he was glad that another officer had volunteered for the task. His strong point was maths and physical geography. He could never understand the attraction to the humanities and arts at college. The English Literature students who swanned about debating dead men's words and feelings freaked him out. He was much more comfortable with straight answers and stuff that had no variables: like emotion.

Emma picked up on his mystification and smiled. She'd volunteered because she loved literature. Plain and simple. But this was a double win: not only was it poetry, but Lakes poetry that she hadn't read since university. The verse, she was convinced, was at the centre of this case, and she'd stayed up way into the night to perfect her brief for DI Porter.

'Do you read poetry, Rob?' Of equal rank, they were comfortable using their first names. Emma was a little senior to him, having been a DC for two years, and so Rob was still well and truly the rookie.

'Erm, not really. My girlfriend likes books, but I've never got into them really. I watch films, but reading makes me think I should be getting out and doing something.'

'So, you see it as a waste of time?'

'Kind of.' Rob smiled. They understood one another.

'Well, I'll tell you what I think. The boss has already said that they're calling cards, and messages. Agreed?'

'Yup.' Rob listened intently, as well as navigating the traffic, which was light through town. They were almost on the outskirts of Penrith and neared the Scaws Estate.

'They're both pretty depressing. Even I'll admit that. But not at first glance. You've got to really be quite keen to dig deep into both of them to analyse their meaning.' She shifted in her seat, animated now. Rob concentrated and tried to follow her meaning.

'See, they're both about how life always comes to an end, or is ruined. Moira's poem – the one about the flower – well, that's quite obvious, without going in to too much detail. It's about all things in nature being fleeting and short-lived, no matter how beautiful they are. The message is that we should enjoy the things that delight us because soon enough, they'll be gone.' She looked at Rob but she couldn't read his face. He looked as though he was simply concentrating on his driving, until he asked, 'So what do you think it means?'

'Well, I think it means that Moira thought too much of herself and deserved to be taught a lesson, after all, the boss said it was about punishment.'

'Christ, he's sick as fuck.'

'Well, yes, there is that. Anyway, the second one – Brandy's – that's slightly different in that it's about how screwed up mankind is.'

'Screwed up?'

'Yes, how we've been given all these amazing things in nature, but we've messed it all up.'

'How have we done that?'

'Well, if you look at nature: the birds, the trees, the sea, for example, everything works in harmony. But once you put us into the equation, things start to go wrong and we've screwed up royally.'

'What the hell has that got to do with a drug addict-cum-prostitute on the Scaws Estate?'

'Exactly that. Everything we touch, we ruin. Look, shit isn't in harmony when we humans get involved.'

'God, that's deep. I mean, this guy is what? A professor or something? Maybe a writer? A teacher?'

'I don't think it's that specific. They could have become obsessed with poetry over the years and it's just their way of expressing their disgust.'

'Disgust?'

'Yes. Disgust. I think that's really important. The killer was disgusted by Moira and Brandy's behaviour in life.'

The rest of the journey took place in silence.

They drove into the Scaws Estate and parked on the street. The conversation in the car was forgotten and they prepared to find out if Brian Wick was home. Rob knocked on the door, but there was no answer. They both peered through a window, which had dirty net curtains hung up. They squinted. From the corner of her eye, Emma saw a shadow of movement and Rob saw it too. It was on the other side of the flat; the sun was shining in and three figures could be spotted in the brightness: they were framed like silhouettes. They needed to know if Brian Wick was one of the figures, and if he had something to hide.

Rob rapped on the door again, loudly. Again, nothing. He kept banging.

Finally, after about five minutes of hammering and peering through the window at the figures, the door was opened. A man stood in the hallway, but it wasn't Brian Wick: they knew from the photograph taken from his record.

'Bick's not here.'

Rob and Emma heard the sound of a window being opened or closed and they barged past the man, running through the flat. The kitchen backed onto a fire escape and as they peered down it, it wobbled and banged under stress from the speed of the escapee. They couldn't see the other two.

'Shit!' said Rob. He walked over to the window and peered out, the scene was one of concrete and garages and yards: he could have gone anywhere. 'Let's go.' Emma wore flat shoes, and she was up for a chase. As they went back through the flat, they saw that the other guy had legged it too.

'Come on.' They ran down a stairwell, that they thought might lead to the back of Wick's flat, and split up. Ten minutes later, they came together at the flat entrance, out of breath and admitting defeat.

'Let's have a look round.' They didn't have a search warrant, but the property was abandoned and left open and technically could be a crime scene, so they had justifiable cause.

The place was a shithole. They began looking in drawers, behind cushions, and in wardrobes, for any hint of Brandy Carter. The place reeked of idleness and contraband.

In the bedroom, the double bed lay unmade. The waste bin contained used condoms and tissues. The sheets were stained. In the wardrobe, in a corner, rolled up and seemingly discarded, there was a holdall, and inside it were enough items to get a female through a weekend, or perhaps longer. There was a toilet bag, some perfume, some jewellery, and some clothes. Emma looked at the size, and she reckoned they'd fit Brandy. Satisfied with what they'd found, they locked the flat with a key they found on the kitchen counter, and left.

'Let's get back and get a drawing done of the guy who answered the door, and let's see if Brian Wick owns a car.'

'Did he strike you as the type of sensitive guy you're looking for, into his poetry?' Rob asked, as they walked back to the car.

Chapter 29

Timothy Cole parked his Aston Martin DB9 in the private garage underneath the house, which overlooked Ullswater from her northern shores. He was one of the leading orthopaedic surgeons in the country, and he could demand thousands for private consultations, so the grand property nicely reflected how far he'd come in the world.

It hadn't always been like that.

His wife enjoyed the trappings of his success, and so did their four children. They had an indoor pool, a steam room, whirlpool and bar outside, along with a games room big enough for two pool tables, and a cinema.

The evening was much the same as all the others, for as far back as Tim could remember: the children tucked away with their various gadgetry – be it in the games room or their own vast bedrooms – and his wife halfway down her first or second bottle of wine. She was bored by how easy everything had become. But not today.

She'd had fight in her once.

And he'd enjoyed making love to her. But now it was all different. He no longer knew her; nor she him. He had no idea if she had lovers. He thought he might quite promote the idea to keep her happy. Anything to keep Karen happy, he thought.

He walked towards the front door and took out his key. He wondered if she would be sober enough to talk to, or if he'd have to wait until the morning to be admonished and grilled about the two dead women, and why the police had violated their private domain. But then, if she took it badly, how would it affect the children? Perhaps he could call the bluff of the police, after all they had nothing on him. If they did, they wouldn't have let him walk free. And now another body had been found, surely they were looking for someone else. But that's what terrified him.

He was fucked.

He caught sight of himself in the huge gilded mirror that hung over a table in the grand entrance hall. He looked haggard. And so he should. He threw his keys in the glass bowl and they clattered. He dropped his briefcase and cast his jacket on to a chair unlovingly.

The house was quiet. The children were so used to their solitary existence that they never questioned it. They came in from school, dropped their bags in the kitchen, kissed their mother over her glass of wine, and slunk to their rooms to do what they do.

He couldn't face his wife, and so he took the stairs and visited the children in their various quadrants. They smiled innocently at the welcome intrusion, innocent to the afternoon's invasion. He sat on their beds, asking questions about their day, and tickled the youngest. He wondered why they didn't play together – they had an instant playgroup – but they preferred to hide away, each in his or her own space.

They'd be called down for supper at some point, and watch their iPads at the table with headphones on, while Karen topped up her glass. Six planets orbiting the same moon, but none paying any attention to the others.

If Timothy Cole could give everything away, in trade for being left alone by the police, he would. He'd do it in the flash of an eye, because, for the first time in his life, he wasn't in control. He wasn't in charge, he wasn't calling the shots, and he wasn't the boss.

Nothing meant anything at all in the face of what they all had to come. He'd be struck off, never able to work again. Karen and the children would be homeless. Her rows and rows of Prada, Alexander McQueen, Valentino, Versace, Armani and Dolce & Gabbana meant nothing. The Louis Vuitton luggage she insisted upon was a trinket in the face of the Crown Prosecution Service, when it believed it had a case. And even if they didn't have a case, they'd make one, and no-one would believe the evil consultant who broke the patient–physician code of ethics. He'd be the next Harold Shipman.

He went to his study and poured himself a large whisky. They called it the study, but he never worked in there. He never worked at home. But, occasionally, he would pretend to so he could enjoy the view. That, and the peace and quiet.

He kept the lights off.

The moon lit the lake. It was almost full, and it shone brighter than anything man-made. The black oily mass beneath beckoned him. He wondered if he had the courage to make it all go away. But that would leave his children to pick up the pieces because his wife wouldn't be capable of doing so.

If only he'd have helped Moira that night, instead of hurting her.

He looked at his vast bookcases and wondered simply if someone would write a book about him one day, and if people would read it. He imagined the middle of the book full of glossy photos of the victims, and some of his family, with caveats about how their lives fell apart because they hadn't known their father's dark secret.

The face of Brandy Carter came to him: she was all over the news. She was a pathetic excuse for a human being, addled and ravaged by drugs and promiscuity, a scourge on the NHS. Of course he remembered her; she had offered him sex in exchange for morphine. It wasn't unheard of; it happened. Morphine, and its various guises came at a handsome price.

He drained his whisky, put down the glass and looked at his hands. The hands that give life also take it away, he thought. His eyes rested on a photo of his children on his desk. He picked it up and stared at it. Their lives were about to be torn apart. Maybe he should take them all with him. He understood, now, why fathers did it. The pain of leaving them behind to suffer was too much.

A thud from upstairs slammed him out of his fantasy, and he rushed from the room. The kitchen was upstairs, along with the lounge, because that's where the best views were. He took the stairs, two at a time, and entered the open plan kitchen-dining area. The lights were dimmed over the table, and the place was totally quiet.

Then he saw her.

She began to laugh.

'Tim! Oh my God, I fell. Bloody hell, help me up. I've only had one glass,' Karen insisted. He went to her and helped her up. Her wine glass was under the table, but intact. He automatically went to the fridge to fill it up.

She was still beautiful.

He went to her and held her.

She pulled back at first, so un-used to tenderness. But then she softened, and allowed herself to fall into his arms, and just be held.

'Tim, are you alright?' she asked. He didn't answer. He held her tighter.

'Tim? Tim, that's too tight,' she said.

'I'm so sorry,' he said.

'What for? Tim? You're not making sense. Ouch, that hurts,' she said.

He started to cry, and his shoulders shook. He squeezed tighter, and Karen tried to get free. She hadn't felt him so close for what felt like years – apart from when he had sex with her when she was asleep, and she woke up at the end – and the proximity was both exciting and repulsive.

'I'm sorry,' he said again. He was sobbing now. Karen struggled to breathe.

'Tim…' she said. 'Tim, I… can't… breathe…'

'I know, it's ok. It won't be long now, Karen. You remind me of my mother.'

Chapter 30

Colin Tate answered the door and didn't look surprised to see the badge of a police detective. He had a bright, polite face, and it caught Kelly off guard; anyone who evades being questioned by the police usually turns out to be aggressive and uncooperative, when they were eventually tracked down.

Colin Tate was anything but. The fact that neither James, nor Emily Tate, had told Kelly about their children's adoptions, niggled her. The man before her was thirty-eight years old, and he'd spent his first sixteen years either in care homes or on the street. It was a fact known commonly in psycho circles that killers with an MO including sex and torture usually had a fucked up childhood, and Colin Tate certainly ticked that box.

'Please come in,' he said, as he opened the door wider.

She'd driven to the Scaws Estate to give the address a try for herself, seeing as the door hadn't been answered in the last four days. He was only a POI at the moment, but the fact that he'd been evasive was flagging warnings in Kelly's head. She'd spent the whole weekend in the office, crunching leads and dismissing each one, and it had left her feeling depressed. Laboratories generally closed down at the weekend and people had to go home to sleep. Today marked their second week on the case, and Cane was getting antsy.

She was on her way to Eden House and took the diversion on a whim. She looked around her at the playgrounds that were vandalised and covered in graffiti, the kids — who should be at school by now — hanging about in gangs, the corridors and alleyways smelling of piss, and the domestic arguments wafting on the air with trans-fat takeaways and cigarette smoke. The wealth of James Tate hadn't permeated very far towards his son, and Kelly wondered how Colin ended up here. Motive indeed. And just round the corner from Brian Wick.

They had nothing further to pin on Timothy Cole, but he remained a POI. Person of Interest wasn't a legal term, as such — not like *suspect* or *material witness* — it simply meant they would remain on the table, so to speak. Kelly had spent the rest of her weekend on the phone talking to old colleagues of the surgeon, trying to uncover the slightest hint of arrogance or complacency associated with the so-called 'God-complex'. So far she'd unearthed nothing of the sort. Surgeons, by the very nature of their field, had to be confident and sure and Timothy Cole had earned respect and admiration over his surprisingly illustrious career. No matter what new angle they tried, Timothy Cole didn't fit their MO. He had a happy childhood, was a straight A student at school and college, had no previous, and didn't even smoke.

'Sorry about the mess. I've just got a new job, and I haven't had much time at home. Can I get you a drink?' Colin said. The guy was all control and charm, the antithesis to his mother.

He looked like his mother but then Kelly had to check herself: Emily Tate wasn't this man's mother. She wondered that, if people spent enough time together, they began to take on the same characteristics. But Colin Tate didn't exude pessimism, in fact quite the opposite. He was clearly down on his luck – a thirty-eight-year-old man with transient employment, a dubious past, and a one-bedroom flat; but she wanted to know more about him. He closed the door behind them.

'I'd love anything cold, please,' Kelly said.

'I think I've got some lemon cordial?' Colin offered.

'That'll be fine, thank you,' she said. She watched as Colin went into the tiny kitchen that must have been a metre and a half squared, and looked around for clean cups.

When he came back, he held two plastic cups of juice (no ice), and he held one out to her, which she took gratefully. There were few seating options, but Colin tidied away a few piles of clothes (by moving them onto a table), and they both managed to sit down.

'Colin, I'm sure you know why I'm here. It's been quite a task getting hold of you.' Kelly was giving him a chance to explain. Colin bowed his head for a moment, and looked at her. 'Yes, I do. Mum told me,' he said. He offered no more than that, so Kelly carried on.

'When was the last time you saw your stepmother, Moira?'

Colin looked at the small window facing the street and sighed. 'Erm… years ago. I mean, I never really had much to do with her, apart from visiting Dad, and I kind of stopped that.'

'Why did you stop visiting your father?'

'It's personal,' Colin said, with finality.

'I'm sorry, could you elaborate? It's important.'

'Why is it important?' Colin asked.

'We're trying to establish who was in Moira's life, and who came and went, and why. A change in your relationship might indicate deterioration, or an escalation, if you see what I mean.' She sipped her cool water and looked around. It was half habit, and half intention. She and Johnny used to do it in bars, trying to work out the personalities behind the veneers, before they split up. She missed him. In Colin, she saw a single man, untidy but functional, unharried by convention and nature. She wondered if Johnny would agree.

'I didn't like her. I thought she was after Dad's money, and that was all. I told Dad what I thought and he said I was on my own. I said that was fine by me, and I never went back. I sent back the cheques he wrote, and I tried to move on.'

'Can you tell us about the incident at the care home in Ulverston?'

Colin was prepared. His mother had warned him.

'It was an accident. I was being bullied, I snapped and pushed the guy off me, he banged his head and he haemorrhaged. He died,' Colin stopped. He looked down at his hands. When he looked back up, his eyes were wet and bloodshot. 'I didn't mean it. It's the worst thing that ever happened, and I've never been able to forget it – no-one has allowed me ever to forget it. I can't keep jobs, I can't keep friends – they always, always find out.'

Kelly saw flashes of anger, which might be explained through frustration – or might not. Colin got to his feet, paced up and down the tiny room, and ran his hands through his hair. It was behaviour one might see in a care home. Institutionalisation.

'Did Moira know about it, Colin?'

'Yes!' he shouted, and spittle flew out of his mouth. 'She told Dad I was scum!' He turned around and faced a wall and spread his hands across the wall. Kelly wished she'd brought someone with her. She took out her mobile phone and checked the signal, pretending she had an incoming call.

'Sorry.' She excused herself and spoke into the phone. In reality, she was logging on to the internet to record her location. She pretended to end the call and turned back to Colin.

'Colin, do you know Brandy Carter?'

'Who? No. Why are you asking me this? Who is she?' Colin's face softened slightly with surprise, and Kelly almost felt sorry for him. He was rash, confused and suffering, but in all probability not a threat to her at all.

'Maybe this will help.' Kelly passed him a photo of Brandy. It puzzled her as to why anyone – given the press coverage – might not have seen Brandy's face or heard her name in the news.

'Oh her! Christ, everyone knows her! She's a...' he faltered.

'She's a what?'

'She's a filthy cunt!' Colin spurted out.

Kelly waited calmly for the moment to pass, and for Colin Tate to compose himself.

'Why is she a cunt, Colin?' Kelly asked. She hated the word and it sat brutally on her tongue. Colin Tate had used it viciously.

'She bullies kids for money. She knew if I ever caught her I'd punch her in her stupid face – that's what she deserved – she ran away every time she saw me,' Colin said.

'She's dead,' Kelly said.

'What?' Colin was dismayed.

'Don't you watch the news, Colin? Her body was found on Saturday morning. She was murdered. In a similar way to Moira.' Kelly took a risk. In lots of ways, Colin Tate reminded her of a child.

'What do you want me to say? Maybe Moira was supplying her with smack? I have no idea if they knew each other. I'm not surprised, though. The girl knew some rough people. I never knew her name was Brandy.'

Colin's anger seemed to have dissipated, for now, and he sat down heavily on a dining chair.

'What do I have to do with all of this?' he said.

'Oh, Colin. Do I have to spell it out? It looks bad. You disliked both women, for fairly profound reasons, and you live in the area in which they disappeared, and you know the Lakes well, don't you?'

Colin looked nonplussed.

'You obviously love the outdoors.' Kelly walked over to the table that was piled high with clothes, and retrieved a picture that had been stood up against a wall. She turned to face Colin and held it up. It was a stunning canvas of a photograph taken of a wooden jetty disappearing into a lake, with mountains framing the background. It was very artistic.

'One of the most famous pictures taken of Derwent Water, ever. And over here,' she said, as she put the picture down and walked across the room, pointing at another picture, this time on the wall.

'A stunning painting of Hardknot Pass.' She waited. 'Gifts or knick-knacks?' Kelly asked.

'I climb,' he said, finally.

'I'd appreciate it should you volunteer a DNA sample, as well as a handwriting sample, Mr Tate,' said Kelly.

'Are you arresting me?' Colin said quietly. He appeared meek once more, and Kelly was taken by how quickly he could switch between moods. She felt an overwhelming pity for him, as if he'd spent his whole life resigned to the fact that he was a good-for-nothing nobody who would never change.

'No, I'm not,' said Kelly. She pulled a pair of gloves out of her bag, pulled them on, found a swab, and went towards him. He pulled back.

'I can take cells from inside your mouth, it takes a second and you won't feel anything.'

Slowly Colin opened his mouth. Kelly ran the swab around the inside of his cheek. Quickly, she sealed it, popped it into her bag, and got out a note pad and pen.

'Please,' she said to him.

'What should I write?' he asked, meekly again, like a child.

'Your name and address will do, and put some words in speech marks for me.'

They could be dealing with a schizophrenic: if he remembered penning the lines of verse, he didn't show it. Colin did as he was asked, and as soon as he handed the piece of paper back to Kelly, she knew one of two things: either Colin Tate was a master of evasion, or he was not their killer.

But that's what her job was all about.

Disappointment.

Chapter 31

Brian Wick walked along the road with his head hunched low into his neck, his hood was pulled tightly over his head – despite the warmth from the sun – and his hands were deep in his jeans pockets, which hung about his hips in a USA gang-style arrangement. His boots were dirty, and he sniffed every other step, fighting a cold, or irritated by too much coke. Monk followed, three or four steps behind.

No-one was startled or moved by the sight. Young men in such garb, boasting the gait of men unfazed by social mores, were common in large towns across Britain. Underneath their clothes, and inside their chests, though, they were anything but ordinary. They'd spent three days deciding what to do next. Their photographs had been released by the local press, and had appeared in newspapers. They dare not go back to their flats, and their families had been warned by the police before they could get to them. Friends hid them and they slept on sofas, in bath tubs and on kitchen floors, but they couldn't do it forever. Neither young man could have known that their details had been entered onto the PNC, and it was only a matter of time before they'd be brought in.

Monk had suggested giving themselves up, but Bick had reminded him that the last time they saw Brandy Carter alive, they'd been facing one another, with her in between. Their DNA would be all over her. Monk had watched CSI, but he didn't think the police were that clever in Britain. Bick's plan was to hitchhike to Manchester, but they needed to grow some facial hair and change their appearance well enough to put distance between their photos and their reality. Bick's beard was coming along nicely, but Monk's was slow.

They took a risk, being in public together, but they were buzzing from the long night of excellent coke and beer. Taken together, their two favourite drugs, when they could get hold of them, enabled them to drink all night and not lose their senses. However, it also meant that they'd forgotten that they were in hiding. They shuffled along towards Casey's flat, but they'd got lost, and they'd walked along the same street four times. Now they were sobering up, and both boys experienced a rising panic as two old women gave them lengthy stares outside the post office.

Bick needed a smoke but he was out so he popped into the off-licence, Monk following meekly. Bick went inside and asked for ten Benson and Hedges, as well as a lighter. He was barely outside when he lit up and passed one to Monk.

There were no sirens.

An unmarked car screeched to a halt outside the off-licence, and the two boys froze. Only then did the response team let their sirens blare and the blues flash. Bick felt his anal sphincter muscle twitch, and his heart began to beat faster than if he was running at full speed. He believed that, at any moment, the organ would jump through his skin onto the pavement below. Monk's hands flew up in the air before his brain engaged, and later, he wouldn't be able to remember the next twenty seconds of his life. Bick's eyes darted about. There were two cars, one contained the uniformed pigs, and the other two plain clothes detectives – one male, one female. He glared at the female. He knew his time was up and he raised his hands. The uniforms approached with caution, instructing the two males to turn around and place their hands behind their backs, which they did. Once cuffed, they were led back to the response car. Kelly got out and walked towards them.

Kelly looked at Brian Wick and knew he called the shots. The meek boy beside him, looking as though he'd pissed himself, was a follower. Kelly had considered the possibility of two killers working together, but it was a rare MO and Emma had seen three figures at the flat. They knew that Brandy had bought cigarettes from the corner shop around eleven p.m. but she could have easily gone back to the flat after that. Another doubt cast a shadow over Kelly's theory: looking at the two boys before her, extraordinarily out of their depth, she doubted if either had even heard of the Lakeland poets. Or, if either, even inside a psychotic episode, could write a sentence. And where was the third man? That said, they could still give Kelly information about the second victim that could turn out to be crucial.

'You're entitled to a lawyer present, Brian,' said Kelly.

'I don't need a fucking lawyer, I haven't done anything,' he replied. Kelly noticed that his eyes were red and he sniffed every ten seconds or so: drugs, she thought. He was probably Brandy's supplier and Kelly had a good idea how she paid for them. She nodded and the young men were helped into the car.

They drove to Penrith police station where interview rooms had been set up. They could hold the men for twenty-four hours, more if they found reasonable evidence to put before DCI Cane and his superiors at Carleton Hall.

Once they'd entered the station, Bick and Monk were relieved of their possessions, processed, and guided into separate rooms. Kelly watched as Brian Wick stared at the other man's back as he was led in the opposite direction. She could tell by his face that they hadn't got a story straight before they'd been caught. Brian Wick had already done two years inside, and Kelly doubted he'd want to go back. She might be able to use it as leverage. She decided to let the two of them stew for a bit while she briefed her team.

She wanted to interview Wick herself. DS Will Phillips would take care of the other, as yet unidentified, man. It was established that he'd been the one who'd answered the door at Wick's flat.

Those who were present from Kelly's team met in the incident room. Kelly spoke.

'We know that Moira and Brandy were killed by the same person. We know that they have a calling card. But I'm sure you will all agree, that when we brought in these two clowns, they probably didn't do it. However, we'll lean on them and see why they ran. Will, I want you to take the dribbling wreck – find a name and run him through the system. I'll take Brian Wick.'

'Guv.' Phillips nodded.

'Kate, can you watch the feed and take notes?'

Kelly walked with DC Phillips and they approached the interview rooms.

Kelly walked into the room where Brian Wick was sweating and trying desperately to deal with the toxins in his body, and sat down. She offered him a drink. He took it gratefully and gulped the whole cup down.

'Thirsty?'

No answer.

'You've been busy. Why the rush to get away, Brian?'

She followed his eyes as he watched her and it made her feel queasy. The scrotum was flirting with her in a murder enquiry. He was a slime-ball, but was he a murderer?

He agreed to have his mouth swabbed for DNA and, as she took it, his eyes watched her face. Close up, his skin was ravaged by toxins, his breath smelled of alcohol, and his body of sweat.

'Where were you between the 12th and the 14th of July, Brian?' she asked.

'On the 12th, I was at my flat, hanging, playing GTA, and I went to bed early,' he said. Kelly expected a long battle.

'What's GTA?' Kelly feigned ignorance. She abhorred games like GTA, and those who played them.

'Grand Theft Auto,' Bick said, smugly.

'Ah, yes, the game where thugs go round raping, beating and killing women, right?' Kelly asked. Wick shifted uncomfortably.

'And when was the last time you saw Brandy Carter alive?' she asked.

'That day. She left the flat when I was asleep and she never came back,' he said.

'And what fun and games did you get up to before she just walked out of your life?' she asked.

Kelly had interviewed scores of men like Brian Wick. They were cocky, too relaxed and always alpha. Brian sat back in his chair, seemingly enjoying himself and Kelly wondered how scum like this survived the womb. She could see his brain working out what he should say next.

How much should he admit to, and when to tell her. She waited.

'Me and Monk had sex with her,' he said. Kelly knew the score: that little gem would explain any DNA found on Brandy.

'There was another one too,' he said. Kelly sat forward.

'What do you mean?' she asked.

'Another person. There were three of us who had sex with her. Don't look at me like that, it wasn't the first time, she was willing, but we didn't kill her,' he said. As he spoke, he looked at Kelly directly and she held his gaze. He was earnest and very convincing. Or an extremely good actor. 'She got stuff in exchange, she wasn't forced.' Bick seemed to Kelly as though he was keen to emphasise this fact.

'So, why did you run?' she asked.

'Because you fuckers never believe me,' he retorted.

'Is it any wonder, when you call us fuckers?' she asked. He didn't answer.

'Do you know what time she left?' she asked.

'I woke up at about eleven for the toilet, and she wasn't there. I thought she might be asleep on the couch, like she sometimes stayed there. But she wasn't, so I went to the toilet and thought she might have gone out for cigarettes, but it was too late by then. So I thought she was in the other room with Monk or Tinny,' he paused.

'Monk or Tinny?' Kelly asked. It made her pity these young men who still called each other names that belonged in the school playground. Their lives were so empty and immature that all they had was X-box, porn and lots of time. She wondered at the lethargy, arrogance and desolation that led young men to shirk a meaningful life for one full of nothing, along with the girls who followed them round; girls like Brandy Carter who led equally depressing existences.

'Monk is Jason, next door with your pal, and Tinny is his brother, Barry,' Bick replied. Kelly made notes. She could see that he was enjoying dobbing in his mates. They had their third man.

'Surname?'

'Copeland.'

'Can you give me an address?' she asked.

'Sure,' he said.

After she wrote it down, she looked at Brian Wick and sighed. Hunches were a detective's enemy, but she knew – just knew – that Brian Wick, despite being a fucktard thug from Wankersville, was not her perp.

'Have you heard of the poet, Shelley, Brian?' she asked. Bick looked wary, as if it was a trick question.

'Is that a friend of Brandy's?' he asked. Kelly closed her eyes.

'What about Aira Force?' she asked.

'Isn't that the new kickboxing game from Sony?' he replied, genuinely excited.

'Have you ever read any poetry at all, Brian, ever?' she asked. Brian searched his brain.

'There was an old woman from…' he began, grinning. Kelly held up her hand.

'Enough. Thanks, Brian,' she said.

Kelly got up and a uniform opened the door for her. In all the time she'd interviewed him, Brian Wick had not once asked about Brandy Carter. He wasn't the slightest bit interested in how a girl that he'd shared his flat with had died. Or where she was now, or how her family was. Kelly didn't know why she wasn't surprised. She went next door to see if Phillips had managed to get a full name for Jason the Monk, and if he had also snitched on his brother. She thought of Brandy Carter's last night alive. Not only had she had group sex for drugs, she'd been brutally murdered and no doubt tortured by somebody else too.

Chapter 32

As Kelly walked to the other interview room to check progress with DC Phillips, she was handed a piece of paper. On it was a note to call a DI from West Yorkshire police. Instinct told her to act upon it sooner rather than later. She knocked on the interview room door and put her head round. The large man, arrested with Bick, was crying and Phillips was standing in the corner with his arms folded.

'Need a word,' Kelly said. Phillips followed her out and shut the door behind him. 'What's he said?' she asked.

'He hasn't actually come out with many comprehendible words yet, but the ones he has are pretty interesting. He's adamant he didn't kill Brandy, but he's sorry for hurting her.'

'Has he given a name? Our lovely Bick has informed me that he's called Jason Copeland, and his brother, Barry Copeland was there too. Apparently all three had intercourse with her the night she disappeared.'

'Christ.'

'Indeed. Our suspect's DNA so far is unquestionably legitimately all over our bodies. Drop that bombshell on young Jason, and tell him his mate has dobbed him in, and see what happens. And ask him where his brother Barry is.'

Phillips nodded.

'Thing is, none of these wasters owns a car or, as far as I can see, has access to one. Our suspect needed a car – the dogs smelled Brandy's scent up to the road at Aira Force car park, and they smelled Moira's up to the road where I parked – as close to the church in Watermillock as possible. These losers don't drive. We've got twelve hours to get as much out of these boys as possible. But I'm chasing twelve vehicle tracks from Aira Force, and CCTV coming and going at the A592 junction, at the Glencoyne caravan Park – they've got the only CCTV along that road,' she said. Phillips understood that he was to delay the boys as long as possible, so they could piece together Brandy's last movements.

'By the way,' Kelly said. 'Look, this is an example of Brian Wick's handwriting,' she said, holding up a piece of paper. The scrawl was that of a five-year-old, hardly a literary enthusiast.

Phillips looked at Kelly and reflected her own frustration. It would be so easy to pin everything on a gang of rampant boys who tortured for kicks, but it wasn't to be their day. Phillips went back into the interview room and Kelly dialled the number of the DI in West Yorkshire who wanted to speak to her. It didn't take long to track him down.

'DI Kelly Porter? Good morning. Look, I received a memo from your constabulary about two murders you've had over there in Cumbria,' said the DI.

'Yes, that's correct, it went out to five northern constabularies. It was a long shot, we have reason to believe that we have a mature killer, but there are no cold cases in Cumbria matching the MO. We've got a few missing persons and I'm chasing them. What have you got for me?'

'Between 2009 and 2012, we had a spree of homicides across the county, and by the time they stopped, two officers had made significant links between all four of them,' said the DI.

'What do you mean, they stopped?'

'Like I said, the last one was four years ago and, since then, there have been no more. Not that we know of.'

'What was the MO?' Kelly asked.

'Torture, mutilation, calling card and sexual rage,' answered the DI.

'What was the calling card?' she asked, her heart beating.

'References to the bible,' he said.

Kelly's mind raced. It wasn't poetry but it was writing: it was communication, and communication that transmitted a message. 'What kind of references?'

'Well, they seemed random at the time, but when we put them together, they all shared the same theme of punishment,' he said. 'It all basically came down to one thing, which is why when I read your directive, my memory was stoked; each woman was killed in the way it said in the bible. I thought it didn't fit at first, because your references are poetry, but I thought I'd contact you anyway,' he said.

'Were the notes handwritten?'

'Yes, they were. There was a delay on making the connection because,' the officer stopped and coughed, as if embarrassed. 'Each murder was committed, or, shall I say discovered, in a different area: West Yorks, South Yorks, North Yorks, and Humberside. It took a while to make the link, but once we did, the writing matched in all four cases. Before that, we'd put together other similarities, but the handwriting was key, and we knew if we could get a suspect, the court case would be on our side.'

'And?'

'We never did.'

There was a pause as each officer contemplated a murderer getting away with his crimes.

'Can you send the files to me?' Kelly asked, quietly crossing her fingers, hoping the case files were still intact.

'Of course, I'll prepare them. It's always bothered the department here, they were horrifically brutal murders and we've never solved them. It stuck with us. Reading over them again, I think they're linked. At the time, it was questioned, because we never found a suspect with handwriting that matched, and that's pretty much all we had. Everything else was circumstantial. See what you think. Call me if you have any questions,' he said.

'I will. Thank you again. Just one question, was the handwriting evidence questioned or was it obvious that it matched, and you just never had someone to compare it to?' asked Kelly.

'I was told that handwriting is as particular as finger-prints, and it was indisputable,' he said.

They hung up. She stood in the corridor and tapped her phone to her lip. She made a note to send the directive once more, thinking that someone else's memory might also be jarred. Killers often move counties to avoid detection, it's the most sensible thing to do, especially before databases were linked. Before HOLMES.

She re-entered the interview room. Bick looked up. He bit his dirty nails.

'Did you hurt Brandy, Brian?' He looked at her and wondered if he should tell the truth or not. She could see his mind operating.

'She didn't *say* we did,' was all he said.

'What does that mean? Do you *think* she was hurt? Jason does, and he's admitted, on record, to hurting her,' she said. She watched him.

'I didn't hurt her, but I think Monk – I mean, Jason – did, he did it… you know… he's a big lad.' Bick smiled. Kelly's gut tightened. She hoped that Brandy Carter was so out of it on drugs on her last evening on this earth, that she had very little knowledge of what happened to her before she died.

'You're going to have to enlighten me, Brian. For the record.' She waited, not wanting to make it easy for him.

Brian swallowed. 'Monk's a bit, like, rough. It's why we call him…'

'Monk,' she finished for him. 'Very droll,' she added. 'Is this some kind of joke to you, Brian? Your girlfriend is dead and you're giggling about naughty Monk names.' The religious reference didn't go unnoticed but Kelly's gut told her it was coincidence.

'She's not my girlfriend,' he said. He seemed disgusted.

'Just someone you had sex with?' she asked.

'Yes,' he replied, as if that made all the difference.

'So, all three of you had sex with her. Jason hurt her, she left, and you never saw her again?' she asked.

'Yup. Exactly,' Brian said, pleased with himself.

Kelly shook her head. 'So, a murder victim comes back with three different sets of DNA, and they match yours, and your pals, and a jury is going to understand? When you were the last people to see her alive?' She omitted the shopkeeper, but Bick didn't need to know that information. What they had so far wouldn't stand up in court, but it didn't hurt to scare the shit out of this thug. Ted had already said that any bodily fluids would have been washed away by the river. But there was still hope.

Bick's face changed, and panic set in. Of course, it sounded ludicrous. He'd thought that by telling the truth, she'd appreciate his honesty and believe his story, but now he heard it back to himself, he realised that it was a pathetic story, and no-one in their right mind would believe them.

'Did you shut her up, Brian?'

'What?'

'Did she have a loose tongue?'

Brian squirmed and Kelly knew that the drugs were wearing off.

'She can't tell anyone what happened anymore, can she?'

'I didn't kill her!'

'Do you always remember what you do when you use?'

Bingo. He looked alarmed. She'd hit a raw nerve. Of course he didn't remember everything he did when he was off his tits. She left.

Phillips was in the corridor.

'He's admitted to having sex with Brandy, and he's confirmed his brother did too. The brother is being brought in now. He's in a mess, I can't get anything else out of him, he keeps repeating over and over that he didn't mean to hurt her,' Phillips said.

Their stories matched. And that was unusual, as well as highly frustrating. It was rare that suspects corroborated so closely under scrutiny. They usually blabbed on each other, desperate to save their own skins. It meant one thing: they were telling the truth. Kelly decided to go up to her office, three floors up, to read the email sent from Yorkshire Police.

'Let them sweat for a bit. Take a break, Will.'

Upstairs, she sat down heavily behind her desk. She switched on her computer and read that she'd received fifty-two emails since the arrest of Brian Wick and Jason Copeland. One caught her eye: it was entitled: Optical Microscopy. The grey fibres were both from the same production line of carpets produced between 1984 and 1999. The carpet was bought in bulk by several local government councils across the country and had now been discontinued. Four areas were mentioned on the list that Kelly recognised: The Scaws Estate, where Brian Wick and Colin Tate lived, Fair Hill, Askham Bridge and Stockham; all in the Penrith area.

Next, she opened the email with the subject highlighted in bold: Yorkshire Police.

There were pages and pages of the stuff. She scanned it, and her brain picked up words and phrases here and there. She pushed her mouse back and forth, looking for links and found them bountiful, as had the officers at the time, but still they hadn't been able to charge anyone. Five suspects had been arrested but all ruled out, courtesy of fingerprints, DNA, shoe size, and, of course, handwriting. She trawled through the columns and rows of tables, charting hundreds, if not thousands, of neck-breaking data: names, addresses, maps, employee records and forensic archives, all routine for an investigation of its size. It was just what she was doing now, and her heart sank. The investigation across Yorkshire had lasted five years and no-one had been caught.

Sexual rage... asphyxiation... note in throat... fractured larynx... petechial haemorrhage... vaginal trauma...

There were passages from Deuteronomy, Isaiah, Hebrews... none of which made any sense to Kelly, a staunch atheist. She thought of The Reverend Neil Thomas.

'He disciplines and He scourges…'
'And the earth will reveal her bloodshed…'
'Fear Him who is able to destroy…'

One case stood out. That of fifty-two-year-old Tania Stewart. It was a classic case of overkill, and Tania had been stabbed seventeen times in her abdomen and fifteen times in her breast area. It was the only case that fitted neither the Yorkshire, nor her own, MO. Why knives? Why Tania?

It was personal.

She read more about Tania Stewart, who'd been warden at a children's home in Whitehaven between 1993 and 1996: until it burned down in that year. Tania Stewart had also been under investigation for misconduct, at the Yorkshire care home where she worked, when she was brutally murdered in her home in May 2010.

By the time Kelly looked at her watch again, she'd spent three hours reading.

Chapter 33

They'd agreed to meet in Pooley Bridge.

The sun had begun its descent and Kelly looked like any other normal person going for a drink on a summer evening. She wore a lemon-coloured sun dress, with small straps over her shoulder, and her hair fell down around her face. She wore a little more makeup than usual, and higher heels. For the first time in weeks, she felt feminine. The case was never very far away from the noise in her head, but at least she could pretend to relax. She enjoyed the feeling of being away from the incident room; it felt illicit.

The Crown was quiet and Johnny sat at the bar. He turned round to see who had opened the door and smiled at her. He wore shorts and flip flops, and Kelly smiled at his nonchalance. She didn't expect anything else. He ran his fingers through his hair and stood to greet her. He pulled out a chair.

'Shall we go outside?' she asked.

'Ok,' he said. 'What would you like?'

'I'll have a glass of bubbles please. I completed on a house today. Will you celebrate with me?' She reached for the keys inside her bag and dangled them in the air. No-one else had put an offer in on the pretty house with the terrace overlooking the river. She was a cash buyer and ready to go: her offer had been accepted yesterday.

'That's great, Kelly. Where is it?'

'Here. It overlooks the river.' She watched him for his reaction, and could tell he was thinking that it could be awkward. Fuck it. It was a free country and they were all grown up.

'Don't worry, Johnny, I have no intention of stalking you. Do you still live here?'

'Yeah, same place,' he said. The barman opened a bottle of prosecco and poured Kelly a glass.

'Make that two.' Johnny started a tab and they walked outside with their drinks. Kelly popped her sunglasses back on and found a table that was still in the sun.

'Cheers, here's to you having your own place at last.' They chinked their glasses together and drank.

'Like the dress.' He was still as direct and abrupt as ever.

'Thanks. Like the flip-flops.'

'They're new, actually.'

Kelly raised her eyebrows. She'd only ever seen him wear flip-flops, trainers or walking boots. His casual attire never bothered her, it showed he didn't feel the need to show off, and it demonstrated his confidence. She liked both characteristics. They sat down.

'How's things, Kelly? You look well,' he said. His eyes took her in and she felt thoroughly gone over, but he always did that.

'I'm good. Work's busy, but I like that.'

'Have you got anything to do with those bodies turning up?'

'Of course. As always, it's my case.'

'Oh Jesus. That's shit. I'm sorry.'

'Not at all. It's what I do, you know that. I don't know how you did your job in the army, Johnny, I couldn't do that, just like you couldn't chase psychos. And this one is a fucking nut job.'

'I think I probably killed plenty of psychos. Doesn't it piss you off that you go to all that effort to pin someone down and they get given five years or something? Life should mean life.'

'I agree, but I'm not a judge or a lawyer. I just do my bit then hand them over. The better the evidence, the tighter the case. That's where my job ends. So what have you been up to?'

'Same. Mountain Rescue. It's been manic this season so far. I'm running the Keswick to Barrow next month.'

'Running it? I thought it was a walk, isn't it forty-odd miles?'

'There are a few nutcases who run it, and I've been roped in to do it for The Mountain Rescue fund. I know I'm just a stupid bloke going through my mid-life crisis.'

Kelly smiled at him.

'Have you bought that Porsche yet?'

'No, but I was thinking about a boat. I'll get the bottle.' He nodded to their empty glasses. Kelly watched him go and checked her phone: all quiet. The incident room was manned by the night shift: everything was covered, but she couldn't help herself. Johnny returned with the bottle.

'I've heard that the guy you're after has been dubbed "The Teacher". What's that all about?' He filled her glass. It was true. News outlets loved a good tag line and Kelly wasn't sure what she made of it: it could be a curse or a handy benefit. Carleton Hall could deal with it: her focus was working the leads.

'We haven't told the press everything, but what we have told them is that we think the women were tortured because they were being punished for something – essentially taught a lesson. The nickname came about from a leak; we think someone on the inside has leaked the information about the poems. Some clever dick at the *Evening Echo* came up with it and will probably win some journo award for it. I suppose it's better than The Lakeland Lunatic, or the Punisher. They can call him what they like, as long as it plays to the ego of the killer and he takes one risk too many, so I can catch the bastard.'

Kelly didn't mind the name tag. It meant that it had caught the attention of the nation, and that meant more people on the lookout for pieces of the puzzle. Newspapers always did it. Headlines were what sold papers, and handy epithets and scary rhyming slang were the bread and butter of news desks everywhere. 'The Teacher' had a certain ring to it, and it suited the MO. It wasn't too offensive, although someone had suggested that it might actually be a teacher – Cane had received complaints from the Department of Education citing gross incitement to hatred against teachers. Kelly insisted that it hadn't come from her office; inside the confines of four walls, they actually called him 'The Poet'. But he wasn't a poet, he was a thief, using someone else's work to brag. It did give a nod to the literary aspect of the murders and Kelly knew that, secretly, DC Emma Hide was intoxicated by the whole poetry angle and her insights were fascinating. Kelly believed that the young DC's hypotheses could very well turn out to be pivotal to the case, but she hadn't told her directly. After learning about the Yorkshire killer; and his calling card, Kelly's intuition told her that the words used to communicate via the deceased, were fundamental to threading all the missing pieces together. As she'd found a hundred times before at this point, Kelly believed that all they needed was right in front of them. The exposure meant more phone calls to the incident room that turned out to be absolute bullshit, but it had to be done and one day, when they least expected it, it'd be worth it. But what niggled her was the leak: they had to find out how the press had discovered the poetry.

'Is that what you think? That he's watching all the news and actually enjoying it?' Johnny asked.

'Yep. That's exactly what I think. If he didn't want the attention, he'd hide the bodies, not leave them to be discovered.' She'd probably said too much if it was anyone else, but Johnny was a private man, not given to sensationalism. She was pretty sure that he'd keep things to himself.

'I've seen some pretty fucked up stuff, but this guy sounds like he's sick – I mean really sick in the head. You deal with society's best don't you?'

'Yep, which is why, when we catch him, he'll probably get Broadmoor.'

'Do you think you'll catch him?'

'Yes,' she said and lowered her sunglasses to look at him, dead in the eye. Kelly would dearly love to get Johnny to go over what they had: he had just the right combination of cynicism, stomach and judgement to cope with the piles of information being generated by her office on an hourly basis.

'Are you sure it's the same guy who did both?' he asked.

'We're sure,' she replied. His inquisitiveness diverted her, and she enjoyed it.

'Don't psychos like that usually go through some kind of shit childhood or something?'

'Normally, yes. But it's no excuse.' Johnny had hit upon something that she'd already planned to explore with her team: their killer, like the Yorkshire killer, had grown into the monster he'd become, and he'd once been a novice – perhaps in a children's home or care home of some sort. There might be medical records about juvenile delin-quency – possibly cruelty to animals, for example – that had been flagged up years ago, waiting to be discovered, and linking their killer to a job, a doctor, a family. A past. Whitehaven was their newest lead.

'I'm not saying it is, it just always surprises me what people do to one another. I once went down a street in Sierra Leone and a woman was lying in the middle of the road, writhing around in agony, it looked like she'd been run over. A vehicle pulled up and reversed over her a couple of times until she stopped moving, then drove off. I don't know why I remember that, but it's one of the things that sticks. Look at ISIS throwing gay men off the roofs of buildings, and you see what we are capable of.'

'We? Johnny, we're not the same as ISIS.'

'Yes we are. If you take away our land, invade us, kill our families, brainwash us from birth and arm us, then most of us would react the same way.'

'Really? Would you? I don't think so. Besides, I don't think that my killer has gone through any of that. I don't think this is some kind of deranged dropout, he's more likely to be inside society than on its periphery.'

'Maybe he went through worse. All I'm saying is that humanity and compassion are all relative.'

'So you're saying killers are made not born?'

'I'm saying that we all have limits. There's only so much a person can go through before we flip.'

'I refuse to believe that all abusers have, at some point, been abused, but it's a good point. Kids who get royally screwed up early enough go on to become evil bastards. Some, not all. Can we change the subject?'

'Sorry. So when do I get to see the house?'

Kelly watched him. His skin was honey-coloured from his work on the fells, and the hairs on his arms were blonde. His hair was flecked with blonde, as well as grey. His face was lined with deep wrinkles showing where he laughed and where he thought. The prosecco was going to her head.

'Why don't we go there now?' They walked back towards the river and Kelly stopped in front of the house. Her house. Johnny's arm brushed against her and he placed his hand on the small of her back as she unlocked the door. He stepped in and she closed the door.

They made it to the foot of the stairs before they began tearing at each other's clothes.

Chapter 34

Professor John Derrent was of slim build, and he wore faded khaki shorts and a beige shirt that had seen better days, reminiscent of a hunting party at the height of The Raj. But he wasn't fazed by the state of his dress, and whether or not it was currently in vogue; he was more interested in two young college students who had decided to tag along with the afternoon's walking tour.

One of them wore shorts so short that he could see the crack of her buttock, when she bent over to check her back pack for water. Both giggled when he smiled and winked at them, as he popped his shades onto the top of his head. Despite his dress sense, and his advancing years, Derrent exuded a confidence only reserved for film stars and TV personalities. He wasn't either, but fancied himself a minor celebrity around the halls and colleges of Lancaster University. When third year students graduated, he kept in touch with a selection of them on Facebook, and insisted on reunions at remote residences in the Lakes, lent to him by friends. A few ex-students kept coming, and John Derrent's supply of willing conquests never seemed to dry up. His taste extended beyond student age too. He had no shortage of partners of a more contemporary background – lecturers mainly, married or not.

His face was tanned and he'd had his teeth whitened at great expense. But he had no wife to pay for, and no kids to leech him dry, so he was free to spend his money on the things that occupied men half his age: women and drugs.

Today he felt an excitement beyond that which normally inspired him. The Teacher had everyone talking, and John Derrent had a special tour planned. He did a quick head count and wrote down names. There was a good smattering of all ages, and it was quite a crowd. He counted seventeen people, including himself and the good reverend. Neil was an odd acquaintance but good for a pint and a natter about literature. The reverend was also partial to the occasional joint, and they'd spent plenty of balmy evenings laying by the lake, gazing at the stars, reciting poetry. Derrent fancied himself as quite the bohemian, and finally, he had something to brag about: not only did he have a newly captive audience, thanks to The Teacher, but he also had insider knowledge, thanks to Sally.

They'd gathered at Howtown jetty, and a steamer had just departed, leaving the place deserted, apart from their group. An elderly couple clicked their cameras, and it was obvious to the professor and the reverend that this was their first visit to the Lakes. Their keenness gave them away, as well as the awe with which they surveyed the view, which encased them from every angle. No matter where they looked, fell and lake assaulted the senses, and made people smile intoxicating smiles.

'Good afternoon, ladies and gentlemen!' Derrent enthused. 'Thank you so much for joining us! As you might well be aware, today's tour is based on William and Dorothy Wordsworth's many walks around beautiful Ullswater. But, sadly, the area where the tour is usually based – just across the lake there – is inaccessible to us today.' He paused and pointed across to the north shore, towards Gowbarrow. 'Sadly, the whole area is still sealed off, after the dreadful incident at the weekend. As we all know, a poor girl was found murdered at Aira Force, and, despite being a tragic tale, it was also one of Wordsworth's favourite places.' Derrent paused again, for effect, and allowed a ripple of sensationalism to travel around the group. The participants all felt as though they were living part of a macabre history, and each national reverted to type: the Japanese clicked their cameras, the Italians checked their sunglasses, and the British pretended not to be ruffled.

A man on his own at the back of the group, quietly took notes, and Derrent felt distinguished in his perceived eminence – he was being taken seriously. Too often, participants gossiped and fidgeted when he was relaying vital information, but not today. Today, everyone paid attention.

'And so today, ladies and gents, we are commencing the tour from the opposite bank: no less significant, and providing us with a new perspective. Who knows? It may turn out to be even more successful.'

Reverend Neil looked over the group with satisfaction, as he would his congregation, and Derrent introduced him. The group was suitably impressed to have a man of the cloth in attendance, and it gave the tour a higher legitimacy and a sense of officialdom.

'If we look over to the north shore, slightly eastwards, we can just make out the small hamlet of Watermillock, the site of yet another grisly reminder of what has befallen the lake in the last week. Yes, another body – the first in fact – was discovered outside the reverend's own church, and I know what you're thinking – a pattern is emerging.

Indeed. When will The Teacher strike again? And where will he leave his next victim?'

Derrent paused and put his hands on his hips, gazing across the lake in an exaggerated manner, encouraging the same from his group. People took selfies, and the quiet man at the back continued making notes.

They began their tour. The plan was to walk the southern shore (instead of the northern one), and end up in a pub in Glenridding, where there would be refreshments and a quiz. It was an impressive hike, and it would take them up and down fells as they went.

Derrent carried a long walking stick, with a handle of deer horn, and he used it deliberately with every stride. The reverend fell into animated conversation with those around him. Some asked questions, others just listened.

'Why is he called The Teacher?' asked a French lady.

'Well,' Derrent began, and winked at Reverend Neil. 'I have it on trusty authority that The Teacher is teaching his victims a lesson as he punishes them.' An appropriate gasp rippled among the group. Derrent enunciated the word punish, as if it was syrup dripping from his lips. The quiet man stopped writing and listened carefully. The French lady recoiled in horror.

'I'll spare you the gorier details, but Moira Tate – the poor woman found in Watermillock – had been horribly disfigured, and not only that.' His voice grew quieter, as if he were telling a horror story around a campfire. 'Not only that, but a warning was left on her body,' he said. A man put his arm around his wife and the two blonde students stood closer together. 'The same is true of poor Brandy Carter, the girl found at Aira Force.'

The professor waited as the sinister details were absorbed by the group. To read something in a newspaper is one thing, but to stand with a university professor and the reverend whose church it was where a body was actually discovered, made it all the more remarkable and personal.

'What kind of warning?' The quiet man spoke, and everyone turned round to watch him, then back again, to listen to Derrent's reply. The sun beat down upon them, but a few shivered and rubbed goose bumps on their arms.

'Poetry,' Derrent said. Gasps rattled around along with the breeze, and Derrent smiled smugly, satisfied that his bombshell had had the desired effect. It was the first time he'd parted with the information, and it made him feel central to the unfolding drama – a place he always liked to be.

Derrent turned swiftly and carried on up the path, dramatically. He felt quite the minor celebrity.

Once past Hallin Fell, Dobbin Wood came into view, and the tip of Aira point could be made out. The quiet man knew this already as he'd hiked here a hundred times before. Gowbarrow Fell dominated the view, and the walkers trudged on, desperate to ask more questions.

'There, over there,' said Derrent, pointing.

'The spot where William and his sister, Dorothy, saw the daffodils; the spot where he penned his most famous words, and the spot where a killer carried a body up to Aira Force,' said Derrent. Neil was used to such claims of grandiose elaboration, and he found today's yarn no less embellished than normal; the punters lapped it up. It was harmless enough and brought good money to bolster the church. Neil would have chance to enthuse about his own passion soon enough; the Lakes poets. They made a good duo; Derrent warmed the crowd and Neil recited the lines, as perfectly as if he read them from a script.

The group gathered at the shoreline and gazed across to Aira Point, from where the Aira Beck meandered its way down the steep hill to the tumbling falls, crashing from the dramatic fell above. The waterfall couldn't be seen from the shore as it was hidden by dense woodland, but with the help of the professor and the reverend, the group could imagine the scene that left such an elemental impression on Wordsworth.

'You can just see the roof of the great Lyulph's Tower, the former hunting lodge of the Dukes of Norfolk, and starting point of Wordsworth's "The Somnambulist".' Derrent went on to detail the sorry tale of the medieval legend of Emma, the woman who'd plunged to her death whilst sleepwalking at Aira Force, and how her ghost still frequented it. His tone rose and fell – poetic in itself – and one could be forgiven for believing that Wordsworth had actually penned most of his poetry whilst in a mythical trance, sat in his suit and top hat, under the trees and amongst the red squirrels and deer, two hundred years ago.

These stories didn't interest the quiet man, who'd reverted to taking notes once more. What interested him was how Professor Derrent knew so much about the demise of Moira Tate and Brandy Carter, and why the reverend had chosen to recite the exact poem, of which an excerpt had been left inside the tongue-less throat of Brandy Carter… '*What man has made of man…*' It allowed the reverend to decry the modern world, and how all of humanity is tarnished and beyond hope – unless we turn to God: his God of course, thought the quiet man, cynically.

Once he was out of these ridiculous hiking clothes and back in uniform, he'd give DI Porter a full report. But for now, he had to endure a pub meal and quiz with this sorry collection of civilians who got off on murder.

Chapter 35

Wendy Porter had been readmitted to The Penrith and Lakes, and Kelly headed to the female medical ward. It was fairly quiet, but Kelly could hear Nikki speaking to a nurse, and it didn't sound as though they were swapping pleasantries about the weather. Kelly's heart sank and she slowed her footsteps.

'What is taking so long?' Nikki was shouting. She was treating the staff like they were idiots. Nikki's demands were unrealistic and the more she pissed off the staff, the more they'd make things difficult: it was human nature. But for some reason Nikki didn't seem to grasp this simple fact.

'Is there a problem?' Kelly said. Nikki turned around, and the sight of Kelly only heightened her irritation.

'Mum's MRI has been delayed again, and no-one in this place seems to be able to do their job properly!' Nikki spat. The nurse took her opportunity to walk away, as she did so, she rolled her eyes at Kelly.

'You won't get anywhere treating them like that, Nikki, I don't care how mad you are,' Kelly said.

'So now you're a fucking doctor as well are you?' Nikki said sarcastically. Kelly wanted to say so much. She even felt the urge to slap her sister's face, but she didn't.

'Is this all about Dave Crawley?' Kelly said.

'What?' Nikki asked.

'You. This.' Kelly gesticulated. 'What is your problem? Why are you so angry? It won't do Mum any good, it won't get things done quicker, and you'll just piss them off so you get ignored more.'

Kelly stood her ground as Nikki squared up to her. She thought at one point that Nikki might hit her. Instead, her sister looked her up and down and simply said, 'You're just you,' and walked away.

'Hang on a minute, what the hell is that supposed to mean?' Kelly asked, following her. She hadn't noticed, but her voice had become as raised as her sister's. A nurse appeared with her hands on her hips. 'Do you mind?'

They were reprimanded like children. Kelly was ashamed.

'I'm sorry,' she said.

Nikki walked away. The nurse went back to her duties, and Kelly was left in the corridor on her own.

Kelly realised that she didn't even know what room her mother was in this time, and went to find a nurse to ask. This time, the same nurse who'd shouted, seemed calmer, and smiled at her, more sympathetic.

'I'm so sorry about that, it was really insensitive,' Kelly said.

'Your mother's in room twenty-five, Kelly. It is Kelly isn't it? It's not long that she was in, is it?'

'No, I'm thinking of moving in and renting a room,' Kelly said. She managed a weak smile but both women knew that it was far from being flippant.

'I wouldn't. Far too many chiefs and not enough Indians around this place,' the nurse said. Kelly understood; the police force was the same. They shared a knowing glance. She went to see her mother but Nikki had beaten her to it.

'I heard you both, you know. Can't you give it a rest? How do you think it makes me feel, knowing that when I'm gone you'll be at each other's throats?' Wendy looked agitated and in pain. Kelly felt wretched.

'I'm sorry, Mum. Everyone's tired, but abusing the staff won't make them any quicker,' Kelly said.

'How dare—' began Nikki.

'Stop it!' Wendy intervened again. 'If you continue to argue, I'll have the staff get rid of both of you, and you won't be welcome back! I mean it, I've had enough. I'm sick enough as it is without listening to your racket.' Wendy finished and laid back onto her pillows, exhausted. Both siblings had more to say, but both had the sense to heed their mother's warning.

'Can I get you a cup of tea, Mum?' asked Kelly.

'No, I've had five already, I think. Can one of you go to the shop and get me some fruit?' Both sisters said yes at the same time, and they looked at one another.

'I'm happy either way, I don't mind,' said Kelly.

'I don't mind either, I'm happy to go,' Nikki said.

'Right, I'll stay here,' said Kelly. Nikki left.

'Have the kids been in, Mum?' Kelly referred to Nikki's three children.

'Yes but they didn't stay for long, I think all the dials and tubes scare them.'

'They won't understand.'

'Why do you and Nikki fight, Kelly? It's torture for me.'

'I don't know, Mum. I hate it too. We were never close really, remember when we were growing up, we always had different friends and different interests, I suppose. The world would be pretty dull if we got on with everyone.' It sounded weak.

'It'd be bloody quiet though!' Wendy said. 'I raised you the same, I did everything the same.' Wendy looked out of the window, wistfully. Kelly realised that her mother was taking the blame.

'Mum, it's not your fault! Christ, we're adults!'

'I worry, Kelly. About when I'm not here.'

'Mum, you're going to be here for a lot longer than any of us!' Kelly said, half believing what she was saying. Wendy looked at her, and managed a smile. They both knew that wasn't true.

'Why don't you rest and I'll try to find out when your scan is,' Kelly said. She left the room and walked along the corridor. She could hold a conversation about a million ways to die, but she couldn't be honest with her own mother. Nikki was on her way back from the shop.

'I need a word,' Kelly said to her. Nikki was unwilling to follow her sister but, eventually, she did. They went into the day room and, thankfully, it was empty.

'Look, I think we should be civil in front of Mum,' Kelly said.

Nikki began to object. Kelly held up her hand.

'Hold on, it doesn't have to be fucking genuine. Just play along, ok? At least let's try and avoid arguing in front of her. We could arrange different visiting times, or something. I don't know. But what I do know is that Mum is sick of it.'

'If you didn't make everything an argument, we wouldn't have the problem in the first place,' Nikki said belligerently.

'For God's sake, Nikki! That's what I mean. Can't we just not have this pathetic competition in the first place? Listen to yourself! Tell me when you're coming and I won't. If it's too difficult for you to be in the same room,

I'll come some other time, I really don't have time for this, just grow up!'

'Who do you think you are?'

Kelly couldn't quite believe what she was hearing. Her sister was levelling up to her again and Kelly couldn't help but laugh. It was the least appropriate thing to do, but she'd had enough.

'I've bought a house,' was all she said. It did the trick, and Nikki stopped in her tracks.

'What?' Nikki asked.

'Like I said, tell me when you're here and I'll come some other time. I won't be at the house for much longer,' Kelly said. She turned to walk away.

'So, now Mum is ill, you make plans for your escape. That's so typical of you, Kelly,' Nikki wasn't giving up. Kelly turned around.

'Look, throw mud wherever you like and for as long as you like. I haven't got time for bullshit. Mum has me, and she has you. Me moving out will give her, and me, breathing space and it's best all round. Don't try and make this into something it's not. Penrith is not exactly fucking Texas. I'm only in Pooley Bridge!' This time, she walked away without turning back. She zoned the noise of her sister's voice out of her head, and went to find someone who could help her.

A group of doctors and nurses wafted along the corridor, like a swarm of bees looking for pollen. Kelly knew that this meant they were doing their rounds. She went back to her mother's room, followed closely by Nikki. The group walked in and looked at Wendy's notes. No-one spoke.

'Mrs Wendy Porter?'

Wendy acknowledged the doctor. She looked small in the presence of such a collection of medical experts, as anyone would. Kelly wanted to speak for her, but she knew that Mum would want to do everything herself. Kelly and Nikki took in all the details for later, when Mum would forget, and ask them to repeat everything.

The blood tests were good, but the doctors were changing Wendy's medication, and it would make her feel sick. Kelly wrote down the name of the drug. They told Wendy that she could expect a three-day stay, as things stood at the moment, while they sorted her medication and organised an MRI. The young doctors took notes, and the nurses scuttled around them like waiting staff. The power of these people unsettled Kelly, and she thought of Timothy Cole again. The entourage left as rapidly as it had appeared, and Kelly looked at her mother. Was this it? Was this the beginning of more and more hospital stays, until finally, she never left?

'Look, there's no point either of you staying here, you heard what they said, they have a plan for the next few days. I have my phone, I am perfectly capable of calling you when I need you. I think I'd like a snooze,' said Wendy.

Kelly couldn't decide if this was Wendy's way of saying she'd like to be left alone, or in fact she was genuinely tired. Both daughters decided to leave, and they kissed their mother and walked to the ward exit in silence.

Kelly took the stairs, Nikki took the lift.

Chapter 36

Johnny sat on his decking reading a book. He was on duty, but it didn't mean he couldn't enjoy the sunshine. He could get a call at any minute.

He loved his job.

It wasn't the kind of thing boys grew up dreaming about – that was more likely to be a soldier, but it was something that adult men often thought about. The isolation, the freedom, the vastness of the terrain – all pitted against a man with a back pack, helping to save people. He'd been told he was saving people when they'd deployed to Iraq. They were helping the Iraqis, they were told. And they believed them.

'Theirs is not to reason why, theirs is but to do and die…'

But officers were supposed to be thinking soldiers, and their burden was their penance. Soldiers were supposed to get PTSD, not officers. Officers were supposed to accept what came with the job: their decisions that got men killed, their choices that maimed teenagers, and their unwavering loyalty to the crown. Johnny remembered the eyes of the father he'd looked into, as the details of his son's death were read out at the inquest. The helicopter had taken too long to get to him and he'd bled out. The lad had been nineteen.

Johnny pushed the thoughts away and replaced them with pleasant ones: of pinning Kelly up against the wall in her empty lounge. There were only a few things that truly relaxed him in life and the other one was being in the fells. Kelly was good at both.

He didn't need much, and what he had delivered most of that. He'd mellowed since leaving the army, and it felt good. No more frenetic, testosterone-driven marches through Wales, no more kowtowing to senior ranks, no more carrying fifty kilos up a mountain in a hundred degrees heat, and no more dead bodies.

That was Kelly's world now, not his, and he had no regrets.

Being on the mountain gave him space and peace, despite his job. It wasn't combat: helicopters were readily available, they didn't take enemy fire, equipment wasn't held up by politics, money flowed in (thanks to charitable donations), and the people rescued were thankful, not hostile.

It was satisfying.

Johnny thought of his daughter. She was too far away. They'd made a go of it, him and his wife, moving from one patch to another, pretending that it was some form of life, always running away from reality. He'd known Carrie was unhappy but they never talked about it. They fell into a routine of ignorance and bliss, and used Josie as a screen behind which to hide.

Josie. She was nearly twelve, and she was beginning to look like a young woman. She'd been through a lot, more than Johnny would like, but he'd told himself that no-one was a perfect parent. They didn't hand out manuals at the birth. You just struggled blindly, making it up as you went along, and hoping for the best.

Johnny closed his eyes, turned his face to the sun, and thoughts of Kelly returned once more.

When his pager rang, he was almost asleep. He stretched and got out of the sun lounger. He called the switch board and spoke to Marie. Johnny covered both Patterdale and Penrith, and someone needed medical assistance on Riggindale Crag, close to High Street. They'd summited and begun their descent, but a female in her sixties had twisted her ankle and couldn't be moved. A group of students had called it in. The helicopter was ready but Riggindale was tricky to navigate and cloud covered a few patches.

It didn't matter how many videos, YouTube posts, Twitter drives and public safety posters they produced each year, the Lake District teams never failed to be dismayed at the amount of ill-prepared walkers who found themselves in trouble each season.

But Johnny didn't judge them too harshly. It had taken him years to qualify for mountain rescue, and it wasn't difficult to underestimate the treachery of the fells.

They'd been working with a new fleet of S92 helicopters, and it was Johnny's job to locate an ideal spot to land. But first he needed to locate the casualty. The group of students who'd made the call had stayed with the couple who, by all accounts, were experienced hikers.

High Street was so named thanks to the Romans, who built their tracks over the open fells rather than through the dense woodland of the valleys. Johnny often wondered what their ancestors would make of the fells now, with the hordes of walkers, helicopters, and litter strewn across the landscape. In under thirty minutes, Johnny would be flying over the popular route, one that often reminded walkers not to take Mother Nature for granted.

Johnny thought about The Teacher as he drove. Kelly didn't need to spell it out that the guy was strong. He'd dumped two bodies, and Johnny knew how heavy a dead body was. Johnny was strong. Not gym-strong, in that he lifted weights above his head three times a week, but instinctively strong. His muscles had borne huge loads over terrain similar to Cumbria for two decades, and for days on end. The common view of soldiers is of them patrolling through villages and towns with rifles, looking for the enemy, and retreating to base when they're finished. The reality is that most of the time, they're carrying equipment weighing close to fifty kilograms for days, and most of that is water.

But the thing that Johnny struggled to get his head round most was the *urge* to hurt a woman, and then dump her like trash. He pondered briefly on which was worse: torture and murder for war, or for enjoyment? He shook his head, and the thoughts along with it.

He parked at the centre, and he could see the helicopter blades whirring. Whatever he needed was on board. He was no medic, but the casualty would be dropped off at the nearest available hospital in good time. The two biggest were Penrith and Lakes, and Furness General in Barrow-in-Furness.

As he climbed into the red and white helicopter, Johnny wondered if Kelly would catch her killer, or if he'd strike again. He shook the hands of two colleagues and wondered if the killer had an ordinary job and an ordinary life. He might go to the same pub every Friday night to play cards. It struck him that anyone he knew could be capable of leading a double life. Wherever he went: the corner shop, the pub, Marie's office, everywhere, people discussed The Teacher.

The great machine lifted and ascended quickly. Johnny looked out of the window and readied a stretcher.

Ullswater sparkled below them and stretched away into the distance. They flew south, over Loadpot Hill and High Kop, and Haweswater came into view. The Lakes looked tiny from the air. To the west, he made out the Isle of Man, to the east, the Yorkshire Dales. It was a beautiful day.

The students had been told to lay down something colourful and wave their arms about, and Johnny was impressed to see a square shape, made from humans, formed below them. He familiarised himself with their location and knew a good spot to land. It would take three of them to carry the injured woman back to the helicopter, but it wouldn't be taxing. Johnny guided the pilot to a flat area, who lowered the machine to the ground. Johnny led the way, and they jumped out and jogged to the woman. She was called Pat.

'Hello, Pat,' Johnny said. Pat smiled bravely. His colleagues spoke to the husband.

Johnny lay down his stretcher and undid the straps. He also made an initial assessment. Pat was in pain, but she was bright and cooperative. The ankle was twisted nastily and Johnny knew from experience that it was broken. Somebody had had the common sense to take off her boot, and the ankle was swollen and purple. Pat was a tough lady. The couple looked prepared: they had adequate equipment, maps, water, and good walking gear. They looked experienced too; it was simply a terribly unlucky accident.

'She slipped as we stepped over that rock, her foot was caught and she went the wrong way,' said the husband.

Unfortunate, thought Johnny.

The three men loaded Pat onto the stretcher, and soon they were back at the helicopter. The husband came on board too, and the students continued their hike, buoyed with exciting stories for the pub later.

As the helicopter lifted off, Johnny's pager buzzed again.

Marie's voice was uncharacteristically quiet.

Johnny was required to escort the police for his next job. Two hikers had reported seeing a body near Hart Crag, a place inaccessible by air or road. There was no confirmation yet as to if it was indeed a body, but Johnny experienced a sensation in his gut that would only be confirmed when he led the officers to the spot.

It hadn't sounded like a prank call, Marie told him. The police had to take the call seriously, and it was Johnny's day to be of service.

He called Kelly.

Chapter 37

'Kelly Porter?' the man asked.

'Yes, speaking,' Kelly replied.

'Ah, good. May I introduce myself? Dr Philip Modus, forensic analyst. Handwriting specialist to be exact. I'm calling from The Minatour Lab in Oldham.'

'Ah, Dr Modus, thanks for getting back to me. Please tell me you have some news.' He had her full attention. She prayed for a break. Testimony from people like Dr Modus was more likely to get the case accepted by the CPS when the time came.

'I do hope so. I do apologise for the delay, we've been snowed under down here, you know.' Kelly had heard it all before. Get on with it, she thought.

'I'm sure you have, Dr Modus.'

'So, the first sample you sent to us – a beautiful example by the way – it was an excerpt from Shelley, am I right?'

'Yes.' This was not going to be a short conversation. But it was worth the extra effort if it bore results. She crossed her fingers.

'Not my favourite, I have to say.'

Kelly impatiently tapped her pen on the desk.

'Anyway, the brain guides the hand, Detective, and this is a fascinating subject. Their emotional energy is off the chart, I wonder – do you have the original? My guess is that the writing can be felt on the underside – like Braille – you see, it depicts much passion in the subject.'

Kelly looked at her watch. Johnny would be on the mountainside now.

'The backwards slant is also unique: 'cool as a cucumber' is the phrase that sprung to mind when I saw it. Now, everyone has their own unique set of characteristics when they write, just like a fingerprint.' Kelly had heard this before too. Every expert in their field swore that their methodology was the most unique, be it dentals, hair follicles, gait analysis, camber of toes, or eye lash direction. And each expert would happily talk for hours on their preferred field of interest, if allowed to. The trick was to show enough respect while at the same time hurrying them along. She didn't say a word.

'So, the dot over the "i" in both cases is just off to the right of the letter: this indicates that the writer finished the sentences before going back to dot the i and cross the t, so to speak.' Dr Modus wasn't sure that Detective Porter was still on the end of her line, and found her lack of response puzzling.

In fact she was concentrating. She'd brought the first sample sent to the Doctor up on her computer screen. She could see what he meant.

'Yes, I can see that, Doctor, what does it mean?' She wanted to know where he was going, and follow his thread but, more than that, to know if he was going to be helpful.

'You've got a forceful character here, angry and in a rush. It's as if they're writing a threatening letter rather than poetry.' Kelly doubted that the Doctor had any idea how important what he had just said might possibly turn out to be.

'How can the writing be cool and angry at the same time?'

'Good question. The execution is cool, the emotion is angry.'

It was a good answer.

'Can you confirm a definite match between the first and second samples, Doctor?' she asked. They'd have to get a second opinion, to tick that box, at a later date.

'Emphatically, yes.'

Bingo. She pumped the air and slapped her desk. A few heads poked round her doorway and she smiled and pointed towards the phone. Such gesticulation from DI Kelly Porter usually meant good news, and a buzz spread around the office. It was their watertight proof that Moira and Brandy were killed by the same sicko.

'Can you tell if the writer is left- or right-handed, Dr Modus?'

'Sometimes, yes. But not always and it's not foolproof. Sometimes (in about one percent of the population) a writer crosses their t in such a definitive way that you can tell if it's been done to the left or the right. I think this person is left-handed, but I couldn't say one hundred percent.'

'What about the eight samples I sent to you marked appendices 1 through to 7, Doctor?' She referred to the samples they'd collected from witnesses of interest so far: James and Colin Tate, Terrance Johnson, the Reverend Neil Thomas, Timothy Cole, plus Brian, Jason and Barry – the jolly trio who, in Kelly's eyes, had abused Brandy's body as badly as had her killer on her last night alive.

'Of course, that's why I called, Detective, I'm afraid none of them are matches.'

'Really?' Kelly felt deflation but, in honesty, not huge surprise.

'Really, Detective. There are several clinchers in all eight cases. I've included it in an email I've prepared, I'll send it this afternoon.'

'Thank you so much, Dr Modus. And the four examples I sent together, under the heading, 'Yorkshire'? I explained that they were from several years ago.' Her fists clenched, and her breathing slowed.

'Of course. These examples were fascinating, and I spent a long time on them, letting a sizeable number of other priorities slide, I have to tell you,' he said, pleased with himself.

'Thank you so much, Doctor. I really appreciate that,' her heart pounded. 'Did you reach any conclusions?' Kelly closed her eyes.

'I think I'm right in saying that a graphologist confirmed that the four cases were a match,' he said. Kelly hadn't explained herself properly, she chided herself. But before she could go further, the doctor was talking again, about how wonderful it was to find such specimens.

'Now, I specialise in handwriting over time, and there is always the possibility that a person's handwriting changes completely from, say, adolescence, to adulthood, but that's not the case here.' Kelly's heart sank.

'The changes are more subtle. I have no doubt at all that the loops, use of punctuation, and personality traits obvious in the text, are all the same work as the first two examples from this month. The slant is all over the place, but when the slant goes back – as it does in the older adult – it's a match. The force is less but one would expect that in, perhaps, an undecided mind, or one that regrets one's actions or is not wholly certain of them at the time. By way of example, the reference to Hebrews 12:5-7, "Those whom the Lord loves, he disciplines, and he scourges…" There are no spelling mistakes, and look at the inverted commas – people either use double or single speech marks and this never really changes throughout their lives – it's a learned behaviour, like all habits.'

Kelly's stomach was churning. It couldn't be, she dared not believe. Surely, this was an enormous break, on a gigantic scale. Now they could pool resources with Yorks and Humberside Police, treble no, quadruple the scale, and nail this bastard, who was running out of places to hide.

'Dr Modus, are you happy to state in a court of law, under oath, that it is in your opinion that the same person penned all six passages?'

'Yes, I am.'

'Thank you,' she said simply. She covered her head with her hand.

'Now, the loops are another thing altogether,' the doctor took off again, and Kelly had to find a way to slam down the phone and call the DI in West Yorks.

'Dr Modus, I've just had a message passed to me, and it's urgent I'm afraid, thank you so much for your help, and I can't wait to read your report in full detail. I'm so sorry I really need to leave it there.'

'Oh, of course, Detective. I understand. Well, I'm glad I was of service and if you need anything explaining, my handwriting is appalling. That's a joke, by the way,' he said. Kelly was glad that she wasn't Mrs Modus.

'Lovely, Doctor, bye now.' She hung up.

It was just the boost they needed.

She called Yorkshire police.

Chapter 38

The quickest way up Hart Crag was to land a helicopter at Boredale but, of the two available, one was in maintenance, and the other – recently occupied by Johnny to get to the lady on High Street – was on its way to Furness General Hospital in Barrow-in-Furness. The next quickest way was for Johnny to hike from Patterdale. He could be up there in twenty-five minutes, but the coppers would take twice that time. Kelly could smash it, but she might not make it here in time to allow them to set off, and he looked at his watch again. The police suggested that one officer go with Johnny and the other wait for the helicopter to drop off the patient and head back, then meet them at Boredale with the medics.

'You need to lose all that mate,' Johnny said to the officer in full kit. The sun was searing, and the climb was notoriously steep. The officer agreed, and gave his stuff to his colleague, who'd hand it over once they were on top.

'Have you got sun cream?' Johnny asked.

The officer shook his head. Johnny reached into his back pack and brought out some factor fifty; he never wore anything less. The officer rubbed it into his face, concentrating on his nose, and handed it back. Johnny drove the short drive to Patterdale and parked in the car park, as close as he could to the small gate at the bottom of the climb. Most of the ascent was exposed to the elements;

there was no shade whatsoever, and it would be hot. Johnny carried three litres of water and gave another to the officer.

It wasn't the first time that Johnny would've seen a dead body on a mountainside, but it was the first time he'd led a mission to ascertain if it was indeed a body in the first place. He tried to think what items could be mistaken for a body, but came up blank. The hikers had not approached the object, but had made the call from a distance of around sixty metres. Johnny knew, from experience, that bodies were most certainly identifiable from sixty metres.

'I'm Johnny, by the way,' he said, and held out his hand for the officer.

'Dan, nice one, mate. Huge respect for you guys, you do an awesome job,' said Dan.

Johnny didn't care much for compliments, but appreciated the sentiment.

'You do much hiking, Dan?' Johnny was trying to gauge the correct pace; he didn't want to kill the bloke. He looked late twenties/early thirties so he should have been fit but these days one never knew. A twenty-year-old could easily look fit but, if they played Xbox all day long and ate burgers, then it wouldn't be long before Johnny could have them blowing out of their arses, on their knees.

'Most weekends, mate. I want to do what you do, when I leave,' Dan said. Thank God, thought Johnny.

They heard a woman's voice and looked behind them. True to her word, Kelly had managed to get into some walking gear and head over to Patterdale. She owed Johnny, big time. Without him, she'd have found out hours later. It could be a hoax, a fake, an animal, or even a mannequin, but Kelly was taking no chances.

Johnny looked at Kelly's body underneath her shorts and small vest top. She'd make it up this hill in less than thirty minutes if the copper kept up. He smiled at her and popped his sunglasses onto his head.

'Detective Porter,' Kelly said and held out her hand to Dan. Dan shook her hand and allowed her to go ahead of him.

Johnny set off hard. They turned a sharp corner past a house, and then the hill stretched upwards ahead. Kelly had been up the path dozens of times. During the summer, it was brown from over use, and bracken framed it: thick, heavy and green. Another twist in the path offered a natural water stop and Johnny sucked hard on his Camelbak, Dan did the same, and Kelly waited. She looked back to the White Lion at Patterdale and it looked tiny already. The ascent was one of the sharpest in the area so it wasn't rammed with walkers, like the lower fells, but they spotted the odd group of friends, and a few couples, descending. They all exchanged hearty greetings, and the walkers carried smiles so wide, Johnny called it the fell face. Eyes enlarged, cheeks red, breathing deep, and a smile threatening to burst off the face meant only one thing: a summit in the lakes.

Finally, they came across a path that levelled out a little and Dan caught his breath. Kelly decided to take a drink. She took off her small back pack, and took out a bottle of water.

Higher up, they crossed a few brooks and Johnny suggested they take advantage of the fresh water, it was crystal clear and full of the earth and her minerals. It was delicious. Dan rubbed some on his face, and they ploughed on.

Johnny noticed that Dan was falling behind, and stopped to wait for him to catch up. Kelly waited higher up. No-one rushed the policeman; the last thing any man wanted to be told, was that their physical prowess was lagging behind another's. Especially when there was an age gap of around twenty years and a woman up ahead. They took more water.

'Look,' Johnny said, pointing south. 'Brotherswater.'

Dan turned and followed Johnny's finger. It was an excuse for another stop. Kelly was growing irritable, and Johnny knew it, but they had no choice but to all ascend together.

The snaking road over Kirkstone Pass was clearly visible, and they even made out caravans clogging the route. To the north, the southern tip of Ullswater looked miles away, yet they didn't feel as though they'd climbed far. They carried on.

They finally reached a level expanse, and Dan took deep breaths as he recovered, his thighs burning. He wished he'd eaten more for lunch. They took on water and enjoyed the wind whipping across the vast grass-land that could take them east to Beda Fell or south to Angletarn Pikes, but they were going north back towards Ullswater, and past Place Fell, to Hart Crag. Dan looked ahead, thinking they might be close, because of the distance they'd climbed vertically. It must be almost two thousand feet, he thought. But they still had a way to go. Kelly strode ahead and Dan began to think that she was some professional hiker or something. Detectives were supposed to languish behind desks, eat cold pizza and drink warm beer.

Johnny handed him a chunk of Kendal Mint Cake and he took it gratefully. 'Cheers, mate,' Dan said. They headed towards another steep ascent, and this one was rocky.

'Almost there now,' said Johnny encouragingly. He watched Kelly ahead. She was bull-headed, like he used to be, and it amused him.

They met several walkers coming the other way, and Dan looked for signs that they'd seen the same view as the two hikers who'd reported the body, but none seemed to. It must be well hidden. Perhaps the hikers were lost, or strayed from the path for some open air fun and games, like a lot of youngsters did. It was rare to find opportunities for outdoor sex these days, and the Lakes offered perhaps more than its fair share. Dan had been called to many a rendezvous to move people along, and it still made him smile. Why people couldn't just use a bed was a question he asked himself over and over again but then he supposed it was the risk of getting caught that they loved.

A dead body would certainly put that fire out.

Dan's thighs wobbled under the strain of the final ascent, and he clambered on hands and knees over the rocks. He was only twenty-nine years old, but he smoked too much, and when he walked at the weekend with the Mrs, they took it slow, had countless breaks, took in the scenery, and ended up in the pub. These two were mountain goats, and he felt embarrassed.

They made it to the top and Johnny pointed to the trig point for Place Fell, it wasn't far now. Hart Crag was just beyond, and hopefully the helicopter could take them all down.

Dan was thankful for the even terrain at the top. A few steps towards Ullswater, and the story was much different. The helicopter could hover up here, but it would be impossible to land, and Hart Crag was another five hundred feet higher.

They stopped for water and another piece of Kendal Mint Cake, then carried on towards the higher fell. In the distance, they heard the chopper, and Johnny took his radio out of his pocket and spoke to Marie. Kelly watched him. They were nearly there.

'They've landed at Boredale, they're waiting for further instruction. Let's see if we can find something,' said Johnny. He spoke into his radio again, 'Marie, where exactly were the hikers when they spotted it?'

'Close to the summit, Johnny, on the north side. Repeat: north edge.' Johnny replaced his radio, and carried on.

'North edge,' he said to Kelly. She nodded. The wind picked up as they became more exposed, the higher they went. Johnny turned around and shouted to Dan, but his voice got lost in the wind and, again, he waited until the policeman caught up. Kelly stopped and took a sweater out of her back pack. She put it on.

'It's round there,' Johnny shouted, pointing north. The climb wasn't as taxing as the first ascending quarter of Place Fell, but the wind made it surprisingly cold.

Johnny stopped abruptly and beckoned behind him with his hand. Dan and Kelly understood, and followed Johnny's gaze. A small elevation above them, and to the north, something looked out of place. The terrain was a mixed fudge of brown and green, as far as the eye could see, until it met the sky, and then it was pure azure blue. Further up, into the hemisphere, it turned silver, with the sun.

But what they saw was none of these colours. It was a grey-white mass, dotted with dark tangles, and the three walkers knew straight away that it was, indeed, a body. Johnny reached for his radio, as did Dan. Kelly called Eden House.

'Marie, I think it's a body. The two officers with me agree. It's twenty feet away from us. I can get to it, but we'll have to make the rescue from the air, you can't land. Repeat, you cannot land,' Johnny added. 'It's definitely female, but she looks young, I'm not even sure she's an adult.' Johnny looked away. There was something so adolescent about the body – maybe it was her hips, or breasts – he didn't know, but he knew that he felt sick.

And angry. His thoughts turned to Josie.

Dan spoke to his colleague, waiting in the helicopter.

'Tell the medics to get ready,' Johnny said. 'We're literally just short of the summit, and we're dropping down to the northern face. There's a huge boulder, Marie. It's above that.'

'Nobody's going anywhere until I've searched the whole scene, including the body, Johnny. It could take me hours,' Kelly said. Johnny nodded, and relayed the message to Marie, who'd have to find some way of putting the helicopter on stand-by for when the search was complete. By then, it might not be available, and the poor girl might have to stay up here overnight.

As they waited, Johnny came to one conclusion: that whoever got this body up here was not just strong, but scary as hell, and he wasn't sure he wanted Kelly going after him. But he also knew that he couldn't stop her.

Chapter 39

The team in the incident room watched the sixty-inch TV screen mounted on the wall. They were silent.

Kelly bit the end of her pen. Rob shook his head and drained his coffee. Others tutted. If Sky TV had ordered a backdrop to perfectly match their coverage, then they'd done a good job and knew important people in high places. Torrential rain drenched the fells, and a woman in a red raincoat stood alone, in front of a Penrith housing estate, with the distant brown mountains brooding behind her. The wind-driven deluge soaked her clothes, and she'd left her raincoat slightly open to further dramatise the brutality of the setting, where three women had been tortured and killed – and the police were doing nothing about it. It was the first rain for two months, and it fell hard, as if on order from Sky News.

The journo's face was heavily made up, and Kelly couldn't help thinking that she must be touched up by the make-up artist between each take, to keep looking that good.

'*The Teacher* seems still to evade Cumbria Police who have not, as yet, given a statement about the latest body to be found here in the Lake District.' She paused to waft dramatically behind her, as if the mountains themselves were to blame. They remained stubbornly silent in answer.

'The latest victim, fourteen-year-old Aileen Bicker-staff, brings the total to three in the space of just one week. Cumbria Police say that they are working a number of leads, but an inside source told me this morning that they have no solid suspects and don't know where to turn next.'

The woman paused again, smiling stoically, and adjusting her hood for just long enough for the general public to think the Cumbria Constabulary a bunch of muppets. Grunts and exclamations went up around the room and Kelly bit the end of her pen clean off.

'Fuckers,' she said, unable to help herself.

'Too right, Guv.'

The screen panned to a small living room, and Kelly let out a groan. 'For God's sake! Who sobered her up?'

Sharon Carter sat meekly on the edge of a sofa, and Kelly wondered how long it had taken the Sky production team to clear a space in her flat.

'My Brands was everything to me,' Sharon sobbed. Dave Kent sat next to her, holding her hand, occasionally looking towards the camera, enjoying his moment of fame.

In the incident room, heads fell into hands through sheer embarrassment, and Kelly's blood boiled.

'You have got to be kidding!' said Kelly.

'What have the police told you so far, Mrs Carter?' It was the same journo, but she wore a tight royal blue dress and her hair was expertly curled around her heavily made up face. The VT was pre-recorded.

'Nothing. They've been here once. I even had to ring up to see her…' said Sharon.

'To see your own daughter?' the journo asked, affronted. Sharon Carter nodded and sniffed. The journo offered her a tissue and it was taken graciously. A footer ran along the bottom of the screen reading:

Sharon Carter — mother of murdered student Brandy Carter. Frustration mounts as families demand answers and killer evades police.

Sharon nodded. Kelly had been informed that Sharon Carter had indeed visited her daughter at the morgue but, despite leaving messages and sending officers to her address, no-one had seen the mother of Brandy Carter since Emma Hide had seen her lying comatose on her stinking sofa.

'What do you want to say to the police, Sharon?' the journo pressed on, occasionally batting her eyelids to the camera, as if interviewing Miss World.

'I just want to know who killed my Brands,' Carter replied, before her face crumpled into a bereaved mess. Her shoulders heaved and the camera panned back to Miss Royal Blue looking pained, as if she was about to volunteer to become the next UN envoy for refugee kids. Even Dave Kent had red eyes.

The piece went back to Miss Royal Blue — now in red again — in the rain, on the council estate. The rain matched everyone's mood.

'The three women, Moira Tate, Brandy Carter, and Aileen Bickerstaff, were all left in the open, to the cruelty of the elements, at various beauty spots around the Lake District, and one thing is for sure, the police are no nearer to catching this callous killer who discards his victims like trash.'

'Trash? When did we go all US of Fucking A?' Kelly said.

'But one thing the police actually do agree on, is that they were all killed by the same person, and they were tortured before they were killed, leading some elements of the press to name the man The Teacher. The Cumbria Constabulary released a statement yesterday about the first two victims, but when we went to their headquarters this morning, no-one would see us. It seems they are a constabulary in crisis. The relatives of these women want answers, but they don't seem to be getting any. Unconfirmed reports from a source close to the enquiry have told us that the killer left poems on the bodies as warnings. The information has not been confirmed or denied by the constabulary, but it gives another sinister twist to the whole saga. The last time we saw anything of this magnitude in such a short space of time was the Suffolk Strangler back in 2006. Police then were just as puzzled, and it took five brutal and shocking deaths to get to the bottom of the case. Will it take five this time? Back to you in the studio.'

The journo stood for a moment, frozen in the rain, beaming into the camera. She was dwarfed by the scenery behind her, and Kelly guessed that was the point. They wanted to make the problem insurmountable so they could keep coming back to it, for more sensational journalism.

Kelly flicked off the TV.

'So, Derrent has been talking to the journos. What has surveillance given us?' she asked. John Derrent had been under police surveillance since the walking tour, joined by a police plant by Kelly.

'He's in a sexual relationship with a Doctor Sally Bradley, Guv. She's Director of Medical Studies at Lancaster University's Faculty of Medicine. It turns out she went to school with Tracy Watkins, who now works as an assistant pathologist in the Carlisle office,' said the quiet officer who'd endured a day with Professor Derrent.

'Ted Wallis's office?' Kelly asked.

'Yes, Guv.'

'Shit,' said Kelly. Her desk phone rang. She left the room. 'Take five,' she said.

It was DCI Cane. She held the receiver away from her ear, as he shouted into it. The incident room was across the corridor, and Kelly figured that they could probably hear too, from where they were.

'Yes, Guv,' she said. She walked gloomily back to the incident room, where her team waited.

'Well, if The Teacher wanted national coverage, he's now got it, and he's probably loving it. I suppose we should be grateful that none of our faces appeared on the news,' she said.

It was only a matter of time before someone got wind of who was leading the investigation. Then, as had happened before, Kelly would be intimately linked to their killer, whether she liked it or not. From that moment on, it would be easy to find out her address, her family members, and her routines. She could be taken off the case.

She needed to up her game.

Kelly addressed the room. She stood in front of the white board and nodded to Rob. He pushed a button on his laptop and a photo came up on the white board. The colours flowed over Kelly's face as she became one with the image behind her: the body of fourteen-year-old Aileen Bickerstaff.

'What do we know, people?' Kelly asked. Hands flew up.

Kelly prompted them, one at a time.

'She's been in and out of the Penrith and Lakes Hospital since she was seven years old with various ailments. *Ailing Aileen*, they called her in the admin office, Guv. Her last operation was to straighten a scoliotic spine,' said one. 'Her mother said she never went anywhere without her cane. It was multi-legged NHS standard issue for her kind of category.'

'Do we think that it was the latest trophy?'

'Yes, Guv.'

'So, the surgery didn't work? How come she was alone when she disappeared? What was the last sighting?'

'The surgery worked initially, Guv. But the worst type of scoliosis never goes away entirely. It was hoped that the surgery would correct the spine for good, but it didn't. She was due more surgery when she matured into adulthood. The last sighting was being dropped off at the public library in town. She was very independent, according to her mother; there's no record of her in the library, it seems she never made it inside.'

'Sightings outside and around the library?'

'None yet, Guv.'

'You'd think a young girl with a walking stick would attract attention.'

'Problem is distinguishing between sticks for mountain walking, and sticks for injuries: they're a common enough sight.'

'But, did she walk with an awkward gait?'

'The mother said she hid it well.'

Kelly nodded. It appeared that Aileen Bickerstaff's ability to stare bad luck in the face and tell it to jog on, aiding her assimilation into the able-bodied general public, could well be part of what made her unmemorable. It was a cruel twist.

'Who performed the operation?' she asked, already guessing the answer.

'Timothy Cole. It says here that no-one else could have done it. She needed thirteen metal plates attached to her vertebrae.'

'We need to get Cole in again. So far, no forensics match him at all. So that leaves us with the possibility that someone wants to frame his backside. Why? I want lists of everybody he's ever worked with. Carry on,' Kelly said.

'Yes, Guv. Her mother and father reported Aileen missing five days ago. The coroner put her time of death at twenty-four hours before the dump, just like the others, so it indicates that she was kept alive somewhere for three days,' said another.

'Why didn't we know about a missing persons?' Kelly asked.

'It was reported in Ambleside, Guv. A uniform on the night shift who'd been on scheduled leave, so he hadn't seen your circular,' an officer said, apologising on the constable's behalf.

'And he didn't think to link the fucking *Teacher*, who everyone from here to China knows about, might have something to do with a missing female in the Lakes?' Kelly spat.

'No, Guv.'

'Please tell me we found something – anything – on the body, apart from what the coroner already noted,' Kelly said. She hadn't had the stomach to attend another autopsy.

'A grey fibre, Guv, and it's a match to the one found on Moira Tate's foot, and under Brandy Carter's nail.'

'That was quick, who put a firework up the lab's arse?' Kelly asked.

'Super Ormond, Guv.'

'You are kidding me?' Kelly said, brightening. Superintendent Neil Ormond only came out of his ivory tower at Carleton Hall for high-profile press releases or golf. DCI Cane must be feeling the heat.

'Who's working the council addresses? I want a list of them now,' she asked.

'There are five hundred and fifty-two,' DS Umshaw said.

'I want them all. They need to be cross-referenced with employees at the hospital. And past employees. Have we looked into the poem?' she asked.

'Yes, Guv. It's Coleridge.' DC Emma Hide walked towards Kelly and showed her the linked email. The image came up on the white board.

'Work without hope draws nectar in a sieve
And Hope without an object cannot live.'

'Emma?' Kelly asked. The whole team had begun to look at DC Hide as their Lakes poetry go-to, and she was stepping up to the new limelight. Kelly watched her.

'It's all about effort, and how human beings just take life for granted, and don't invest in their own wellbeing, but just expect the earth to care for them.' It was a brave shout, espousing philosophy in the middle of a police investigation, but the room was absolutely silent when DC Hide spoke. 'The theme of punishment is clear in all three murders now, and the poetry is telling us their sins, i.e. why they deserved their fates. Aileen Bickerstaff's sin was that she was a burden on society, it smacks of Darwinism, Guv.'

'So that was Ailing Aileen's sin: she sucked the NHS dry,' said Kelly. 'How current. The Teacher is an apt epithet. Who came up with it?'

'It was used once by the *Evening Echo* and then the *Westmorland Gazette*, but Professor Derrent has been increasing his Instagram followers using its hashtag, and now everyone's using it.'

'He'll like it.' Kelly thought aloud. 'Thanks everybody. You're all doing an amazing job. Keep your eyes peeled on the news: they can be great allies. Carry on with the fantastic work, and apologise on my behalf to your families, I know the long hours are taking their toll. DS Umshaw, it's your turn to get home on time tonight. Spend some time with the girls and get some rest.'

Kate Umshaw nodded. Kelly was rotating their hours so no-one burned out. Every member of her team was willing to go the extra mile, but she couldn't have officers missing detail through fatigue. She left the room and called Ted Wallis.

'No I'm not joking,' she said to him. 'Tracy Watkins, one of your assistants, is the leak.'

Kelly thought back to the afternoon that she and Johnny had approached Aileen's body, not knowing then that she was a mere fourteen years old. As they'd approached her, they'd noticed a nasty, raw scar on the girl's hip, and it was only when Ted Wallis called her after the autopsy, that he'd told her what was inside. He'd found the poem sewn into her, after one of her old scars had been reopened.

Chapter 40

Kelly made her way to the ward where her mother had been for three days. She walked like an automaton to the allotted bed. This week's bed.

It was empty.

Blind panic set in, and Kelly ran frantically from the room, shouting randomly, looking for a nurse or a doctor. A nurse stepped in her way and caught her by both arms, head on, and she stopped, breathless, and shocked.

'My...' Kelly said.

'It's alright, Kelly, erm, Miss Porter – she's fine. We wanted to give her an ultrasound on her heart, before allowing her to go home. Relax. She's ok,' said the nurse. The nurse wasn't tall, but she was solid, and Kelly was thankful for someone to, literally, run in to. Kelly managed a weak smile.

'Come on,' said the nurse. 'I'll make you a cup of tea, sit down here,' she ordered, ushering her back to the room where her mother should have been. Kelly was unaccustomed to taking orders, but she did as she was told, and it felt good not to have to think. Her head hurt, as well as her body. She longed to lie down and close her eyes, drifting away, slowly, on a gentle breeze. She was thankful that Nikki wasn't here. They'd stayed true to their word, and made an effort to visit their mother separately. When they found themselves in the same room, one of them left.

The nurse left her sitting in a hard armchair, adjacent to her mother's empty bed. Kelly appreciated that the NHS was short on cash, but she marvelled at the lack of comfort and taste when choosing ward furniture. She sat back, willing herself to breathe slower, in an attempt to calm her beating heart.

She was losing it.

She was terrified of failure. If she didn't catch this sick bastard soon, her reputation would be in tatters and another woman would die. Despite her tan, she had dark circles under her eyes and her skirt felt looser than normal. She hated losing weight; it made her feel weak.

The nurse came back to the room and handed her a proper mug of tea – rather than one from a machine – and she was grateful. The nurse must have a thousand and one things to do, but she'd recognised the need of someone else, and that compassion was the thing Kelly loved most about nurses, most of them.

'I'm sure I'm holding you up. You must have other things to do. Don't worry about me, I'm fine,' Kelly said. She wondered if the ruse would work. When a woman uses the word fine, it usually meant WARNING: STORM AHEAD. Kelly joked that fine was actually an acronym for *Fucked-up, Insecure, Neurotic and Emotional.* Woman to woman, it meant: please stay a while, I need you.

The nurse put her hand on Kelly's, and smiled.

'I know you're ok. You need to slow down, that's all. You can't save everyone,' the nurse said, and left quietly. Kelly stared at the door for a long time and sipped her tea. It was warm and sweet, and Kelly felt the goodness spread through her body, and she relaxed a little.

By the time her mother was brought back to the ward, Kelly was fast asleep in the uncomfortable chair.

'Mum,' Kelly said, dazed and disoriented, rubbing her eyes and stretching. 'My god, what time is it?' She looked at her watch and groaned inwardly. She'd been asleep for more than an hour. She needed to get going.

'Kelly, love. You must have needed it,' her mother said. 'I watched the news with the nurses last night; they don't know what they're talking about. You just carry on doing what you're doing. You'll get him, Kelly, I know you will.' Her mother's voice was deliberately impassioned, and Kelly felt her insides stir with gratitude. But the feeling soon turned sour, as she took in the appearance of her mother. For the first time since diagnosis, Wendy Porter looked very slightly yellow. And they all knew what that meant. Her face was slightly sunken, and her eyes lacked vigour.

'The new medicine worked, I can go home tomorrow,' said Wendy brightly.

Kelly smiled at her mother's resolve. Whatever was thrown at her; she bounced back with determination; it was a lesson that most of us could learn from. She went to her mother and embraced her.

Kelly knew she'd have to move into her new house at some point, but was waiting for the right time to announce it. Wendy showed no sign that Nikki might have told their mother about the move out of spite; that was at least positive. Furniture had begun to arrive at the property in Pooley Bridge, and Kelly had browsed new bathroom fittings. As always, this wasn't a good time. Wendy put her arms around her daughter's waist and closed her eyes.

'Why didn't you tell me about your house?' she said. Kelly's heart sank. So she knew after all.

'Oh Mum, I… Nikki shouldn't have told you.'

'Why not? I'm pleased for you, Kelly. It's the right thing to do. At your age, I had two children and a husband to look after. You need to get a move on, you know, and you're not going to meet anyone living with your mum,' Wendy said. Kelly hadn't really thought about it like that.

'Now you can stop sneaking around.' Kelly went to say something, but Wendy held her hand up and shook her head.

'Promise me you'll catch this man, Kelly. He's used his life for awful things, and he's well and living, and taking and hurting and killing. And I've done everything right: been nice to people, respectful, worked in hospital having needles stuck into me when I should be out in the sunshine, enjoying myself. It's not fair.'

'I will, Mum. I promise.'

'Well then, off you go,' Wendy said, and sat down on her bed. 'I'm not going anywhere today.'

Her mother was giving her a blessing. She was ordering her to go to work. She was saying: *it's ok to leave. Go and make it count.*

As she left the hospital, and climbed into her car, she received a message from DS Umshaw, and replayed it.

Timothy Cole, along with his family, had gone missing.

Chapter 41

DC Phillips talked as Kelly drove. Her right foot pushed further down on the accelerator, and as she squeezed it lower, her aggravation faded. When she was focused on something – anything – she didn't feel it, but in the confines of the car, and with traffic slowing them down, Kelly was tormented by things she couldn't change in her personal life, as well as in the case.

They were driving to Whitehaven and took the A66. Summer had returned to the fells after the blip of rain that had marred the dry run. Blencathra and then Skiddaw shone resplendent in the changing light. Kelly could have done with a hard hike up either right now, but there was no let-up in the case, and the need to show progress was no more pressing than now with a suspect AWOL and leads sending them in all directions. She was aware of Phillips' slight discomfort and slowed a little.

'Tell me about the care home, Will.' He went through his notes.

'1996 – The Whitehaven Home for Children and Adolescents burned down, killing two staff and three children. Tania Stewart was a day warden – a kind of house mistress – there. After the fire, she worked in a Workington home until 1999, moving to Yorkshire, where she worked until her death.'

'So, the fire – what were the conclusions of the enquiry?'

If she could have chosen a time in which to make this cross country journey to the coastal town of Whitehaven, the middle of a late-July day would be her last choice. Ordinarily, it would take an hour. Today, it would more likely take two.

'Accident,' Phillips said.

'How long did it take them to come up with that little gem?' she asked.

'A day.'

'What?'

'A day. It stinks,' Phillips articulated what Kelly was thinking.

'Tell me about Tania Stewart,' she said.

He looked at his notes.

'She was fifty-two when she was murdered. The detective in charge was convinced of overkill, and that her killer was known to her. She had fifteen stab wounds to her breasts – seven to the right, eight to the left – and seventeen to her abdomen. Classic rage. I phoned the care home in Workington but it had closed down. However, I managed to track three patients' relatives and a colleague. Each one said the same thing: that she was cruel.'

'How?' asked Kelly.

'The relatives complained to the company owners on five separate occasions, they cited rationing water as a discipline method, poor hygiene and drastic changes to their relatives' personalities.'

'Who was the colleague?'

'A student nurse who was training there. She's in her thirties now, but she was very clear. She said she was scared to say anything at the time, but she saw Stewart hit her patients and take food away. There was one occa-sion where Stewart made a patient clean faeces off the floor. Apparently the patient had an accident and Stewart smeared it all over the floor, then made the woman clean it.'

'Jesus, why didn't the girl report her?' Kelly asked. But she already knew why – institutional bullying would be terrifying for an eighteen-year-old, new to the profession.

'She said she was scared to. She left soon after. She didn't know that Stewart was dead. When I told her, she sort of implied that she wasn't at all surprised. She said, and I quote, "Probably one of her old patients did it, or their families."'

'Do any of our suspects so far have links to care homes, apart from Colin Tate?'

'Only him, but none of the forensics match him. It's the same story: all the suspects have elements that match – MO, motive, opportunity, knowledge of the victims – but none of them tick all the boxes. It's as if, taken altogether, we'd have the perfect suspect,' he said. Since the search on the Cole residence, the whole family had vanished into thin air, and all units were looking out for them. It was baffling.

'What the hell are we missing?' she asked. But it was rhetorical. She was thinking aloud.

'What about his handwriting?' asked DC Phillips.

'Dr Modus said that even though every sample was different, and he agreed that Cole has the capacity and intelligence to change styles easily, and has done so, he found no characters in any of the notes supplied. He said, in all his career, he's never come across a person who can omit every single trait and produce an entirely new style.

They always carry something from one style to the next, even if they're doing it deliberately.'

'So why run?'

They fell silent as they approached Keswick, the turn off was rammed and they were glad to avoid the town itself. They carried on west, towards Bassenthwaite Lake, and the traffic thinned a little. The southern side of Skiddaw sat covered in sunshine, and both detectives looked up, longingly.

'When's the last time you were up there?' Kelly asked, following his gaze and reading his thoughts. Their personal lives had ceased to exist.

'Oh ages.'

'How's Katrina taking it?' she asked.

'She's good, she's always busy anyway.' Kelly knew that DC Phillips and his wife, Katrina, had yet to start a family, and so they were both fairly flexible for now. She studied her junior and noticed that his eyes were tired and the wrinkles around them looked deeper than they had recently. He also had dark shadows underneath. She felt a pang of guilt.

'Does Katrina like to hike, Will?'

'Not really, it's usually me and the dog.'

'What is it?'

'She's a border Collie. Millie. She's seven, and she's done a hundred and twenty Wainwrights.'

'No!'

'Yes. We've got just under a hundred to go. I keep hoping she'll make it.' His face relaxed and his eyes shone for the first time that day. They all longed for normality.

'How's your mum, boss?'

Kelly was thrown but touched. The question was genuine, but she couldn't have personal stuff getting in the way; it would make her soft around the edges.

'Mum's back at home, thank you. Thanks for asking, Will. She's dying. She knows it, we know it. It's about keeping her comfortable.' Kelly stared ahead. Bassenthwaite Lake took her mind off the conversation. Will looked out of the window.

'So why don't you hand the case to someone else? And spend more time with her?' he said.

'Because she wants me to catch The Teacher.' Kelly smiled mischievously and Phillips didn't know if his boss was joking. Something told him she wasn't.

'What a legend,' he said. There was a companionable silence until Kelly broke it.

'I don't think it's Cole.'

'I know. Someone who knows him?'

'Yes.'

'So, the hospital?'

'Yes. I'm hoping that something from today will provide us with something to connect a name from the care homes to the hospital.'

'Anything from his rental properties?'

'No, Guv. They've all got tenants and none have the issued grey carpet, even though three of them are ex-council and fit the timeline.'

'I wonder if it could be an ex-patient of his. Someone who was let down by him.'

'Like it,' Phillips said.

'Maybe he hasn't always been the eminently successful surgeon that he is today: even perfectionists make mistakes.'

'I'll call DS Umshaw. She's coordinating the search of the hospital staff database.'

Chapter 42

A reporter stood outside the Church of All Saints, on the Pike Road, Penrith. Mourners lined the streets on either side. A hush descended on the crowd when the hearse arrived, flanked by five black sedans carrying the family of Aileen Bickerstaff.

Johnny had sat on the mountainside for two hours, while Dan spoke into his radio, and Kelly gathered evidence and took photographs. She'd even sketched the scene, by hand, on a drawing pad, noting carefully where everything was. The helicopter had left three times for emergencies, but each time it came back and hovered above them, waiting for Kelly's lead.

The wind had picked up on top of Hart Crag, and Johnny couldn't help glance at what was left of the young girl, occasionally. Her torso was weirdly bent, and deep marks were left on her neck. He recalled the moment when Kelly had noticed the scar on the girl's hip, where her underwear should have been.

The scar was sewn up with black thread. The wound was infected and the skin had begun to turn green. Thick yellow pus had dried into the stitching, and, against the pure white skin, looked oddly inhuman. He thought at the time that a human isn't made of those colours: dark green, orangey-yellow and white. A human is made of pink, beige, brown and cream – colours that hint of life, of warmth, energy and spirit. There was no spirit left in the girl's carcass, and that's how he thought of it.

He'd dreamt of her body all that week.

Especially the colours.

He dreamt of black worms crawling out of the green skin, and of the whole thing slitting apart, and yellow goo bleeding out and running onto him. For the first time in years, he'd dreamt of war.

He'd only looked at her face once.

Her eyes were closed, and he was thankful. Her hair was wet and tangled – thanks to a day or two out there, he suspected. She looked asleep, and he hoped that she hadn't suffered for long. He thought of Kelly and how many bodies she'd seen like this.

Johnny had seen bodies ripped in two, laying on the side of the road in Iraq. He'd seen bodies headless and rotting, hung from bridges in Sierra Leone. And he'd seen bodies piled up, being nibbled on by dogs, in Bosnia.

This girl was different. She'd been left all alone in that desolate place and he wanted to hold her and bring her back to life. He couldn't imagine anything happening to Josie. Johnny didn't want to know the details, and he hadn't asked Kelly any questions.

Bile rose in his throat as he thought of the girl's family. Kelly said that some families wanted to know every last detail about their loved one's final moments, and others requested only the basic information. Johnny wondered, as he stood up in front of the pew, as Aileen's body was carried in to the church, if Annie and Joe Bickerstaff had wanted to know what he knew – that Aileen had met a terrible death.

Speakers had been placed outside the church, so that hundreds could share the service.

Annie and Joe Bickerstaff walked behind the coffin, and Johnny thought he might be sick. Kelly never went to funerals unless she was expressly invited. She said it reminded the families of the brutality of the victim's death, rather than the beauty of their life, which is not what funerals were supposed to do. Her face in the congregation would be further torture to the family. Johnny understood completely, but he had to go. He had to listen to the eulogy and the history of the girl he'd first met on the mountainside, because he had to try to rid himself of the images that refused to disappear in the middle of the night.

A road block had been put in place, at Kelly's request, and no traffic disturbed the tranquillity of the site. Behind the church, where traffic could still be heard, a navy blue Volkswagen Touran sat, engine running, windows closed, and parked momentarily. The closed windows looked odd, it was another searing hot day, and most people celebrated the fact with open windows. The occasional convertible taunted onlookers with its Hollywood-style swagger, as the drivers marked the highlight of their year.

But Johnny saw none of this. And no-one took any notice of the Touran as it pulled away from the curb, behind the church, and turned left out of the town, towards Pooley Bridge and Ullswater. Its final destination was Coniston Lake, or a location close by, where daffodils grew in the spring.

The driver turned the radio up and took a bite from a sandwich. A debate on Radio Four had caught their attention, and it would make the drive more pleasant. But nothing could spoil the afternoon.

Staff Nurse Nicola Tower was a heavy fat bitch. Manoeuvring her into the boot of the Touran had been

266

a cumbersome task, but not insurmountable. It had been easier getting her in when she'd been alive. The nurse had happily accepted a lift after her shift, and had talked and talked as usual, her great gob opening and closing, droning on and on, giving the world her opinions on her patients, their families and her colleagues. Mistakenly, she believed that her views mattered, that anyone cared about her vitriol, so unshaken was she in her self-importance.

She'd even accepted the invite for a cup of tea.

As the electric garage had closed behind them, Nicola hadn't stopped for breath, and continued talking about the weather, celebrities, Brexit and other trifling affairs she deemed too important to keep her trap shut about. Once on the sofa, the nurse filled it, sitting with her legs open, unable to close them fully; inviting attention to herself and her obese frame. She was a shame on her profession. A stain, a scourge. A problem.

Problems needed solutions.

The final straw was the fluttering of the nurse's eyes, flirting and encouraging; wanting more than a cup of tea and a lovingly served biscuit on a pretty plate.

Her smile had waned when the belt was pulled so tightly from behind that it knocked her backwards over the sofa. Nicola had heaved against it with all her might, her mounds of flesh wobbling and jerking as her nurse's tunic rode up, exposing her great white belly. But the grip of the belt was vice-like. It was a relief when Nicola passed out, not because the perpetrator was tired, more because it gave a respite to the racket of her voice.

Nicola had lovely plump veins that took the chlorpromazine well: it would last about half an hour. Meanwhile, there was an excellent programme on Radio Two about Wilfred Owen. Certainly not the best war poet (Hardy's

Drummer Hodge would be difficult to beat), but Owen would do for now until the anti-psychotic wore off and Nicola began to contemplate her future.

As the Touran headed south, the news interrupted the radio programme. The Teacher was the main news item. Of course.

The Teacher.

It was disappointing.

It lacked authority and status. But it was unsurprising, given the lack of imagination and predictability displayed by laymen generally.

Chapter 43

Whitehaven Police Station was a drab affair. Its archive was well ordered but, like any other basement register, it was situated in the bowels of the building. But at least it was cool in there. Kelly steeled herself to delve deep into the chronicles of cases decades old, and she was glad she'd brought a sweater.

She and DC Phillips had been greeted by PC Wright, who'd offered them coffee, and as much time as they needed. Kelly wanted to read the case file herself. Meanwhile, Phillips had three addresses to visit. Two were in Whitehaven, and one in Workington. Three separate relatives of three clients all cared for at some point by Tania Stewart.

'Did you manage to talk to anyone in Yorkshire about the misconduct case she was facing?' Kelly asked, before he departed.

'Yes, same thing: cruelty and bullying. Five families brought the complaint, and the local authority had no choice but to suspend her while they investigated.'

'And she was killed how far into the investigation?' she asked.

'She was suspended in the April of 2010, and the local paper ran a piece on it. She was murdered in May,' he replied.

'And no-one was ever charged?'

'No, Guv.'

'Right, Will. I'll see you back here. I'll be going nowhere for a while.'

'I'll be back about four.' He left.

In the silent room, underneath the street, Kelly began her search, and it wasn't long before she located the twenty-year-old file on the fire.

The police officer in charge had long retired, but that's what she expected. The case hadn't even shown up on the computer file, so it had never been written up. She knew that in the case of old investigations – especially so-called open and shut ones – it was seen as a waste of time.

The file wasn't thick, just as she'd also expected, and it was maddeningly sparse on detail. It didn't say if an accelerant was found; it didn't mention the original source of the blaze; and it didn't give any indication that anyone interviewed suspected foul play. She ran a check of the night nurse on duty, Ms Sara Moyles, and the janitor, Mr Fred White, who died apparently trying to rescue her. She jotted down their last addresses and then tried to find as many of the children's details as possible. She also looked for any links between the night staff and Tania Stewart. She suspected that Tania Stewart hadn't suddenly become a sadist in 2010 when she'd first been accused of cruelty, she might have been abusing her position for years. Ripe for abuse, children's homes up and down the country had been common targets for sexual predators until very recently. Kelly wondered what Sara Moyles and Fred White had been up to on the night of the fire.

There were seven statements from children. Kelly flicked through them. Three children had perished in the blaze, but there was only one autopsy. Kelly tutted and rolled her eyes.

The cause of death noted on the single autopsy was toxic smoke inhalation. She couldn't find anything on the other two children. One was a girl and one was a boy. She was staggered that an investigation could conclude the deaths of two children and not reference at least a coroner's report for them. After the fire, the children remaining in the home had been shipped off to other institutions.

The autopsy on Fred White concluded the same as for the child – poisonous smoke inhalation – but Sara Moyles died of a broken neck, before her lungs had a chance to fill with smoke. A note in the file said that it was assumed that Moyles had fallen whilst trying to escape the blaze, and White tried to rescue her before being overcome himself. There was no statement from Tania Stewart, who being day staff, hadn't been on shift. Despite this, it would have been customary to gather statements from all staff, given the devastation of the fire. Stewart moved on after that.

Kelly took a screenshot of the two children unaccounted for, and the name of the coroner. Perhaps Ted Wallis could unearth some old files for her.

She thanked PC Wright, and decided to walk to the site of the old home. Her neck was stiff from hunching over and, to her amazement, it was almost three o'clock and she was hungry.

The home had been rebuilt as offices several times, and an ugly mixture of glass and metal sat where once there had been a graceful home; she'd seen pictures, and it had been a grand Victorian pile. Houses now backed onto the establishment, but in 1996 there were just fields behind the home – perfect for an arsonist to hide in.

The names of the two children, unaccounted for, were embedded in her brain and she walked back to the police station, stopping at a small corner shop on the way to buy a sad-looking boxed sandwich. She called Phillips.

'Boss,' he said. He was breathless, and it sounded as though he was running.

'Yes, Will? I'm just on my way back to the station now,' she said.

'The three relatives were more than happy to tell everything they knew about Nurse Stewart. Rumour had it that she started the fire herself, to cover up what was going on there. They alluded to local gossip at the time along the lines that Stewart knew that the night shift, i.e. Moyles and White, were basically left up to their own devices with the children. I have a name of a man who used to attend the home. He's a recluse, chances are he won't want anyone looking into his business, but at the time of the fire, he was only fifteen. His history is a text book rendition of delinquency. He was fostered by a local family, and they had all sorts of problems with him – petty theft, cruelty to animals, and arson. He set their garage on fire when he was seventeen, and he was moved to different care arrangements. He was seen as the local thug, and kept getting into trouble. He moved from family to family after that.'

The news piqued Kelly's interest. 'Where are you? Are you on your way back?'

'That's not all. I spoke to the niece of a woman who had a life changing fall while in the charge of Tania Stewart in Workington, in 1999. She said it was well known that Stewart believed in sterilisation for orphans and euthanasia for the elderly. The woman was scared out of her wits, but she did tell officers investigating accusations of abuse, just before Stewart left to go and work in Yorkshire. She slipped through the loop of coordinated police checks, and her history stayed back here in the North West. No-one in Yorkshire knew what she was like,' he said.

'Do you know where the old resident lives?' she asked.

'Penrith.'

'Name?'

'Douglas Alexander.'

It wasn't one of the names of the children from the Whitehaven fire, whose fate was, as yet, uncertain. But it was another lead.

Chapter 44

Sarah Tate's original statement had been taken by two uniforms, and it had been perfunctory and standard. Nothing had flagged red lights to Kelly, and it had been filed away with all the others.

Until now.

They'd had a call from her wanting to meet with a detective and Kelly's interest was stoked. She'd set aside half an hour or so to meet with the woman, and Rob was available to assist.

She was a small woman in her late thirties who fiddled with the corners of her jacket, which she'd thrown over her arm as an afterthought. They sat in an interview room in Eden House and waited for Ms Tate to get whatever it was that was bothering her off her chest. They were calm and patient, though inside Kelly began to regret setting aside time, and her mind wandered to other things she had to do. The woman had been fetched coffee and water in an attempt to make her feel relaxed. As relaxed as one could be in a police interview cell.

'I'm worried about my brother.' Sarah finally began speaking.

'Colin? Why is that, Sarah?' Kelly asked. Once again, she had to remind herself that the small meek woman before her was not related to any of her family, but she bore an uncanny resemblance to her adoptive mother,

Emily. They shared the same mannerisms and both took up minimal space in the room. Sarah didn't overtly share Emily's misery, but her brow was furrowed, and her mouth turned down at the corners.

'He has problems dealing with emotion, you know. I don't see him very often, but I saw him yesterday, and he's basically shut himself away in his flat. He let me in eventually, but he's in a complete mess.'

Kelly clasped her hands together and placed them on the table. A fan whirred in the corner and she was desperate for some air. 'And why do you think he might be acting like that?'

'It's because you think he had something to do with Moira's murder,' said Sarah.

'Right. That can explain why persons of interest who have been interviewed by the police become jittery. It's quite normal. No-one wants to be associated with such a crime. Colin is only one line of enquiry. We can't rule anything out until we've consolidated all the evidence, but let me assure you, that I'll let Colin know as soon as we make a decision either way. We did explain that to him.'

Colin Tate was a minor part of the puzzle, but his adoptive sister didn't need to know that. The fact was that they had virtually nothing on the man. His feet literally didn't fit, his DNA didn't match, his handwriting certainly didn't match – he could hardly string together a sentence on paper – and he had no links to the other women. Their most promising lead to date was the elusive Timothy Cole who had either gone walkabout with his family, or killed them. And even then his links to the women were so glaringly obvious that the man was either stupid or innocent.

'Is there anything else that we should know?' asked Kelly. Sarah Tate was nervous for sure, but she could be holding back. The cues from her face were worrying; she twitched and grimaced oddly, as if she was play-acting, or very scared.

'We went to meet Moira, in Penrith.' It was blurted out, but instantly, Sarah Tate's face broke. It had been a huge burden, Kelly could tell. She looked at Rob, who was taking notes. Sarah looked between both of them. Kelly didn't answer, or show that she was affected by the news. She merely allowed Sarah to continue.

'You have our attention,' Kelly said.

'We agreed to meet her in a pub, near the hospital. She agreed, it was all arranged. She never turned up.'

'Why have you only told us this now, Sarah?'

'We knew what you'd think. Colin is innocent! He's so scared that he'll get framed for this like so many other things in his life. It's putting so much strain on him, I'm scared he'll do something stupid. He can't know I've been here.' Sarah looked frantic and Kelly felt pity for her. She allowed Sarah to calm down.

'Would you like a tissue?' Kelly pushed the generic box wheeled out for interviewees towards Sarah, who took one gratefully. She was beginning to relax.

'What day was it? Your meeting with Moira, I mean,' Kelly asked.

'It was the Monday, the eighth. Just before she was found on the Wednesday. She didn't call and cancel, and she didn't answer her phone when we tried.' Sarah's shoulders sagged and she sniffed into the tissue.

'You blocked caller ID?' asked Kelly. Several incoming calls on Moira's records had shown prior to the phone

276

ceasing all comms, late on the Monday evening. One of them was a no caller ID call: the Tate siblings.

'Yes,' Sarah replied. Kelly tapped her pen.

'What was the meeting about?' Kelly asked.

'She'd agreed to be a kind of go-between for my father and Col. I begged her to do it. Colin is... special. He's vulnerable, and my dad is old-fashioned. They never should have fallen out, but they did, and he turned to Moira. It was all a terrible coincidence but Col blamed Dad, and vice-versa. I think Moira liked the drama.'

'So, why would she agree to act as peace maker?' Kelly asked.

'Because I promised to sign over my trust fund,' Sarah said.

Kelly and Rob stopped what they were doing. If Sarah noticed, she didn't show it. Kelly didn't have to communicate her thoughts to her junior. Money, greed, selfishness... Motive. Kelly gathered herself and went back to Sarah.

'So she doesn't show up. Which pub and what time?' Rob made notes.

'The Red Cock, King Street. 9 p.m.'

Kelly calculated the times when Moira had been roaming the streets, ranting down the phone to Timothy Cole. He said he last spoke to her about 10 p.m. so she could have easily have made her meeting; a meeting that she stood to gain from handsomely.

'How much is your trust fund worth? I assume that Colin no longer has one?' Kelly asked.

At this point, Rob received a call and looked at his boss.

'Go and take it.' He left the room, apologising to the two women. Kelly knew that he was expecting an important call.

'My dad stopped Colin's but he never closed it. When Dad passes away, I know it will go to Colin, he never changed his will, and deep down, I know he never would. They're both worth £100,000.'

'Each?'

'Yes.'

'There's no way Moira would have missed that meeting by choice. Why would you let £100,000 go to Moira?'

'To show my dad that we love him more than the money.'

Chapter 45

The phone call to Rob's mobile was from Douglas Alexander, who was willing to meet a male officer for a brief conversation. Kelly thought she could change his mind, and they left Eden House after they'd thanked Sarah Tate for her courage in coming forward.

'Jesus, Rob. This family. It just keeps getting filthier. You know, the fingers thing: it fits with the greed idea. But there are no connections between the Tates and the other victims. It's as if whoever is doing this knows these people, and is playing them all together in some kind of macabre production. This is what happened to Yorkshire Police. They went round and round in circles, turning up zero forensics that actually matched the killer. Case unsolved.'

Kelly's shoes tapped harshly on the tiled floor, and Rob knew her well enough now to know that she was perplexed. He remained quiet. They reached the Audi and got in. Kelly slammed her door harder than necessary and Rob hid a smirk. He looked out of the window. Newton Rigg was a five minute drive.

Douglas Alexander was a tower of a man. He worked lumbering timber in a yard just to the north of Penrith, near the Newton Rigg estate. Kelly and Rob watched as the man casually threw planks the size of railway sleepers over his shoulders as if they were tea towels. He worked shirtless and his body was tanned and muscular. Kelly couldn't help feel a pang of pity as she watched. It would be easy to dismiss the man as a drop out, a layabout, a social misfit. So much in life was left to chance, and either one of them could easily have ended up where Douglas Alexander was. Stats such as these were so often the back-ground music to their job: kids who'd missed the right launch time – and then the boat completely – who ended up being adults in the wrong place, and at the wrong time.

They walked towards the site, and Douglas stopped what he was doing. Kelly knew he could tell who they were, and that they didn't belong here. It was their clothes, their demeanour, and probably the man's own experience of institutions and the law. Kelly watched him grab a rag and wipe his hands and his brow. His back muscles rippled and shone, and Kelly looked at his body: his physique was stunning. Rob had said that over the phone the man came across as articulate and intelligent. Kelly wondered what other surprises he had for them.

'Douglas?' Rob asked. He'd asked for a male and Kelly encouraged Rob to give the impression that he was the lead detective.

Douglas nodded and gave a half-smile. He looked at Kelly warily, and she felt examined. Douglas knitted his brow. Rob introduced himself, and they shook hands.

'I asked for a male detective only.'

'I know, Douglas. This is my inspector.'

'Kelly Porter.' She held out her hand, and it was taken. Douglas's grip was strong and manly. It smacked of confidence. Kelly matched it. He eyed her, and she passed some sort of test. He nodded.

'Let's go inside the brew shed.'

They followed him. It was quite cool inside the shed, and the windows were open. Metal chairs and tables were scattered about, and jackets, kit and lunch boxes littered the place. Douglas cleared a space for them. Kelly could see that he was mindful that the shed wasn't somewhere he'd want to take a lady. There was something endearingly sensitive about him.

'Sorry,' he said to her.

'Not a problem, Douglas. It is alright if I call you Douglas?' she checked.

'Call me Doug. I can make you tea, but I can't guarantee a clean mug, so I wouldn't bother if I were you.'

'No problem, at least you're honest,' she said. Doug pulled out three metal chairs and they sat down. The guy was pretty calm, and it reminded Kelly of the saying about still waters…

'Doug, like I said on the phone, we'd really like to ask you some questions about your time at the Whitehaven Home for Children and Adolescents.' Rob lead again.

Doug flinched, just perceptibly. If they'd blinked they would have missed it.

'Do you remember two kids who were there about the same time as you – Brian Leith and Amy Gardener?'

'Sure I do. They were killed in the fire.'

'We're not so sure,' Rob said. This had a strange effect on Doug, who began to smile.

'Really?' asked Doug. 'Why do you say that?'

'No bodies were found, not even traces, and they were assumed dead, not confirmed dead. The fire was pretty hot, it is possible that they left no trace but it's highly unusual. How well did you know Brian Leith, Doug?'

Kelly watched Rob, he was growing in confidence and she liked that. He was comfortable in charge. More importantly, Doug was loosening up.

'As well as I knew anyone in there. We talked about running away, maybe, you know to get away from those fucking animals.' He stopped smiling. 'We all talked about setting fire to the place ourselves, so I always believed Brian or Amy did it and ran away. I hope they did.' The smile returned.

'Why, Doug? What happened there?' Rob asked. Doug looked out of the window and didn't speak for several minutes. Neither Kelly nor Rob pushed him.

'Can you ask the lady to wait outside?' Doug finally asked. Damn. He still couldn't open up.

'I'm difficult to shock, Doug,' Kelly said.

'I bet you are, Kelly. But it's non-negotiable I'm afraid. I can't say what I have to say and look a lady in the eye.' He held her gaze. Rob looked between them. They were about the same age: his boss and the giant man, but Doug was like something from another era: he was a gentleman.

Kelly gathered her things.

'It's not personal,' Doug said.

'I know.' She smiled at him warmly and left.

Rob turned back to the man. Doug looked at his hands and wrung them together. He took a long, deep breath and began talking.

It was forty-five minutes before Rob emerged from the shed, and the colour had left his cheeks.

Kelly waited for him by a wall.

'Jesus, what did he tell you?'

'I wrote it all down, and he checked it and signed it. I'll tell you in the car.'

When they were back in the car, Rob turned to Kelly and said, 'We need to find Brian Leith.'

Chapter 46

The drive to Coniston was leisurely. The exact spot where
Wordsworth had penned his celebration of daffodils would
stay forever unknown, but people guessed. Most said
Ullswater; after all, his lines had been penned years after his
walk with Dorothy there by the lake. Some said Coniston.

The Touran stopped at a deserted spot, close to the
lake. The water was still and flat, like a pure sheet of
expensive crystal. A light breeze moved small branches
gently up and down. No-one ever came here, apart from
the odd ranger to make sure there were no campfires.

It was getting worse, like Byron said. The Lakes was
ruined by people: a scourge of sick-minded, vain, hypo-
critical and superficial hordes, intent on banality and
infirmity. People were messy and noisy, and they interrupted the silence on the fells. The great swarms, which
descended every summer, abused the beauty and ruined
the sanctity of the peaks. Images of Moira came back,
and with them, the feeling of consummate power. The
strap tightening around Brandy's throat, Aileen begging
for forgiveness…

With Nicola Tower quiet for once, the selection of
words could begin. It had to match the candidate: each
was unique. The grass was warm, under the tree, and
nothing stirred but the odd cloud in the sky. No children
frolicked, no lovers rowed up and down in wooden boats,

no motor boats roared, no steamers disturbed the water, and no Harrier jets left thunder in their wake. The lake was perfect, like the Old Man of Coniston himself, behind them. Peace was absolute, and with it came clarity of thought.

It had to be Wordsworth.

And with him, she'd become one with the land again. Like poor Drummer Hodge.

It had been Old Albert's favourite too.

They throw in Drummer Hodge, to rest
Uncoffined, just as found:
His landmark is a kopje crest
That breaks the veldt around…
Yet portion of that unknown plain
Will Hodge forever be…

Nicola was still quiet after the sun went down behind Coniston Old Man. The Touran had driven around the lake a few times and had returned after sundown to avoid the last rangers.

She was heavy, as was to be expected. That's why it was important to park as close to the trees as possible, and use the shifting skate. It made a huge difference, and meant that Nicola could be positioned in the perfect spot.

She fell on to the skate with a thud, and it probably broke a few bones, but it didn't matter now to Nicola; she wouldn't feel a thing. The moon was a waning crescent, and the heavy cloud conspired with it to provide excellent cover. The Touran's lights had been switched off since turning off the B5285, at Guards Woods. Rangers looking for illegal campers or fly tippers would have checked the area earlier, and might check again before dawn, depending on their mood. Most people respected the laws of the National Trust.

The lake beckoned, and its black silky surface looked like deep inky oil – so different from this afternoon. This side of Coniston was by far the quietest, and that was the reason for the location. Each candidate had to be matched perfectly to their final resting place. This place was about as quiet as could be found inside the National Park, and that's why Nicola would have hated it. The serenity, intoxicating calm and regal beauty was the perfect place to introduce Nicola to what she might have been.

Humble.

Moira was left forever exposed (her worst nightmare) in the middle of a village, outside the institution she loathed – the church. Brandy was submerged in clean, fresh running water, to cleanse her of the filth she allowed into her. Poor Ailing Aileen was left overlooking the exquisite perfection of the Lake District, to make sure she never forgot about Nature's law: that weaklings are a nuisance, and cannot be allowed to drain the resources of others. Now, Nicola, possibly the most irritating woman on the planet, had no-one to talk to anymore, in one of the most isolated locations in the Lakes.

The shifting skate was silent, having being oiled well, and it glided over the dirt easily, towards the lake.

There it was.

No yellow heads sat plump on long green stilts in summer, but it didn't matter. Nicola was about to become part of this place, like Drummer Hodge, and, in the spring, when the daffodils announced their arrival, she will have helped them on. It was perfect.

She smelled.

That was the problem with summer.

Nicola wouldn't stay up. She kept leaning maddeningly over to one side. The woman was as exasperating in death as she'd been in life. Finally, she stayed where she was put for her photograph. Her great breasts hung over her huge belly, down to her thighs, but were now cool as ice, and not inviting at all. Her head bent down towards her chest, and her arms were arranged either side of her body. It was as if she was asleep. The cosmetic work could have been better, but it was the thought that counted.

The area was popular with dog walkers, and with the smell she was exuding already, it wouldn't be long before Nicola Tower became famous: her lifelong dream. These moments spent saying goodbye were always a little disappointing; an anti-climax. The tracks left by the shifting skate were kicked over on the way back to the car, and the boot door slammed down. It was a shame it was all over. Until the next time.

As the car's engine came to life, a single fat black fly landed on one of Nurse Tower's wounds, and began its work.

Chapter 47

Kelly woke with a start.

At first, she didn't know where she was. Then, after a few moments, and her eyes adjusting, she realised that she was in her new house, in her new bedroom, with new bedsheets.

She laid back luxuriously and stretched. She looked at her window and the sunlight beyond and sank deeper into her pillow. She felt at peace. But soon, reality hit and she remembered that she had to drag herself out of bed and get to work.

She turned her head, Johnny's chest rose and fell rhythmically. She'd got in late. Very late in fact, but Johnny said he'd still come over. He'd brought takeaway, and they'd sat on crates. Her bed was the first thing to be delivered, the sofas would take weeks.

She looked around the room: her clothes were all over the floor, together with Johnny's. Well at least they'd had a bed this time. She smiled and stretched again. The thought of hauling her body out of bed was completely unappealing. She supposed that her new coffee machine might be a consolation. Johnny still hadn't moved, so she slipped out of bed and went to the bathroom for a shower. When she came back to the bedroom to get dressed, the bed was empty and she heard noises downstairs. She opened her windows and looked down at the river. She'd never get bored of the view. Perhaps she could bring Mum over later to sit on the terrace. Wendy was out of hospital again and every time she came out, she seemed to bounce right back.

Kelly hadn't seen Nikki all week, and for that she was thankful.

She towel dried her hair and got dressed. Her bedroom had built-in wardrobes and they were full already. She selected a white blouse and a patterned skirt. It wasn't a frivolous pattern, but it was a little more interesting than just a single colour. The skirt was a sensible check, and she matched it with brown leather sandals. The stairs were wood with no carpet and her heels clunked noisily on them. The space was lavish compared to her mother's terrace and she felt extravagant.

'Good morning,' she said, as she joined Johnny in the kitchen.

'I thought you'd be up and out early,' he said. 'I've made you an omelette.'

'You spoil me! Thank you very much, are you joining me?'

'I'm making another one now.'

'I'll wait then.' She got cutlery from the sink (she only had two of everything, donated by Wendy, so far), and took it, and her omelette, outside. More crates had been turned upside down, and she used one as a table and pulled up two more as seats. It was warm already, and it was only seven a.m.

Johnny joined her and they ate in silence.

'You make a good omelette.'

Her phone buzzed and she looked at the screen. It was Matt, Nikki's husband.

'Oh God, I'm ignoring that.'

'Who is it?' Johnny asked.

'My brother-in-law. It won't be important. My sister will have put him up to it.'

'Why would she do that?'

'It's a long, boring story. Let's just say, we don't get on.'

'I'm an only child, it's a lot less complicated.'

Kelly's phone rang again. She tutted, it was Matt again.

'You better answer it, it doesn't look like he's going to stop trying,' Johnny said. She did so.

'Kelly Porter.' She was always formal with Matt because she didn't know how much poisoned honey Nikki had fed him, so she kept a distance.

Johnny watched as Kelly's demeanour changed. She sat upright and then stood up. Now she was pacing. He watched her. Families, he thought. Such a pain in the arse. But then he wondered if Josie would ever feel like that about him, and be irritated by his phone calls.

'Matt, calm down. I think you're over reacting. Look, she'll be with a friend.' Kelly shrugged her shoulders towards Johnny, who began clearing away. He had to get going as well. Kelly listened.

'Yesterday she was supposed to meet a friend, she didn't show up. She didn't come home last night, and she's not answering her phone.'

'Who was she supposed to meet, and what time?'

'Her friend, Katy Crawley. Around four o'clock.'

'So, when was the last time you saw her?'

Kelly searched her memory and played her days back, trying to work out what day it was. It was Friday.

'Before that, about two o'clock,' Matt said. 'The kids are in meltdown, your mum hasn't seen her either.'

'How did she seem, Matt? Was she stressed or upset about anything? You know Katy Crawley can be a bit of a drain, did you know that Nikki has been giving her money?'

'I sort of knew, Kelly, but I don't see what that has to do with her going off and not being here for her kids.'

'I know, I'm just thinking aloud. Are you sure Katy is telling the truth? Maybe Nikki wanted a break and is getting her to cover for her?'

'Why would she do that?'

'I don't know, Matt. I'm just thinking like a copper would.'

Thinking like a copper would…

'Matt. Will you let me make some calls and I'll get right back to you?' They hung up. Kelly rang her sister's phone. The tone was dead. Then she rang her mother.

'Mum, I've just spoken to Matt.'

'I've been up all night, Kelly. She wouldn't go off and tell no-one where she'd gone. She wouldn't leave the kids, and Matt, and…' said Wendy.

'Has Matt spoken to the police?' Kelly asked her mother.

'No, I don't think so, do you think we should?' Wendy sounded more alarmed.

'I'll do it, leave it to me.'

'Do you think she's ok, Kelly?'

'I don't know, Mum. I'll keep you updated, I promise. Has she done this before? I mean, had she been acting strangely or saying she wanted to get away for a bit?'

'No.'

'When is the last time you spoke?'

'Yesterday. She was going to get the rest of my things from the hospital. I forgot to tidy my cupboard. I'm such a fool.'

'Alright, Mum. Listen, I'll get back to you, alright?'

She hung up.

Working backwards, Nikki's last known trip was to the hospital.

A shadow crept over Kelly's day; a day that had started so perfectly.

'I'm making a move,' said Johnny. Their goodbyes were always rushed and she felt regret.

'Right, of course. Thanks for breakfast, and er… dinner,' she said.

He walked over to her and put one hand on her jaw and cupped her face. He bent over to kiss her and she allowed him.

'Let me know when you'd like to do it again,' he said.

'I will. Soon.'

'Good.' He left and Kelly watched his back. She stood like that for a few seconds after the door had banged, and then she remembered what she had to do.

Chapter 48

The ambulance parked as close to the trees as possible, after a search of the area by the forensic team. They worked quietly. They all watched the news. They'd all heard of The Teacher.

At first, fascination and tantalising gossip had dominated the news, verging on sickening vicarious replay. But even that was turning sour, and the atmosphere at the Tourist Board was now one of panic. Visitors were cancelling in their thousands, and buses, boats, restaurants and bars were empty.

They wouldn't be able to keep this one out of the news for long either. Number four.

She'd been picked at by small carnivores, which had been attracted by the open wounds around her midriff. Great slices of flesh had been removed from her belly and at first glance it looked like the cuts had been made by a seamstress, preparing to make a prom dress smaller for the excited teenager who'd lost so much weight, especially for the event. But it wasn't a dressmaker's dummy. It was a woman. Another woman.

The team was made up of five forensic examiners and, today, Ted Wallis had come along. Senior pathologists usually didn't have the time or the inclination to visit scenes in the field, but this was different. Ted had autopsied every victim and this time he wanted to see her in-situ. Such context wasn't necessary, but Ted was inextricably linked to these women now, and he wanted to see the killer caught. And he also wanted to help Kelly. Perhaps he'd see something at the scene that was new, something that he would never see in the morgue.

He looked at the soil, rummaged through bushes, and took photos. His team was perfectly capable of carrying out these tasks for him, but he worked alongside them, performing the duties he'd trained for thirty years ago. He used stepping plates, so as not to disturb vital evidence. Defence barristers were getting pickier year on year, and a tiny detail could stump him on the stand. These days, juries wanted to see the scene for themselves, in as much detail as possible.

Ted was old school, and he'd brought along with him a sketch pad and pencil, which he used to sketch the scene. It always helped to jog the memory if it was required later.

He stopped and bent down. There were tyre tracks in the mud, and despite being covered with loose soil, they were still visible. The hot weather had preserved them beautifully and they were nice and hard – perfect for plaster. He ordered an imprint. Leading from the tyre tracks were other tracks, smaller ones, and Ted couldn't work out what had made them. He had them filled with plaster too, and they'd be sent to a track expert along with the tyre tracks.

His mind was focused, and he was unaware of members of his team watching him. It wasn't every day that someone as senior as Ted Wallis could be studied in the field, and they were distracted by him. They watched his methodical movements, and the way he looked at certain items from different angles. It took him over forty-five minutes to get close to the body, so busy was he examining everything else around her first.

A tent had been erected around the scene, and cars could be heard in the distance. It was an isolated spot but people walked dogs here, and soon it would become a thoroughfare for animals with three hundred million nose receptors. He couldn't allow that to happen, and the police were busy securing the area.

She'd been found by a park ranger, desperate for the toilet and caught short, looking for somewhere off the road. He'd given a statement to the uniform, first on to the scene. Ted could still smell his vomit, which lay in a pile ten feet away from the body.

Kelly Porter had been informed, and she was on her way. Ted had called her personally.

For now, his aim was to find a piece of paper.

He noted the stillness of the place. It was bewitching. He imagined a figure, most likely under the cover of night, arranging the bulky frame of this woman. Had he said anything? Had he taken his time? How long had he planned this location to be her final resting place? As always, he struggled with the motive behind the act. No matter how old Ted got, he could never rationalise such depravity. He looked at the incisions. Fat had been removed from under them, and Ted wondered if the killer thought he was doing her a favour. Plastic surgery for free. The victim was clean, Ted could tell straight away. Her nails were scrubbed, and her wounds weren't suppurating. There were various marks all over her body, and Ted wouldn't know what had caused them, or if they were inflicted ante- or post-mortem, until he had her on the slab. Washing indicated intimacy, he noted. He spotted marks around her neck, and they looked consistent with the other victims. He heard rustling behind him and turned around. Kelly walked towards him. She was grim-faced and she stared beyond him, towards the victim.

He wondered how close Kelly's team was to solving these crimes, but he wouldn't ask her. Ted knew that sometimes crimes went unsolved for decades. It was taking a toll on the young detective's face.

'Kelly,' he said, simply.

'Ted.' Kelly's eyes never left the victim.

'I haven't found a note yet, take a look. She has the same ligature marks round her neck, wrists and ankles. We found tyre tracks and another smaller track, possibly a lifting device.'

'I know her,' said Kelly. 'She worked at Penrith and Lakes Hospital, she nursed my mother.'

Ted stopped what he was doing, and stared at Kelly.

'Do you know her name?'

'Yes, she's called Nicola. Nicola Tower. She was a staff nurse, full of life, always joking around, perhaps a little too much sometimes. She was, how can I put it? Wonderfully tactless.' Kelly's voice was dead pan.

The answer was right under her nose. She'd walked the same wards, she'd said hello to the same patients, she'd probably made a coffee at the same machine as the killer, but, as she wracked her brain for images of anyone matching their profile, Kelly continually came up blank. She'd thought it might be a hospital porter, a visitor, a consultant, the man selling newspapers and chocolate bars; anyone would do. They'd been through the staff lists, the patient lists, including outpatients, and through auxiliary staff. Thousands of people went through the doors of the Penrith and Lakes Hospital. Hundreds of vehicles came and went, and any one of them could be responsible for the series of murders on the shoulders of Kelly Porter and her team. She'd thought of closing the hospital, but that was out of the question. She'd put officers on every entrance, scoured CCTV footage, and personally spoken to over five hundred people.

And still no-one knew where Timothy Cole was.

'Why did you come down here, Ted?' She looked away from Nicola Tower. Something gnawed at her gut.

'Do I need to answer that, Kelly? I trust my team implicitly, but I needed to see it this time for myself, to see if I could spot something, anything significant. I can see how much this is taking out of you. I thought I could help.'

'I'm fine Ted,' she lied. He didn't believe her. 'I think we are looking at number four, Kelly. Kelly?' He watched her, trying to get her attention, but she'd zoned out again and her face was blank. He watched as she walked towards the nurse she'd called Nicola.

'What has The Teacher said this time? What was her crime?'

'I don't know, Kelly. I won't know until I get her back to the morgue. Do you want me to guess?'

Kelly nodded. She already had her own theory.

'Moira was missing her fingers; Brandy was missing her tongue, Aileen missing her cane, and now Nicola is missing a lot of her flesh.'

Kelly looked at the body and she hadn't noticed before. Her mind had wandered to the women before death – and during expiry – and how they'd suffered. She was overlooking the detail that now offered itself to her.

'Flesh?'

'Look. He took her fat deposits, Kelly. Her hips, inner thighs, belly and some back fat.'

'Oh, Jesus.'

'Quite. It's as if he's given her a fat-reducing operation; make of that what you will.'

'Vanity.'

'Yes.'

'My sister has gone missing.'

He stared at her.

'Kelly? You don't think it's linked do you?'

'I've spent so much time in the hospital this month, it's like my second home. So has Nikki. So has my mother. The victims are all connected to the hospital. Each one of them seemed to have known their killer: else why would they have agreed to go with them? He needs a vehicle to do this,' she pointed at Nicola Tower. 'Nikki has been missing for twenty-four hours, but she's a mother, Ted. She'd never leave her children. I have to go.'

'Where?'

'God knows. First I need to report it formally.'

'You're remarkably calm, Kelly.'

'I've got no choice. Tell me when you find the poem.'

Ted nodded. He knew, as well as Kelly, that there'd be one: and it was probably lodged inside one of the botched fat removal wounds. He watched Kelly walk away, and called over a junior. He had to get the body on his slab so he could find the poem.

298

Chapter 49

Kelly increased her steps as she returned to her car. She called her sister's mobile again. No answer.

No matter how much she denied it, no matter how much she willed the thoughts away; and no matter how many times she pretended that Nikki had bunked at Katy's last night, drinking wine and drowning their sorrows until the early hours, Kelly knew; she knew that whoever roamed the corridors of the Penrith and Lakes looking for imperfections and human frailty – or whatever else it was that The Teacher pretended was wrong with the planet – Nikki was not ok. Every fibre of her body told her. Next, she called Missing Persons. She hadn't worked the section for years, but she vaguely knew the routines.

Nikki Morden was reported missing shortly after midday.

Kelly sat in her Audi and stared at the lake. Coniston was serene and calm, unlike Ullswater, which always had some form of power vehicle ploughing up and down the water. There were isolated sections, but Kelly knew that the killer would never have got away with dumping a body so close to the larger, more tourist-oriented lake. He knew the lakes very well indeed. Probably born or raised here; and that put to bed the idea that their suspect might be connected with the transient summer workforce, or labourers on the numerous building sites, paid by the hour.

The care home angle bugged her. Brian Leith had disappeared off the face of the earth after the fire in Whitehaven. How could that be? Unless he was dead like they all presumed. Same for the girl called Gardener. Maybe she was chasing shadows and the two teenagers had perished after all. Was she clutching at straws? It was highly likely that she was suffering from fatigue, and that it was clouding her judgement. She called DS Umshaw.

'Kate. Have we found Brian Leith yet?'

'No, Guv. But we do have an old photo. It's been generated and digitalised for release to the press, with your go ahead. DCI Cane is here.'

Kelly rolled her eyes. Cane wouldn't snoop around Eden House for a nice cup of coffee; he was getting twittery. She dismissed the development until she could properly deal with it, face to face.

'Has Brian Leith popped up in any of our searches of NHS trusts in Yorkshire between 2009 and 2012?'

'Not yet, Guv.'

'Right, I'm on my way. The fourth victim – not confirmed yet, but it looks like it, Kate – is a staff nurse from the Penrith and Lakes called Nicola Tower. Get her next of kin ready to be informed will you? I don't know when I'll be back, Coniston is heating up and the traffic will be choked. Tell the notification to go ahead without me. Maybe DCI Cane would like to do it?'

Umshaw stifled a smirk. 'Yes, Guv.'

'The coroner is here and he's taken tracks from a vehicle, two in fact. I want the tracks from Aira Force chased, who's free?'

Umshaw sighed. 'I'll find someone.'

300

'Kate, there's something I need to tell you, but I don't want the rest of the team in on it just yet. They'll know soon enough. The press is going to have a field day.'

'Guv?'

'My sister, Nikki, is missing. Given the hospital link, I need to consider the possibility that our Teacher knows me. It sounds crazy and egotistical, but my mother was nursed by Nicola Tower, and Catherine Tring was nursed on a ward that my mum stayed on two weeks ago.'

'I don't know what to say.'

'That's not like you, Kate. That cheers me up a little.' Kelly tried her best to laugh, because it was true; Kate Umshaw always had a word ready, whether it was welcome or not.

'We've inputted the NHS trusts from all four Yorkshire areas, as well as the council houses fitted with the carpet. Oh and we've got the results back on the earth found in Moira's mouth and nose.'

'Please give me some good news.' Kelly closed her eyes and sat back in her seat. The forensic officers in suits were still processing the scene behind her car.

'The samples were sent to a palynologist…'

'A what?'

'A pollen expert – it narrows down the search for the origin of soil.'

'Oh.'

'They confirmed that the soil in Moira's ears, nose and mouth isn't indigenous to Watermillock. In fact, it's a mixture of bog standard garden centre organic compost, mixed with domestic earth from the Penrith area, notably from either Scaws, Redgill, or Askham Bridge.'

'Scaws again?'

'Right.'

'And Timothy Cole's rental properties came up blank?'

'Yes. They're simply in the wrong part of town. Of course, anyone can buy garden centre compost, but it's what was mixed with it that was narrowed down so specifically.'

Kelly knew that forensic soil analysis was one of the things that would stand indisputably in court. Sediment, colour, structure, mineral content and density couldn't be contested. The science was absolute. Now all they needed to do was find the garden it had come from.

'Border force?' All airports, sea ports and rail networks had been given Timothy Cole's details, as well as those of his wife and children.

'Nothing.'

Kelly exhaled deeply. She felt impotent.

'What's Cane up to?'

'Practising his fire-breathing.'

'Keep him busy.'

'I've got over five hundred NHS staff names to give him if he gets pesky.'

'See you soon.' Kelly rang off. She dismissed her junior officer's minor impertinence; everybody did it, and it was a natural stress buster. Shit travels downwards and Cane would say the same about Super Ormond, given half the chance.

She couldn't complain. Super Ormond had granted her more boots on the ground since the body count had gone up. Not that it had made much difference. Their killer seemed to have planned everything like a production, some kind of macabre summer play in which no-one knew the outcome but him. They were all being directed and staged until he decided to stop, and that didn't seem likely. Her only consolation was that, in her experience, killers this voracious and brazen always made mistakes.

She spent the journey back to Penrith working out exactly what to ask for from her bosses. They'd already arranged a search of the Coniston area, combing for witnesses. Geographically, The Teacher was making her life harder by the day. She drew a map in her mind and turned up the music. Coniston was thirty miles away from Ullswater – where the other three women had been found. What was The Teacher up to?

With a sickening knot in her stomach, her thoughts turned to her sister, and she knew that she'd have to add her family to the data this afternoon. They were now in the loop, as peripheral interest or not, they were leads.

Kelly went over the times she'd visited the hospital – for work or family visiting. Momentarily, she thought herself mad – mad that she'd found herself at the centre of this circus. She figured that, during the countless hours she'd spent at the Penrith and Lakes Hospital, be it for personal or professional reasons, she knew that she'd been watched. *They'd* been watched. And she had reached the awful conclusion in her mind that Nikki Morden was highly likely to be the next victim. She searched her memory, hoping for some detail to click into place, someone who'd had contact with both her mother and her sister. If The Teacher had Nikki, that meant that he'd selected her – he'd watched her, and worked her out. He'd got to know her routines, her habits, her weaknesses and her family. Nikki only ever stayed near their mother, she didn't wander around the hospital, unless to go to the shop. That meant the killer had come to them, in that room.

And got to know their mother.

Chapter 50

Kelly's team assembled at six p.m. for the last brief of the day. She studied them. There were at least seven detectives whom she didn't know, and hadn't got time to get to know. They remained simply names as she dished out jobs. They'd been loaned officers from Glasgow and Lancashire and her small incident room was looking cramped. They nursed cups of water and mugs of coffee. Outside, the story had stoked the interest of the international press, and tents had been erected, remaining there through the night, waiting for information. They felt like insects in a bell jar, examined and directionless.

DS Kate Umshaw perched on a table, having given up her seat, studying a document. Her eyes looked more sunken than normal and she'd wafted in on a cloud of cigarette smoke, stronger than usual indicating that she'd sucked on two in the time it took for one. DC Phillips flicked through a bundle of photographs and sighed from time to time. He ate a sandwich bought hastily from Boots on the High Street. DC Emma Hide looked fresh as always. She looked after herself. Even when called into work at eight a.m. Hide would manage a visit to the gym. She reminded Kelly of herself in her London days, but without the booze: Hide never touched a drop. The tide was changing in the force. Whereas ten years ago officers unwound by getting hammered, today they were more likely to enter a triathlon or a marathon. Emma was training for the Grisedale Grind and she had her sights set on winning the title of the Lady of the Forest. It was a brutal four kilometre, fifteen hundred foot toil through Whinlatter Forest and then up the spine of Grisedale Pike. Eden House's money was on Emma, who now sat in a chair with her head in a book recommended by her old English Tutor about the Romantic Movement in the Lake District. Kelly walked to the white board and everybody in the room looked up.

Cane was still there. He'd come in to her office earlier, when she'd returned, after a hellish journey through the centre of the Lakes, and he'd rightly demanded an update. She'd been rehearsing what she'd say all the way back.

'Sir. It's clear that the victimology in each case is some kind of sin.'

He hadn't questioned her rather metaphysical approach, he'd simply nodded. She'd recounted each snippet of poetry, and quoted DC Hide's immaculate analysis on each.

'It appears that The Teacher got to know each victim quite well, sir. We did think we were on to something with a hospital janitor called Paul Bamber – he's local, has access to all wards (he delivers papers and snacks), he's a gym bunny, and he's somewhat of a loner, but he's got solid alibis for the period of Moira's disappearance and that of Aileen Bickerstaff, and they check out. I've got everyone working the council property lead and I'm chasing the vehicles tracks. I think we're going to catch him the good old fashioned way, Eddie.'

'Crunching data.'

'Exactly.'

'It's tedious, Kelly. I know. I'm behind you, you know that – but Super Ormond is under the hammer here.'

'Yes, I'm well aware of that, but I'm also aware that – as yet – Super Ormond hasn't sent me a fucking transformer, or a super hero to help.'

Cane coughed to stifle his laugh.

'He wants to know why, in this day and age of DNA and advanced technology, we're still working paper leads.'

Kelly didn't respond, she merely held his gaze. She knew that he knew that keeping her any longer was detrimental to what they were both trying to achieve.

'You've been here all afternoon, you know how hard my team is working.'

'I know. But you're in charge, so the buck stops with you.'

His words still stung when she stood in front of her team at six o'clock. Dozens of faces stared at her, looking for answers that she couldn't yet give. She was torn. What she wanted to be doing right now was taking Matt's statement about Nikki's last known whereabouts, and arranging the foot search. But she knew that if she allowed her judgement to be clouded, she'd be taken off the case. She was perilously close as it was but if she kept her head she knew they wouldn't want to lose her; she, more than anyone, knew the case so far inside out, backwards, forwards, sideways, and blindfolded. Not that it was doing them much good.

'Good evening everybody. I've got a few updates. HR at the Penrith and Lakes hospital sent me this just an hour ago.' She tapped her laptop and the email came up on the white board. 'I've copied everybody in.' Her eyes were fuzzy and she rubbed them. Cane stood at the back of the room, holding a coffee.

'It's a list of everyone who has ever worked with Timothy Cole. If you look at the third page, you'll see the name of a hospital porter called Paul Bamber. His name pops up three times in the space of six years. He worked at the Royal in Hull, he worked at Furness General – which is where Cole works once a month – and he's working at the Penrith and Lakes. He has access to any ward, any time because part of his job is moving patients around by wheelchair. All staff on wards 5 and 7, as well as the fracture clinic, know him to chat to. He's a gym bunny and visits the hospital gym regularly, which is free to staff.'

Kelly pressed a button and Paul Bamber's photograph appeared on the board. 'Thirty-seven years of age, white male. Umshaw and Phillips: I want you two on nurseries, schools, parents, siblings, career history and previous.'

'Now, the gym has been checked by DC Shawcross, and he's well known there. He's there every day, and he holds the record for the most pull-ups; his upper body strength is nothing short of impressive. He lives in Stockham, next door to the Scaws Estate. It's an ex-council property, and it's on our list of places supplied with the grey carpet. He's being paid a visit as we speak. His details are also chugging through the PNC. The only sticking point is that his alibis for two of the abductions check out. He remains a POI.'

One major detail bothered Kelly about the new suspect: she'd never met the guy. But, then she had to remind herself that her theory about the killer knowing her, and her mother and sister, was just that – a theory. Nikki might be in the Bahamas with her new lover. Kelly hoped that she was. Word had spread throughout Eden House and Kelly was aware of lingering looks and sympathetic stares, and she didn't like it. She had to face it head on.

'We have a new missing person.' A photograph of Nikki came up on the white board. A few whispers were stifled, and Cane watched his SIO carefully.

'Nikki Morden. Yes, she's my sister — to put that one to bed straight away. Which is why I'm keen to nail the theory that he knew all of his victims. You all know that I virtually live at the Penrith and Lakes; so does my sister. Nicola Tower nursed my mother, and my mother also spent time on the same ward as Catherine Tring, though not at the same time. We're convinced that my sister wouldn't leave her kids without word; her phone is dead and she hasn't used her bank card. If you're wondering about motive; my sister enjoyed tearing a strip off the nursing staff — publicly and loudly. She was last seen on Thursday morning, yesterday. The evidence and the MO both suggest that she's being held somewhere — close to the Scaws Estate — see the report on the soil. For the record, I can't ever remember meeting Paul Bamber.'

Kelly didn't vocalise what everybody was thinking: that the MO of The Teacher also suggested that, if he had Nikki Morden, then, right now, she'd be either dead or close to it.

Kelly stayed professional, and brought up the report on the board. The atmosphere in the room became maudlin, but she pretended not to notice. She couldn't have her position compromised else she'd never find Nikki.

'We've also got an update on the tyre tracks from the Nicola Tower site. The small tracks belong to a shifting skate. It has three sets of wheels and can shift loads of up to one and a half tons. It seems that even Mr Universe couldn't manoeuvre Nicola satisfactorily. The larger tracks are from a Volkswagen Touran. I need someone to pull the hospital CCTV for the VW. This is our strongest lead yet. They match the tracks taken from Aira Force car park. VW Tourans aren't exactly rare, so it really is a needle in a haystack but it's something. We're trying to get the tyres narrowed down to a supplier.'

Kelly waited for her team to finish reading and adding notes. They'd soon be given their next assignments and many of them wouldn't get home until way after nightfall tonight.

Her stamina was flagging. She desperately wanted to close her eyes but her evening spread out before her like a gaping Milky Way, deep in space. There was no way she was going anywhere before ten o'clock. She doubted she'd get any sleep at all tonight. After work, she'd head straight to Matt's. She had no idea what he'd told the kids.

Nikki's disappearance hadn't been released to the press, but knowing the size of Katy Crawley's mouth and the chances of her wanting her five minutes of fame on TV, it wouldn't be long. Having dished out work and deciding who was going where to check what, Kelly thanked everyone and walked back to her office, closing the door behind her. She sat at her desk and put her head in her hands. She could have drifted off there and then, and she rubbed her eyes again. Her mind spun. Names, places, faces, wounds, characters of the alphabet and dark sinister rooms eddied in and out of her conscious. She saw vivid images and pressed her temples, willing the noise to stop.

When she looked up, she stared straight ahead. A nagging detail made her switch on her computer and she pulled up a file. She sat up straight with renewed vigour and pressed a few buttons, finding the right email.

It was the file of an employee at the Penrith and Lakes. One who'd been looked at, time and again, but overlooked. It was crazy, she knew, but she had to make sure.

She checked the names of the children resident at the time of the Whitehaven fire, and wrote some notes. Next she checked on the history of one child in particular. The child had been put into care after the death of the mother. The mother's death had been ruled an accident; she was partial to a sherbet or seven. She'd fallen downstairs and broken her neck. The injuries were very similar to those of Ms Sara Moyles from the Whitehaven care home. The child took the father's name, not the mother's and that's where they'd slipped through the piles of paper.

Kelly tapped more details into her computer and wrote more notes. After the mother's death, the property was consumed by fire, similar to another blaze only a few years previous which had consumed another property five doors down the street. Again, it had been seen as an accident. The guy was old and incapacitated. He could never have got out.

The death of Albert Ferguson had not been seen as suspicious. But Kelly noted that he was on the sex offender's register. The mother, five doors down, had given a statement. Her name was Pearl Richmond. Other neighbours at the time had supported the fact that Mrs Richmond was in and out of the Ferguson property regularly. Kelly went into the incident room and began hunting for something. Everybody carried on as normal. She found what she was looking for: an employment file from the Penrith and Lakes. DCI Cane looked up and watched her. She walked back to her office. Cane followed her.

She sat down and opened the employment file. The first page was a CV, and on the second was clipped a photograph.

Cane banged on her door.

Chapter 51

'Kelly Porter.' Kelly answered her phone, ignoring the door. DCI Cane walked in anyway. Kelly held up her hand and he waited impatiently, listening to her conversation. She put the caller on speaker phone. Cane pulled up a chair and sat down.

'Miss Porter? It's James Tate. Do you have time to talk?'

'Mr Tate? How can I help?' Kelly hadn't spoken to the husband of the first victim (the first they'd been allowed to find) for what seemed like a very long time. In fact, it was barely two weeks.

'Good evening, Detective. Can you talk? I know it's a tad late, but I think there's something that might be of interest to you.'

'Yes, of course I can. I'm in my office. How may we help?'

'Splendid, I was hoping I'd catch you. I only ever seem to catch up on my calls when I'm driving. It's a beautiful evening.'

Cane furrowed his brow and Kelly shrugged her shoulders. She mouthed 'I don't know' and looked out of the window.

'It certainly is a beautiful evening, Mr Tate. Unfortunately I'm not outside but I can see from my window.'

'Ah, I'm sure you are quite busy. I won't keep you long. I heard about the dreadful goings on. It's quite appalling.'

'It is, Mr Tate. Do you have any news for us?' Kelly was hopeful that he, or a member of his family, might have remembered something.

'I doubt it, I'm afraid, it's just a query that I thought you might be able to help me with.'

'Go on.'

Cane paced up and down. Kelly felt irritated and looked away from him, turning her back and staring out of the window.

'I've been sorting through Moira's estate,' Mr Tate carried on. Kelly's stomach tightened. Death is only the beginning for the loved ones, the fallout goes on for years. A vision of Moira's body, naked and cleaned, dumped on the grass outside the parish church of All Saints, came to her.

'I'm sorry, Mr Tate. How's it been?'

'To be perfectly honest with you, a nightmare. Moira's estate was easy, it's her mother's that's caused the headache.'

'Really?'

Kelly's mind wandered to her sister and she wondered if Matt had heard anything. Uniforms had been dispatched to visit Nikki's friends, her place of work, the children's schools, as well as shops and supermarkets, and so far they'd all drawn a blank. Kelly could only approach the case like she approached everything and she had to let all of the officers involved do their jobs. She could only make a difference if she kept her head. Mr Tate was still talking.

Kelly rubbed her shoulder with her free hand. She'd forgotten about Cane.

'Well, apart from taking an eternity for the lawyers to verify everything, and her signing ninety percent over to her grandson – Moira would be turning in her grave –

we're having trouble finding another benefactor, and I was hoping you could help.'

It was an odd request, but Kelly was happy to do what she could.

'I'll do what I can.'

'Catherine left ten percent of her entire estate – and let me tell you, detective, that is a lot of money...' Kelly did the calculations in her head, and she already knew that Warren Downs stood to gain just short of five hundred thousand pounds. That meant that the other benefactor was looking at around fifty grand. Kelly wondered where the old lady had got her money from, but she hadn't asked.

'Mr Tate, if you don't mind me asking, how did Catherine end up with such a fortune?'

'Moira helped her with some lucky investments. Her last husband was fairly wealthy, and Catherine just got lucky, thanks to Moira.'

'I didn't know Moira was a market expert.' She winced, instantly regretting the insensitive remark, but Mr Tate didn't seem to notice.

'She wasn't, but some friend of hers was. She would be spitting feathers if she could see what has happened to it.'

'She knew, Mr Tate. Catherine told Moira what she intended to do with her money.' The line went quiet.

'Mr Tate?'

'For heaven's sake call me James.'

'James.'

'Did she know about the nurse?' he asked.

'What nurse?'

'The other benefactor: it's a nurse who treated her apparently. There's a letter in the will. It was added two weeks before Catherine died. I've transferred the money, but now my calls are not getting through.'

'You've transferred the money?' Kelly asked.

'All the details were on the letter.'

'Isn't that odd? Didn't you contest it? A terminally-ill patient making a nurse benefactor, two weeks before she died, is surely grounds for contest, James.'

'I honestly didn't think of that. I was just following Catherine's wishes.'

'What's the name of the nurse?' Kelly asked. A creeping sensation down her back made Kelly's hands sticky at the wheel.

She put the phone down and turned around to come face to face with Cane.

'Christ!' Kelly caught her breath.

'Sorry. I've been here the whole time,' he said. 'What is it, Kelly? Who was that?'

Chapter 52

Over the last two weeks – and most of those in the last couple of days – almost seventy police men and women had notched up over thirteen thousand working hours. Hundreds of volunteers canvassed neighbours, looked into tips and leads, and hundreds more tourists prolonged their holidays to volunteer to search woodland, fields and fells. The mountain rescue, over every one of their twelve areas, clocked up hours of overtime to search the most inaccessible areas of the Lakes, to see if any shred of evidence could be found around the dump sites. They each had a list, and day by day scoured the countryside looking for shreds of evidence, meanwhile holding down their day jobs.

Today, Johnny took Hart Crag.

He walked slowly. His brief was to notice anything out of the ordinary, anything that didn't belong on a mountainside. Johnny had spent hundreds of hours out here in the wilderness, either for pleasure or to save someone's life, and he knew the contours and crannies of most peaks. Despite the pressing importance of his searches, and those of his colleagues, he also took time to admire the beauty surrounding him.

The fell was silent and no-one ventured to this particular peak today; either that, or they'd been already and gone home. It was, after all, six o'clock in the evening, and the sun's glow was turning to silver. He took the Boredale

Hause route this time, just in case he found something that had been overlooked. The Lake District National Park was fairly anomalous regarding typical human behaviour, in that people tended to keep it tidy. Whether out of respect, or the fact that most visitors weren't British, wasn't something looked into by a select committee of researchers. It was just a fact. The mountains were almost pristine. Johnny came across the odd apple core, and a few cigarette butts, but nothing stood out.

The area was easy to search in the sense that it was exposed, however, some of the elevations were a challenge, and the tourists trying to get to where a body had been dumped were usually frustrated. He'd hiked the steep and satisfying Hawk Crag, and was now coming up on his final destination. The sun was falling behind Helvellyn to the west and the wind picked up. Kelly had told him to look under bushes and rocks that seemed out of place, and he did so, as he walked slowly towards the summit of Hart Crag.

The vision of the girl sitting there, as if taking a break from her climb, came back to him. He remembered her uneven breasts, and the paleness of her skin. He couldn't get Aileen out of his head.

He'd touched her cheek, not knowing if she was real, but he'd recoiled from her and wiped his hand unconsciously. They'd played a song that he didn't know at her funeral, but it didn't matter: it did what it was intended to do – make the congregation cry. He remembered thinking that he would ensure that no-one sang sad songs at his funeral. It was different to the other funerals he'd attended. Funerals of soldiers.

Military funerals were distinct, in that the army tended to take over and no-one knew who the young man behind the flag really was. The family knew: the sister, the aunt, and the dad – they all knew. But the congregation (mainly of other military personnel and their families) were there to honour a colleague. The atmosphere was that of the brave, courageous warrior, and warriors didn't cry.

He did see soldiers cry, just once. It was at the funeral of a twenty-two-year-old who'd been blown up at a checkpoint in Afghanistan, two days after becoming a father. The boys – as Johnny called them – lived in bunks together, six or eight a throw, for seven months. They weren't just family, they were flesh and blood. Muckers.

He tripped over a clump of bracken and swore. He wasn't concentrating. Fat lot of good he'd be to Kelly, if he just came up here and wandered aimlessly, day dreaming and feeling sorry for himself. He stopped and looked around. He was almost at the location where Aileen had been found.

He walked round the largest boulder and was startled to find a figure sitting in the exact spot. For a moment, Johnny's body filled with electricity, but then he calmed and laughed it off. The figure had the same reaction, and they laughed together.

'God, Sorry!' Johnny said. 'I nearly had a heart attack,' he added.

The figure stood up.

'I didn't expect to see anyone up here so late,' said the stranger.

'I prefer it when it's quiet,' Johnny said.

His military past, always just under the surface, even now, rose up in him and something told him not to divulge the reason for his visit.

'Me too,' said the stranger.

Johnny committed details to memory: the shortness of the hair that wasn't yet grey or thinning, the walking boots, the height, eye colour and face shape. Johnny thought it an unusual place to take a break: above the boulder, in the most exposed and dangerous place on the fell.

A silence descended, and the figure stood up.

'Enjoy the rest of your walk. I've finished here,' the stranger said. Johnny thought about asking what he'd finished, but he kept his mouth closed. He moved backwards to let the stranger pass, and he caught a whiff of pungent masculinity. It took him by surprise. It seemed primeval, base, and guttural. It was like the scent an animal gives off when informing a rival to back off.

Johnny stood still.

The stranger moved away, towards the Place Fell route. They didn't look back.

Quickly, Johnny pulled out his phone and zoomed in as much as he could, before taking a photograph. It wasn't very good, but it was something.

He turned back to where the stranger had been sitting, and noticed something in the spot where they'd sat so peacefully. He went closer and bent over. The sun had caught the metal and made it shine.

It was a gold pen.

And it was engraved.

Chapter 53

Sometimes, Kelly thought she'd have been better suited to the Wild West. Clint Eastwood never had to wait for warrants. As she waited, she took a call from Ted Wallis.

He'd found a poem inside the body of Nicola Tower.

It was the confirmation they needed to make Nicola officially their fourth victim. Reporters had been camping outside the Penrith and Lakes, as well as Carleton Hall: now they'd get a new tidbit. The Lake District National Park was becoming world famous for more than its bid to become a UNESCO world heritage site.

'What do you mean inside her, Ted?' Kelly asked. Ted coughed. In the forty years he'd been dissecting bodies, he'd performed perhaps fifteen hundred autopsies, and only a hundred of those were for the police. The job at hand had always engaged him enough in its detail, to turn off his emotions and concentrate on precision. An autopsy was the last communication a homicide victim might send, and this noble pursuit drove him on, beyond the horror, beyond the gore, the stench and the brutality.

But today, he'd removed his head set, and his glasses, and wiped his brow. He couldn't ever remember doing that, apart from when he'd autopsied Lottie Davis.

'It was rammed into her throat so forcefully, Kelly, that it broke three cervical vertebrae,' he said.

Kelly paused for a few seconds, letting the news sink in.

'Can you read it, Ted?'

He'd stood over her body and unfolded the piece of paper with gloved hands, as he had all the others, and peered at the brown dried blood. The words were fresh in his mind.

'Yes. I won't forget it in a hurry. It's Wordsworth. The Prelude. It reads: 'Gently did my soul put off her veil'. It's about ridding oneself of pretension, Kelly. I've become an avid reader of the Lakes poets recently.' Kelly thought that was the nicest thing she'd heard in days. He had her back.

'The Prelude is generally accepted as Wordsworth's autobiography, Kelly. Do you think that's significant?'

'Emma said something about that.'

'Emma?'

'Yes, sorry. DC Hide, one of my detectives. Something about the narcissism of romantic poetry, and how birth and death are pivotal to life. Every time he kills, he's reborn somehow.'

'Like a journey?'

'Yes. Like a cleansing. Like teaching and learning.'

'So the journalists are on to something.'

'Maybe, Ted. Or maybe I'm just going crazy. I take it you swabbed for semen?' she asked.

'Of course,' Ted replied.

'I don't think it will make a difference.'

'What do you mean?' he asked. He was affronted, as if Kelly was giving up on him; giving up on herself.

'There is never any seminal fluid on the victims, is there?'

'It's always difficult to preserve the integrity of DNA when it's exposed to the elements, Kelly. You must know that. We'll find some that hasn't been degraded, and we'll be able to use it in court, don't you worry.'

'I'm not explaining myself properly. I don't think you've found any seminal fluid, Ted, because there is none.'

Ted laughed out loud, and instantly regretted it. 'What do you mean?'

The penny dropped and Ted caught on. 'Because objects were used instead?' He'd seen it many times before. 'Sexual aversion perhaps?'

'Yes, absolutely. Like I said all along. The sex thing is separate; incidental almost. It's the punishment which is paramount. *Gently did my soul put off her veil. Naked as in the presence of her God.*'

'Yes, I read the whole thing too. It's very beautiful,' he said, and it was.

'I have a new theory.'

'I'm all ears.'

It was getting late. The chances of finding a senior magistrate to sign the search warrant at this hour was slim, and Cane had told her to make the circumstantial as convincing as she could. At the moment, it was a mixture of hunch, conjecture, coincidence and a few leaps of faith. Cane wasn't confident enough to take it to Ormond, but he was willing to get a warrant, if (it was a big if) they could get one signed tonight. Tomorrow was Saturday, and their time was running out.

Failing that, Kelly was prepared to walk into the Penrith and Lakes and confront the sister of the ward directly. They had an address, but no-one was home.

The address, on the Scaws Estate, was an ex-council property, and a database search confirmed that it had cheap grey carpet laid in the correct timeframe for their fibres.

The profile of The Teacher had been blown wide open.

The Coniston anomaly also bothered Kelly and she hadn't been able to give anyone – least of all Cane – an explanation for it.

Until she'd phoned the hospital.

A conference was organised for the weekend. It was for medical professionals learning new modules on palliative care. But that wasn't the point. The conference was being held at a sprawling five star hotel near Coniston, and their new suspect was on the guest list.

Chapter 54

Nikki shivered.

She lay on a concrete floor, staring up at the ceiling. The inside of the roof was covered in rusted metal railings and structural beams. The ceiling itself was flat and, in one corner, water ran down the wall. The source of the water was a small crack, and this is how Nikki knew if it was day or night. She could no longer see daylight, and so she knew it was evening. She'd had nothing to eat or drink, her mouth tasted of metal, and her tongue was swollen. She knew that she was in some kind of out-building, like a garage, and it was boiling hot. Her head pounded, and she'd begun to drift in and out of consciousness. She thought that she might have been drugged.

Anger and rage had given way to fear and panic, and now, her only thoughts were of her daughters.

Her biggest fear was that no-one would ever know where she was.

She'd got in the car willingly. Why wouldn't she? The floor was cool, but she didn't mind. She rocked back and forth, trying to make the raging thirst lessen in her thumping head.

She'd never wished so much to see Kelly Porter's face.

She'd tried shouting and banging, but one of her legs was attached to a wall by a series of plastic straps, which tightened when pulled. Her ankle pulsed with pain and the strap had bitten deep into her leg. Occasionally, she examined it for signs of infection: it was scabby, but there was no pus, just cuts. She'd stopped shouting hours ago as her throat and lips dried up, and so now, simply swallowing was an effort.

She'd tried to talk to her captor initially, for the sake of reason and compassion, but she soon realised that any attempt to converse earned her a punch to the side of her head. She'd persevered at first, but now she remained quiet. It was perfectly obvious that no-one could hear her from the outside. And she was scared.

She'd always thought herself tough. Her and her friends strutted round the clubs and bars of Penrith in an impenetrable pack, as a warning to anyone brave enough to ask them to make a space at the bar, or wait their turn in the lavatory.

This was different: she wasn't in control.

Her captor only spoke to give orders: 'hands up,' 'sit down,' 'shut up,' for example.

After two separate blows to the temple with a fist the size of a cabbage, Nikki did exactly as she was told.

She wondered if Kelly would even bother looking for her. Surely they'd find her, if Kelly was all that she was cracked up to be. She must know where she was. She must.

But how could she if Nikki didn't know herself?

Nikki tried to work out the logic of what was happening to her over and over, simply because it didn't make sense. She went from thinking that it was all a mistake, to considering the possibility that it was planned. Each time she returned to the conclusion that it was all a mistake, but she knew that communication was no longer an option: the fist hurt too much. Dried blood clung to the skin where it had split at the side of her head. The worst part was the thinking. Nikki rarely had time to think, and now it hurt her head, and she realised why she never did it. The faces of her children came and went, keeping her warm and fairly lucid. She thought of the programmes she watched on crime and investigation: she'd enjoyed watching sadistic killers evading the police on the special casefiles every week – actually *enjoyed* it. Now it repulsed her, and she didn't think she could ever watch another programme about a woman being taken, held and... She couldn't think beyond her current state.

She stared at the crack in the ceiling. The sun was shining, and she wondered if the children were playing outside. Or if her disappearance had been on the news. She *felt* their tears. They'd be terrified. She'd never left them for this long.

She looked around her, and tried to distract herself with details: the oil stain, the smell of petrol, the cement, and the tools. But this garage wasn't used for a car – well not at the moment anyway.

Her eyes settled on a sheet of newspaper on the floor, which hadn't moved since she'd been in here. She'd read it a thousand times, for something to do. She'd memorised the articles on it, and she could recite them without looking. She knew the names of the reporters, the names and emails of the editors, and the people in the three photographs who'd become her companions.

The three women were dead, of course, all killed by The Teacher. Moira Tate looked well off, and in control. Nikki imagined her as a mother, all proper and bossy. Then thoughts of her own mother made her eyes close tightly, tears stinging behind them. She forced herself back into the imaginary world of the people in the newspaper. She wondered what Moira sounded like when she spoke.

Brandy Carter looked like a chav. She was someone who Wendy Porter would not have had for a playdate with her girls. Nikki managed a smile, and blood seeped out of a cracked lip.

Fourteen-year-old Aileen Bickerstaff was different. The same age as her own daughter, Charlie. Nikki whispered to her gently, like a loving mother. To take the pain away, Nikki examined all the objects in the garage one by one, imagining how each might help her. She looked for things to throw, things to cut and things to make noise. But each time she searched, she realised that they were all out of her reach.

She remembered Kelly saying that the vast majority of people who were abducted were taken by someone they knew. So it was only a matter of time before she was found. Wasn't it? She remembered a lot of what Kelly said, now, in here.

The garage lock clanked against metal, and Nikki held her breath. The door was wrenched open and slammed shut again.

It wasn't anyone coming to rescue her.

It was her captor, walking towards her, holding something. It was only a foot away when Nikki realised that the item was a syringe. She panicked and struggled, and received a blow to her jaw for her efforts.

As the needle sank in, she wondered if she'd ever see her family again.

Chapter 55

The Dippen Wood Estate was a working farm as well as a hotel, conference and banqueting provider, and an exclusive leisure complex for private members. Currently, there were one hundred and seventy-nine paying residents on site, plus thirty-two gym members either in the pool, spa or the gym itself. Twenty-three members of staff were on duty.

Cane had insisted on coming. Kelly had assumed that he'd want to get home, but he'd been sucked into the urgency that had gripped Eden House and he was going nowhere. Phillips, Hide and Shawcross were tasked with searching the Scaws Estate house, and Kate Umshaw accompanied Kelly. They'd been given three squad cars by Ormond.

There was an after-dinner lecture scheduled for eight-forty-five p.m. and their suspect was on the list. They'd checked ahead and all seventeen members from the Penrith NHS Trust had checked in to their rooms. Kelly knew that the chances of the Scaws Estate address holding her sister, and the Dippen Wood harbouring The Teacher was a notion borne of pure romantic zeal that would make Wordsworth blush. But it was a shot.

The roads had been quieter as the Lakes tourists retired to their apartments for the night after a glorious day on the fells or in the trinket shops of Windermere. They'd reached the hotel in under an hour. Phillips kept them updated by radio.

CCTV footage of Nikki leaving the hospital at midday on Thursday afternoon had been pulled and examined. It proved she was there but, beyond that, the trail went dead. Kelly had no idea why Nikki would be at the hospital until her mother confirmed that she was collecting a prescription for her. A photograph had been prepared from the footage and released to the press, along with the old photograph of Brian Leith.

They slowed their cars, and parked at the edge of the main car park. Kelly instructed the uniforms to wait for instructions. She wanted to make sure that the lecture had commenced before they entered the building. She and Cane walked to the main entrance, and DS Umshaw waited in the car. They approached the main desk, which wasn't at all busy, and looked around. A few people sat at the bar, ordering late post dinner drinks, and the restaurant was busy. They were expected, and shown in to an office behind the counter. The night manager awaited them and was ready to show them to wherever they needed to go. She'd already prepared the details requested by the officers as they made their way to the hotel: the member of the conference, given room number 247, had checked in and had ordered room service at just gone eight p.m.

The manager confirmed that she could take the two detectives to the light and effects landing, above the auditorium to get a closer look at those in attendance.

'It's quite normal to hold lectures this late. They'll all pile into the bar afterwards, and we'll struggle to turf them out by early morning. NHS staff are the worst. Excuse me.'

The manager thought she was being helpful with her extra offerings of information. Kelly was grateful. They were led behind reception, to a staff staircase, emerging above the two halls used for conferences. They could hear the speaker.

'Are you sure we can't be seen up here?' Kelly asked.

'Positive. Look, the lights are pointed towards the front of the stage and to the audience.' Kelly and Cane followed her finger and were satisfied that they could search the attendees without being spotted.

Their suspect was not in the lecture.

'Take us to the room.'

The manager nodded and Kelly informed DS Umshaw to organise the uniforms; she wanted both main entrances covered, as well as the gym, spa and orangerie. She didn't need to remind them of their need for subtlety. Two officers, armed with tasers, were to be escorted to the room.

The gloves were off. Kelly didn't need a photograph, she'd never ever forget the face. Her teeth clenched unwittingly, as she walked beside Cane for the short journey downstairs to the second floor.

They stopped outside room 247.

Kelly indicated to the manager to return to reception, after handing her the master key. A uniform banged on the door. There was no answer. He tried again.

Kelly inserted the key card and opened the door. The two uniforms went inside ahead of her, and Cane followed behind. The room was empty.

Not just of a body or a resident; it was completely empty. There was no luggage, no toiletries, no personal items; no indication that anyone had checked into the room. Kelly strode to the door and checked the number. They had the correct room.

Her shoulders slumped.

'I'll go back to the conference organiser,' Kelly said. 'I'm going to speak to them, to see if our guest actually ever turned up in person or checked in somehow remotely,' she said. Kelly contemplated the embarrassing possibility that their suspect was never at the Dippen Wood hotel complex at all, but had somehow engineered the whole thing.

'Let's check the site car parks for the blue Touran. Does the hotel have CCTV?' She looked at the officers, who looked at one another. One took the initiative and went to reception to find the manager.

Kelly called Phillips. No-one had showed up at the residence either and they definitely had not been on shift at the hospital.

Kelly spotted a female toilet and left Cane to coordinate officers. She wanted to punch something.

Chapter 56

In Penrith, officers entered the address on the Scaws Estate. An officer, who'd attended the Less Destructive Entry course, tried to limit the damage breaking in through the front door. They were unsuccessful.

The house had been bought back in 2012. It looked ordinary from the outside. It was in a rough area of Penrith, but it was kept well. It was an ex-council property. The exterior, from what they could make out in the dark, was non-descript, but tidy.

Once secured by uniformed officers, and confirmation was received that it was indeed unoccupied by the resident, it was indicated to the detectives that it was safe for them to enter. They suited and booted, and checked their equipment. Forensic officers entered first. A photographer prepared his lenses and positioned two cameras in a crisscross over his chest. Phillips, Shawcross and Hide accompanied them.

The entrance hall was plain. The carpet was well-worn (not grey), and it led into a kitchen on the right and a lounge on the left. They spread out. Phillips opened drawers and looked for handwriting, diaries, books, and anything out of place. In the lounge, a huge tapestry hung on one wall, but this was the only nod to taste; everything else was incredibly bland. They were looking for grey fibres, as well as bed sheets, weapons and stains.

They'd been told to seize any trainers, shoes, items possibly containing DNA (toothbrushes, discarded tissues, anything that might have been in the owner's mouth or on their person), and fingerprints. They were also looking for signs of sexual deviance, such as porn, or books on sadism. As well as poetry.

In the kitchen, a beautiful set of prints was pulled from a wine glass, and in the sitting room, another set was taken off the TV remote.

Rob went upstairs and found two forensic specialists kneeling. They were picking up fibres from a carpet with tweezers. The carpet was grey. It was also well worn and covered in stains that were being treated for blood proteins and examined under ultra violet light.

In the bedrooms, sheets were taken and beds looked under, but everything seemed normal so far. The accepted theory from their boss was that the murders took place at a location where the killer had plenty of time, and felt comfortable. But, so far, it didn't look as though this was it. Inside a wardrobe, laid neatly in pairs, were several pairs of trainers. The shoes, like the clothing, were masculine, and Rob looked for a size. They were all size seven, and three pairs were Nikes. He turned them over, one by one, and stopped at the third pair. There, on the tread, in exactly the same place committed to Rob's memory from the print, was a small stone lodged into a crack.

There was plenty more to gather, bag and tag, and items were placed carefully into containers or bags. The house was silent as officers wrote notes on labels and gathered detritus from every corner of every room. Rob showed the trainers to Phillips and they knew they were in the right place. It regrouped their resolve and they continued searching. Every possible piece of physical evidence needed to be gathered and one of those pieces that may seem insignificant now could well turn into that one piece of critical evidence that could swing a jury.

'Where's the entrance to the garage?' Rob asked Emma. 'Have you seen it?' he asked again. She shook her head. They went to find Phillips and show him the plans of the property. The building plans of the council properties, obtained from the council archive, showed that the garages were attached from the inside. Over the years, it could have easily been blocked up. But Rob wanted to be sure. Phillips helped them search around. The plans clearly showed a door linking the garage to the house, and it was situated in the lounge. They went in and stared at the wall. But instead of a door, hung a huge great tapestry. The same one they'd merely glanced at when they first came in the room.

It looked old and very expensive. 'The door should be here.'

They studied the artwork and took in the skill and the labour that must have gone in to producing such a thing. It reminded Emma of Hampton Court and a school trip she'd been on. Those tapestries were priceless and she wondered how a nurse on an NHS salary could afford such a thing. If it was genuine.

It captivated them, and they stared at it. It wasn't particularly beautiful, but it was beguiling. There were worn patches, here and there, and as they got closer, they could smell the age in its fibres. The main content of the image was branches and leaves of all colours and sizes, and they were fringed with gold. The odd bird could be spotted resting among the foliage. But the emphasis of the tapestry was the scene in the middle. An animal – it could have been a goat or a pony – was being attacked by four wolf-like creatures with sharp teeth and evil grins. They were fantastical creatures, none of which were real. But it was unsettling nonetheless. There was no blood, no gore, and no evidence of pain or anguish. The animal in the middle had simply given up and accepted its fate.

'I think we're done,' a voice startled them. It was one of the forensic officers.

'No, we're not. We need to get into the garage,' Phillips said. 'Help us with this will you?' Rob and Emma took one end of the tapestry and Phillips took the other. It was thick and very heavy, but they managed to pull it away from the wall.

Behind it, hidden all along, was a door.

Chapter 57

Kelly leant over the sink and stared into the mirror. They'd come such a long way. Literally. All of the pieces fitted: lack of semen, history of child offending, professional knowledge, access to all the victims, and the employment history. The only thing they were waiting for was a handwriting sample from HR back in Penrith, and a DNA sample. But first, they had to find their suspect. Kelly kicked the sink stand.

'Fuck, fuck, fuck,' she said. She stood up and walked to a cubicle. It was Friday night, she wanted to sit by the fire and eat takeaway with Johnny, and have him take her to bed, and not have to get up at some godforsaken hour in the morning to face the same old shit.

The ladies' toilet was empty and Kelly was thankful. She had to gather her thoughts and get back to Cane. She'd screwed up but not entirely: it was his idea to tag along all this way. The absence of their suspect only heightened the likelihood that they were hiding something. She'd spoken to Phillips and there was no sign of them at home either. They hadn't called in sick or given any excuse or valid reason to miss the conference, but it was clear that they had no intention of attending.

The restroom was peaceful and Kelly sat on the closed toilet lid in her cubicle for a long time. They were so close.

She heard the sound of somebody coming in and decided to make a move. She couldn't sit moping here all night. Besides, Cane was waiting for her. She left the cubicle and went to wash her hands. Somebody was pissing, and she checked herself in the mirror. She walked to the basket of immaculately pressed towels and took one. She dried her hands, glancing briefly over her shoulder at the woman leaving the cubicle.

Kelly fumbled for her phone, but it dropped to the floor.

'Hello, Kelly. You've found me.'

Kelly eyed her. She was just an ordinary woman: a little frumpy, hair greying, face wrinkling, plain shoes, and non-descript clothes. Kelly couldn't speak. She remembered Rob telling her about Paul Bamber's impressive pull-up record, and the one next to it: the female record was fifteen and belonged to the dowdy woman in front of her.

'Haven't you got anything to say to me?' said Nurse Amy Richmond, formerly Amy Gardener, and God knows what else.

Kelly pulled her badge. 'I'm arresting you under suspicion of mur—'

Amy laughed. 'Really? But then you'll never know where your sister is, will you?'

Cold assaulted Kelly's body, as she realised the truth, and her dilemma.

'We all have choices, Kelly. How much do you love her? Not much by what I've seen, and I don't blame you! It's such a pointless emotion, love. She whines a lot, doesn't she? That was the final straw for me, trying to tell me how to do my job.'

The whole time Amy had been talking, she hadn't blinked once. Kelly's skin felt cold, and her arm hair stood up. She wanted to say so much; she'd imagined this moment so many times, but now nothing came out of her mouth. Looking at the woman, it was incomprehensible that she could have done those things.

'Why?' she whispered. 'Why?' Kelly heard herself hiss: she couldn't help it.

'Shut up!' Amy spat.

Kelly stood back. Amy's eyes were murderous and Kelly realised that she'd just witnessed the other side to Nurse Richmond: the side that answered her very simple question. Amy's teeth were stained. She folded her arms across her ample chest, and spread her legs. She wore a grey sweat suit, suited to the gym. Her eyes never left Kelly, and she still hadn't blinked. Now she looked capable of killing. For the first time in what seemed like half an hour – but was probably more like ten seconds – Kelly began to think. The initial paralysis that had consumed her on coming face to face with Amy Richmond was dissipating, and she began to formulate a plan. She gathered her anger under control, and assessed her situation. If she stalled Amy Richmond for a while, she might get some answers, maybe even a confession. But, in that time, her sister might be dying. On the other hand, she could call the nurse's bluff and hope that Nikki was unharmed and easy to find. Amy had said that she might 'find her'. She had to hold on to that.

'You're thinking about it, aren't you? We're so similar, you and I, Kelly. You can't stand freeloaders either can you? People who don't deserve to waste our time? Have I given you an entertaining couple of weeks? The Teacher! How unimaginative.'

Kelly couldn't believe what she was hearing, and her anger erupted again.

'I have nothing in common with you. You're a fucking murderer! A monster. You tortured those women, how could you?'

Amy laughed. 'Oh don't deny it, you've loved every minute of piecing together my puzzle. I watched you get more and more excited. I really like your mother, she's a good person, and you should spend more time with her.' Nurse Amy was back and Kelly felt vomit rise from her stomach.

She had to keep her emotions under control. She *had* to stay ahead of this lunatic, who was talking like they were old friends.

Kelly thought again of the board in the gym, when Rob had gone to check out Paul Bamber. Next to his name, he'd told her that the female champion was also named. Kelly had barely listened at the time, she'd been busy taking notes from a file. Rob had told her as an aside, because they had to face it: it was an incredible achievement: Amy Richmond could do fifteen pull ups, and blasted anyone else's efforts out of the park. Kelly had thought her cumbersome and overweight, under her ample uniform, but now she realised that the bulk was solid muscle. She remembered bumping in to her in the corridor and rubbing her arm afterwards; Amy hadn't moved an inch.

She remembered the sweet tea, made so lovingly, and marvelled at how those same hands could have tortured, mutilated and murdered four women; more.

'Why?' Kelly asked again, stalling. Someone was bound to come in soon, and Kelly might be able to either raise the alarm or apprehend the suspect herself. Kelly couldn't do fifteen pull-ups but she had a captive sister and a dying mother, and that would move mountains.

'Why not?' replied Amy.

'Because of the suffering! The harm, you're a woman!' Kelly's words were coming too fast for her mouth, and she hurtled them out like machine gun fire. She wished she had a gun right now; Amy Richmond would be dead.

'A woman? So what?'

Kelly looked at the nurse. For the first time since they'd met, face to face, something struck her that she hadn't thought of before. Amy Richmond, in her grey clothes, short hair, regular round face and chubby cheeks, was androgynous. It hadn't mattered what gender their killer was: and it didn't matter now. The same things that led men to maim and kill had strangled and kidnapped this child too, a long time ago. The hate. The miswired brain. She wasn't a man or a woman, she was a psychopath.

'There are police all over the hotel. You don't stand a chance.'

'I do if you help me. And don't flatter me, you're on your own.'

Kelly's heart sank, but she'd expected it.

'Did you kill your mother?' Kelly asked.

'Yes. Why? I did the neighbourhood a favour.'

Kelly's guts turned over.

'Albert Ferguson?'

Amy knew that Kelly couldn't be recording their conversation because her phone was on the floor, and she'd been caught by surprise after a long, satisfying urination.

'He was a paedophile.' She could have been discussing road sweeping.

'Did he abuse you, Amy?'

The cackle surprised Kelly, and she couldn't figure out what was so funny.

'You've been profiling me, haven't you? Have you been watching CSI, Kelly? Albert Ferguson was a pervert. But he was rich. He kept eighty grand stuffed under his filthy mattress. What would you have done?'

Kelly didn't know what to say. She had interviewed few true psychos. Plenty of thugs – in fact lacking a brain to fuck up – who could kill her with a punch, but few authentic, undisputed maniacs.

She was way out of her depth.

'Why the poetry?'

'I'm bored now, it's time to leave, come on.'

Kelly looked down, and ran her hands through her hair. She bent down to get her phone, but Amy stepped forward and kicked it with such ferocity that it flew against the wall and broke into two pieces. Kelly held her breath. She had to keep telling herself that Nurse Amy, who'd nursed her mother, made sweet tea, and qualified as a nurse, was, in fact, a brutal serial killer.

Kelly nodded quickly. She had no choice.

'Good, now you've made the right choice, let's go. My car is in a car park below this window,' Amy said.

Kelly stood rooted to the spot. She hadn't thought of how they would leave the building, she'd just assumed that they'd leave out of the toilet entrance and straight into the waiting custody of her uniforms.

Amy put her hands in a cup for Kelly, offering her a bunk up, as if they were playing together in a park. Kelly stared at her, repulsed by the thought of touching her, even through the bottom of her shoe.

'No thanks,' she said, and pushed a fancy upholstered stool underneath the window. It wasn't difficult to reach the window and open it. Kelly got through easily and jumped down to the path below, but Amy took a while to manoeuvre her broad shoulders through the gap. Only now was Kelly a witness to the woman's incredible strength. Kelly thought about running to raise the alarm but then she thought of Nikki. She had no choice, and she had no phone.

'We're partners now,' Amy said, as she jumped down from the window. The woman's frame and unlikely athleticism was reminiscent of a silverback gorilla horsing around with its young. Amy smiled and Kelly, once again, felt utter abhorrence.

They were round the back of the hotel complex and there was just enough light to make out a blue Touran, which was parked next to what looked like an estate car. They were the only two cars in the small car park. But Amy didn't get into the blue Touran. Instead she got into the other car, and Kelly's heart sunk again.

Amy wasn't stupid.

Kelly felt as though she were stuck in treacle, with options running out fast. She was about to go rogue with a brutal sadist – who was also highly likely to be psychotic – and she had no way of telling anyone.

She hoped she'd made the right decision.

Chapter 58

Cane was irritated, and he pondered what they could've missed. DS Umshaw watched him and wished that DI Porter would get back; Cane made her jumpy. She also felt protective towards her boss and she sensed that Cane blamed her for the nurse not being here. No-one could believe the theory at first – or had it been that they daren't believe? The repulsion of contemplating that it could be a woman was too much. But, more than any other suspect, DI Porter had connected the ifs, wheres, whys and leads like none of the others. Even the signature on her employment contract bore resemblance to the inscribed lines of poetry left with the victims.

DI Porter had ascertained that the description of the woman who'd picked up the nurse's ID was a close match to their suspect, and so they had to remain hopeful that the suspect was here; or had been here and left. Umshaw refused to believe that Porter had made a mistake. She looked at her watch: it was gone ten o'clock.

The manager approached them and passed on a message that the Touran they'd been looking for had been located. Cane and Umshaw exchanged looks and they looked up and down the corridors again.

'Where did she say she was going?'

'To the lav, Guv.'

'Go and get her, will you? We need to get this car compounded.'

Kate went in the direction that Kelly had gone and entered the ladies' toilet.

'Boss?' she called. None of the cubicles were in use, but she did notice that it was chilly, then she saw the open window. Instinct told her to peek out of the window and outside, she saw several uniforms standing around the blue Touran. It was the only vehicle outside the window. As she went to leave the room, she spotted something under one of the sinks and bent down to look: it was a mobile phone without its back. She recognised it as police issue and her gut turned over. She looked around for the missing back and saw it under beside the waste bin. It fitted. She turned on the phone and knew straight away who it belonged to. Her boss used the same screensaver that she'd used for over six months now: it was a winter shot of Wastwater. One might think it was taken in Switzerland or Norway, so striking was the image. Kelly Porter had shown everyone in the office.

Umshaw went to find Cane.

'Sir,' she said. Cane nodded. She handed him the phone.

'It's DI Porter's. It was in the restroom. She's gone.'

He looked nonplussed.

'Follow me,' instructed Umshaw. He did so. She took him into the restroom and showed him the view outside the window.

He turned back to the DS, who spoke. 'I'd bet my life, sir, she's gone with her because of her sister, and in a different car.'

Cane didn't know the procedure for the abduction of a police officer, because he'd never witnessed it. The rule book was about to be re-written.

'Get the manager back: we need to see the CCTV of the driveway. If you're right, they won't still be here.'

Umshaw ran back to reception and tasked the manager. It didn't take long for them to find the image of the Mazda Estate leaving the hotel complex with two women in the front: one thick set and short haired (driving), and one dark haired and sat unusually forward.

'Clever girl,' said Umshaw under her breath.

Cane covered his eyes with his fingers and rubbed them. This was a disaster. He bit his knuckle. Kelly Porter was in the most dangerous situation of her life, and he was the one who was ultimately responsible. The plate number was run through the ANPR, and the vehicle had been rented from a firm in Ambleside three days ago. All units were put on standby. It wouldn't take long to find them: Amy Richmond's time was running out.

Chapter 59

'Find some step ladders,' Phillips said.

'They'll be in the garage, surely,' replied the forensic officer. Rob put his head on the heavy tapestry. It smelled damp and musty, and it made Rob recoil.

'Let's go in from the outside,' said Emma. They let the tapestry fall. They'd tried the door but it was, unsurprisingly, locked. The squad cars were still in attendance. They never left a scene until it was fully processed, especially when the owner could turn up at any minute. And particularly when the owner was a fucking nutcase.

Outside, the cool air enabled them to catch their breath from the stale air of the interior. They dripped in sweat under their forensic overalls and they chugged water from bottles they'd brought along. They checked their options: they had cutting equipment, and three strapping police officers with a combined force of probably, a third of a ton. They'd get into the garage one way or another. The garage was padlocked several times. Phillips checked the area and he noticed a single tyre print on a small patch of grass, perhaps four metres away from the front of the garage. He ordered a cast to be made.

The uniformed officers heaved, pushed, and swore frequently. They were frequently sent on courses about how to respect someone's property on entering, and they all thought it was bullshit. If a crim refused them entry, or they were responsible for crimes to make a fully-grown adult heave, then they deserved to get their doors smashed in. The lawyers disagreed, and criminals sued the police from the comfort of their cells. This was different. It would come out of Penrith Serious Crime Unit's budget, and Phillips gave them the go ahead. They needed to see inside the garage. Three padlocks had already been smashed, and crow bars were being used to apply incredible force to the sides of the metal door.

Finally, it cracked open and hung lopsided, waiting for their next move. The three uniformed officers stepped aside. One held out his hand. They hadn't come this far for the detectives to go charging into danger. The same rules applied. They would secure the garage first. An officer urged them to step back, and he did so, though, they were desperate to see what was inside.

'Police. Is anyone in there?' An officer flicked on a powerful torch and the three of them wriggled under the damaged door. Inside the garage, the men looked quickly in all directions and the torch illuminated every corner. They weren't interested in detail, their minds were solely focused on if there was a human present, or not.

There wasn't.

The officers forced the door from the inside, and the detectives could then come forward. They walked quickly to the garage and took in the scene. At first glance, it looked like any other garage. There were racks and cabinets along one wall, the floor was stained with oil, cobwebs clogged dark corners, and rags were tossed here and there.

Then they saw the chains.

They were bolted to a wall and on the end of each of them were bundles of cable ties. A loud cracking shocked them and they spun round to witness the inner door being trashed. Amy Richmond's tapestry was about to be ruined whether it was an original or not; Emma couldn't care less. It was dragged from its mount and fell into a heap. A ripping sound could be heard, as the strain of being moved caused a huge tear to open up down the middle of the art work. No-one remarked.

'We need swabs here.'

A light switch was located, and the garage was illuminated. Near the shackles, a dirty blanket was crumpled on the floor. As they looked closer, what appeared to be left over biscuit pieces were stuck to it. A dark stain tinged one of the corners, and the whole thing was bagged. A newspaper laid discarded next to the blanket. Rob looked at it; it was an article about the first three victims.

On a shelf, a tray was laid out messily, as if it had been rifled through in haste. Various cutting tools were noted: a Stanley knife, a few kitchen knives, scissors, bits of glass, and what looked like a scalpel. Next to the tray was a box. With a gloved hand, Rob opened it.

Inside was an array of syringes and bottles of clear liquid marked 'Largactil'. Elsewhere, rolls of plastic sheeting were found, as well as plastic cable ties. Several plastic boxes, like the ones used for children's toys, were stacked neatly in a corner. When they were opened, they contained mainly books, and some magazines. Phillips suggested they look through the titles there, in the garage, rather than taking the whole lot. It would take time, but he wanted to be thorough for DI Porter.

They took a box each.

Rob's contained a whole load of envelopes, and when he looked inside, most of the envelopes contained photographs. There were thousands of them. Some were discoloured and clearly old, but others were more recent. All of them were of landscapes, and, from what Rob could see, they were scenes in the Lake District. Occasionally, he came across one with shapes scribbled on it. He held one up to the light and squinted. Behind the scribble, barely recognisable, was a human form. Every time he came across one with a scribble, he held it up and found the same. The owner of the collection didn't like people much. Rob wondered who had first hired Nurse Richmond, and why no-one spotted that she was off-the-charts weird. He'd never met her, but Kelly had. But, then, she hadn't spotted it either. Rob was convinced that his psycho-radar was excellent, but it had never been put to the test. He wondered what Amy was like in person. Perhaps they'd caught her already. He hadn't heard from Kelly for hours, so that meant she was busy. Emma called him.

In her box, referenced, filed, titled and annotated, were hundreds, if not thousands, of poems. They glanced over them and looked at the handwriting.

That's when they knew for sure.

Chapter 60

'How long do you reckon she's got, Kelly?' Amy asked.

They were driving towards Penrith, and Kelly's eyes darted about, trying to get eye contact with a fellow motorist who might recognise the panicked face of a hostage. Fat chance. No-one looked at her. Everybody was engrossed in their own worlds, checking phones, reading maps or sleeping. No-one stared idly out of the window, waiting for the opportunity to report a woman in distress. No-one would care anyway. These days, someone frantically begging for help – even with just their eyes – would be taken as perhaps a trap. Everybody was full of distrust. And so well they might be, thought Kelly.

'What?' Kelly asked.

The question took her by surprise. All the way from Coniston, Amy had wanted to chat like old friends. Her level of delusion was terrifying.

'Your mum. I reckon four weeks. I'm good at this. I just know. Come on, what do you think?' Amy pushed on.

'Are you out of your mind?' asked Kelly.

Amy looked surprised. 'No. Are you?' she asked.

It was a serious question, and Kelly couldn't think of anything to say. She was angry. Angry because her mother was dying, angry that monsters like this were free on the streets, but mostly angry that she hadn't seen it coming. She noticed that her nails were biting into the palms of her hands and she relaxed them a little. Once she did so, she was able to think more clearly, and she realised that she had to put her personal feelings aside and use this as her opportunity to get inside the head of her killer. Everything could be used at trial and, even though she wasn't recording, the witness statement of an officer of the law who'd been kidnapped would be almost as good a testimony. If she made it that far.

If she survived.

For the first time, Kelly imagined herself tied up and butchered by this piece of shit wanting to be her friend. She'd seen, first-hand, what Nurse Richmond was capable of. She asked herself if she was scared and she couldn't answer.

'Why the sex thing?' Kelly asked.

Amy's hands tightened on the wheel.

'Don't do that,' Amy said.

'What? I'm simply asking you a very straightforward question. I want to know. It's the reason we all thought you a man,' said Kelly. 'If you're allowed to ask me personal questions, then I can too.'

Amy relaxed again and smiled.

'I know, that was funny. The Teacher. Typical though. It just shows how prejudiced you lot really are. Maybe I should have just gone on letting you think that.'

'Oh, but you wouldn't have done that, Amy. You wanted the attention for yourself didn't you?' Kelly pushed.

Amy frowned again.

'So, why the sex stuff? Do you get a kick out of it? Are you batting for the other side?' Kelly pressed on. Her anger had turned to recklessness, but if she got a rise out of Amy, it would be worth it.

'I didn't do that, I don't want to talk about that,' Amy said. Her voice had changed and she'd stopped concentrating on the road. Kelly began to realise her mistake, but it was too late.

'They did that to themselves. They liked it, they told me,' Amy continued. She swerved dangerously and someone registered their rage with their horn. The noise startled Amy and she straightened up. Kelly's heart pounded in her chest. She couldn't believe what she'd just heard. Her recklessness turned to repulsion, then curiosity. She wondered if they'd found her phone yet, and worked out why she'd gone AWOL. There was no way of knowing. She needed to continue stalling Amy.

'What else did they tell you? Apart from they liked it?' Kelly asked. Her throat constricted over the words and she felt bile rise in her throat. She felt as though she were disgracing the dead, speaking of them like this, but she forced the thoughts aside.

Chatty Amy was back. And her driving calmed.

'Oh, we talked a lot. They were sorry,' Amy said.

'Sorry for what?' asked Kelly. She was trying not to punch the woman in the face. She wanted to do a lot more, but then she'd never find Nikki.

Nikki.

'Don't you know anything, Kelly? Why am I surrounded by idiots?' Amy blasted. Another side to the nurse emerged and, so far, Kelly had counted four or five different versions of Amy. Right now, in the car, going over eighty miles per hour, she realised that she needed calm Amy back. Her moods were so volatile that Kelly couldn't be sure what was coming next.

'Well, I do think I've worked it out, but I was just checking. By the way, I like the poetry,' Kelly said. Her teeth clenched and she looked away. *Come on*, she thought, *someone look at the fucking car*. Ordinarily, several perverted lorry drivers would have ogled her by now, but today they weren't interested.

'I'm a poet,' Amy gushed, the anger gone once more.

'Really?' Kelly feigned interest. 'What's it about? No don't tell me, heaven and hell?'

'Nope. Try again.'

Kelly was playing guessing games with a killer who liked to torture, but she couldn't dwell on the implications of that right now. Amy was like a child. Or, at least, this Amy was like a child: loving the attention and the game.

'The Lake District?' Kelly guessed again.

'Nope.' They neared Penrith.

'Women who deserve to be punished. A wild stab in the dark there.' Kelly tried to laugh but nothing came out of her throat.

'Bingo! You're good. We get along great, don't we?' Amy beamed.

Emotion, Kelly observed. That was the last thing she expected.

The rest of the drive went along in a similar vein. Kelly learned that Amy had never done anything bad in her entire life. She'd gotten revenge, she'd taken what was hers, she'd taught people lessons, and she'd done people favours. But she'd never made a mistake, and she'd never done anything wrong. Kelly listened. The child was back until, without notice, killer Amy capriciously reappeared.

'I used to think the Bible was poetic, but I changed my mind. They're all liars and cowards.' Amy's voice turned callous and hostile.

Kelly preferred Amy the child, who was predictable and benign. Maybe Amy had never grown up, maybe that's what psychopathy was: a childlike, immature state that one was stuck in before learning to become an adult. It was another theory. She wondered what Margaret Steiner would say when she found out that they'd all been wrong. The whole time.

'Did you like working in Yorkshire?'

Amy didn't answer.

Kelly wondered where they were. She recognised the estate, but they were certainly nowhere near the house that Rob and Emma should have finished searching by now. She wondered if they'd found the room where Amy played out her fantasies in her diseased brain.

But then Amy pressed a button and a garage door began to open.

Oh shit. She had two houses.

Kelly was torn. One part of her felt terror because no-one knew where she was. The other part of her felt hope that she might see her sister alive. She imagined having to tell her mother that her daughter was dead, but she pushed the thought away.

They reversed in, and Amy continued to chat away merrily. Kelly expected to be asked if she'd like a cup of tea. The garage door closed and the light outside faded, along with Kelly's hopes of being found. Amy must have a plan, and it was her job to work out what it was so that she could stop it.

The engine was turned off, and Amy jumped out of the car. Kelly looked around the garage for something with which to knock out her captor. She did some quick figuring in her head and decided against it; she still didn't know where Nikki was.

'Let's have some tea,' said Amy, and Kelly followed her into the house, as the garage door shut behind them.

Chapter 61

The mood at Eden House was grim.

Cane spoke to Super Ormond on the phone in Kelly's office. The team waited for instructions from him. Their most senior officer was DS Kate Umshaw and she stood in front of the white board, staring at it.

'There's another address we've missed.'

The ball game had just flipped onto its head. Time was against them as they scoured notes, logs and entries for a second address. A sense of unease spread across the room and Kelly's absence was palpable. Amy Richmond had no registered second address, and she and Kelly had vanished. The ANPR showed the hired Mazda at two points between Coniston and Penrith: they were here, somewhere.

Downstairs, an impatient, scruffy looking guy was causing a fuss and asking questions about Kelly Porter, and the desk staff were having trouble getting rid of him. Rob accompanied DS Umshaw down to check it out. He was refusing to leave and he was also claiming that he'd seen Amy Richmond: the nurse wanted by the police.

'Can I help?' Umshaw asked. The man was being held back by two uniforms.

'Where's Kelly?'

'Who are you? Look, sir, we really haven't got time for this. I'm going to have to have you escorted off the premises,' she said. If the guy had information, he better tell them now.

'I'm her boyfriend,' the man said.

The detectives froze. DI Porter never spoke of her personal life, not that she was obliged to divulge it. But the guy might be lying. Kelly had been on TV and any number of weirdos could now come out of the woodwork claiming to know her.

'My name is Johnny Frietze, Patterdale Mountain Rescue. I was the one who found Aileen Bickerstaff's body. Is it true that The Teacher is a woman? A nurse at the hospital?'

Neither detective answered; he could be a journo.

'I can't divulge that information,' Umshaw said finally, weighing him up. 'Check with the file,' she instructed Rob.

'Look,' Johnny said, handing the detective his mobile phone. 'I went up Hart Crag yesterday. I needed to clear my head, and Aileen…' he trailed off. 'I know that Kelly was asking for anyone to give information – anything at all – about seeing anything unusual. I thought I'd go up there, you never know when something unusual will pop up.'

'If you wait here, I'll get someone to take a statement from you,' Kate Umshaw said calmly, and handed his phone back.

'Wait!' Johnny was desperate.

'Look, she was up there in the exact same spot Aileen was left, and I mean the *exact* spot. I should know. After she left, I found a pen. Here, look for yourself.'

Kate Umshaw looked at the pen and turned it over in her hands. It was quite beautiful, and it was engraved. It read: 'Ode to the West Wind'.

More fucking poetry. They'd all become experts and she knew enough to know that it was another poem by Shelley. She looked over her shoulder at Rob, who nodded: Johnny Frietze checked out. She showed him the pen. Emma Hide had quoted it in her studies of The Prelude. It was about autumn killing everything before a long winter.

'Please tell me that she hasn't got Kelly, like the news is saying?' Johnny asked.

'Can you show us some ID?'

Johnny fumbled in his pockets and pulled out his wallet. He found his driver's licence and showed it to the detectives. DS Umshaw looked at him gravely.

'We didn't say that. What you heard on the TV is conjecture. We're looking for the nurse, and one of our officers is suspected to have become...'

'Right. Bullshit. I've called her phone a hundred times.'

Kate hesitated.

'You're Kate, Right? I can tell. She rates you. I can help.'

Johnny's rage was all in his eyes; his demeanour smacked of passion and something else besides. It was a focus that Kate Umshaw saw in her boss's face several times a day and it softened her towards the scruffy man.

'What are you doing about it?'

'Everything we can.'

Johnny's shoulders sank.

'Has there been a mistake?' he asked.

'No.'

'How...? Kelly wouldn't... she couldn't...' Johnny trailed off.

'We have reason to believe that Amy Richmond has DI Porter's sister.'

Now it made sense. He thought quickly. He'd been trained for being held as a hostage, and the prospect was terrifying. He knew that Kelly was mentally strong enough to cope with what was thrown at her, but he couldn't allow himself to imagine the physical damage that was possible to inflict on a human body. He'd seen it plenty. Images of young women with their breasts sliced off in Rwanda entered his head, uninvited.

'I need to help,' Johnny finally said. He swallowed hard.

'I can't possibly let you do that,' DS Umshaw said.

'Why not? I've known the investigation from the beginning. I've seen what she can do. And I have a secret weapon,' Johnny said.

'What's that?'

'I'm not one of you.'

It wasn't unprecedented. Civilians helped police with their enquiries all the time. But Johnny was no ordinary civilian, as it turned out. He was ex-military.

He was asked to wait, and the two detectives walked away. The next twenty minutes dragged by intolerably for Johnny, who was impatient by nature. In the army, you didn't wait for the enemy to come knocking: you went out to find them. He paced up and down and made the staff nervous. Finally, a woman in plain clothes approached him and asked him to follow her. They went upstairs and Johnny looked around. There were dozens of officers all busy on phones, or discussing things intensely, or tapping away at computers.

'Detective Umshaw has asked me to get you to go through these,' she said. 'It's a pile of names and addresses.' Johnny looked at her blankly.

'We have as many officers as we have available working on this case, Mr Frietze, and this is part of what we do. You could help us by trawling through this lot for the name, Amy Richmond. There's about four hundred pages,' she said.

'I can't do that, what the hell is the point? We should be out there looking!' Johnny said angrily.

'Where exactly?' she asked. Johnny was stumped. 'Surely you know where she lives, she works at the hospital for Christ sake!'

'You're absolutely right, but we've already searched it, and no-one's home,' said the female officer. The horrible realisation began to sink in: Amy Richmond had taken Kelly somewhere else. They could be anywhere. The press and police were crawling all over Cumbria and beyond. They couldn't be out in the open; they'd have been spotted by now. In Johnny's mind, that would be Kelly's best chance: luring Amy into the open.

'We need to know where to look,' said the officer. 'You can help us, as another pair of hands, or you can do nothing.'

Johnny took the pile of papers.

'This is what our DI does, Mr Frietze. This is what will find her. And it will save time. Of course we all want to go out there on the streets and look in every flat and garage, but only this will pin point an address. This is what she would want. That's why she went with Richmond, because she knows we'll find her, but only by being sure. I appreciate your frustration. Let me know if you spot anything, I'll be next door. By the way, my name is Emma.' She held out her hand and Johnny took it. She left the pile of papers.

Johnny looked at the heaps of paper. It was a print out of all rental property in Penrith, collated from Estate Agents, and up to date. There were thousands of names of owners and tenants. Johnny wanted to hit something. He could never work for anybody crunching data. He wanted to hold a gun, plan an attack and carry it out, not sit at a desk, trawling through bits of information that may never add up. He bit his tongue, sat down heavily, spread the sheets in front of him, and began scanning.

Chapter 62

The garage door locked behind her and Kelly hoped they'd been spotted by a nosy neighbour. The street had been quiet. Again, she wondered if anyone had missed her yet. She looked at her watch and it was gone eleven p.m. Surely Cane or Umshaw would have worked it out by now. Kate knew she was going to the ladies. She had absolute faith in her DS. She hoped Cane listened to her and had it all over the news. She had no idea if Ormond would risk the element of surprise, though, just for her. She had to believe that he would. That's all she had. She thought about the missed calls she'd had from Johnny all day, and wished she'd answered them. She wanted to hear his voice. He had such a singular way with words that made her bombproof to the worst psycho loons.

Kelly had been desperate to put the radio on in the car, but Amy said she preferred to listen to her own thoughts. It freaked Kelly out, but she had to admit that Amy's head was probably full of voices. The fact that she'd been brought to a residence they didn't know about worried her. It was a brazen move, and Amy's confidence was astounding: so much so that it was reckless, and that was a good thing for Kelly. It meant that her plan might be just as rash, and thus faulty.

'Why have we come here, Amy? The police will be crawling everywhere looking for you. You could have left the country by now. Why are you still here?' Kelly stalled for as long as possible, because the minute it was realised what had happened, they'd be looking for them. It could take days.

Or they might be too late.

They had enough evidence on Amy to put her away for life, and it was a serious question. Most genuinely committed criminals would be on the run by now. But in the short space of time she'd spent with Amy, Kelly had worked out that her brain worked differently to most of the criminals she knew. Ordinary criminals were simply risk-takers of varying degrees, whereas Amy was completely miswired. Amy had already accepted her fate: she knew it was almost over. She knew that the kidnap of a police officer was the pinnacle of whatever she'd planned; there was nowhere left to go after that. Amy had been working up to this point all her life and Kelly could see the satisfaction on her face. She had to stall her and, so far, the only thing that had derailed Amy's focus had been to talk about the seedier and more unsavoury elements of her ghastly trail of destruction. Kelly could never get her head round why most killers could snub out life with impunity but found it difficult to talk about. In her mind it made them weak and, if they were weak, they were vulnerable.

Kelly wondered what would be Amy's next move; apparently, right now, it was to make tea. It made Kelly nauseous when she thought of the last time she'd been served tea by the nurse. Her skin crawled as she remembered Nurse Richmond touching her. She thought of Brandy Carter's tongue, Moira Tate's fingers, Aileen's wounds, and Nicola's botched surgery. Those hands now made her tea. Again.

'I wanted you to see my house,' Amy said.

The answer threw Kelly, but, as she was learning, little of what Amy said, made actual sense.

'But this isn't your address, Amy.'

'And that's our little secret. We're completely safe here, and we won't be disturbed.'

Kelly swallowed involuntarily, but her tongue stuck to the roof of her mouth. Undisturbed doing what?

'What do you think of Timothy Cole?'

'That arrogant bastard!' Milk spilled on the sparse kitchen counter and Kelly took in her breath, waiting for what might come next. She was doing a good job of distracting the nurse. She took in her surroundings. The house was in darkness without natural light. They were shut away behind blinds or electric light. Only the fridge had cast out a slight illumination. Kelly's eyes were adjusting and she looked around. Amy had her back to her and Kelly considered grabbing a knife and disabling her.

'You worked with him in Yorkshire, too. What did he do to piss you off? Did you choose his patients on purpose? You almost got away with framing an innocent man.' Kelly pushed. They still didn't know where Tim Cole was; part of her thought Amy was about to tell her.

'He thought he knew everything. He doesn't.'

'Do you know where he is, Amy? Did you hurt his family?'

'Tempting. Not worth the effort.' Amy smiled. 'I'm playing with you! I have no idea where they are. Did you lose them, Kelly? Tut tut. Shoddy. I'm sure they'll be in one of his many lake houses that you don't know about. I'm glad he was scared enough to run.'

Kelly noticed Amy tense again. It came from nowhere, and Kelly tensed and backed away. Amy rounded on her, holding the teapot. The lid clattered to the tiled floor and smashed. She held Kelly's gaze. It was a scrutiny of distaste, but, within seconds, Amy's eyes had changed again, and she looked dismayed by the mess, and a comely nurse once more. Kelly felt exhausted.

Amy looked at her feet and placed the teapot back onto the counter. Kelly didn't move. Amy set about tidying up the shards of pottery and Kelly decided to help. She knelt down and their fingers touched. A shot of adrenaline hit Kelly and she felt like getting the nurse by her hair and ramming the teapot into her face and bashing her with it over and over again. She breathed, and carried on gathering bits of smashed pot. Amy resumed tea-making duties and Kelly looked around.

The house was completely empty apart from the kitchen. The lack of furnishings made even the tiniest sound echo, and Kelly felt chilly. She wondered if she'd get an opportunity to attack. She'd only get one.

'So which was your favourite?' Amy asked.

Kelly didn't understand the question. 'Sorry? My favourite what?'

'Sacrifice, lesson, candidate... purification if you like?' Amy said, pouring hot water. Kelly thought about running over and grabbing the kettle, throwing boiling hot water over the woman, but her brain quickly performed a risk assessment and ruled it out: she could easily become the victim instead. In under thirty seconds, the plan was dismissed.

'Sacrifice? Purification?' Kelly asked.

'Well, somebody who needs removing, of course. Like Aileen, like Moira, for example. Which one was your favourite?'

Amy stirred sugar into the hot liquid. Kelly felt as though she was outside her own body, and she swayed very slightly. She wasn't sure if she was actually living her own reality or it was a dream. She grabbed the counter with one hand to steady herself, and took a deep breath.

'Amy, this isn't a game. You tortured those women.'

'Well, now, you're wrong. Torture is relative. You could say that I helped them, and the rest of us,' Amy said cheerily, as if discussing walking socks, and whether to wear them inside or outside boots. Again, Kelly fantasised about having a gun.

'Mine was—' Amy began to speak.

'Stop!' Kelly held up her hand. 'I don't want to know. Please, I don't want to know. I think you're sick, you need help. Hand yourself in. They'll find you soon anyway. You've stayed in Penrith! I wouldn't be surprised if they're on their way now. It's all over.' She was pleading with a murderer — something she never envisaged happening.

Amy stopped stirring.

'But no-one knows we're here.'

And Kelly knew it to be true.

'Amy, where's my sister?'

Kelly watched the other woman closely. It was as if a veil of vapour had descended upon her: Amy's face had gone from jovially discussing sugar in tea, to the look of an anger so intense it was all-consuming. Kelly backed away. Chatty, childlike Amy had disappeared again. Kelly's eyes darted here and there. She decided to call Amy's bluff, she had nothing to lose.

'They do know! The police — we all knew. We knew about this place, they'll be on their way now. I guarantee it. Hand yourself in and I'll protect you!'

366

As quickly as it had come, the veil lifted, and Amy turned around and continued to stir the tea.

'Let's sit down,' Amy said, and left the room after handing Kelly a mug.

Again, Kelly had the unsettling sense of being outside her own body. For the second time in as many weeks, she'd been made tea by The Teacher. Her free hand moved towards her jacket, to where her phone would usually sit. She felt naked without it. She wished she carried some kind of GPS that she could set off, but she'd never contemplated kidnap. A second thought seized her: there was nowhere to sit. She'd spotted no furniture at all in the two rooms they'd passed. Maybe there was another room.

She followed Amy, who walked towards a door at the end of the hallway. The hall was dark and windowless, and Kelly struggled to make out shapes. She watched Amy's back: it was broad and firm. The grey sweat suit made Amy look like a man. Kelly thought of what her victims felt as she leant over them and taunted them about their lessons. Moira would have gone willingly with the nurse who cared for her mother. Brandy would have got into anyone's car offering drugs and Amy had access. Aileen might remember the kind nurse from her countless visits, and Nicola might have accepted a lift home from a colleague. It had all happened under their noses. But it had begun years ago, with the woman who fell down the stairs.

'Why did you kill your mother, Amy?'

Amy stopped in the hall. Kelly still had no idea what Amy's plan was, because even psychos have plans.

Kelly looked at her mug of tea, there'd be no point throwing it at the woman in front of her: it would simply bounce off. She had no idea where the front door was, and she knew that the garage was locked. There was nothing on the walls – no pictures or mirrors – that could potentially be used as weapons. She looked down at her shoes; they were heeled but it would take some strength to cause any damage, and Amy would easily overpower her if she worked out her intention.

Kelly listened for traffic. She heard no sirens. She was kidding herself that they'd ever be found. Not before it was too late. And she still didn't know where Nikki was. She refused to think about the possibility that Nikki was already dead. She thought about Johnny: what would he do? Had he been in a similar situation in combat? Face to face with an enemy fighter, with no weapons, and no way out? What would he do if faced with an opponent of obvious greater strength?

She had no idea. He'd probably go for it anyway.

But Kelly wasn't a man. She couldn't do what men could do.

But Amy could.

Amy began walking again, and Kelly kept following. And thinking.

Amy stopped in front of the door, then turned around. 'You might want a sip of that tea,' she said to Kelly.

Kelly looked at the tea and her hand shook slightly, sending the pale brown liquid over the edges on to the floor.

'Oh Christ! I'm sorry,' Kelly said, as if she'd spilled some wine at a friend's house. She questioned her reality once more, and she realised that she was also questioning her sanity. It was quite plausible that in the last couple of days, she'd actually become insane, and what she was experiencing at the moment was simply a manifestation of that fact. Amy smiled at her and Kelly found it repulsive.

Amy turned round again and took a key from her pocket, and faced the door once more.

'I didn't think you wanted it.' Killer Amy was back.

The key turned and the lock clicked.

Amy opened the door without removing the key from its lock.

Very quietly, Kelly placed her dripping mug on the floor.

Within a second, she'd reached Amy and kicked her into the room from behind.

She grabbed the door, slammed it shut, and locked it. She removed the key and slipped it into her pocket.

Kelly shook violently and she willed herself calm. She scrabbled around her tired brain, trying to make sense of something – anything. Think! Think, she told herself. She ran around the tiny house, going in and out of rooms, opening drawers, finding nothing and closing them. Then, she retraced her steps to the garage, and beyond that there was a front door.

It was locked.

She went back to the kitchen and looked around. There was a small step ladder leaning against the wall and she took it and hammered it against the window of the front door. She repeated the slamming four or five times and then stopped, exhausted.

Then she realised that, in her smug excited psychotic haste, Amy Richmond had left her mobile phone on the kitchen counter. Kelly grabbed it and dialled the first number that came into her head. She didn't know any colleagues' numbers by heart.

At Eden House, Johnny didn't recognise the number. He was about to ignore it, but he pressed the green symbol, curious.

'Johnny, thank god,' Kelly whispered.

'Kelly!' Johnny shouted, attracting three or four officers from the next room. They rushed in and stood around him. He held out his hand, indicating for them to be quiet.

'Shut up and listen!' Kelly said. She reeled off the address, memorised as they pulled into the street, and hung up. She'd heard something.

'Kelly!' Johnny shouted, but she'd gone.

Kelly's hand shook.

'Oh, Kelly,' shouted a voice. It was Amy. Her voice was buoyant, maniacal even.

Kelly's chest heaved with the effort of smashing the ladder against the door, and from making contact with the outside world, and hearing Johnny's voice. She listened. And turned towards the door at the end of the corridor.

'I think you've just made a big mistake, Kelly.' Amy's voice was taunting and high pitched. 'You really should come and open the door.'

Then Kelly heard a scream from the same room.

It was Nikki.

Chapter 63

Penrith was awash with high visibility vests, as officers went door to door in their search.

But now they had an address. And they knew that Kelly Porter was still alive. Eden House emptied in under thirty minutes, and Johnny got lost in the rush. He spotted the one who had introduced herself as Emma and followed her. The others were busy talking rapidly and barking orders and instructions. In the distance, Johnny heard sirens. He felt helpless.

'Let's go!' Officers shouted, bodies ran in all directions, and radios cackled.

Johnny wondered if anyone had a decent weapon, or if they intended to take on The Teacher with a few truncheons and the odd taser.

He didn't expect to be offered a lift and so he ran. He knew the way. He'd run for the best part of a hundred miles wearing only stiff army boots, in a monsoon and in the dark before now. He'd lost three of the five men he led that night, but they'd made their final destination.

Penrith was a small town and Johnny knew how to cut off main roads and traffic lights. Even with blues, the coppers would probably arrive at the same time he did.

He didn't watch the detectives leave. And they didn't see him pull on a pair of trainers, casually left under someone's desk. In their haste, the scruffy man who said he was DI Porter's boyfriend was forgotten.

Super Ormond authorised three Armed Response Teams to attend the scene, and DCI Cane hitched a lift with DS Umshaw. DC Hide drove.

They'd all heard their DI on speaker phone as the garbled message was played back over and over. At least it proved who Johnny Frietze was. Out of everyone on the team, Kelly Porter had called him.

Ten of Penrith's fourteen units were put out to attend the scene using blues. As they stepped outside, sirens could be heard in the distance as all over the town, blue lights raced to the Redgill estate. It was right next door to Scaws.

Johnny's lungs screamed.

He took the back of Hoad Hill and jumped garden fences all the way, for about a mile, until it took him to the outskirts of the town. His unexpected run was accompanied by sirens all over town. He saw a helicopter overhead and knew from the noise of its blades that it was press, not police. If only the police were as well-resourced as Sky News, he thought; they'd perhaps catch baddies quicker.

As he ran over two roundabouts, causing three cars to swerve, he knew he was close. The Scaws Estate loomed up on his left, and, this close to midnight, it looked every inch its sinister den of vice. The Redgill Estate was a mile away.

His arms pumped, and the unfamiliar trainers rubbed his feet in the absence of socks. He ignored the pain. He'd driven into Redgill by mistake once and he knew it to be a rabbit warren of flats and old people's bungalows. It was also where Penrith's dropouts scored most of their gear. It wasn't the kind of place that anyone would want to find themselves after dark, at this hour, unless on the lookout for a hit. But it didn't matter much. By the time he entered the estate, flashing lights were beginning to overtake him and he saw Emma staring out of a car window at him, her mouth gaping open.

He waved.

Seven vehicles were already there by the time he arrived, and a small crowd had gathered. Twitter had exploded all over the country, as people posted the locations of police vehicles and selfies. The hashtag #TheTeacher had gone viral, and some reports said that it had been used seven hundred thousand times already this evening. Videos of the scene were trending on Instagram, and half the battle for the police at the scene was keeping civilians away; already they were using tape and physical presence to do so. Johnny forced his way to the front and headed to where the car carrying Emma had gone.

He was stopped at the tape by a burly uniform and he shouted Emma at the top of his voice. She turned and spoke to a colleague for a few seconds and then she approached him.

'We can't let you any closer, Johnny. I know what you're thinking. You have to let the Armed Response Teams deal with it. There's nothing you can do. It's the same for us. Let them do their job. No-one can get close until they've gone in. You know that.'

'At least let me go beyond the rubber-neckers. Come on!'

Emma looked around and lifted the tape. She took him to a vehicle and ordered him to stay put.

'For God's sake, don't let me down, I'll get sacked.'

Johnny did as he was told for now.

Chapter 64

Wendy watched the news.

In front of her, on the screen, she saw pictures of two women. One was a nurse who she knew well and the other was her daughter. From what she could make out, the nurse was wanted by the police, and Kelly had somehow found herself held within the house with her. She was puzzled.

Then a photograph of Nikki came on the screen.

Wendy's head hurt, and she was beginning to experience chest pain. She called Kelly's number but it was dead. Then, like she did every hour or so she called Nikki's number, but that was also dead. She felt powerless and kept in the dark, and it frustrated her. Perhaps she should call 999 and ask them. But that might mean the difference between some poor soul being helped or not.

She had a sinking feeling that she needed help, and no amount of drugs could alleviate her symptoms. It felt like her heart was breaking. But she was convinced that something else was going on. She felt very unwell, she knew that for sure, but she was struggling to work out how much was her illness and how much of it was her emotions.

Questions muddled her brain, such as: why were so many police involved for just one person? She instinctively knew that she was watching a serious situation develop, but she had no idea why. Perhaps the nurse was in trouble and Kelly was helping her, she thought. But then she remembered that the police spokesperson had explicitly called Amy Richmond 'dangerous' on TV.

Dangerous. Wendy didn't think it possible. Besides, Kelly was involved in a serious case at the moment, so it baffled her further as to why she would get involved in something else.

'The nurse, Amy Richmond, is a suspect in the investigation into the four murdered women, here in Cumbria, over the last few weeks. It's not clear what Amy Richmond's connection to the case is, but the police are urging people to stay away from the area — or if they live nearby, lock the door and stay inside,' a reporter said.

He stood on the corner of a street, sirens wailing and lights flashing behind him. People pushed past him, and uniformed police could be seen herding people away from the scene. Wendy looked beyond the policeman to the houses, and she recognised it as the Redgill estate. A house was surrounded but the cameras couldn't get close enough for Wendy to make out details.

Wendy replayed the words over in her mind. A suspect? How could the nurse be a suspect? She thought. Wendy had been nursed by the woman for a long time, and she liked to think that she'd got to know her. She'd shared her thoughts and feelings with her, and the nurse had sat on her bed and held her hand. Every time she was admitted, the nurse made a point of looking after her. Wendy had told her stories about the girls, and about how it broke her heart that they didn't get along.

The nurse had been gentle and kind, and had listened to it all patiently.

And besides, everyone called The Teacher a man. It was a silly name, and insensitive to the families to give him a nickname. Kelly said it was necessary, helpful even, she said it helped focus the public. Wendy tried Kelly's number again, knowing that she'd get the same tone. She put her phone down and closed her eyes. She wished she knew what was going on. Her phone buzzed and she grabbed it, hoping that it might be one of her girls.

It was Matt.

'Wendy?' he said. She could hear sirens and people shouting.

'Where are you?'

'I'm at home, I've got the TV on, are you watching?'

'That's on loud!' she said. 'Yes, I'm watching, but I can't understand it, Matt. Do you know what's going on?'

'I went to the police station and they wouldn't tell me details, but they said that they are looking for Kelly and the nurse.'

'Well, that's what it said on TV, but why would they be looking for the nurse? And why don't they know where Kelly is?'

'Mam,' he said. He'd always called her Mam.

'The nurse that is on TV – she nursed me, Matt – I know her. She's lovely, she must be in some kind of trouble, and that's why Kelly is with her. Is that helpful? Should I speak to someone?'

'Mam, I think it's a bit more complicated than that. They think the nurse is the one who has been killing those women.' He let the words sink in.

'No! Surely not. That's a mistake. How could they get it so wrong? Is Kelly with her? She wouldn't be with her if that was the case, now would she?'

Matt closed his eyes. He should have gone round there in person. He didn't want to leave the kids. They'd been without their mother for almost two nights now and he couldn't give them any answers. He didn't know what to do. He didn't know anyone he could ask to come and sit with them. Her so-called friends were either out on the town or glued to the TV. It was Friday night, after all.

'Wendy, just sit tight. I'm coming. I'll be there as soon as I can, and I'll explain everything.'

Matt put his phone down and went upstairs to speak to Charlie. She was fourteen and they often left her with the younger children. But this was different.

'Dad,' she said quietly. The other two were in bed.

'Charlie, your gran is on her own, and I need to go and see her.' Charlie looked at him, panicking at first, but then she steeled herself and nodded.

'I'll be ok, Dad. Will you call me if…?' She stopped. He went to her and gave her a hug, even she wasn't too old for that. She sniffed. She had an iPhone and an iPad, and her friends talked. She knew exactly what was going on in the news.

'Lock the doors. Where's your phone?' he asked.

'It's here,' she said, picking it up.

'Right, don't let it out of your sight, and don't answer the door.'

'I know the rules, Dad,' she said.

Wendy opened the door and Matt thought she'd aged dramatically since Nikki had gone missing. She stood back to let him in and he stepped into the lounge. He helped her back to her bed, and busied himself with plumping pillows and checking her water jug. It gave him something to do, somebody to look after and fill his mind with other things apart from his wife and the mother of his kids.

The whole way over to her house, he'd mulled over in his head what he was going to tell her. He tried to work out what Nikki would tell her mother. He wasn't sure he knew, so he did what he thought was best: he skirted the issue and they watched the news.

There was a flurry of movement behind the reporter, and she held her earpiece.

'The police have entered the property! We can tell you, exclusively, that several armed police have entered the property here on Redgill estate in Penrith. Will the weeks of expectation come to an end here tonight? The house is suspected to hold Amy Richmond and Detective Inspector Kelly Porter of the Cumbria Constabulary. It is believed that Ms Porter was handling the case of The Teacher.' At this point, the hashtag #TheTeacher appeared in the bottom left hand corner of the screen.

'Why are they doing that?' Wendy asked.

'Oh, it's Twitter, Mam. People all over the country are talking about it on social media.'

'What's Twitter?'

Matt laughed and squeezed her hand: a reprieve to all the madness. He wished he didn't know what Twitter was either. How lovely that would be.

'We have reason to believe now that the nurse, Amy Richmond, is the prime suspect in the case of the murder of four women here in Cumbria. Questions are being asked about the constabulary looking for a man during the whole enquiry, when all along they were searching for a woman, and a nurse at that. Here with us now, is a criminal psychologist who believes that it's an easy assumption to make,' said the reporter. The screen panned out to a small man with glasses, and he looked at the reporter. He was interviewed about various techniques

378

and beliefs that flew over the heads of Wendy and Matt, and probably the rest of the population too.

'That's absolute rubbish!' said Wendy. 'Of course the nurse didn't do that! How can they say that, Matt?'

'I don't know, Mam,' he replied.

The camera turned back to the reporter, and the screen changed to stock pictures of the four spots where the bodies had been found. Matt rolled his eyes. He wanted to know what was happening inside the house. Clearly the press didn't have a clue.

The camera quickly went back to the live scene on the Redgill estate, and the reporter paused and held her earpiece.

'It's unclear at the moment what's happening inside the property, and about the whereabouts of Detective Inspector Kelly Porter. We are being told that there is also a third person at the property. We'll keep you updated as we get more information, live, here in Penrith, outside the home of Amy Richmond, the prime suspect in the murder of four women – a case that police thought centred round a man all along. Back to the studio.'

Wendy looked at Matt and she held on to his arm. Her eyes widened and he didn't know what to say. He looked at her, but he couldn't help her, he had no answers.

His phone rang.

It was Charlie.

Chapter 65

Kelly put Amy's phone back on the counter and froze. There was another scream, and she ran to the door. She took the key from her pocket.

'Nikki!' Kelly screamed through the door.

'Kelly!' Nikki replied.

Kelly had no idea what she was about to find on the other side of the door, but she had no time to consider it. Whatever Amy's plan was, she had to confront it head on. Now she knew for sure that Nikki was here, and that she was alive, and it was what she'd been waiting for all along. Now Amy Richmond was expendable. She was no longer useful.

The reason Kelly had agreed to go with her in the first place had just expired. And she was pissed off.

She unlocked the door and opened it.

'Kelly!' Nikki screamed again.

Her eyes darted around, expecting to be set upon by Amy, but the assault never came. The room was darker even than the hall, but Kelly's eyes began to adjust, and she saw Amy standing next to a bed. She had her arms folded: Kelly had seen the pose so many times, thinking it innocuous. Not today.

She was smiling and this worried Kelly because it smacked of confidence, and the only thing that Amy wanted to be confident about right now was that she was well and truly in control. Kelly wondered how that might be, and she kept looking around for clues.

'It's over, Amy,' Kelly said quietly. 'Nikki, you're going to be fine. Don't struggle. You're going to be alright, isn't that right, Amy?'

Kelly's eyes adjusted even more and she walked to the bed very slowly. She could see that her sister was naked and she clenched her fists. A table was laid out near the bed. On it sat various items of surgical equipment. Kelly held her breath. She had no plan, no idea what her next move might be. Worse, she didn't know what Amy's next move would be either.

Sirens could be heard in the distance. Kelly decided to try to distract Amy. She tried her hardest not to look at her sister's body. Even now, she wanted to preserve her sister's dignity, if she had any left. She had no idea what Nikki had been through so far. She took another step towards the bed.

'You shouldn't have come back to Penrith, Amy. You could have been miles away by now, in another country perhaps,' Kelly said.

'I couldn't miss the end, Kelly. Are you going to watch?'

Kelly's heart began to beat faster, and she looked around for something with which to attack. The sirens were deafening now, blue lights squeezing through gaps under doors and around windows, as if they were surrounded by some sort of weird disco nightmare. The light danced on Nikki, but Kelly couldn't work out if she was injured. She looked alright – apart from the terror in her eyes – but she needed to be sure.

'Nikki, are you hurt?'

'Shut up, Kelly. You need to stop doing that, or I'll make sure you suffer when your time comes. It's not in my nature to be mean, but you're winding me up the wrong way.'

'A lot of people seem to do that, Amy. You're quite touchy, aren't you? What did Albert do to you? Or was it your mother? Of course it was a woman who did despicable things to you, that's why you have done it back to them.'

'Shut up!'

Amy took a step towards the bed and Nikki struggled. The loudspeaker startled them both.

'This is the police! The property is surrounded. We require you to come out peacefully, or we will enter with force. I repeat, we will enter using force…'

More sirens whirred and Kelly wondered how many vehicles Cane had got authorised. It buoyed her: they stood a chance of getting out of here alive.

'Oh dear. Time's up, I'm afraid,' said Amy, who turned around and picked up a knife.

Kelly had never fought anyone carrying a knife before, but she knew the dangers. She'd trained for it, but never encountered the real thing. Not even in London. Most have-a-go thugs who carried knives had no idea how to use them properly. But Amy Richmond did.

'Don't do that!' Kelly shouted.

She was out of ideas: not that she'd had any anyway. Nikki screamed and started to thrash about. Amy raised a knife and Kelly launched at her. Amy must have weighed twice as much as her, but the nurse went flying. Kelly didn't hear a clatter of metal and so she surmised that the nurse still carried the weapon. Amy crashed against the table and fell over on to the floor, but she was up in under two seconds. She launched at Kelly, who side-stepped her. The nurse was quick and spun round to launch another attack.

Kelly moved away in time.

They glared at one another.

Killer Amy was back. Nikki began to cry.

'That bed is three feet away and you're five feet away. I can get this into her chest before you can get to me,' Amy said. Her smile was other-worldly.

They heard the sound of breaking wood and glass, and Kelly seized the moment. She barged at Amy, head down, and took her round the waist. Amy pulled back her arm as she was falling backwards, with Kelly on top of her. She brought the knife down and it connected. Kelly squealed in pain, but she butted her elbow in Amy's face and was up before the nurse. At last, the nurse's bulk was going against her. Kelly kicked the nurse's arm and the knife flew out of her hand. Amy flung herself at Kelly's legs and tackled her. Kelly went down with a thump. She wriggled her legs as fast and lithely as she could, and got free. But Amy wasn't done. She ran to the table and picked up a smaller knife. She turned round towards Nikki.

Kelly ran as fast as she could and jumped into the air and kicked Amy's back with both feet. Amy landed on Nikki and brought her hand up.

'No!' shouted Kelly. Amy brought her hand down but she missed. Kelly got hold of her hair and pulled with all her strength. Amy punched her in the guts and Kelly was fully winded. She could barely breathe, never mind move. In a slow motion fog, Kelly saw Amy stand up and smile at her, while at the same time, pull the knife above her head.

'In here!' whispered Kelly, unable to do anything else. She threw her weight in one mighty force around the trunk of her body and managed to kneel up. She made one last attempt to block Amy's path, and then she heard lots of voices and banging, and shouting fill the room.

Guns pointed at Amy and, for a moment, Kelly thought she was going to stab her sister anyway, and be blown away in the process. But instead, she held the knife out and smiled broadly.

'Don't move!' the officer nearest shouted.

Kelly still lay on the bed, on top of her sister. Amy was stood beside them. For a moment, Kelly thought Amy might still have a go.

'Identify yourself!'

Kelly's throat burned and her ribs screamed in pain. Nikki was frozen in shock.

'DI Porter.' Kelly managed to rasp. She crawled to the bed. She had no interest in what happened to Amy Richmond from here on in. Nikki was in shock and breathing erratically.

'We need a medic!' The officer spoke into his radio and another made the arrest. Amy Richmond was cuffed and taken out of the room escorted by four officers. Three more remained and one asked Kelly if she was alright. She nodded. 'I don't know about my sister. Could you please take off your jacket so I can at least get her covered up,' Kelly asked. The officer stood down his weapon and took off his jacket. Kelly covered her sister and looked for something with which to cut her restraints, but as she did so, she noticed a large stain underneath her that was steadily getting bigger.

–

As Amy Richmond was driven away from the scene, she looked out of the window and smiled for the cameras. Editors up and down the country salivated at the journalistic gold before them: a female serial killer, and one who loved the limelight. It was a dream combination. Twitter hits on #TheTeacher around the world reached ninety million, and psychologists, neurologists, psychiatrists and all sorts of self-styled 'experts' came forward to give their opinion on how a woman could turn into a monster. New hashtags began: #AmyEvil, #Deathpenalty, and #savekellyporter were the most popular.

–

Inside number fourteen Portland Walk, Redgill, South End, medics worked quietly. Officers manned the doorway, and tents were erected between the front of the house and waiting ambulances. Emma Hide allowed Johnny to wait just outside the house. Umshaw had already gone in.

'Where's DI Porter?' she asked. The officer nodded in the direction of the room at the back of the house, and Emma looked at Johnny.

'Wait here. I'll be out soon. I promise.'

Johnny ran his hands through his hair and thought about rushing past the young detective and finding out for himself, but he'd cost her her job, for the sake of waiting perhaps a minute. He nodded.

She went in.

A stream of light shone from a single window that had been opened, and the evening glow made the scene look eerie. Medics surrounded a bed and a figure on it was hooked up to various IVs, but Emma could tell that she was lifeless, perhaps unconscious. Next to her, holding her hand, was Kelly, and next to her, Kate Umshaw. Kelly was being attended to by a medic and winced as something was pressed into her side.

'You have to get into the ambulance now,' Kate said sternly to Kelly, who didn't want to leave her sister. She turned round.

'I'll stay with your sister, I won't leave her, I promise,' she said. Kelly stood up and walked slowly to the door. She'd refused a wheelchair; smiling weakly at Emma.

'Boss, your friend, Johnny – the one you called – he's outside.'

Kelly made it to the door, but faltered, and the medic ordered a stretcher. Kelly looked round at the bed one last time, before she lay down on the portable bed. She was wheeled out, and before she was outside, she passed out.

Emma made sure that Johnny Frietze was the one to accompany her to the hospital. She wished there was an alternative to The Penrith and Lakes.

Chapter 66

Kelly was in theatre for four hours. When she came round, she stared into the faces of Johnny and her mother. She focused, still groggy, and tried to speak. Wendy was in a wheelchair and she was pulled up to her daughter's bedside as close as she could get.

'Shhh,' she said. Kelly's eyes closed again.

Next time she woke up, she felt better but very hungry. Wendy was still there, holding her hand. And she saw Johnny standing behind her mother, thinking it was a dream.

'Chicken,' Kelly said. Wendy looked behind herself at Johnny, who shrugged. 'I'll go,' he said. But first, he came to the bed and kissed Kelly on her lips. Wendy Porter smiled.

'What day is it?' Kelly asked.

'It's Sunday. You came in here yesterday, in the early hours.'

'Nikki…' Kelly said to her mother.

'Ok. It's ok. I know. I know. Johnny stayed with me the whole time. You did everything you could, Kelly. I'm so proud of you,' she said.

'But I…' Kelly said, trying to get up. She fell back in pain.

'You've had surgery, Kelly. You need to rest,' Wendy said.

'I saw…'

'I know. Rest now. I'll wake you up with chicken.'

'Mum?'

'Yes, darling?'

'I'm sorry.'

'I love you, Kelly.'

'I love you, too.'

Epilogue

They were on the summit of Scafell Pike. It was their tenth Wainwright in three weeks.

Wastwater shimmered to the south west, and it snaked round to the left and disappeared into the distance. In the opposite direction, Great Gable stood tall and commanding, the most reliable of them all: its inoffensive dome giving it the air of a teddy bear's belly. To the south east, they could even make out Windermere.

Kelly sat very still and turned her face to the autumn sun. It was her highest and longest climb since the summer and she felt good. She felt strong. The doctors had told her to listen to her body, and that she'd know when she was ready. Johnny sat next to her but didn't speak. He looked southwards to see if he could make out Coniston Old Man. Kelly looked at him. Josie was coming to stay, and she was nervous. They were only sharing dinner together, Kelly wouldn't stay. Neither had suggested it.

Kelly was ravenous and rooted about in her back pack for something to eat. She pulled out a foil parcel and unwrapped it. She'd brought a hoisin duck wrap and she devoured it. She glugged at a bottle of water and got her breath back. She'd lost some fitness but it would come back soon enough.

'Ready? I could sit here all day, but I said I'd be there at three,' Johnny said.

'I know. Yes, I'm ready. I'll swing by about six, yes?' Johnny nodded. She could tell he was nervous too, and it touched her.

'How are you feeling?' he asked.

'Actually brilliant. It wasn't easy but I got up.'

'Impressive.'

They descended easily and stopped to take in the best views that they'd missed on the way up, either due to Kelly trying to keep pace, or simply because they'd had their backs to them. They snapped photos on their phones and stopped for water.

'Do you want to go straight home?' he asked.

'Yes, I'm going to the hospital to see Mum.'

It took less than an hour to descend and it was strange being back at sea level. It was like being in a parallel universe for a moment, stopped in perfection. Only those who knew the Lakes understood. Johnny drove her home and she showered quickly. Her house was almost decorated, and she had sofas, over one of which she threw her coat.

Afterwards, she picked through her mail and put on some music. The terrace was still warm despite being October.

Kelly noticed an envelope that looked private. Her address was printed but there were no official markings on it. She decided to open it first: the other stuff was just bills and adverts. Something different was exciting. She rarely received anything interesting through the post. The last surprise she'd had like this was a hand written letter from her sister. Nikki found it easier to thank her this way, although Kelly didn't want thanking. What she did wasn't an act of bravery or courage, it was just instinct. The card sat on the window sill in the kitchen and Kelly re-read it occasionally. Nikki had spent two months in hospital.

Even now, when she was in the Penrith and Lakes hospital, Kelly couldn't entirely settle around the nurses. And if the truth be known, the nurses found it difficult to settle around her: she was a constant reminder of the shame Amy Richmond had brought on their profession.

The Trust had introduced new measures to vet staff, and CCTV had been installed inside drug stores and private rooms. Some thought it an invasion of privacy, but others – like Kelly – believed that if they'd had it before, they might be able to prove that Catherine Tring had been helped on her way to a death even the palliative team didn't expect so soon.

She looked at the envelope in her hands and opened it.

It contained a folded piece of paper and Kelly knew that it was handwritten. She opened it and her hands began to shake. It had been sent from Broadmoor in Berkshire.

It read, 'Dear Kelly, I do hope you are well, I think of you often. How is your mother? I always liked her. I've sent you one of my favourite poems…'

Kelly dropped the letter. She'd seen the handwriting a thousand times before.

Acknowledgements

I would firstly like to thank my agent, Peter Buckman, for his never ending encouragement and faith; also Louise Cullen and the team at Canelo for their passion and meticulous attention to detail. For their fascinating insight, Harry Chapfield, Cumbria Constabulary (ret'd), Inspector Paul Redfearn, London Met Police, and DI Rob Burns, Beds Police. I want to thank the Lemons: you know who you are, I love you. And finally Mike, Tilly and Freddie for being neglected at odd times of the day; I couldn't have done this without you.

CANELOCRIME

Do you love crime fiction and are always on the lookout for brilliant authors?

Canelo Crime is home to some of the most exciting novels around. Thousands of readers are already enjoying our compulsive stories. Are you ready to find your new favourite writer?

Find out more and sign up to our newsletter at canelocrime.com